Dear Reader,

I've always enjoyed a good romance in which kids are involved. You see, I *know* kids. Wayne and I managed to produce four within a five-year span—and I lived to tell about it.

When it came to writing about girls, I had my own two daughters, who were a terrific source of reference. How well I remember the days when Jody, age thirteen, carried Oil of Olay in her purse. (One is never too young to ward off age lines, you know!) It's easy to laugh about it now, but back then Jody was serious about premature aging. Naturally, Jenny, a year younger, added her own bit of comic relief. One day I found her practicing scowls so she could look like rock singer Billy Idol. Wayne and I sadly realized that we were spending thousands of dollars to straighten the teeth of a teenager who intended never to smile again.

As I mentioned, my husband and I survived, and just as important, so did Jody and Jenny, who are both raising daughters of their own. There *is* justice in this world, isn't there?

I hope you enjoy *Lone Star Lovin'* and *Yours and Mine*. The stories were inspired by two of the most gifted little conspirators I've ever known. The daughters in these stories want just one thing: for their moms and dads to find happiness. As everyone who's ever raised children is well aware, kids are often way ahead of us!

Warmest regards,

Debbie Macomber

P.S.: I love to hear from readers. You can write me at P.O. Box 1458, Port Orchard, WA 98366. Or visit my Web site at www.debbiemacomber.com.

DEBBIE MACOMBER

Darling Daughters

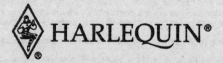

TORONTO • NEW YORK • LONDON
AMSTERDAM • PARIS • SYDNEY • HAMBURG
STOCKHOLM • ATHENS • TOKYO • MILAN • MADRID
PRAGUE • WARSAW • BUDAPEST • AUCKLAND

ISBN 0-373-83512-4

DARLING DAUGHTERS

Copyright © 2002 by Harlequin Books S.A.

The publisher acknowledges the copyright holder of the individual works as follows:

YOURS AND MINE
Copyright © 1989 by Debbie Macomber

LONE STAR LOVIN'
Copyright © 1993 by Debbie Macomber

CONTENTS

For Simone Hartman,
the sixteen-year-old German girl
who came to live with us to learn about America.
Instead, she taught us about love, friendship,
Wiener schnitzel and fun...German style.
We love you, Simone!

One

"**M**om, I forgot to tell you, I need two dozen cupcakes for tomorrow morning."

Joanna Parsons reluctantly opened her eyes and lifted her head from the soft feather pillow, squinting at the illuminated dial of her clock radio. "Kristen, it's after eleven."

"I know, Mom, I'm sorry. But I've *got* to bring cupcakes."

"No, you don't," Joanna said hopefully. "There's a package of Oreos on the top shelf of the cupboard. You can take those."

"Oreos! You've been hiding Oreos from me again! Just what kind of mother are you?"

"I was saving them for an emergency—like this."

"It won't work." Crossing her arms over her still-flat chest, eleven-year-old Kristen sat on the edge of the mattress and heaved a loud, discouraged sigh.

"Why not?"

"It's got to be cupcakes, home-baked chocolate ones."

"That's unfortunate, since you seem to have forgotten to mention the fact earlier. And now it's about four hours too late for baking anything. Including chocolate cupcakes." Joanna tried to be fair with Kristen, but being a single parent wasn't easy.

"Mom, I know I forgot," Kristen cried, her young voice rising in panic, "but I've got to bring cupcakes to class tomorrow. It's important! Really important!"

"Convince me." Joanna used the phrase often. She didn't want to seem unyielding and hard-nosed. After all, she'd probably forgotten a few important things in her thirty-odd years, too.

"It's Mrs. Eagleton's last day as our teacher—remember I told you her husband got transferred and she's moving to Denver? Everyone in the whole class hates to see her go, so we're throwing a party."

"Who's *we*?"

"Nicole and me," Kristen answered quickly. "Nicole's bringing the napkins, cups and punch, and I'm supposed to bring homemade cupcakes. Chocolate cupcakes. Mom, I've just got to. Nicole would never forgive me if I did something stupid like bring store-bought cookies for a teacher as wonderful as Mrs. Eagleton."

Kristen had met Nicole almost five months before at the beginning of the school year, and the two girls had been as thick as gnats in August from that time on. "Shouldn't the room mother be organizing this party?" That made sense to Joanna; surely there was an adult who would be willing to help.

"We don't have one this year. Everyone's mother is either too busy or working."

Joanna sighed. Oh, great, she was going to end up baking cupcakes until the wee hours of the morning. "All right," she muttered, giving in to her daughter's pleading. Mrs. Eagleton *was* a wonderful teacher, and Joanna was as sorry as Kristen to see her leave.

"We just couldn't let Mrs. Eagleton move to Denver

without doing something really nice for her," Kristen pressed.

Although Joanna agreed, she felt that Oreos or Fig Newtons should be considered special enough, since it was already after eleven. But Kristen obviously had her heart set on home-baked cupcakes.

"Mom?"

Even in the muted light, Joanna recognized the plea in her daughter's dark brown eyes. She looked so much like Davey that a twinge of anguish worked its way through Joanna's heart. They'd been divorced six years now, but the pain of that failure had yet to fade. Sometimes, at odd moments like these, she still recalled how good it had felt to be in his arms and how much she'd once loved him. Mostly, though, Joanna remembered how naive she'd been to trust him so completely. But she'd come a long way in the six years since her divorce. She'd gained a new measure of independence and self-respect, forging a career for herself at Columbia Basin Savings and Loan. And now she was close to achieving her goal of becoming the first female senior loan officer.

"All right, honey." Joanna sighed, dragging her thoughts back to her daughter. "I'll bake the cupcakes. Only next time, please let me know before we go to bed, okay?"

Kristen's shoulders slumped in relief. "I owe you one, Mom."

Joanna resisted the urge to remind her daughter that the score was a lot higher than one. Tossing aside the thick warm blankets, she climbed out of bed and reached for her long robe.

Kristen, flannel housecoat flying behind her like a flag unfurling, raced toward the kitchen, eager to do what she could to help. "I'll turn on the oven and get everything ready," she called.

"All right," Joanna said with a yawn as she sent her foot searching under the bed for her slippers. She was mentally scanning the contents of her cupboards, wondering if she had a chocolate cake mix. Somehow she doubted it.

"Trouble, Mom," Kristen announced when Joanna entered the well-lighted kitchen. The eleven-year-old stood on a chair in front of the open cupboards above the refrigerator, an Oreo between her teeth. Looking only mildly guilty, she ate the cookie whole, then shook her head. "We don't have cake mix."

"I was afraid of that."

"I guess we'll have to bake them from scratch," Kristen suggested, reaching for another Oreo.

"Not this late, we won't. I'll drive to the store." There was an Albertson's that stayed open twenty-four hours less than a mile away.

Kristen jumped down from the chair. The pockets of her bathrobe were stuffed full of cookies, but her attempt to conceal them failed. Joanna pointed toward the cookie jar, and dutifully Kristen emptied her pockets.

When Kristen had finished, Joanna yawned again and ambled back into her bedroom.

"Mom, if you're going to the store, I suppose I should go with you."

"No, honey, I'm just going to run in and out. You stay here."

"Okay," Kristen agreed quickly.

The kid wasn't stupid, Joanna thought wryly. Winters in eastern Washington were often merciless, and temperatures in Spokane had been well below freezing all week. To be honest, she wasn't exactly thrilled about braving the elements herself. She pulled on her calf-high boots over two pairs of heavy woollen socks. Because the socks were so thick, Joanna could only zip the boots up to her ankles.

"Mom," Kristen said, following her mother into the bedroom, a thoughtful expression on her face. "Have you ever thought of getting married again?"

Surprised, Joanna looked up and studied her daughter. The question had come from out of nowhere, but her answer was ready. "Never." The first time around had been enough. Not that she was one of the walking wounded, at least she didn't think of herself that way. Instead, her divorce had made her smart, had matured her. Never again would she look to a man for happiness; Joanna was determined to build her own. But the unexpectedness of Kristen's question caught her off guard. Was Kristen telling her something? Perhaps her daughter felt she was missing out because there were only the two of them. "What makes you ask?"

The mattress dipped as she sat beside Joanna. "I'm not exactly sure," she confessed. "But you could remarry, you know. You've still got a halfway decent figure."

Joanna grinned. "Thanks...I think."

"I mean, it's not like you're really old and ugly."

"Coming from you, that's high praise indeed, considering that I'm over thirty."

"I'm sure if you wanted to, you could find another man. Not like Daddy, but someone better."

It hurt Joanna to hear her daughter say things like that about Davey, but she couldn't disguise from Kristen how selfish and hollow her father was. Nor could she hide Davey's roving eye when it came to the opposite sex. Kristen spent one month every summer with him in Seattle and saw for herself the type of man Davey was.

After she'd finished struggling with her boots, Joanna clumped into the entryway and opened the hall cupboard.

"Mom!" Kristen cried, her eyes round with dismay.

"What?"

"You can't go out looking like that!" Her daughter was pointing at her, as though aghast at the sight.

"Like what?" Innocently Joanna glanced down at the dress-length blue wool coat she'd slipped on over her rose-patterned flannel pajamas. Okay, so the bottoms showed, but only a little. And she was willing to admit that the boots would look better zipped up, but she was more concerned with comfort than fashion. If the way she looked didn't bother her, then it certainly shouldn't bother Kristen. Her daughter had obviously forgotten why Joanna was venturing outside in the first place.

"Someone might see you."

"Don't worry, I have no intention of taking off my coat." She'd park close to the front door of the store, run inside, head for aisle three, grab a cake mix and be back at the car in four minutes flat. Joanna didn't exactly feel like donning tights for the event.

"You might meet someone," Kristen persisted.

"So?" Joanna stifled a yawn.

"But your hair... Don't you think you should curl it?"

"Kristen, listen. The only people who are going to be in the grocery store are insomniacs and winos and maybe a couple of pregnant women." It was highly unlikely she'd run into anyone from the bank.

"But what if you got in an accident? The policeman would think you're some kind of weirdo."

Joanna yawned a second time. "Honey, anyone who would consider making cupcakes in the middle of the night has a mental problem as it is. I'll fit right in with everyone else, so quit worrying."

"Oh, all right," Kristen finally agreed.

Draping her bag strap over her shoulder, Joanna opened the front door and shivered as the arctic wind of late January wrapped itself around her. Damn, it was cold. The grass was so white with frost that she wondered, at first, if it had snowed. To ward off the chill, she wound Kristen's purple striped scarf around her neck to cover her ears and mouth and tied it loosely under her chin.

The heater in her ten-year-old Ford didn't have a chance to do anything but spew out frigid air as she huddled over the steering wheel for the few minutes it took to drive to the grocery store. According to her plan, she parked as close to the store as possible, turned off the engine and dashed inside.

Just as she'd predicted, the place was nearly deserted, except for a couple of clerks working near the front, arranging displays. Joanna didn't give them more than a fleeting glance as she headed toward the aisle where baking goods were shelved.

She was reaching for the first chocolate cake mix to come into sight when she heard footsteps behind her.

"Mrs. Parsons! Hello!" The shrill excited voice seemed to ring like a Chinese gong throughout the store.

Joanna hunched down as far as she could and cast a furtive glance over her shoulder. Dear Lord, Kristen had been right. She was actually going to bump into someone who knew her.

"It's me—Nicole. You remember me, don't you?"

Joanna attempted a smile as she turned to face her daughter's best friend. "Hi, there," she said weakly, and raised her right hand to wave, her wrist limp. "It's good to see you again." So she was lying. Anyone with a sense of decency would have pretended not to recognise her and casually looked the other way. Not Nicole. It seemed as though all the world's eleven-year-olds were plotting against her tonight. One chocolate cake mix; that was all she wanted. That and maybe a small tub of ready-made frosting. Then she could return home, get those cupcakes baked and climb back into bed where most sane people were at this very moment.

"You look different," Nicole murmured thoughtfully, her eyes widening as she studied Joanna.

Well, that was one way of putting it.

"When I first saw you, I thought you were a bag lady."

Loosening the scarf that obscured the lower half of her face, Joanna managed a grin.

"What are you doing here this late?" the girl wanted to know next, following Joanna as she edged her way to the checkout stand.

"Kristen forgot to tell me about the cupcakes."

Nicole's cheerful laugh resounded through the store like a yell echoing in an empty sports stadium. "I was watching Johnny Carson with my dad when I remembered I hadn't bought the juice and stuff for the party. Dad's waiting for me in the car right now."

Nicole's father allowed her to stay up that late on a school night? Joanna did her utmost to hide her disdain. From what Kristen had told her, she knew Nicole's parents were also divorced and her father had custody of Nicole. The poor kid probably didn't know what the word discipline meant. No doubt her father was one of those weak-willed liberal parents so involved in their own careers that they didn't have any time left for their children. Imagine a parent letting an eleven-year-old wander around a grocery store at this time of night! The mere thought was enough to send chills of parental outrage racing up and down Joanna's backbone. She placed her arm around Nicole's shoulders as if to protect her from life's harsher realities. The poor sweet kid.

The abrupt whoosh of the automatic door was followed by the sound of someone striding impatiently into the store. Joanna glanced up to discover a tall man, wearing a well-cut dark coat, glaring in their direction.

"Nicole, what's taking so long?"

"Dad," the girl said happily, "this is Mrs. Parsons—Kristen's mom."

Nicole's father approached, obviously reluctant to acknowledge the introduction, his face remote and unsmiling.

Automatically Joanna straightened, her shoulders stiffening with the action. Nicole's father was exactly as she'd pictured him just a few moments earlier. Polished, worldly, and too darn handsome for his own good. Just like Davey. This was exactly the type of man she went out of her way to avoid. She'd been burned once, and no relationship was worth what she'd endured. This brief encounter with Nicole's father told Joanna all she needed to know.

"Tanner Lund," he announced crisply, holding out his hand.

"Joanna Parsons," Joanna said, and gave him hers

for a brisk cold shake. She couldn't take her hand away fast enough.

His eyes narrowed as they studied her, and the look he gave her was as disapproving as the one she offered him. Slowly his gaze dropped to the unzipped boots flapping at her ankles and the worn edges of the pajamas visible below her wool coat.

"I think it's time we met, don't you?" Joanna didn't bother to disguise her disapproval of the man's attitude toward child-rearing. She'd had Nicole over after school several times, but on the one occasion Kristen had visited her friend, the child was staying with a baby-sitter.

A hint of a smile appeared on his face, but it didn't reach his eyes. "Our meeting is long overdue, I agree."

He seemed to be suggesting that he'd made a mistake in allowing his daughter to have anything to do with someone who dressed the way she did.

Joanna's gaze shifted to Nicole. "Isn't it late for you to be up on a school night?"

"Where's Kristen?" he countered, glancing around the store.

"At home," Joanna answered, swallowing the words that said home was exactly where an eleven-year-old child belonged on a school night—or any other night for that matter.

"Isn't she a bit young to be left alone while you run to a store?"

"N-not in the least."

Tanner frowned and his eyes narrowed even more. His disapproving gaze demanded to know what kind of mother left a child alone in the house at this time of night.

Joanna answered him with a scornful look of her own.

"It's a pleasure to meet you, Mr. Lund," she said coolly, knowing her eyes relayed a conflicting message.

"The pleasure's mine."

Joanna was all the more aware of her dishevelled appearance. Uncombed and uncurled, her auburn hair hung limply to her shoulders. Her dark eyes were nice enough, she knew, fringed in long curling lashes. She considered them her best asset, and purposely glared at Tanner, hoping her eyes were as cold as the blast from her car heater had been.

Tanner placed his hands on his daughter's shoulders and drew her protectively to his side. Joanna was infuriated by the action. If Nicole needed shielding, it was from an irresponsible father!

Okay, she reasoned, so her attire was a bit outlandish. But that couldn't be helped; she was on a mission that by rights should win her a nomination for the mother-of-the-year award. The way Tanner Lund had implied that *she* was the irresponsible parent was something Joanna found downright insulting.

"Well," Joanna said brightly, "I have to go. Nice to see you again, Nicole." She swept two boxes of cake mix into her arms and grabbed what she hoped was some frosting.

"You, too, Mrs. Parsons," the girl answered, smiling up at her.

"Mr. Lund."

"Mrs. Parsons."

The two nodded politely at each other, and, clutching her packages, Joanna walked regally to the checkout stand. She made her purchase and started back toward the car. The next time Kristen invited Nicole over,

Joanna mused on the short drive home, she intended to
spend lots of extra time with the girls. Now she knew
how badly Nicole needed someone to nurture her, to
give her the firm but loving guidance every child deserved.

The poor darling.

Two

Joanna expertly lowered the pressure foot of her sewing machine over the bunched red material, then used both hands to push the fabric slowly under the bobbing needle. Straight pins, tightly clenched between her lips, protruded from her mouth. Her concentration was intense.

"Mom." A breathless Kristen bounded into the room.

Joanna intercepted her daughter with one upraised hand until she finished stitching the seam.

Kristen stalked around the kitchen table several times, like a shark circling its kill. "Mom, hurry, this is really important."

"Wlutt?" Joanna asked, her teeth still clamped on the pins.

"Can Nicole spend the night?"

Joanna blinked. This wasn't the weekend, and Kristen knew the rules; she had permission to invite friends over only on Friday and Saturday nights. Joanna removed the pins from her mouth before she answered. "It's Wednesday."

"I know what day it is." Kristen rolled her eyes towards the ceiling and slapped the heel of her hand against her forehead.

Allowing his daughter to stay over at a friend's house

on a school night was exactly the kind of irresponsible parenting Joanna expected from Tanner Lund. Her estimation of the man was dropping steadily, though that hardly seemed possible. Earlier in the afternoon, Joanna had learned that Nicole didn't even plan to tell her father she and Kristen were going to be performing in the school talent show. The man revealed absolutely no interest in his daughter's activities. Joanna felt so bad about Tanner Lund's attitude that she'd volunteered to sew a second costume so Nicole would have something special to wear for this important event. And now it seemed that Tanner was in the habit of farming out his daughter on school nights, as well.

"Mom, hurry and decide. Nicole's on the phone."

"Honey, there's school tomorrow."

Kristen gave her another scornful look.

"The two of you will stay up until midnight chattering, and then in the morning class will be a disaster. The answer is no!"

Kristen's eager face fell. "I promise we won't talk. Just this once, Mom. Oh, please!" She folded her hands prayerfully, and her big brown eyes pleaded with Joanna. "How many times do I ask you for something?"

Joanna stared incredulously at her daughter. The list was endless.

"All right, forget I asked that. But this is important, Mom, real important—for Nicole's sake."

Every request was argued as urgent. But knowing what she did about the other little girl's home life made refusing all the more difficult. "I'm sorry, Kristen, but not on a school night."

Head drooping, Kristen shuffled toward the phone.

"Now Nicole will have to spend the night with Mrs. Wagner, and she hates that."

"Who's Mrs. Wagner?"

Kristen turned to face her mother and released a sigh intended to evoke sympathy. "Her baby-sitter."

"Her father makes her spend the night at a baby-sitter's?"

"Yes. He has a business meeting with Becky."

Joanna stiffened and felt a sudden chill. "Becky?"

"His business partner."

I'll just bet! Joanna's eyes narrowed with outrage. Tanner Lund was a lowlife, kicking his own daughter out into the cold so he could bring a woman over. The man disgusted her.

"Mrs. Wagner is real old and she makes Nicole eat health food. She has a black-and-white TV, and the only programs she'll let Nicole watch are nature shows. Wouldn't you hate that?"

Joanna's mind was spinning. Any child would detest being cast from her own bed and thrust upon the not always tender mercies of a baby-sitter. "How often does Nicole have to spend the night with Mrs. Wagner?"

"Lots."

Joanna could well believe it. "How often is 'lots'?"

"At least twice a month. Sometimes even more often than that."

That poor neglected child. Joanna's heart constricted at the thought of sweet Nicole being ruthlessly handed over to a woman who served soybean burgers.

"Can she, Mom? Oh, please?" Again Kristen folded her hands, pleading with her mother to reconsider.

"All right," Joanna conceded, "but just this once."

Kristen ran across the room and hurled her arms

around Joanna's neck, squeezing for all she was worth. "You're the greatest mother in the whole world."

Joanna snorted softly. "I've got to be in the top ten percent, anyway," she said, remembering the cupcakes.

"ABSOLUTELY NOT," Tanner said forcefully as he laid a neatly pressed shirt in his open suitcase. "Nicole, I won't hear of it."

"But, Dad, Kristen is my very best friend."

"Believe me, sweetheart, I'm pleased you've found a soulmate, but when I'm gone on these business trips I need to know you're being well taken care of." And supervised, he added mentally. What he knew about Kristen's mother wasn't encouraging. The woman was a scatterbrain who left her young daughter unattended while she raided the supermarket for nighttime goodies—and then had the nerve to chastise him because Nicole was up a little late. In addition to being a busybody, Joanna Parsons dressed like a fruitcake.

"Dad, you don't understand what it's like for me at Mrs. Wagner's."

Undaunted, Tanner continued packing his suitcase. He wasn't any happier about leaving Nicole than she was, but he didn't have any choice. As a relatively new half owner of Spokane Aluminum, he was required to do a certain amount of traveling. More these first few months than would be necessary later. His business trips were essential, since they familiarised him with the clients and their needs. He would have to absorb this information as quickly as possible in order to determine if the plant was going to achieve his and John Becky's five-year goal. In a few weeks, he expected to hire an assistant who would assume some of this responsibility, but for now the task fell into his hands.

Nicole slumped onto the edge of the bed. "The last time I spent the night at Mrs. Wagner's she served baked beef heart for dinner."

Involuntarily Tanner cringed.

"And, Dad, she made me watch a special on television that was all about fungus."

Tanner gritted his teeth. So the old lady was a bit eccentric, but she looked after Nicole competently, and that was all that mattered.

"Do you know what Kristen's having for dinner?"

Tanner didn't care to guess. It was probably something like strawberry ice cream and caramel-flavored popcorn. "No, and I don't want to know."

"It isn't sweet-and-sour calf liver, I can tell you that."

Tanner's stomach turned at the thought of liver in any kind of sauce. "Nicole, the subject is closed. You're spending the night with Mrs. Wagner."

"It's spaghetti and meatballs and three-bean salad and milk and French bread, that's what. And Mrs. Parsons said I could help Kristen roll the meatballs—but that's all right, I'll call and tell her that you don't want me to spend the night at a home where I won't be properly looked after."

"Nicole—"

"Dad, don't worry about it, I understand."

Tanner sincerely doubted that. He placed the last of his clothes inside the suitcase and closed the lid.

"At least I'm *trying* to understand why you'd send me to someplace like Mrs. Wagner's when my very best friend *invited* me to spend the night with her."

Tanner could feel himself weakening. It was only one night and Kristen's weird mother wasn't likely to be a dangerous influence on Nicole in that short a time.

"Spaghetti and meatballs," Nicole muttered under her breath. "My all-time favourite food."

Now that was news to Tanner. He'd thought pizza held that honour. He'd never known his daughter to turn down pizza at any time of the day or night.

"And they have a twenty-inch colour television set." Tanner hesitated.

"With remote control."

Would wonders never cease? "Will Kristen's mother be there the entire night?" he asked.

"Of course."

His daughter was looking at him as though he'd asked if Mrs. Parsons were related to ET. "Where will you sleep?"

"Kristen has a double bed." Nicole's eyes brightened. "And we've already promised Mrs. Parsons that we'll go straight to bed at nine o'clock and hardly talk."

It was during times such as this that Tanner felt the full weight of parenting descend upon his shoulders. Common sense told him Nicole would be better off with Mrs. Wagner, but he understood her complaints about the older woman as well. "All right, Nicole, you can stay at Kristen's."

His daughter let out a whoop of sheer delight.

"But just this once."

"Oh, Dad, you're the greatest." Her arms locked around his waist, and she squeezed with all her might, her nose pressed against his flat stomach.

"Okay, okay, I get the idea you're pleased with my decision," Tanner said with a short laugh.

"Can we leave now?"

"Now?" Usually Nicole wanted to linger at the apartment until the last possible minute.

"Yes. Mrs. Parsons really did say I could help roll the meatballs, and you know what else?"

"What?"

"She's sewing me and Kristen identical costumes for the talent show."

Tanner paused—he hadn't known anything about his daughter needing a costume. "What talent show?"

"Oops." Nicole slapped her hand over her mouth. "I wasn't going to tell you because it's on Valentine's day and I know you won't be able to come. I didn't want you to feel bad."

"Nicole, it's more important that you don't hide things from me."

"But you have to be in Seattle."

She was right. He'd hate missing the show, but he was scheduled to meet with the Foreign Trade Commission on the fourteenth regarding a large shipment of aluminum to Japan. "What talent do you and Kristen have?" he asked, diverting his disappointment for the moment.

"We're lip-synching a song from Heart. You know, the rock group?"

"That sounds cute. A fitting choice, too, for a Valentine's Day show. Perhaps you two can be persuaded to give me a preview before the grand performance."

Her blue eyes became even brighter in her excitement. "That's a great idea! Kristen and I can practise while you're away, and we'll show you when you come back."

It was an acceptable compromise.

Nicole dashed out of his bedroom and returned a couple of minutes later with her backpack. "I'm ready anytime you are," she announced.

Tanner couldn't help but notice that his daughter looked downright cheerful. More cheerful than any of the other times he'd been forced to leave her. Normally she put on a long face and moped around, making him feel guilty about abandoning her to the dreaded Mrs. Wagner.

By the time he picked up his briefcase and luggage, Nicole was waiting at the front door.

"Are you going to come in and say hello to Mrs. Parsons?" Nicole asked when Tanner eased his Mercedes into Kristen's driveway fifteen minutes later. Even in the fading late-afternoon light, he could see that the house was newly painted, white with green shutters at the windows. The lawn and flower beds seemed well maintained. He could almost picture rose bushes in full bloom. It certainly wasn't the type of place he'd associated with Kristen's loony mother.

"Are you coming in or not?" Nicole asked a second time, her voice impatient.

Tanner had to mull over the decision. He wasn't eager to meet that unfriendly woman who wore unzipped boots and flannel pajamas again.

"Dad!"

Before Tanner could answer, the door opened and Kristen came bowling out of the house at top speed. A gorgeous redhead followed sedately behind her. Tanner felt his jaw sag and his mouth drop open. No, it couldn't be! Tall, cool, sophisticated, this woman looked as though she'd walked out of the pages of a fashion magazine. It couldn't be Joanna Parsons—no way. A relative perhaps, but certainly not the woman he'd met in the grocery store that night.

Nicole had already climbed out of the car. She paused as though she'd forgotten something, then ran around to his side of the car. When Tanner rolled down his window, she leaned over and gave him one of her famous bear hugs, hurling her arms around his neck and squeezing enthusiastically. "Bye, Dad."

"Bye, sweetheart. You've got the phone number of my hotel to give Mrs. Parsons?"

Nicole patted her jeans pocket. "It's right here."

"Be good."

"I will."

When Tanner looked up, he noted that Joanna was standing behind her daughter, her hands resting on Kristen's shoulders. Cool, disapproving eyes surveyed him. Yup, it was the same woman all right. Joanna Parsons's gaze could freeze watermelon at a Fourth of July picnic.

Three

"Would you like more spaghetti, Nicole?" Joanna asked for the second time.

"No, thanks, Mrs. Parsons."

"You asked her that already," Kristen commented, giving her mother a puzzled look. "After we've done the dishes, Nicole and I are going to practise our song."

Joanna nodded. "Good idea, but do your homework first."

Kristen exchanged a knowing look with her friend, and the two grinned at each other.

"I'm really glad you're letting me stay the night, Mrs. Parsons," Nicole said, as she carried her empty plate to the kitchen sink. "Dinner was great. Dad tries, but he isn't much of a cook. We get take-out food a lot." She wandered back to the table and fingered the blue-quilted place mat. "Kristen told me you sewed these, too. They're pretty."

"Thank you. The pattern is really very simple."

"They have to be," Kristen added, stuffing the last slice of toasted French bread into her mouth. "'Cause Mom let me do a couple of them."

"You made two of these?"

"Yeah," Kristen said, after she'd finished chewing. Pride beamed from her dark brown eyes. "We've made lots of things together since we bought the house. Do you have any idea how expensive curtains can be? Mom made the entire set in my room—that's why everything matches."

"The bedspread, too?"

"Naturally." Kristen made it sound like they'd whipped up the entire set over a weekend, when the project had actually taken the better part of two weeks.

"Wow."

From the way Nicole was staring at her, Joanna half expected the girl to fall to her knees in homage. She felt a stab of pity for Nicole, who seemed to crave a mother's presence. But she had to admit she was thrilled by her own daughter's pride in their joint accomplishments.

"Mom sews a lot of my clothes," Kristen added, licking the butter from her fingertips. "I thought you knew that."

"I… No, I didn't."

"She's teaching me, too. That's the best part. So I'll be able to make costumes for our next talent show." Kristen's gaze flew from Nicole to her mother then back to Nicole. "I bet my mom would teach you how to sew. Wouldn't you, Mom?"

"Ah…"

"Would you really, Mrs. Parsons?"

Not knowing what else to say, Joanna agreed with a quick nod of her head. "Why not? We'll have fun learning together." She gave an encouraging smile, but she wondered a bit anxiously if she was ready for a project like this.

"That would be great." Nicole slipped her arm around Kristen's shoulders. Her gaze dropped as she hesitated. "Dinner was really good, too," she said again.

"I told you what a great cook my mom is," Kristen boasted.

Nicole nodded, but kept her eyes trained to the floor. "Could I ask you something, Mrs. Parsons?"

"Of course."

"Like I said, Dad tries real hard, but he just isn't a very good cook. Would it be rude to ask you for the recipe for your spaghetti sauce?"

"Not at all. I'll write it out for you tonight."

"Gee, thanks. It's so nice over here. I wish Dad would let me stay here all the time. You and Kristen do such neat things, and you eat real good, too."

Joanna could well imagine the kind of meals Tanner Lund served his daughter. She already knew that he frequently ordered out, and the rest probably came from the frozen-food section of the local grocery. That was if he didn't have an array of willing females who did his cooking for him. Someone like this Becky person, the woman he was with now.

"Dad makes great tacos though," Nicole was saying. "They're his specialty. He said I might be able to have a slumber party for my birthday in March, and I want him to serve tacos then. But I might ask him to make spaghetti instead—if he gets the recipe right."

"You get to have a slumber party?" Kristen cried, her eyes widening. "That's great! My mom said I could have two friends over for the night on my birthday, but only two, because that's all she can mentally handle."

Joanna pretended an interest in her leftover salad, stirring her fork through the dressing that sat in the bottom of the bowl. It was true; there were limits to her mothering abilities. A house full of screaming eleven- and twelve-year-olds was more than she dared contemplate on a full stomach.

While Nicole finished clearing off the table, Kristen loaded the dishwasher. Working together, the two completed their tasks in only a few minutes.

"We're going to my room now. Okay, Mom?"

"Sure, honey, that's fine," Joanna said, placing the leftovers in the refrigerator. She paused, then decided to remind the pair a second time. "Homework before anything else."

"Of course," answered Kristen.

"Naturally," added Nicole.

Both vanished down the hallway that led to Kristen's bedroom. Watching them, Joanna grinned. The friendship with Nicole had been good for Kristen, and Joanna intended to shower love and attention on Nicole in the hope of compensating her for her unsettled home life.

Once Joanna had finished wiping down the kitchen counters, she made her way to Kristen's bedroom. Dutifully knocking—since her daughter made emphatic comments about privacy these days—she let herself in. Both girls were sitting cross-legged on the bed, spelling books open on their laps.

"Need any help?"

"No, thanks, Mom."

Still Joanna lingered, looking for an excuse to stay and chat. "I was placed third in the school spelling bee when I was your age."

Kristen glanced speculatively toward her friend. "That's great, Mom."

Warming to her subject, Joanna hurried to add, "I could outspell every boy in the class."

Kristen closed her textbook. "Mrs. Andrews, our new teacher, said the school wasn't going to have a spelling bee this year."

Joanna walked into the room and sat on the edge of

the bed. "That's too bad, because I know you'd do well."

"I only got a B in spelling, Mom. I'm okay, but it's not my best subject."

A short uneasy silence followed while both girls studied Joanna, as though waiting for her to either leave or make a formal announcement.

"I thought we'd pop popcorn later," Joanna said, flashing a cheerful smile.

"Good." Kristen nodded and her gaze fell pointedly to her textbook. This was followed by another long moment of silence.

"Mom, I thought you said you wanted us to do our homework."

"I do."

"Well, we can't very well do it with you sitting here watching us."

"Oh." Joanna leaped off the bed. "Sorry."

"That's all right."

"Let me know when you're done."

"Why?" Kristen asked, looking perplexed.

Joanna shrugged. "I…I thought we might all sit around and chat. Girl talk, that sort of thing." Without being obvious about it, she'd hoped to offer Nicole maternal advice and some much needed affection. The thought of the little girl's father and what he was doing that very evening was so distasteful that Joanna had to force herself not to frown.

"Mom, Nicole and I are going to practise our song once we've finished our homework. Remember?"

"Oh, right. I forgot." Sheepishly, she started to walk away.

"I really appreciate your sewing my costume, Mrs. Parsons," Nicole added.

"It's no trouble, Nicole. I'm happy to do it."

"Speaking of the costumes," Kristen muttered, "didn't you say something about wanting to finish them before the weekend?"

"I did?" The look Kristen gave her suggested she must have. "Oh, right, now I remember."

The girls, especially her daughter, seemed relieved when Joanna left the bedroom. This wasn't going well. She'd planned on spending extra time with them, but it was clear they weren't keen on having her around. Taking a deep breath, Joanna headed for the living room, feeling a little piqued. Her ego should be strong enough to handle rejection from two eleven-year-old girls.

She settled in the kitchen and brought out her sewing machine again. The red costumes for the talent show were nearly finished. She ran her hand over the polished cotton and let her thoughts wander. She and Kristen had lived in the house only since September. For the six years following the divorce, Joanna had been forced to raise her daughter in a small apartment. Becoming a home owner had been a major step for her and she was proud of the time and care that had gone into choosing their small one-storey house. It had required some repairs, but nothing major, and the sense of accomplishment she'd experienced when she signed her name to the mortgage papers had been well worth the years of scrimping. The house had only two bedrooms, but there was plenty of space in the backyard for a garden, something Joanna had insisted on. She thought that anyone studying her might be amused. On the one hand, she was a woman with basic traditional values, and on the other, a goal-setting businesswoman struggling to succeed in a male-dominated field. Her boss would have found it difficult to understand that the woman who'd set her sights on the position of senior loan officer liked the feel of wet dirt under her fingernails. And he would have been surprised to learn that she could take a simple piece of bright red cotton and turn it into a dazzling costume for a talent show.

An hour later, when Joanna was watching television and finishing up the hand stitching on the costumes, Kristen and Nicole rushed into the living room, looking pleased about something.

"You girls ready for popcorn?"

"Not me," Nicole said, placing her hands over her stomach. "I'm still full from dinner."

Joanna nodded. The girl obviously wasn't accustomed to eating nutritionally balanced meals.

"We want to do our song for you."

"Great." Joanna scooted close to the edge of the sofa, eagerly awaiting their performance. Kristen plugged in her ghetto blaster and snapped in the cassette, then hurried to her friend's side, striking a pose until the music started.

"I can tell already that you're going to be great," Joanna said, clapping her hands to the lively beat.

She was right. The two did astonishingly well, and when they'd finished Joanna applauded loudly.

"We did okay?"

"You were fabulous."

Kristen and Nicole positively glowed.

When they returned to Kristen's bedroom, Joanna followed them. Kristen turned around and seemed surprised to find her mother there.

"Mom," she hissed between clenched teeth, "what's with you tonight? You haven't been yourself since Nicole arrived."

"I haven't?"

"You keep following us around."

"I do?"

"Really, Mom, we like you and everything, but Nicole and I want to talk about boys and stuff, and we can't very well do that with you here."

"Oh, Mrs. Parsons, I forgot to tell you," Nicole inserted, obviously unaware of the whispered conversation going on between Kristen and her mother. "I told my dad about you making my costume for the talent show, and he said he wants to pay you for your time and expenses."

"You told your dad?" Kristen asked, and whirled around to face her friend. "I thought you weren't going to because he'd feel guilty. Oh, I get it! That's how you got him to let you spend the night. Great idea!"

Joanna frowned. "What exactly does that mean?"

The two girls exchanged meaningful glances and Nicole looked distinctly uncomfortable.

"What does what mean?" Kristen repeated the question in a slightly elevated voice Joanna recognized immediately. Her daughter was up to one of her schemes again.

Nicole stepped in front of her friend. "It's my fault, Mrs. Parsons. I wanted to spend the night here instead of with Mrs. Wagner, so I told Dad that Kristen had invited me."

"Mom, you've got to understand. Mrs. Wagner won't let Nicole watch anything but educational television, and you know there are special shows we like to watch."

"That's not the part I mean," Joanna said, dismissing their rushed explanation. "I want to know what you meant by not telling Mr. Lund about the talent show because he'd feel guilty.''

"Oh…that part." The two girls glanced at each other, as though silently deciding which one would do the explaining.

Nicole raised her gaze to Joanna and sighed, her thin shoulders moving up and down expressively. "My dad won't be able to attend the talent show because he's got a business meeting in Seattle, and I knew he'd feel terrible about it. He really likes it when I do things like the show. It gives him something to tell my grandparents about, like I was going to be the next Madonna or something."

"He has to travel a lot to business meetings," Kristen added quickly.

"Business meetings?"

"Like tonight," Kristen went on to explain.

"Dad has to fly someplace with Mr. Becky. He owns half the company and Dad owns the other half. He said it had to do with getting a big order, but I never listen to stuff like that, although Dad likes to explain every little detail so I'll know where he's at and what he's doing."

Joanna felt a numbing sensation creeping slowly up her spine. "Your dad owns half a company?"

"Spokane Aluminum is the reason we moved here from West Virginia."

"Spokane Aluminum?" Joanna's voice rose half an octave. "Your dad owns half of Spokane Aluminum?" The company was one of the largest employers in the Northwest. A shockingly large percentage of their state's economy was directly or indirectly tied to this company. A sick feeling settled in Joanna's stomach. Not only was Nicole's father wealthy, he was socially prominent, and all the while she'd been thinking... Oh, dear heavens. "So your father's out of town tonight?" she asked, feeling the warmth invade her face.

"You knew that, Mom." Kristen gave her mother another one of those searching gazes that suggested Joanna might be losing her memory—due to advanced age, no doubt.

"I...I thought—" Abruptly she bit off what she'd been about to say. When Kristen had said something about Tanner being with Becky, she'd assumed it was a woman. But of course it was *John* Becky, whose name was familiar to everyone in that part of the country. Joanna remembered reading in the *Review* that Becky had taken on a partner, but she hadn't made the connection. Perhaps she'd misjudged Tanner Lund, she reluctantly conceded. Perhaps she'd been a bit too eager to view him in a bad light.

"Before we came to Spokane," Nicole was saying now, "Dad and I had a long talk about the changes the move would make in our lives. We made a list of the good things and a list of the bad things, and then we talked about them. One bad thing was that Dad would be gone a lot, until he can hire another manager. He doesn't feel good about leaving me with strangers, and we didn't know a single person in Spokane other than Mr. Becky and his wife, but they're real old—over forty, anyway. He even went and interviewed Mrs. Wagner before I spent the night there the first time."

The opinion Joanna had formed of Tanner Lund was crumbling at her feet. Evidently he wasn't the irresponsible parent she'd assumed.

"Nicole told me you met her dad in the grocery store when you bought the mix for the cupcakes." Kristen shook her head as if to say she was thoroughly disgusted with her mother for not taking her advice that night and curling her hair before she showed her face in public.

"I told my dad you don't dress that way all the time," Nicole added, then shifted her gaze to the other side of the room. "But I don't think he believed me until he dropped me off tonight."

Joanna began to edge her way toward the bedroom door. "Your father and I seem to have started off on the wrong foot," she said weakly.

Nicole bit her lower lip. "I know. He wasn't real keen on me spending the night here, but I talked him into it."

"Mom?" Kristen asked, frowning. "What did you say to Mr. Lund when you met him at the store?"

"Nothing," she answered, taking a few more retreating steps.

"She asked my dad what I was doing up so late on a school night, and he told me later that he didn't like her attitude," Nicole explained. "I didn't get a chance to tell you that I'm normally in bed by nine-thirty, but that night was special because Dad had just come home from one of his trips. His plane was late and I didn't remember to tell him about the party stuff until after we got home from Mrs. Wagner's."

"I see," Joanna murmured, and swallowed uncomfortably.

"You'll get a chance to settle things with Mr. Lund when he picks up Nicole tomorrow night," Kristen stated, and it was obvious that she wanted her mother to make an effort to get along with her best friend's father.

"Right," Joanna muttered, dreading the confrontation. She never had been particularly fond of eating crow.

Four

Joanna was breading pork chops the following evening when Kristen barrelled into the kitchen, leaving the door swinging in her wake. "Mr. Lund's here to pick up Nicole. I think you should invite him and Nicole to stay for dinner...and explain about, you know, the other night."

Oh, sure, Joanna mused. She often invited company owners and acting presidents over for an evening meal. Pork chops and mashed potatoes weren't likely to impress someone like Tanner Lund.

Before Kristen could launch into an argument, Joanna shook her head and offered the first excuse that came to mind. "There aren't enough pork chops to ask him tonight. Besides, Mr. Lund is probably tired from his trip and anxious to get home."

"I bet he's hungry, too," Kristen pressed. "And Nicole thinks you're a fabulous cook, and—"

A sharp look from her mother cut her off. "Another night, Kristen!"

Joanna brushed the bread crumbs off her fingertips and untied her apron. Inhaling deeply, she paused long enough to run a hand through her hair and check her reflection in the window above the sink. No one was going to mistake her for Miss America, but her appearance was passable. Okay, it was time to hold her head high, spit the feathers out of her mouth and get ready to down some crow.

Joanna forced a welcoming smile onto her lips as she stepped into the living room. Tanner stood awkwardly just inside the front door, as though prepared to beat a hasty retreat if necessary. "How was your trip?" she ventured, straining to make the question sound cheerful.

"Fine. Thank you." His expression didn't change.

"Do you have time for a cup of coffee?" she asked next, doing her best to disguise her unease. She wondered quickly if she'd unpacked her china cups yet. After their shaky beginning, Joanna wasn't quite sure if she could undo the damage. But standing in the entryway wouldn't work. She needed to sit down for this.

He eyed her suspiciously. Joanna wasn't sure she should even try to explain things. In time he'd learn she wasn't a candidate for the loony bin—just as she'd stumbled over the fact that he wasn't a terrible father. Trying to tell him that she was an upstanding member of the community after he'd seen her dressed in a wool coat draped over pajamas, giving him looks that suggested he be reported to Children's Protective Services, wasn't exactly a task she relished.

Tanner glanced at his wristwatch and shook his head. "I haven't got time to visit tonight. Thanks for the invitation, though."

Joanna almost sighed aloud with relief.

"Did Nicole behave herself?"

Joanna nodded. "She wasn't the least bit of trouble. Nicole's a great kid."

A smile cracked the tight edges of his mouth. "Good."

Kristen and Nicole burst into the room. "Is Mr. Lund going to stay, Mom?"

"He can't tonight…"

"Another time…"

They spoke simultaneously, with an equal lack of enthusiasm.

"Oh." The girls looked at each other and frowned, their disappointment noticeable.

"Have you packed everything, Nicole?" Tanner asked, not hiding his eagerness to leave.

The eleven-year-old nodded reluctantly. "I think so."

"Don't you think you should check my room one more time?" Kristen suggested, grabbing her friend's hand and leading her back toward the hallway.

"Oh, right. I suppose I should." The two disappeared before either Joanna or Tanner could call them back.

The silence between them hummed so loudly Joanna swore she could have waltzed to it. But since the opportunity had presented itself, she decided to get the unpleasant task of explaining her behavior out of the way while she still had her nerve.

"I think I owe you an apology," she murmured, her face flushing.

"An apology?"

"I thought…you know… The night we met, I assumed you were an irresponsible parent because Nicole was up so late. She's now told me that you'd just returned from a trip."

"Yes, well, I admit I did feel the sting of your disapproval."

This wasn't easy. Joanna swallowed uncomfortably and laced her fingers together forcing herself to meet his eyes. "Nicole explained that your flight was delayed and she forgot to mention the party supplies when you picked her up at the baby-sitter's. She said she didn't remember until you got all the way home."

Tanner's mouth relaxed a bit more. "Since we're both being truthful here, I'll admit that I wasn't overly impressed with you that night, either."

Joanna dropped her gaze. "I can imagine. I hope you realise I don't usually dress like that."

"I gathered as much when I dropped Nicole off yesterday afternoon."

They both paused to share a brief smile and Joanna instantly felt better. It hadn't been easy to blurt all this out, but she was relieved that they'd finally cleared the air.

"Since Kristen and Nicole are such good friends, I thought, well, that I should set things right between us. From everything Nicole's said, you're doing an excellent job of parenting."

"From everything she's told me, the same must be true of you."

"Believe me, it isn't easy raising a preteen daughter," Joanna announced. She rubbed her palms together a couple of times, searching for something brilliant to add.

Tanner shook his head. "Isn't that the truth?"

They laughed then, and because they were still awkward with each other the sound was rusty.

"Now that you mention it, maybe I could spare a few minutes for a cup of coffee."

"Sure." Joanna led the way into the kitchen. While Tanner sat down at the table, she filled a mug from the pot keeping warm on the plate of the automatic coffee maker and placed it carefully in front of him. Now that she knew him a bit better, she realised he'd prefer that to a dainty china cup. "How do you take it?"

"Just black, thanks."

She pulled out the chair across the table from him, still feeling a little ill at ease. Her mind was whirling. She didn't want to give Tanner a second wrong impression now that she'd managed to correct the first one. Her worry was that he might interpret her friendliness as a sign of romantic interest, which it wasn't. Building a new relationship was low on her priority list. Besides, they simply weren't on the same economic level. She worked for a savings-and-loan institution and he was half owner of the largest employer in the area. The last thing she wanted was for Tanner to think of her as a gold digger.

Joanna's thoughts were tumbling over themselves as she struggled to find a diplomatic way of telling him all this without sounding like some kind of man hater. And without sounding presumptuous.

"I'd like to pay you," Tanner said, cutting into her reflections. His cheque-book was resting on the table, Cross pen poised above it.

Joanna blinked, not understanding. "For the coffee?"

He gave her an odd look. "For looking after Nicole."

"No, please." Joanna shook her head dismissively. "It wasn't the least bit of trouble for her to stay the night. Really."

"What about the costume for the talent show? Surely I owe you something for that."

"No." Once more she shook her head for emphasis. "I've had that material tucked away in a drawer for ages. If I hadn't used it for Nicole's costume, I'd probably have ended up giving it away later.''

"But your time must be worth something.''

"It was just as easy to sew up two as one. I was happy to do it. Anyway, there'll probably be a time in the future when I need a favour. I'm worthless when it comes to electrical outlets and even worse with plumbing.''

Joanna couldn't believe she'd said that. Tanner Lund wasn't the type of man to do his own electrical repairs.

"Don't be afraid to ask,'' he told her. "If I can't fix it, I'll find someone who can.''

"Thank you,'' she said, relaxing. Now that she was talking to Tanner, she decided he was both pleasant and forthright, not at all the coldly remote or self-important man his wealth might have led her to expect.

"Mom,'' Kristen cried as she charged into the kitchen, "did you ask Mr. Lund yet?''

"About what?''

"About coming over for dinner some time.''

Joanna felt the heat shoot up her neck and face until it reached her hairline. Kristen had made the invitation sound like a romantic tryst the three of them had been planning the entire time Tanner was away.

Nicole, entering the room behind her friend, provided a timely interruption.

"Dad, Kristen and I want to do our song for you now.''

"I'd like to see it. Do you mind, Joanna?''

"Of course not.''

"Mom finished the costumes last night. We'll change and be back in a minute,'' Kristen said, her voice high with excitement. The two scurried off. The minute they were out of sight, Joanna stood up abruptly and refilled her cup. Actually she was looking for a way to speak frankly to Tanner, without embarrassing herself—or him. She thought ironically that anyone looking at her now would be hard put to believe she was a competent loan officer with a promising future.

"I think I should explain something," she began, her voice unsteady.

"Yes?" Tanner asked, his gaze following her movements around the kitchen.

Joanna couldn't seem to stand in one place for long. She moved from the coffeepot to the refrigerator, finally stopping in front of the stove. She linked her fingers behind her back and took a deep breath before she trusted herself to speak. "I thought it was important to clear up any misunderstanding between us, because the girls are such good friends. When Nicole's with Kristen and me, I want you to know she's in good hands."

Tanner gave her a polite nod. "I appreciate that."

"But I have a feeling that Kristen—and maybe Nicole, too—would like for us to get to know each other, er, better, if you know what I mean." Oh Lord, that sounded so stupid. Joanna felt herself grasping at straws. "I'm not interested in a romantic relationship, Tanner. I've got too much going on in my life to get involved, and I don't want you to feel threatened by the girls and their schemes. Forgive me for being so blunt, but I'd prefer to have this out in the open." She'd blurted it out so fast, she wondered if he'd understood. "This dinner invitation was Kristen's idea, not mine. I don't want you to think I had anything to do with it."

"An invitation to dinner isn't exactly a marriage proposal."

"True," Joanna threw back quickly. "But you might think...I don't know. I guess I don't want you to assume I'm interested in you—romantically, that is.'' She slumped back into the chair, pushed her hair away from her forehead and released a long sigh. "I'm only making matters worse, aren't I?"

"No. If I understand you correctly, you're saying you'd like to be friends and nothing more."

"Right." Pleased with his perceptiveness, Joanna straightened. Glad he could say in a few simple words what had left her breathless.

"The truth of the matter is, I feel much the same way," Tanner went on to explain. "I was married once and it was more than enough."

Joanna found herself nodding enthusiastically. "Exactly. I like my life the way it is. Kristen and I are very close. We just moved into this house and we've lots of plans for redecorating. My career is going nicely."

"Likewise. I'm too busy with this company to get involved in a relationship, either. The last thing I need right now is a woman to complicate my life."

"A man would only come between Kristen and me at this stage."

"How long have you been divorced?" Tanner asked, folding his hands around his coffee mug.

"Six years."

The information appeared to satisfy him, and he nodded slowly, as though to say he trusted what she was telling him. "It's been five for me."

She nodded, too. Like her, he hadn't immediately jumped into another relationship, nor was he looking for one. No doubt he had his reasons; Joanna knew she had hers.

"Friends?" Tanner asked, and extended his hand for her to shake.

"And nothing more," Joanna added, placing her hand in his.

They exchanged a smile.

"SINCE MR. LUND can't be here for the talent show on Wednesday, he wants to take Nicole and me out for dinner next Saturday night," Kristen announced. "Nicole said to ask you if it was all right."

"That's fine," Joanna returned absently, scanning the front page of the Saturday evening newspaper. It had been more than a week since she'd spoken to Tanner. She felt good about the way things had gone that afternoon; they understood each other now, despite their rather uncertain start.

Kristen darted back into the kitchen, returning a minute later. "I think it would be best if you spoke to Mr. Lund yourself, Mom."

"Okay, honey." She'd finished reading Dear Abby and had just turned to the comics section, looking for Garfield, her favourite cat.

"Mom!" Kristen cried impatiently. "Mr. Lund's on the phone now. You can't keep him waiting like this. It's impolite."

Hurriedly Joanna set the paper aside. "For heaven's sake, why didn't you say so earlier?"

"I did. Honestly, Mom, I think you're losing it."

Whatever *it* was sounded serious. The minute Joanna was inside the kitchen, Kristen thrust the telephone receiver into her hand.

"This is Joanna," she said.

"This is Tanner," he answered right away. "Don't feel bad. Nicole claims I'm losing *it* too."

"I'd take her more seriously if I knew what *it* was."

"Yeah, me too," Tanner said, and she could hear

the laughter in his voice. "Listen, is dinner next Saturday evening all right with you?"

"I can't see a problem at this end."

"Great. The girls suggested that ice-cream parlour they're always talking about."

"The Pink Palace," Joanna said, and managed to swallow a chuckle. Tanner was really letting himself in for a crazy night with those two. Last year Kristen had talked Joanna into dinner there for her birthday. The hamburgers had been as expensive as T-bone steaks, and tough as rawhide. The music was so loud it had impaired Joanna's hearing for an entire week afterward. And the place was packed with teenagers. On the bright side, though, the ice cream was pretty good.

"By the way," Joanna said, "Nicole's welcome to stay here when you're away next week."

"Joanna, that's great. I didn't want to ask, but the kid's been at me ever since the last time. She was worried I was going to send her back to Mrs. Wagner."

"It'll work best for her to stay here, since that's the night of the talent show."

"Are you absolutely sure?"

"Absolutely. It's no trouble at all. Just drop her off—and don't worry."

"Right." He sounded relieved. "And don't wear anything fancy next Saturday night."

"Saturday night?" Joanna asked, lost for a moment.

"Yeah. Didn't you just tell me it was all right for the four of us to go to dinner?"

Five

"I really appreciate this, Joanna," Tanner said. Nicole stood at his side, overnight bag clenched in her hand, her eyes round and sad.

"It's no problem, Tanner. Really."

Tanner hugged his daughter tightly. He briefly closed his eyes and Joanna could feel his regret. He was as upset about missing his daughter's talent-show performance as Nicole was not to have him there.

"Be good, sweetheart."

"I will."

"And I want to hear all the details about tonight when I get back, okay?"

Nicole nodded and attempted a smile.

"I'd be there if I could."

"I know, Dad. Don't worry about it. There'll be plenty of other talent shows. Kristen and I were thinking that if we do really good, we might take our act on the road, the way Daisy Gilbert does."

"Daisy who?" Tanner asked, and raised questioning eyes to Joanna, as if he expected her to supply the answer.

"A singer," was the best Joanna could do. Kristen had as many cassette tapes as Joanna had runs in her tights. She found it impossible to keep her daughter's favourite rock stars straight. Apparently Tanner wasn't any more knowledgeable than she was.

"Not just *any* singer, Mom," Kristen corrected impatiently. "Daisy's special. She's only a little older than Nicole and me, and if she can be a rock star at fifteen, then so can we."

Although Joanna hated to squelch such optimism, she suspected that the girls might be missing one minor skill if they hoped to find fame and fortune as professional singers. "But you don't sing."

"Yeah, but we lip-synch real good."

"Come on, Nicole," Kristen said, reaching for her friend's overnight bag. "We've got to practise."

The two disappeared down the hallway and Joanna was left alone with Tanner.

"You have the telephone number for the hotel and the meeting place?" he asked.

"I'll call if there's a problem. Don't worry, Tanner, I'm sure everything's going to be fine."

He nodded, but a tight scowl darkened his face.

"For heaven's sake, stop looking so guilty."

His eyes widened in surprise. "It shows?"

"It might as well be flashing from a marquee."

Tanner grinned and rubbed the side of his jaw with his left hand. "There are only two meetings left that I'll have to deal with personally. Becky's promised to handle the others. You know, when I bought into the company and committed myself to these trips, I didn't think leaving Nicole would be this traumatic. We both hate it—at least, she did until she spent the night here with you and Kristen the last time."

"She's a special little girl."

"Thanks," Tanner said, looking suitably proud. It was obvious that he worked hard at being a good father, and Joanna felt a twinge of conscience for the assumptions she'd made about him earlier.

"Listen," she murmured, then took a deep breath, wondering how best to approach the subject of dinner. "About Saturday night…"

"What about it?"

"I thought, well, it would be best if it were just you and the girls."

Already he was shaking his head, his mouth set in firm lines of resolve. "It wouldn't be the same without you. I owe you, Joanna, and since you won't accept payment for keeping Nicole, then the least you can do is agree to dinner."

"But—"

"If you're worried about this seeming too much like a date—don't. We understand each other."

Her responding smile was decidedly weak. "Okay, if that's the way you want it. Kristen and I'll be ready Saturday at six."

"Good."

JOANNA WAS PUTTING the finishing touches to her makeup before the talent show when the telephone rang.

"I'll get it," Kristen yelled, racing down the hallway as if answering the phone before the second ring was a matter of life and death.

Joanna rolled her eyes toward the ceiling at the importance telephone conversations had recently assumed for Kristen. She half expected the call to be from Tanner, but then she heard Kristen exclaim, "Hi, Grandma!" Joanna smiled softly, pleased that her mother had remembered the talent show. Her parents were retired and lived in Colville, a town about sixty miles north of Spokane. She knew they would have attended the talent show themselves had road conditions been better. In winter, the families tended to keep in touch by phone because driving could be hazardous. No doubt her mother was calling now to wish Kristen luck.

Bits and pieces of the conversation drifted down the hallway as Kristen chatted excitedly about the show, Nicole's visit and their song.

"Mom, it's Grandma!" Kristen yelled. "She wants to talk to you."

Joanna finished blotting her lipstick and hurried to the phone. "Hi, Mom," she said cheerfully. "It's nice of you to call."

"What's this about you going out on a date Saturday night?"

"Who told you that?" Joanna demanded, groaning silently. Her mother had been telling her for years that she ought to remarry. Joanna felt like throttling Kristen for even mentioning Tanner's name. The last thing she needed was for her parents to start pressuring her about this relationship.

"Why, Kristen told me all about it, and sweetie, if you don't mind my saying so, this man sounds just perfect for you. You're both single parents. He has a daughter, you have a daughter, and the girls are best friends. The arrangement is ideal."

"Mother, please, I don't know what Kristen told you, but Tanner only wants to thank me for watching Nicole while he's away on business. Dinner on Saturday night is not a date!"

"He's taking you to dinner?"

"Me and Kristen and his daughter."

"What was his name again?"

"Tanner Lund," Joanna answered, desperate to change the subject. "Hasn't the weather been nasty this week? I'm really looking forward to spring. I was thinking about planting some annuals along the back fence."

"Tanner Lund," her mother repeated, slowly drawling out his name. "Now that has a nice solid feel to it. What's he like, sweetie?"

"Oh, honestly, Mother, I don't know. He's a man. What more do you want me to say?"

Her mother seemed to approve that piece of information. "I find it interesting that that's the way you view him. I think he could be the one, Joanna."

"Mother, please, how many times do I have to tell you? I'm not going to remarry. Ever!"

A short pause followed her announcement. "We'll see, sweetie, we'll see."

"AREN'T YOU GOING to wear a dress, Mom?" Kristen gave her another of those scathing glances intended to melt a mother's confidence into puddles of doubt. Joanna had deliberated for hours on what to wear for this evening out with Tanner and the girls. If she chose a dress, something simple and classic like the ones she wore to the office, she might look too formal for a casual outing. The only other dresses she owned were party dresses, and those were so outdated they were almost back in style.

Dark wool pants and a wheat-colored Irish cableknit sweater had seemed the perfect solution. Or so Joanna had thought until Kristen looked at her and frowned.

"Mom, tonight is important."

"We're going to the Pink Palace, not the Spokane House."

"I know, but Mr. Lund is so nice." Her daughter's gaze fell on the bouquet of pink roses on the dining-room table, and she reverently stroked a bloom. Tanner had arranged for the flowers to be delivered to Nicole and Kristen the night of the talent show. "You can't wear slacks to dinner with the man who sent me my first real flowers," she announced in tones of finality.

Joanna hesitated. "I'm sure this is what Mr. Lund expects," she said with far more confidence than she felt.

"You think so?"

She hoped so! She smiled, praying that her air of certainty would be enough to appease her sceptical daughter. Still, she had to agree with Kristen: Tanner *was* nice. More than nice—that was such a weak word. With every meeting, Joanna's estimation of the man grew. He'd called on Friday to thank her for minding Nicole, who'd gone straight home from school on Thursday afternoon since her father was back, and mentioned he was looking forward to Saturday. He was thoughtful, sensitive, personable, and a wonderful father. Not to mention one of the best-looking men she'd ever met. It was unfortunate, really, that she wasn't looking for a husband, because Tanner Lund could easily be a prime candidate.

The word husband bounced in Joanna's mind like a ricocheting bullet. She blamed her mother for that. What she'd told her was true—Joanna was finished with marriage, finished with love. Davey had taught her how difficult it was for most men to remain faithful, and Joanna had no intention of repeating those painful lessons. Besides, if a man ever did become part of her life again, it would be someone on her own social and economic level. Not like Tanner Lund. But that didn't mean she was completely blind to male charms. On the contrary, she saw handsome men every day, worked with several, and had even dated a few. However, it was Tanner Lund she found herself thinking about lately, and that bothered Joanna. It bothered her a lot.

The best thing to do was nip this near relationship in the bud. She'd go to dinner with him this once, but only this once, and that would be the end of it.

"They're here!" The drape swished back into place as Kristen bolted away from the large picture window.

Calmly Joanna opened the hall closet and retrieved their winter coats. She might appear outwardly composed, but her fingers were shaking. The prospect of seeing Tanner left her trembling, and that fact drained away what little confidence she'd managed to accumulate over the past couple of days.

Both Tanner and Nicole came to the front door. Kristen held out her hands, and Nicole gripped them eagerly. Soon the two were jumping up and down like pogo sticks gone berserk.

"I can tell we're in for a fun evening," Tanner muttered under his breath.

He looked wonderful, Joanna admitted grudgingly. The kind of man every woman dreams about—well, almost every woman. Joanna longed to think of herself as immune to the handsome Mr. Lund. Unfortunately she wasn't.

Since their last meeting, she'd tried to figure out when her feelings for Tanner had changed. The roses had done it, she decided. Ordering them for Kristen and Nicole had been so thoughtful, and the girls had been ecstatic at the gesture.

When they'd finished lip-synching their song, they'd bowed before the auditorium full of appreciative parents. Then the school principal, Mr. Holliday, had stood at their side and presented them each with a beautiful bouquet of long-stemmed pink roses. Flowers Tanner had wired because he couldn't be there to watch their act.

"Are you ready?" Tanner asked, holding open the door for Joanna.

She nodded. "I think so."

Although it was early, a line had already begun to form outside the Pink Palace when they arrived. The minute they pulled into the parking lot, they were accosted by a loud, vibrating rock-and-roll song that might have been an old Jerry Lee Lewis number.

"It looks like we'll have to wait," Joanna commented. "That lineup's getting longer by the minute."

"I had my secretary make reservations," Tanner told her. "I heard this place really grooves on a Saturday night."

"Grooves!" Nicole repeated, smothering her giggles behind her cupped palm. Kristen laughed with her.

Turner leaned his head close to Joanna's. "It's difficult to reason with a generation that grew up without Janis and Jimi!"

Janis Joplin and Jimi Hendrix were a bit before Joanna's time, too, but she knew what he meant.

The Pink Palace was exactly as Joanna remembered. The popular ice-cream parlor was decorated in a fifties theme, with old-fashioned circular booths and outdated jukeboxes. The waitresses wore billowing pink skirts with a French poodle design and roller-skated between tables, taking and delivering orders. Once inside, Joanna, Tanner and the girls were seated almost immediately and handed huge menus. Neither girl bothered to read through the selections, having made their choices in the car. They'd both decided on cheeseburgers and banana splits.

By the time the waitress, chewing on a thick wad of bubble gum, skated to a stop at their table, Joanna had made her selection, too.

"A cheeseburger and a banana split," she said, grinning at the girls.

"Same here," Tanner said, "and coffee, please."

"I'll have a cup, too," Joanna added.

The teenager wrote down their order and glided toward the kitchen.

Joanna opened her purse and brought out a small wad of cotton wool.

"What's that for?" Tanner wanted to know when she pulled it apart into four fluffy balls and handed two of them to him, keeping the other pair for herself.

She pointed to her ears. "The last time I was here, I was haunted for days by a ringing in my ears that sounded suspiciously like an old Elvis tune."

Tanner chuckled and leaned across the table to shout, "It does get a bit loud, doesn't it?"

Kristen and Nicole looked from one parent to the other then shouted together, "If it's too loud, you're too old!"

Joanna raised her hand. "Guilty as charged."

Tanner nodded and shared a smile with Joanna. The smile did funny things to her stomach, and Joanna pressed her hands over her abdomen in a futile effort to quell her growing awareness of Tanner. A warning light flashed in her mind, spelling out danger.

Joanna wasn't sure what had come over her, but whatever it was, she didn't like it.

Their meal arrived, and for a while, at least, Joanna could direct her attention to that. The food was better than she remembered. The cheeseburgers were juicy and tender and the banana splits divine. She promised herself she'd eat cottage cheese and fruit every day at lunch for the next week to balance all the extra calories from this one meal.

While Joanna and Tanner exchanged only the occasional remark, the girls chattered happily throughout dinner. When the waitress skated away with the last of their empty plates, Tanner suggested a movie.

"Great idea!" Nicole cried, enthusiastically seconded by Kristen.

"What do you think, Joanna?" asked Tanner.

She started to say that the evening had been full enough—until she found two eager young faces looking hopefully at her. She couldn't finish her sentence; it just wasn't in her to dash their good time.

"Sure," she managed instead, trying to insert a bit of excitement into her voice.

"*Teen Massacre* is showing at the mall," Nicole said, shooting a glance in her father's direction. "Donny Rosenburg saw it and claims it scared him out of his wits, but then Donny doesn't have many."

Kristen laughed and nodded, apparently well-acquainted with the witless Donny.

Without the least bit of hesitation, Tanner shook his head. "No way, Nicole."

"Come on, Dad, everyone's seen it. The only reason it got an adult rating is because of the blood and gore, and I've seen that lots of times."

"Discussion is closed." He spoke without raising his voice, but the authority behind his words was enough to convince Joanna she'd turn up the loser if she ever crossed Tanner Lund. Still, she knew she wouldn't hesitate if she felt he was wrong, but in this case she agreed with him completely.

Nicole's lower lip jutted out rebelliously, and for a minute Joanna thought the girl might try to argue her case. But she wasn't surprised when Nicole yielded without further argument.

Deciding which movie to see involved some real negotiating. The girls had definite ideas of what was acceptable, as did Tanner and Joanna. Like Tanner, Joanna wasn't about to allow her daughter to see a movie with an adult rating, even if it was "only because of the blood and gore."

They finally compromised on a comedy that starred a popular teen idol. The girls thought that would be "all right," but they made it clear that *Teen Massacre* was their first choice.

Half an hour later they were inside the theater, and Tanner asked, "Anyone for popcorn?"

"Me," Kristen said.

"Me, too, and could we both have a Coke and chocolate-covered raisins, too?" Nicole asked.

Tanner rolled his eyes and, grinning, glanced toward Joanna. "What about you?"

"Nothing." She didn't know where the girls were going to put all this food, but she knew where it would end up if she were to consume it. Her hips! She sometimes suspected that junk food didn't even pass through her stomach, but attached itself directly to her hip bones.

"You're sure?"

"Positive."

Tanner returned a moment later with three large boxes of popcorn and other assorted treats.

As soon as they'd emptied Tanner's arms of all but

one box of popcorn, the girls started into the auditorium.

"Hey, you two, wait for us," Joanna called after them, bewildered by the way they'd hurried off without waiting for her and Tanner.

Kristen and Nicole stopped abruptly and turned around, a look of pure horror on their young faces.

"You're not going to sit with us, are you, Mom?" Kristen wailed. "You just can't!"

"Why not?" This was news to Joanna. Sure, it had been a while since she'd gone to a movie with her daughter, but Kristen had always sat with her in the past.

"Someone might see us," her daughter went on to explain, in tones of exaggerated patience. "No one sits with their parents any more. Not even woosies."

"Woosies?"

"Sort of like nerds, only worse!" Kristen said.

"Sitting with us is obviously a social embarrassment to be avoided at all costs," Tanner muttered.

"Can we go now, Mom?" Kristen pleaded. "I don't want to miss the previews."

Joanna nodded, still a little stunned. She enjoyed going out to a movie now and again, usually accompanied by her daughter and often several of Kristen's friends. Until tonight, no one had openly objected to sitting in the same row with her. However, now that Joanna thought about it, Kristen hadn't been interested in going to the movies for the past couple of months.

"I guess this is what happens when they hit sixth grade," Tanner said, holding the auditorium door for Joanna.

She walked down the center aisle and paused by an empty row near the back, checking with Tanner before she entered. Neither of them sat down, though, until they'd located the girls. Kristen and Nicole were three rows from the front and had slid down so far that their eyes were level with the seats ahead of them.

"Ah, the joys of fatherhood," Tanner commented, after they'd taken their places. "Not to mention motherhood."

Joanna still felt a little taken aback by what had happened. She thought she had a close relationship with Kristen, and yet her daughter had never said a word about not wanting to be anywhere near her in a movie theatre. She knew this might sound like a trivial concern to some, but she couldn't help worrying that the solid foundation she'd spent a decade reinforcing had started to crumble.

"Joanna?"

She turned to Tanner and tried to smile, but the attempt was unconvincing.

"What's wrong?"

Joanna fluttered her hand weakly, unable to find her voice. "Nothing." That came out sounding as though she might burst into tears any second.

"Is it Kristen?"

She nodded wildly.

"Because she didn't want to sit with us?"

Her hair bounced against her shoulders as she nodded again.

"The girls wanting to be by themselves bothers you?"

"No...yes. I don't know what I'm feeling. She's growing up, Tanner, and I guess it just hit me right between the eyes."

"It happened to me last week," Tanner said thoughtfully. "I found Nicole wearing a pair of tights. Hell, I didn't even know they made them for girls her age."

"They do, believe it or not," Joanna informed him. "Kristen did the same thing."

He shook his head as though he couldn't quite grasp the concept. "But they're only eleven."

"Going on sixteen."

"Has Kristen tried pasting on those fake fingernails yet?" Tanner shuddered in exaggerated disgust.

Joanna covered her mouth with one hand to hold back an attack of giggles. "Those press-on things turned up every place imaginable for weeks afterward."

Tanner turned sideways in his seat. "What about makeup?" he asked urgently.

"I caught her trying to sneak out of the house one morning last month. She was wearing the brightest eye shadow I've ever seen in my life. Tanner, I swear if she'd been standing on a shore, she could have guided lost ships into port."

He smiled, then dropped his gaze, looking uncomfortable. "So you do let her wear makeup?"

"I'm holding off as long as I can," Joanna admitted. "At the very least, she'll have to wait until seventh grade. That was when my mother let me. I don't think it's so unreasonable to expect Kristen to wait until junior high."

Tanner relaxed against the back of his seat and nodded a couple of times. "I'm glad to hear that. Nicole's been after me to 'wake up and smell the coffee,' as she puts it, for the past six months. Hell, I didn't know who to ask about these things. It really isn't something I'm comfortable discussing with my secretary."

"What about her mother?"

His eyes hardened. "She only sees Nicole when it's convenient, and it hasn't been for the past three years."

"I...I didn't mean to pry."

"You weren't. Carmen and I didn't exactly part on the best of terms. She's got a new life now and apparently doesn't want any reminders of the past—not that I totally blame her. We made each other miserable. Frankly, Joanna, my feelings about getting married again are the same as yours. One failed marriage was enough for me."

The theatre lights dimmed then, and the sound track started. Tanner leaned back and crossed his long legs, balancing one ankle on the opposite knee.

Joanna settled back, too, grateful that the movie they'd selected was a comedy. Her emotions were riding too close to the surface this evening. She could see herself bursting into tears at the slightest hint of sadness—for that matter, joy. Bambi traipsing through the woods would have done her in just then.

Joanna was so caught up in her thoughts that when Tanner and the others around her let out a boisterous laugh, she'd completely missed whatever had been so hilarious.

Without thinking, she reached over and grabbed a handful of Tanner's popcorn. She discovered that the crunchiness and the buttery, salty flavor suited her mood. Tanner held the box on the arm between them to make sharing easier.

The next time Joanna sent her fingers digging, they encountered Tanner's. "Sorry," she murmured, pulling her hand free.

"No problem," he answered, tilting the box her way. Joanna munched steadily. Before she knew it, the popcorn was gone and her fingers were laced with Tanner's, her hand firmly clasped in his.

The minute he reached for her hand, Joanna lost track of what was happening on the screen. Holding hands seemed such an innocent gesture, something teenagers did. He certainly didn't mean anything by it, Joanna told herself. It was just that her emotions were so confused lately, and she wasn't even sure why.

She liked Tanner, Joanna realised anew, liked him very much. And she thoroughly enjoyed Nicole. For the first time since her divorce, she could imagine getting involved with another man, and the thought frightened her. All right, it terrified her. This man belonged to a different world. Besides, she wasn't ready. Good grief, six years should have given her ample time to heal, but she'd been too afraid to lift the bandage.

When the movie was over, Tanner drove them home. The girls were tired, but managed to carry on a lively backseat conversation. The front seat was a different story. Neither Tanner nor Joanna had much to say.

"Would you like to come in for coffee?" Joanna asked when Tanner pulled into her driveway, although she was silently wishing he'd decline. Her nerves continued to clamor from the hand holding, and she wanted some time alone to organise her thoughts.

"Can we, Dad? Please?" Nicole begged. "Kristen and I want to watch the Saturday Night videos together."

"You're sure?" Tanner looked at Joanna, his brow creased with concern.

She couldn't answer. She wasn't sure of anything just then. "Of course," she forced herself to say. "It'll only take a minute or two to brew a pot."

"All right, then," Tanner said, and the girls let out whoops of delight.

Occasionally Joanna wondered if their daughters would ever get tired of one another's company. Probably, although they hadn't shown any signs of it yet. As far as she knew, the two girls had never had a serious disagreement.

Kristen and Nicole disappeared as soon as they got into the house. Within seconds, the television could be heard blaring rock music, which had recently become a familiar sound in the small one-storey house.

Tanner followed Joanna into the kitchen and stood leaning against the counter while she filled the automatic coffee maker with water. Her movements were jerky and abrupt. She felt awkward, ungraceful—as though this was the first time she'd ever been alone with a man. And that was a ridiculous way to feel, especially since the girls were practically within sight.

"I enjoyed tonight," Tanner commented, as she removed two cups from the cupboard.

"I did, too." She tossed him a lazy smile over her shoulder. But Tanner's eyes held hers, and it was as if she was seeing him for the first time. She half turned toward him, suddenly aware of how tall and lean he was, how thick and soft his dark hair. With an effort, Joanna looked from those mesmerising blue eyes and returned to the task of making coffee, although her fingers didn't seem willing to cooperate.

She stood waiting for the dark liquid to filter its way into the glass pot. Never had it seemed to take so long.

"Joanna."

Judging by the loudness of his voice, Tanner was standing directly behind her. A beat of silence followed before she turned around to face him.

Tanner's hands grasped her shoulders. "It's been a long time since I've sat in a movie and held a girl's hand."

She lowered her eyes and nodded. "Me, too."

"I felt like a kid again."

She'd been thinking much the same thing herself.

"I want to kiss you, Joanna."

She didn't need an analyst to inform her that kissing Tanner was something best avoided. She was about to tell him so when his hands gripped her waist and pulled her away from the support of the kitchen counter. A little taken aback, Joanna threw up her hands, as if to ward him off. But the minute they came into contact with the muscled hardness of his chest, they lost their purpose.

The moment Tanner's warm mouth claimed her lips, she felt an excitement that was almost shocking in its intensity. Her hands clutched the collar of his shirt as she eagerly gave herself up to the forgotten sensations. It had been so long since a man had kissed her like this.

The kiss was over much too soon. Far sooner than Joanna would have liked. The fire of his mouth had ignited a response in her she'd believed long dead. She was amazed at how readily it had sprung back to life. When Tanner dropped his arms and released her, Joanna felt suddenly weak, barely able to remain upright.

Her hand found her chest and she heaved a giant breath. "I...don't think that was a good idea."

Tanner's brows drew together, forming a ledge over his narrowed eyes. "I'm not sure I do, either, but it seemed right. I don't know what's happening between us, Joanna, and it's confusing the hell out of me."

"You? I'm the one who made it abundantly clear from the outset that I wasn't looking for a romantic involvement."

"I know, and I agree, but—"

"I'm more than pleased Kristen and Nicole are good friends, but I happen to like my life the way it is, thank you."

Tanner's frown grew darker, his expression both baffled and annoyed. "I feel the same way. It was a kiss, not a suggestion we live in sin."

"I...really wish you hadn't done that, Tanner."

"I apologise. Trust me, it won't happen again," he muttered, and buried his hands deep inside his pockets. "In fact it would probably be best if we forgot the entire incident."

"I agree totally."

"Fine then." He stalked out of the kitchen, but not before Joanna found herself wondering if she *could* forget it.

Six

A kiss was really such a minor thing, Joanna mused, slowly rotating her pencil between her palms. She'd made a criminal case out of nothing, and embarrassed both Tanner and herself.

"Joanna, have you had time to read over the Osborne loan application yet?" her boss, Robin Simpson asked, strolling up to her desk.

"Ah, no, not yet," Joanna said, her face flushing with guilt.

Robin frowned as he studied her. "What's been with you today? Every time I see you, you're gazing at the wall with a faraway look in your eye."

"Nothing's wrong." Blindly she reached toward her In basket and grabbed a file, although she hadn't a clue which one it was.

"If I didn't know better, I'd say you were daydreaming about a man."

Joanna managed a short, sarcastic laugh meant to deny everything. "Men are the last thing on my mind," she said flippantly. It was a half-truth. Men in the plural didn't interest her, but *man*, as in Tanner Lund, well, that was another matter.

Over the years Joanna had gone out of her way to avoid men she was attracted to—it was safer. She dated occasionally, but usually men who might be classified

as pleasant, men for whom she could never feel anything beyond a mild friendship. Magnetism, charm and
sex appeal were lost on her, thanks to a husband who'd
possessed all three and systematically destroyed her
faith in the possibility of a lasting relationship. At least,
those qualities hadn't piqued her interest again, until
she met Tanner. Okay, so her dating habits for the past
few years had been a bit premeditated, but everyone
deserved a night out now and again. It didn't seem fair
to be denied the pleasure of a fun evening simply because she wasn't in the market for another husband. So
she'd dated, not a lot, but some and nothing in the past
six years had affected her as much as those few short
hours with Nicole's father.

"Joanna!"

She jerked her head up to discover her boss still
standing beside her desk. "Yes?"

"The Osborne file."

She briefly closed her eyes in a futile effort to clear
her thoughts. "What about it?"

Robin glared at the ceiling and paused, as though
pleading with the light fixture for patience. "Read it
and get back to me before the end of the day—if that
isn't too much to ask?"

"Sure," she grumbled, wondering what had put
Robin in such a foul mood. She picked up the loan
application and was halfway through it before she realised the name on it wasn't Osborne. Great! If her day
continued like this, she could blame Tanner Lund for
getting her fired.

When Joanna arrived home three hours later she was
exhausted and short-tempered. She hadn't been herself
all day, mainly because she'd been so preoccupied with
thoughts of Tanner Lund and the way he'd kissed her.

She was overreacting—she'd certainly been kissed before, so it shouldn't be such a big deal. But it was. Her behaviour demonstrated all the maturity of someone Kristen's age, she chided herself. She'd simply forgotten how to act with men; it was too long since she'd been involved with one. The day wasn't a complete waste, however. She'd made a couple of important decisions in the last few hours, and she wanted to clear the air with her daughter before matters got completely out of hand.

"Hi, honey."

"Hi."

Kristen's gaze didn't waver from the television screen where a talk-show host was interviewing a man—at least Joanna thought it was a man—whose brilliant red hair was so short on top it stuck straight up and so long in front it fell over his face, obliterating his left eye and part of his nose.

"Who's that?"

Kristen gave a deep sigh of wonder and adolescent love. "You mean you don't know? I've been in love with Simply Red for a whole year and you don't even know the lead singer when you see him?"

"No, I can't say that I do."

"Oh, Mom, honestly, get with it."

There *it* was again. First she was losing *it* and now she was supposed to get with *it*. Joanna wished her daughter would decide which she wanted.

"We need to talk."

Kristen reluctantly dragged her eyes away from her idol. "Mom, this is important. Can't it wait?"

Frustrated, Joanna sighed and muttered, "I suppose."

"Good."

Kristen had already tuned her out. Joanna strolled into the kitchen and realised she hadn't taken the hamburger out of the freezer to thaw. Great. So much for the tacos she'd planned to make for dinner. She opened and closed cupboard doors, rummaging around for something interesting. A can of tuna fish wasn't likely to meet with Kristen's approval. One thing about her daughter that the approach of the teen years hadn't disrupted was her healthy appetite.

Joanna stuck her head around the corner. "How does tuna casserole sound for dinner?"

Kristen didn't even look in her direction, just held out her arm and jerked her thumb toward the carpet.

"Soup and sandwiches?"

Once more Kristen's thumb headed downward, and Joanna groaned.

"Bacon, lettuce and tomato on toast with chicken noodle soup," she tried. "And that's the best I can do. Take it or leave it."

Kristen sighed. "If that's the final offer, I'll take it. But I thought we were having tacos."

"We were. I forgot to take out the hamburger."

"All right, BLTs," Kristen muttered, reversing the direction of her thumb.

Joanna was frying the bacon when Kristen joined her, sitting on a stool while her mother worked. "You wanted to talk to me about something?"

"Yes." Joanna concentrated on spreading mayonnaise over slices of whole-wheat toast, as she made an effort to gather her scattered thoughts. She cast about for several moments, trying to come up with a way of saying what needed to be said without making more of it than necessary.

"It must be something big," Kristen commented. "Did my teacher phone you at work or something?"

"No, should she have?" She raised her eyes and scrutinised Kristen's face closely.

Kristen gave a quick denial with a shake of her head. "No way. I'm a star pupil this year. Nicole and I are both doing great. Just wait until report-card time, then you'll see."

"I believe you." Kristen had been getting top marks all year, and Joanna was proud of how well her daughter was doing. "What I have to say concerns Nicole and—" she hesitated, swallowing tightly "—her father."

"Mr. Lund sure is good-looking, isn't he?" Kristen said enthusiastically, watching for Joanna's reaction.

Reluctantly Joanna nodded, hoping to sound casual. "I suppose."

"Oh, come on, Mom, he's a hunk."

"All right," Joanna admitted slowly. "I'll grant you that Tanner has a certain amount of...appeal."

Kristen grinned, looking pleased with herself.

"Actually it was Mr. Lund I wanted to talk to you about," Joanna continued, placing a layer of tomato slices on the toast.

"Really?" The brown eyes opened even wider.

"Yes, well, I wanted to tell you that I...I don't think it would be a good idea for the four of us to go on doing things together."

Abruptly Kristen's face fell with surprise and disappointment. "Why not?"

"Well...because he and I are both really busy." Even to her own ears, the statement sounded illogical, but it was difficult to tell her own daughter that she was frightened of her attraction to the man. Difficult to explain why nothing could come of it.

"Because you're both busy? Come on, Mom, that doesn't make any sense."

"All right, I'll be honest." She wondered whether an eleven-year-old could grasp the complexities of adult relationships. "I don't want to give Nicole's dad the wrong idea," she said carefully.

Kristen leaned forward, setting her elbows on the kitchen counter and resting her face in both hands. Her gaze looked sharp enough to shatter diamonds. "The wrong idea about what?" she asked.

"Me," Joanna said, swallowing uncomfortably.

"You?" Kristen repeated thoughtfully, a frown creasing her smooth brow. She relaxed then and released a huge sigh. "Oh, I see. You think Mr. Lund might think you're in the marriage market."

Joanna pointed a fork at her daughter. "Bingo!"

"But, Mom, I think it would be great if you and Nicole's dad got together. In fact, Nicole and I were talking about it just today. Think about all the advantages. We could all be a real family, and you could have more babies... I don't know if I ever told you this, but I'd really like a baby brother, and so would Nicole. And if you married Mr. Lund we could take family vacations together. You wouldn't have to work, because... I don't know if you realise this, but Mr. Lund is pretty rich. You could stay home and bake cookies and sew and stuff."

Joanna was so surprised that it took her a minute to find her voice. Openmouthed, she waved the fork jerkily around. "No way, Kristen." Joanna's knees felt rubbery, and before she could slip to the floor, she slumped into a chair. All this time she'd assumed she was a good mother, giving her daughter everything she needed physically and emotionally, making up to Kristen as much as she could for her father's absence. But she apparently hadn't done enough. And Kristen and Nicole were scheming to get Joanna and Tanner together. As in married!

Something had to be done.

She decided to talk to Tanner, but an opportunity didn't present itself until much later that evening when Kristen was in bed, asleep. At least Joanna hoped her daughter was asleep. She dialled his number and prayed Nicole wouldn't answer.

Thankfully she didn't.

"Tanner, it's Joanna," she whispered, cupping her hand over the mouthpiece, taking no chance that Kristen could overhear their conversation.

"What's the matter? Have you got laryngitis?"

"No," she returned hoarsely, straining her voice. "I don't want Kristen to hear me talking to you."

"I see. Should I pretend you're someone else so Nicole won't tell on you?" he whispered back.

"Please." She didn't appreciate the humor in his voice. Obviously he had yet to realise the seriousness of the situation. "We need to talk."

"We do?"

"Trust me, Tanner. You have no idea what I just learned. The girls are planning on us getting married."

"Married?" he shouted.

That, Joanna had known, would get a reaction out of him.

"When do you want to meet?"

"As soon as possible." He still seemed to think she was joking, but she couldn't blame him. If the situation were reversed, no doubt she would react the same way.

"Kristen said something about the two of them swimming Wednesday night at the community pool. What if we meet at Denny's for coffee after you drop Nicole off?"

"What time?" He said it as though they were planning a reconnaissance mission deep into enemy territory.

"Seven-ten." That would give them both a few extra minutes to make it to the restaurant.

"Shall we synchronise our watches?"

"This isn't funny, Tanner."

"I'm not laughing."

But he was, and Joanna was furious with him. "I'll see you then."

"Seven-ten, Wednesday night at Denny's," he repeated. "I'll be there."

ON THE EVENING of their scheduled meeting, Joanna arrived at the restaurant before Tanner. She already regretted suggesting they meet at Denny's, but it was too late to change that now. There were bound to be other customers who would recognise either Tanner or her, and Joanna feared that word of their meeting could somehow filter back to the girls. She'd been guilty of underestimating them before; she wouldn't make the same mistake a second time. If Kristen and Nicole did hear about this private meeting, they'd consider it justification for further interference.

Tanner strolled into the restaurant and glanced around. He didn't seem to recognise Joanna, and she moved her sunglasses down her nose and gave him an abrupt wave.

He took one look at her, and even from the other

side of the room she could see he was struggling to hold in his laughter.

"What's with the scarf and sunglasses?"

"I'm afraid someone might recognise us and tell the girls." It made perfect sense to her, but obviously not to him. Joanna forgave him since he didn't know the extent of the difficulties facing them.

But all he said was, "I see." He inserted his hands in the pockets of his overcoat and walked lazily past her, whistling. "Should I sit here or would you prefer the next booth?"

"Don't be silly."

"I'm not going to comment on that."

"For heaven's sake," Joanna hissed, "sit down before someone notices you."

"Someone notices me? Lady, you're wearing sunglasses at night, in the dead of winter, and with that scarf tied around your chin you look like an immigrant fresh off the boat."

"Tanner," she said, "this is not the time to crack jokes."

A smile lifted his features as he slid into the booth opposite her. He reached for a menu. "Are you hungry?"

"No." His attitude was beginning to annoy her. "I'm just having coffee."

"Nicole cooked dinner tonight, and frankly I'm starving."

When the waitress appeared he ordered a complete dinner. Joanna asked for coffee.

"Okay, what's up, Sherlock?" he asked, once the coffee had been poured.

"To begin with I…I think Kristen and Nicole saw you kiss me the other night."

He made no comment, but his brow puckered slightly.

"It seems the two of them have been talking, and from what I gather they're interested in getting us, er, together."

"I see."

To Joanna's dismay, Tanner didn't seem to be the slightest bit concerned by her revelation.

"That troubles you?"

"Tanner," she said, leaning toward him, "to quote my daughter, 'Nicole and I have been talking and we thought it would be great if you and Mr. Lund got together. You could have more babies and we could go on vacations and be a real family and you could stay home and bake cookies and stuff.'" She waited for his reaction, but his face remained completely impassive.

"What kind of cookies?" he asked finally.

"Tanner, if you're going to turn this into a joke, I'm leaving." As far as Joanna was concerned, he deserved to be tormented by two dedicated eleven-year-old matchmakers! She started to slide out of the booth, but he stopped her with an upraised hand.

"All right, I'm sorry."

He didn't sound too contrite, and she gave a weak sigh of disgust. "You may consider this a joking matter, but I don't."

"Joanna, we're both mature adults," he stated calmly. "We aren't going to let a couple of eleven-year-old girls manipulate us!"

"Yes, but—"

"From the first, we've been honest with each other. That isn't going to change. You have no interest in remarriage—to me or anyone else—and I feel the same way. As long as we continue as we are now, the girls don't have a prayer."

"It's more than that," Joanna said vehemently. "We need to look past their schemes to the root of the problem."

"Which is?"

"Tanner, obviously we're doing something wrong as single parents."

He frowned. "What makes you say that?"

"Isn't it obvious? Kristen, and it seems equally true for Nicole, wants a complete family. What Kristen is really saying is that she longs for a father. Nicole is telling you she'd like a mother."

The humour drained out of Tanner's eyes, replaced with a look of real concern. "I see. And you think this all started because Kristen and Nicole saw us kissing?"

"I don't know," she murmured, shaking her head. "But I do know my daughter, and when she wants something, she goes after it with the force of a bulldog and won't let up. Once she's got it in her head that you and I are destined for each other, it's going to be pretty difficult for her to accept that all we'll ever be is friends."

"Nicole can get that way about certain things," he said thoughtfully.

The waitress delivered his roast beef sandwich and refilled Joanna's coffee cup.

Maybe she'd overreacted to the situation, but she couldn't help being worried. "I suppose you think I'm making more of a fuss about this than necessary," she said, flustered and a little embarrassed.

"About the girls manipulating us?"

"No, about the fact that we've both tried so hard to

be good single parents, and obviously we're doing something wrong.''

"I will admit that part concerns me."

"I don't mind telling you, Tanner, I've been in a panic all week, wondering where I've failed. We've got to come to terms with this. Make some important decisions."

"What do you suggest?"

"To start with, we've got to squelch any hint of personal involvement. I realize a certain amount of contact will be unavoidable with the girls being such close friends.'' She paused and chewed on her bottom lip. ''I don't want to disrupt their relationship.''

"I agree with you there. Being friends with Kristen has meant a good deal to Nicole."

"You and I went months without talking to each other," Joanna said, recalling that they'd only recently met. "There's no need for us to see each other now, is there?"

"That won't work."

"Why not?"

"Nicole will be spending the night with you again next Thursday—that is, unless you'd rather she didn't."

"Of course she can stay."

Tanner nodded, looking relieved. "To be honest, I don't think she'd go back to Mrs. Wagner's anymore without raising a big fuss."

"Taking care of Nicole is one thing, but the four of us doing anything together is out of the question."

Once more he nodded, but he didn't look pleased with the suggestion. "I think that would be best, too."

"We can't give them any encouragement."

Pushing his plate aside, Tanner reached for his water glass, cupping it with both hands. "You know, Joanna,

I think a lot of you." He paused, then gave her a teasing smile. "You have a habit of dressing a little oddly every now and then, but other than that I respect your judgment. I'd like to consider you a friend."

She decided to let his comment about her choice of clothing slide. "I'd like to be your friend, too," she told him softly.

He grinned, and his gaze held hers for a long uninterrupted moment before they both looked away. "I know you think that kiss the other night was a big mistake, and I suppose you're right, but I'm not sorry it happened." He hesitated, as though waiting for her to argue with him, and when she didn't, he continued. "It's been a lot of years since I held a woman's hand at a movie or kissed her the way I did you. It was good to feel that young and innocent again."

Joanna dropped her gaze to her half-filled cup. It had felt right for her, too. So right that she'd been frightened out of her wits ever since. She could easily fall in love with Tanner, and that would be the worst possible thing for her. She just wasn't ready to take those risks again. They came from different worlds, too, and she'd never fit comfortably in his. Yet every time she thought about that kiss, she started to shake from the inside out.

"In a strange sort of way we need each other," Tanner went on, his look thoughtful. "Nicole needs a strong loving woman to identify with, to fill a mother's role, and she thinks you're wonderful."

"And Kristen needs to see a man who can be a father, putting the needs of his family before his own."

"I think it's only natural for the two of them to try to get us together," Tanner added. "It's something we should be prepared to deal with in the future."

"You're right," Joanna agreed, understanding exactly what he meant. "We need each other to help provide what's lacking in our daughters' lives. But we can't get involved with each other." She didn't know any other way to say it but bluntly.

"I agree," he said, with enough conviction to lay aside any doubt Joanna might still hold.

They were silent for a long moment.

"Why?"

Strangely, Joanna knew immediately what he was asking. She had the same questions about what had happened between him and Nicole's mother.

"Davey was—is—the most charming personable man I've ever met. I was fresh out of college and so in love with him I didn't stop to think." She paused and glanced away, not daring to look at Tanner. Her voice had fallen so low it was almost a whisper. "We were engaged when my best friend, Carol, told me Davey had made a pass at her. Fool that I was, I didn't believe her. I thought she was jealous that Davey had chosen me to love and marry. I was sick that my friend would stoop to anything so underhand. I always knew Carol found him attractive—most women did—and I was devastated that she would lie that way. I trusted Davey so completely that I didn't even ask him about the incident. Later, after we were married, there were a lot of times when he said he was working late, a lot of unexplained absences, but I didn't question those, either. He was building his career in real estate, and if he had to put in extra hours, well, that was understandable. All those nights I sat alone, trusting him when he claimed he was working, believing with all my heart that he was doing his utmost to build a life for us...and then learning he'd been with some other woman."

"How'd you find out?"

"The first time?"

"You mean there was more than once?"

She nodded, hating to let Tanner know how many times she'd forgiven Davey, how many times she'd taken him back after he'd pleaded and begged and promised it would never happen again.

"I was blind to his wandering eye for the first couple of years. What they say about ignorance being bliss is true. When I found out, I was physically sick. When I realised how I'd fallen for his lies, it was even worse, and yet I stuck it out with him, trusting that everything would be better, everything would change…someday. I wanted so badly to believe him, to trust him, that I accepted anything he told me, no matter how implausible it sounded.

"The problem was that the more I forgave him, the lower my self-esteem dropped. I became convinced it was all my fault. I obviously lacked something, since he…felt a need to seek out other women."

"You know now that's not true, don't you?" His voice was so gentle, so caring, that Joanna battled down a rush of emotion.

"There'd never been a divorce in my family," she told him quietly. "My parents have been married nearly forty years, and my brothers all have happy marriages. I think that was one of the reasons I held on so long. I just didn't know how to let go. I'd be devastated and crushed when I learned about his latest affair, yet I kept coming back for more. I suppose I believed Davey would change. Something magical would happen and all our problems would disappear. Only it never did. One afternoon—I don't even know what prompted it.… All I knew was that I couldn't stay in the marriage any longer. I packed Kristen's and my things and walked out. I've never been back, never wanted to go back.''

Tanner reached for her hand, and his fingers wrapped warmly around hers. A moment passed before he spoke, and when he did, his voice was tight with remembered pain. ''I thought Carmen was the sweetest, gentlest woman in the world. As nonsensical as it sounds, I think I was in love with her before I even knew her name. She was a college cheerleader and a homecoming queen, and I felt like a nobody. By chance, we met several years after graduation when I'd just begun making a name for myself. I'd bought my first company, a small aluminum window manufacturer back in West Virginia. And I was working night and day to see it through those first rough weeks of transition.

''I was high on status,'' Tanner admitted, his voice filled with regret. ''Small-town boy makes good—that kind of stuff. She'd been the most popular girl in my college year, and dating her was the fulfilment of a fantasy. She'd recently broken up with a guy she'd been involved with for two years and had something to prove herself, I suppose.'' He focused his gaze away from Joanna. ''Things got out of hand and a couple of months later Carmen announced she was pregnant. To be honest, I was happy about it, thrilled. There was never any question whether I'd marry her. By then I was so in love with her I couldn't see straight. Eight months after the wedding, Nicole was born...'' He hesitated, as though gathering his thoughts. ''Some women are meant to be mothers, but not Carmen. She didn't even like to hold Nicole, didn't want anything to do with her. I'd come home at night and find that Carmen had neglected Nicole most of the day. But I made excuses for her, reasoned everything out in my own mind—the unexplained bruises on the baby, the fear I saw in Nicole's eyes whenever her mother was around. It got so bad that I started dropping Nicole off at my parents', just so I could be sure she was being looked after properly.''

Joanna bit the corner of her lip at the raw pain she witnessed in Tanner's eyes. She was convinced he didn't speak of his marriage often, just as she rarely talked about Davey, but this was necessary if they were to understand each other.

''To be fair to Carmen, I wasn't much of a husband in those early months. Hell, I didn't have time to be. I was feeling like a big success when we met, but that didn't last long. Things started going wrong at work and I damn near lost my shirt.

''Later,'' he continued slowly, ''I learned that the entire time I was struggling to hold the company together, Carmen was seeing her old boyfriend, Sam Dailey.''

''Oh, Tanner.''

''Nicole's my daughter, there was no doubting that. But Carmen had never really wanted children, and she felt trapped in the marriage. We separated when Nicole was less than three years old.''

''I thought you said you'd only been divorced five years?''

''We have. It took Carmen a few years to get around to the legal aspect of things. I wasn't in any rush, since I had no intention of ever marrying again.''

''What's happened to Carmen since? Did she remarry?''

''Eventually. She lived with Sam for several years,

and the last thing I heard was they'd split up and she married a professional baseball player.''

"Does Nicole ever see her mother?" Joanna remembered that he'd said his ex-wife saw Nicole only when it was convenient.

"She hasn't in the past three years. The thing I worry about most is having Carmen show up someday, demanding that Nicole come to live with her. Nicole doesn't remember anything about those early years—thank God—and she seems to have formed a rosy image of her mother. She keeps Carmen's picture in her bedroom and every once in a while I'll see her staring at it wistfully." He paused and glanced at his watch. "What time were we supposed to pick up the kids?"

"Eight."

"It's five after now."

"Oh, good grief." Joanna slung her bag over her shoulder as they slid out of the booth and hurried towards the cash register. Tanner insisted on paying for her coffee, and Joanna didn't want to waste time arguing.

They walked briskly toward their cars, parked beside each other in the lot. "Joanna," he called, as she fumbled with her keys. "I'll wait a couple of minutes so we don't both arrive at the same time. Otherwise the girls will probably guess we've been together."

She flashed him a grateful smile. "Good thinking."

"Joanna." She looked at him questioningly as he shortened the distance between them. "Don't misunderstand this," he said softly. He pulled her gently into the circle of his arms, holding her close for a lingering moment. "I'm sorry for what Davey did to you. The man's a fool.'' Tenderly he brushed his lips over her forehead, then turned and abruptly left her.

It took Joanna a full minute to recover enough to get into her car and drive away.

Seven

"Mom," Kristen screeched, "the phone's for you."

Joanna was surprised. A call for her on a school night was rare enough, but one that actually got through with Kristen and Nicole continually on the line was a special occasion.

"Who is it, honey?" No doubt someone interested in cleaning her carpets or selling her a cemetery plot.

"I don't know," Kristen said, holding the phone to her shoulder. She lowered her voice to whisper, "But whoever it is sounds weird."

"Hello." Joanna spoke into the receiver as Kristen wandered toward her bedroom.

"Can you talk?" The husky male voice was unmistakably Tanner's.

"Y-yes." Joanna looked toward Kristen's bedroom to be certain her daughter was out of earshot.

'Can you meet me tomorrow for lunch?''

"What time?"

"Noon at the Sea Galley."

"Should we synchronise our watches?" Joanna couldn't resist asking. It had been a week since she'd last talked to Tanner. In the meantime she hadn't heard a word from Kristen about getting their two families together again. That in itself was suspicious, but Joanna had been too busy at work to think about it.

"Don't be cute, Joanna. I need help."

"Buy me lunch and I'm yours." She hadn't meant that quite the way it sounded and was grateful Tanner didn't comment on her slip of the tongue.

"I'll see you tomorrow then."

"Right."

A smile tugged at the edges of her mouth as she replaced the telephone receiver. Her hand lingered there for a moment as an unexpected tide of happiness washed over her.

"Who was that, Mom?" Kristen asked, poking her head around her bedroom door.

"A…friend, calling to ask if I could meet…her for lunch."

"Oh." Kristen's young face was a study in scepticism. "For a minute there I thought it sounded like Mr. Lund trying to fake a woman's voice."

"Mr. Lund? That's silly," Joanna said with a forced little laugh, then deftly changed the subject. "Kristen, it's nine-thirty. Hit the hay, kiddo."

"Right, Mom. 'Night."

"'Night, sweetheart."

"Enjoy your lunch tomorrow."

"I will."

Joanna hadn't had a chance to walk away from the phone before it pealed a second time. She gave a guilty start and reached for it.

"Hello," she said hesitantly, half expecting to hear Tanner's voice again.

But it was her mother's crisp clear voice that rang over the wire. "Joanna, I hope this isn't too late to call."

"Of course not, Mom," Joanna answered quickly. "Is everything all right?"

Her mother ignored the question and asked one of her own instead. "What was the name of that young man you're dating again?"

"Mother," Joanna said with an exasperated sigh, "I'm not seeing anyone. I told you that."

"Tanner Lund, wasn't it?"

"We went out to dinner *once* with both our daughters, and that's the extent of our relationship. If Kristen let you assume anything else, it was just wishful thinking on her part. One dinner, I swear."

"But, Joanna, he sounds like such a nice young man. He's the same Tanner Lund who recently bought half of Spokane Aluminum, isn't he? I saw his name in the paper this morning and recognised it right away. Sweetie, your dad and I are so pleased you're dating such a famous successful man."

"Mother, please!" Joanna cried. "Tanner and I are friends. How many times do I have to tell you, we're not dating? Kristen and Tanner's daughter, Nicole, are best friends. I swear that's all there is to—"

"Joanna," her mother interrupted. "The first time you mentioned his name, I heard something in your voice that's been missing for a good long while. You may be able to fool yourself, but not me. You like this Tanner." Her voice softened perceptively.

"Mother, nothing could possibly come of it even if I was attracted to him—which I'm not." Okay, so that last part wasn't entirely true. But the rest of it certainly was.

"And why couldn't it?" her mother insisted.

"You said it yourself. He's famous, in addition to being wealthy. I'm out of his league."

"Nonsense," her mother responded in a huff.

Joanna knew better than to get into a war of words with her stubborn parent.

"Now don't be silly. You like Tanner Lund, and I say it's about time you let down those walls you've built around yourself. Joanna, sweetie, you've been hiding behind them for six years now. Don't let what happened with Davey ruin your whole life."

"I'm not going to," Joanna promised.

There was a long pause before her mother sighed and answered, "Good. You deserve some happiness."

AT PRECISELY NOON the following day, Joanna drove into the Sea Galley parking lot. Tanner was already there, waiting for her by the entrance.

"Hi," she said with a friendly grin, as he walked toward her.

"What, no disguises?"

Joanna laughed, embarrassed now by that silly scarf and sunglasses she'd worn when they met at Denny's. "Kristen doesn't know anyone who eats here."

"I'm grateful for that."

His smile was warm enough to tunnel through snow drifts, and as much as Joanna had warned herself not to be affected by it, she was.

"It's good to see you," Tanner added, taking her arm to escort her into the restaurant.

"You, too." Although she hadn't seen him in almost a week, Tanner was never far from her thoughts. Nicole had stayed with her and Kristen when Tanner flew to New York for two days in the middle of the previous week. The Spokane area had been hit by a fierce snowstorm the evening he left. Joanna had felt nervous the entire time about his traveling in such inclement weather, yet she hadn't so much as asked him about his flight when he arrived to pick up Nicole. Their conversation had been brief and pleasantly casual, but her relief that he'd got home safely had kept her awake for hours. Later, she'd been furious with herself for caring so much.

The Sea Galley hostess seated them right away and handed them thick menus. Joanna ordered a shrimp salad and coffee. Tanner echoed her choice.

"Nicole's birthday is next week," he announced, studying her face carefully. "She's handing out the party invitations today at school."

Joanna smiled and nodded. But Tanner's eyes held hers, and she saw something unidentifiable flicker there.

"In a moment of weakness, I told her she could have a slumber party."

Joanna's smile faded. "As I recall, Nicole did mention something about this party," she said, trying to sound cheerful. The poor guy didn't know what he was in for. "You're obviously braver than I am."

"You think it was a bad move?"

Joanna made a show of closing her eyes and nodding vigorously.

"I was afraid of that," Tanner muttered, and he rearranged the silverware around his place setting a couple of times. "I know we agreed it probably wouldn't be a good idea for us to do things together. But I need some advice—from a friend."

"What can I do?"

"Joanna, I haven't the foggiest idea about entertaining a whole troop of girls. I can handle contract negotiations and make split-second business decisions, but I panic at the thought of all those squealing little girls sequestered in my apartment for all those hours."

"How do you want me to help?"

"Would you consider..." He gave her a hopeful look, then shook his head regretfully. "No. I can't ask that of you. Besides, we don't want to give the girls any more ideas about the two of us. What I really need is some suggestions for keeping all these kids occupied. What do other parents do?"

"Other parents know better."

Tanner wiped a lock of dark brown hair from his brow and frowned. "I was afraid of that."

"What time are the girls supposed to arrive?"

"Six."

"Tanner, that's too early."

"I know, but Nicole insists I serve my special tacos, and she has some screwy idea about all the girls crowding into the kitchen to watch me."

Now it was Joanna's turn to frown. "That won't work. You'll end up with ten different pairs of hands trying to help. There'll be hamburger and cheese from one end of the place to the other."

"I thought as much. Good Lord, Joanna, how did I get myself into this mess?"

"Order pizza," she tossed out, tapping her index finger against her bottom lip. "Everyone loves that."

"Pizza. Okay. What about games?"

"A scavenger hunt always comes in handy when things get out of hand. Release the troops on your unsuspecting neighbours."

"So far we've got thirty minutes of the first fourteen hours filled."

"Movies," Joanna suggested next. "Lots of movies. You can phone early and reserve a couple of new releases and add an old favourite like *Pretty in Pink*, and the girls will be in seventh heaven."

His eyes brightened. "Good idea."

"And if you really feel adventurous, take them roller-skating."

"Roller-skating? You think they'd like that?"

"They'd love it, especially if word leaked out that they were going to be at the rink Friday night. That way, several of the boys from the sixth-grade class can just happen to be there, too."

Tanner nodded, and a smile quirked the corners of his mouth. "And you think that'll keep everyone happy?"

"I'm sure of it. Wear 'em out first, show a movie or two second, with the lights out, of course, and I guarantee you by midnight everyone will be sound asleep."

Their salads arrived and Tanner stuck his fork into a fat succulent shrimp, then paused. "Now what was it you said last night about buying you lunch and making you mine?"

"It was a slip of the tongue," she muttered, dropping her gaze to her salad.

"Just my luck."

They laughed, and it felt good. Joanna had never had a relationship like this with a man. She wasn't on her guard the way she normally was, fearing that her date would put too much stock in an evening or two out. Because their daughters were the same age, they had a lot in common. They were both single parents doing their damnedest to raise their daughters right. The normal dating rituals and practised moves were unnecessary with him. Tanner was her friend, and it renewed Joanna's faith in the opposite sex to know there were still men like him left. Their friendship reassured her— but the undeniable attraction between them still frightened her.

"I really appreciate your suggestions," he said, after

they'd both concentrated on their meals for several moments. "I've had this panicky feeling for the past three days. I suppose it wasn't a brilliant move on my part to call you at home, but I was getting desperate."

"You'll do fine. Just remember, it's important to keep the upper hand."

"I'll try."

"By the way, when *is* Hell Night?" She couldn't resist teasing him.

He gave a heartfelt sigh. "Next Friday."

Joanna slowly ate a shrimp. "I think Kristen figured out it was you on the phone last night."

"She did?"

"Yeah. She started asking questions the minute I hung up. She claimed my 'friend' sounded suspiciously like Mr. Lund faking a woman's voice."

Tanner cleared his throat and answered in a high falsetto. "That should tell you how desperate I was."

Joanna laughed and speared another shrimp. "That's what friends are for."

Eight

"**M**om, hurry or we're going to be late." Kristen paced the hallway outside her mother's bedroom door while Joanna finished dressing.

"Have you got Nicole's gift?"

"Oh." Kristen dashed into her bedroom and returned with a gaily wrapped oblong box. They'd bought the birthday gift the night before, a popular board game, which Kristen happened to know Nicole really wanted.

"I think Mr. Lund is really nice to let Nicole have a slumber party, don't you?"

"Really brave is a more apt description. How many girls are coming?"

"Fifteen."

"Fifteen!" Joanna echoed in a shocked voice.

"Nicole originally invited twenty, but only fifteen could make it."

Joanna slowly shook her head. He'd had good reason to feel panicky. With all these squealing, giddy pre-adolescent girls, the poor man would be certifiable by the end of the night. Either that or a prime candidate for extensive counselling.

When they arrived, the parking area outside Tanner's apartment building looked like the scene of a rock concert. There were enough parents dropping off kids to cause a minor traffic jam.

"I can walk across the street if you want to let me out here," Kristen suggested, anxiously eyeing the group of girls gathering outside the building.

"I'm going to find a parking place," Joanna said, scanning the side streets for two adjacent spaces—so that she wouldn't need to struggle to parallel park.

"You're going to find a place to leave the car? Why?" Kristen wanted to know, her voice higher pitched and more excited than usual. "You don't have to come in, if you don't want. I thought you said you were going to refinish that old chair Grandpa gave us last summer."

"I was," Joanna murmured with a short sigh, "but I have the distinct impression that Nicole's father is going to need a helping hand."

"I'm sure he doesn't, Mom. Mr. Lund is a really organised person. I'm sure he's got everything under control."

Kristen's reaction surprised Joanna. She would have expected her daughter to encourage the idea of getting the two of them together.

She finally found a place to park and they hurried across the street, Kristen apparently deep in thought.

"Actually, Mom, I think helping Mr. Lund might be a good idea," she said after a long pause. "He'll probably be grateful."

Joanna wasn't nearly as confident by this time. "I have a feeling I'm going to regret this later."

"No, you won't." Joanna could tell Kristen was about to launch into another one of her little speeches about babies, vacations and homemade cookies. Thankfully she didn't get the chance, since they'd entered the building and encountered a group of Kristen's other friends.

Tanner was standing in the doorway of his apartment, already looking frazzled when Joanna arrived. Surprise flashed through his eyes when he saw her.

"I've come to help," she announced, peeling off her jacket and pushing up the sleeves of her thin sweater. "This group is more than one parent can reasonably be expected to control."

He looked for a moment as though he wanted to fall to the ground and kiss her feet. "Bless you."

"Believe me, Tanner, you owe me for this." She glanced around at the chaos that dominated the large apartment. The girls had already formed small groups and were arguing loudly with each other over some subject of earth-shattering importance—like Bruce Springsteen's age, or the real colour of Billy Idol's hair.

"Is the pizza ready?" Joanna asked him, raising her voice in order to be heard over the din of squeals, shouts and rock music.

Tanner nodded. "It's in the kitchen. I ordered eight large ones. Do you think that'll be enough?"

Joanna rolled her eyes. "I suspect you're going to be eating leftover pizza for the next two weeks."

The girls proved her wrong. Never had Joanna seen a hungrier group. They were like school of piranha attacking a hapless victim, and within fifteen minutes everyone had eaten her fill. There were one or two slices left of four of the pizzas, but the others had vanished completely.

"It's time for a movie," Joanna decided, and while the girls voted on which film to see first Tanner started dumping dirty paper plates and pop cans into a plastic garbage sack. When the movie was finished, Joanna calculated, it would be time to go skating.

Peace reigned once Tom Cruise appeared on the television screen and Joanna joined Tanner in the bright cheery kitchen.

He was sitting dejectedly at the round table, rubbing a hand across his forehead. "I feel a headache coming on."

"It's too late for that," she said with a soft smile. "Actually I think everything is going very well. Everyone seems to be having a good time, and Nicole is a wonderful hostess."

"You do? She is?" He gave her an astonished look. "I keep having nightmares about pillow fights and lost dental appliances."

"Hey, it isn't going to happen." Not while they maintained control. "Tanner, I meant what I said about the party going well. In fact, I'm surprised at how smoothly everything is falling into place. The kids really are having a good time, and as long as we keep them busy there shouldn't be any problems."

He grinned, looking relieved. "I don't know about you, but I could use a cup of coffee."

"I'll second that."

He poured coffee into two pottery mugs and carried them to the table. Joanna sat across from him, propping her feet on the opposite chair. Sighing, she leaned back and cradled the steaming mug.

"The pizza was a good idea." He reached for a piece and shoved the box in her direction.

Now that she had a chance to think about it, Joanna realized she'd been so busy earlier, serving the girls, she hadn't managed to eat any of the pizza herself. She straightened enough to reach for a napkin and a thick slice dotted with pepperoni and spicy Italian sausage.

"What made you decide to give up your evening to help me out?" Tanner asked, watching her closely.

"Kristen told Nicole that you had a hot date tonight. You were the last person I expected to see."

Joanna wasn't sure what had changed her mind about tonight and staying to help Tanner. Pity, she suspected. "If the situation were reversed, you'd lend me a hand," she replied, more interested in eating than conversation at the moment.

Tanner frowned at his pizza. "You missed what I was really asking."

"I did?"

"I was trying to be subtle about asking if you had a date tonight."

Joanna found that question odd. "Obviously I didn't."

"It isn't so obvious to me. You're a single parent, so there aren't that many evenings you can count on being free of responsibility. I would have thought you'd use this time to go out with someone special, flap your wings and that sort of thing." His frown grew darker.

"I'm too old to flap my wings," she said with a soft chuckle. "Good grief, I'm over thirty."

"So you aren't dating anyone special?"

"Tanner, you know I'm not."

"I don't know anything of the sort." Although he didn't raise his voice, Joanna could sense his disquiet.

"All right, what's up?" She didn't like the looks he was giving her. Not one bit.

"Nicole."

"Nicole?" she repeated.

"She was telling me that other day that you'd met someone recently. 'A real prince' is the phrase she used. Someone rich and handsome who was crazy about you—she claimed you were seeing a lot of this guy. Said you were falling madly in love."

Joanna dropped her feet to the floor with a loud thud and bolted upright so fast she nearly tumbled out of the chair. She was furiously chewing her pepperoni-and-sausage pizza, trying to swallow it as quickly as she could. All the while, her finger was pointing, first toward the living room where the girls were innocently watching *Top Gun* and then at Tanner who was staring at her in fascination.

"Hey, don't get angry with me," he said. "I'm only repeating what Kristen supposedly told Nicole and what Nicole told me."

She swallowed the piece of pizza in one huge lump. "They're plotting again, don't you see? I should have known something was up. It's been much too quiet lately. Kristen and Nicole are getting devious now, because the direct approach didn't work." Flustered, she started pacing the kitchen floor.

"Settle down, Joanna. We're smarter than a couple of school kids."

"That's easy for you to say." She pushed her hair away from her forehead and continued to pace. Little wonder Kristen hadn't been keen on the idea of her helping Tanner tonight. Joanna whirled around to face him. "Well, aren't you going to say something?" To her dismay, she discovered he was doing his best not to chuckle. "This isn't a laughing matter, Tanner Lund. I wish you'd take this seriously!"

"I am."

Joanna snorted softly. "You are not!"

"We're mature adults, Joanna. We aren't going to allow two children to dictate our actions."

"Is that a fact?" She braced both hands against her hips and glared at him. "I'm pleased to hear you're such a tower of strength, but I'll bet a week's pay that it wasn't your idea to have this slumber party. You probably rejected the whole thing the first time Nicole suggested it, but after having the subject of a birthday slumber party brought up thirty times in about thirty minutes you weakened, and that was when Nicole struck the fatal blow. If your daughter is anything like mine, she probably used every trick in the book to talk you into this party idea. Knowing how guilty you felt about all those business trips, I suppose Nicole brought them up ten or twelve times. And before you knew what hit you, there were fifteen little girls spending the night at your apartment.''

Tanner paled.

"Am I right?" she insisted.

He shrugged and muttered disparagingly, "Close enough.''

Slumping into the chair, Joanna pushed the pizza box aside and forcefully expelled her breath. ''I don't mind telling you, I'm concerned about this. If Kristen and Nicole are plotting against us, then we've got to form some kind of plan of our own before they drive us out of our minds. We can't allow them to manipulate us like this.''

''I think you may be right.''

She eyed him hopefully. ''Any suggestions?'' If he was smart enough to manage a couple of thousand employees, surely he could figure out a way to keep two eleven-year-olds under control.

Slouched in his chair, his shoulders sagging, Tanner shook his head. ''None. What about you?''

''Communication is the key.''

''Right.''

''We've got to keep in touch with each other and keep tabs on what's going on with these two. Don't believe a thing they say until we check it out with the other.''

''We've got another problem, Joanna,'' Tanner said, looking in every direction but hers.

''What?''

''It worked.''

''What worked?'' she asked irritably. Why was he speaking in riddles?

''Nicole's telling me that you'd been swept off your feet by this rich guy.''

''Yes?'' He still wasn't making any sense.

''The purpose of that whole fabrication was to make me jealous—and it worked.''

''It worked?'' An icy numb feeling swept through her. Swallowing became difficult.

Tanner nodded. ''I kept thinking about how much I liked you. How much I enjoyed talking to you. And then I decided that when this slumber party business was over, I was going to risk asking you out to dinner.''

''But I've already told you I'm not interested in a romantic relationship. One marriage was more than enough for me.''

''I don't think that's what bothered me.''

''Then what did?''

It was obvious from the way his eyes darted around the room that he felt uncomfortable. ''I kept thinking about another man kissing you, and frankly, Joanna, that's what bothered me most.''

The kitchen suddenly went so quiet that Joanna was almost afraid to breathe. The only noise was the faint sound of the movie playing in the other room.

Joanna tried to put herself in Tanner's place, wondering how she'd feel if Kristen announced that he'd met a gorgeous blonde and was dating her. Instantly she felt her stomach muscles tighten. There wasn't the slightest doubt in Joanna's mind that the girls' trick would have worked on her, too. Just the thought of Tanner's kissing another woman produced a curious ache, a pain that couldn't be described—or denied.

"Kissing you that night was the worst thing I could have done," Tanner conceded reluctantly. "I know you don't want to talk about it. I don't blame you—"

"Tanner," she interjected in a low hesitant voice, which hardly resembled her own. "It would have worked with me, too."

His eyes were dark and piercing. "Are you certain?"

She nodded, feeling utterly defeated yet strangely excited. "I'm afraid so. What are we going to do now?"

The silence returned as they stared at one another.

"The first thing I think we should do is experiment a little," he suggested in a flat emotionless voice. Then he released a long sigh. "Almost three weeks have passed since the night we took the girls out, and we've both had plenty of time to let that kiss build in our minds. Right?"

"Right," Joanna agreed. She'd attempted to put that kiss completely out of her mind, but it hadn't worked, and there was no point in telling him otherwise.

"It seems to me," Tanner continued thoughtfully, "that we should kiss again, for the sake of research, and find out what we're dealing with here."

She didn't need him to kiss her again to know she was going to like it. The first time had been ample opportunity for her to recognise how strongly she was attracted to Tanner Lund, and she didn't need another kiss to remind her.

"Once we know, we can decide where to go from there. Agreed?"

"Okay," she said impulsively, ignoring the small voice that warned of danger.

He stood up and held out his hand. She stared at it for a moment, uncertain. "You want to kiss right now?"

"Do you know of a better time?"

She shook her head. Good grief, she couldn't believe she was doing this. Tanner stretched out his arms and she walked into them with all the finesse of tumbleweed. The way she fit so snugly, so comfortably into his embrace worried her already. And he hadn't even kissed her yet.

Tanner held her lightly, his eyes wide and curious as he stared down at her. First he cocked his head to the right, then abruptly changed his mind and moved it to the left.

Joanna's movements countered his until she was certain they looked like a pair of ostriches who couldn't make up their minds.

"Are you comfortable?" he asked, and his voice was slightly hoarse.

Joanna nodded. She wished he'd hurry up and do it before one of the girls came crashing into the kitchen and found them. With their luck, it would be either Kristen or Nicole. Or both.

"You ready?" he asked.

Joanna nodded again. He was looking at her almost anxiously as though they were waiting for an imminent explosion. And that was exactly the way it felt when Tanner's mouth settled on hers, even though the kiss was infinitely gentle, his lips sliding over hers like a soft summer rain, barely touching.

They broke apart, momentarily stunned. Neither spoke, and then Tanner kissed her again, moving his mouth over her parted lips in undisguised hunger. His hand clutched the thick hair at her nape as she raised her arms and tightened them around his neck, leaning into him, absorbing his strength.

Tanner groaned softly and deepened the kiss until it threatened to consume Joanna. She met his fierce urgency with her own, arching closer to him, holding onto him with everything that was in her.

An unabating desire flared to life between them as he kissed her again and again, until they were both breathless and shaking.

"Joanna," he groaned, and dragged in several deep breaths. After taking a long moment to compose himself, he asked, "What do you think?" The question was murmured into her hair.

Joanna's chest was heaving, as though she'd been running and was desperate for oxygen. "I...I don't know," she lied, silently calling herself a coward.

"I do."

"You do?"

"Good Lord, Joanna, you taste like heaven. We're in trouble here. Deep trouble."

Nine

The pop music at the roller-skating rink blared from huge speakers and vibrated around the room. A disc jockey announced the tunes from a glass-fronted booth and joked with the skaters as they circled the polished hardwood floor.

"I can't believe I let you talk me into this," Joanna muttered, sitting beside Tanner as she laced up her rented high-top white skates.

"I refuse to be the only one over thirty out there," he replied, but he was smiling, obviously pleased with his persuasive talents. No doubt he'd take equal pleasure in watching her fall flat on her face. It had been years since Joanna had worn a pair of roller skates. *Years.*

"It's like riding a bicycle," Tanner assured her with that maddening grin of his. "Once you know how, you never forget."

Joanna grumbled under her breath, but she was actually beginning to look forward to this. She'd always loved roller-skating as a kid, and there was something about being with Tanner that brought out the little girl in her. *And the woman,* she thought, remembering their kiss.

Nicole's friends were already skating with an ease

that made Joanna envious. Slowly, cautiously, she joined the crowd circling the rink.

"Hi, Mom." Kristen zoomed past at the speed of light.

"Hi, Mrs. Parsons," Nicole shouted, following her friend.

Staying safely near the side, within easy reach of the handrail, Joanna concentrated on making her feet work properly, wheeling them back and forth as smoothly as possible. But instead of the gliding motion achieved by the others, her movements were short and jerky. She didn't acknowledge the girls' greetings with anything more than a raised hand and was slightly disconcerted to see the other skaters giving her a wide berth. They obviously recognised danger when they saw it.

Tanner glided past her, whirled around and deftly skated backward, facing Joanna. She looked up and threw him a weak smile. She should have known Tanner would be as confident on skates as he seemed to be at everything else—except slumber parties for eleven-year-old girls. Looking at him, one would think he'd been skating every day for years, although he claimed it was twenty years since he'd been inside a rink. It was clear from the expert way he soared across the floor that he didn't need to relearn anything—unlike Joanna, who felt as awkward as a newborn foal attempting to stand for the first time.

"How's it going?" he asked, with a cocky grin.

"Great. Can't you tell?" Just then, her right foot jerked out from under her and she groped desperately for the rail, managing to get a grip on it seconds before she went crashing to the floor.

Tanner was by her side at once. "You okay?"

"About as okay as anyone who has stood on the edge and looked into the deep abyss," she muttered.

"Come on, what you need is a strong hand to guide you."

Joanna snorted. "Forget it, fellow. I'll be fine in a few minutes, once I get my sea legs."

"You're sure?"

"Tanner, for heaven's sake, at least leave me with my pride intact!" Keeping anything intact at the moment was difficult, with her feet flaying wildly as she tried to pull herself back into an upright position.

"Okay, if that's what you want," he said shrugging, and sailed away from her with annoying ease.

Fifteen minutes later, Joanna felt steady enough to join the main part of the crowd circling the rink. Her movements looked a little less clumsy, a little less shaky, though she certainly wasn't in complete control.

"Hey, you're doing great," Tanner said, slowing down enough to skate beside her.

"Thanks," she said breathlessly, studying her feet in an effort to maintain her balance.

"You've got a gift for this," he teased.

She looked up at him and laughed outright. "Isn't that the truth! I wonder if I should consider a new career as a roller-skating waitress at the Pink Palace."

Amusement lifted the edge of his sensuous mouth. "Has anyone ever told you that you have an odd sense of humour?"

Looking at Tanner distracted Joanna, and her feet floundered for an instant. "Kristen does at least once a day."

Tanner chuckled. "I shouldn't laugh. Nicole tells me the same thing."

The disc jockey announced that the next song was

for couples only. Joanna gave a sigh of relief and aimed her body toward the nearest exit. She could use the break; her calf muscles were already protesting the unaccustomed exercise. She didn't need roller-skating to remind her she wasn't a kid.

"How about it, Joanna?" Tanner asked, skating around her.

"How about what?"

"Skating together for the couples' dance. You and me and fifty thousand preteens sharing centre stage." He offered her his hand. The lights had dimmed and a mirrored ball hanging in the middle of the ceiling cast speckled shadows over the floor.

"No way, Tanner," she muttered, ignoring his hand.

"I thought not. Oh well, I'll see if I can get Nicole to skate with her dear old dad." Effortlessly he glided toward the group of girls who stood against the wall flirtatiously challenging the boys on the other side with their eyes.

Once Joanna was safely off the rink, she found a place to sit and rest her weary bones. Within a couple of minutes, Tanner lowered himself into the chair beside her, looking chagrined.

"I got beat out by Tommy Spenser," he muttered.

Joanna couldn't help it—she was delighted. Now Tanner would understand how she'd felt when Kristen announced she didn't want her mother sitting with her at the movies. Tanner looked just as dejected as Joanna had felt then.

"It's hell when they insist on growing up, isn't it?" she said, doing her best not to smile, knowing he wouldn't appreciate it.

He heaved an expressive sigh and gave her a hopeful

look before glancing out at the skating couples. "I don't suppose you'd reconsider?"

The floor was filled with kids, and Joanna knew the minute she moved onto the hardwood surface with Tanner, every eye in the place would be on them.

He seemed to read her mind, because he added, "Come on, Joanna. My ego has just suffered a near-mortal wound. I've been rejected by my own flesh and blood."

She swallowed down a comment and awkwardly rose to her feet, struggling to remain upright. "When my ego got shot to bits at the movie theatre, all you did was share your popcorn with me."

He chuckled and reached for her hand. "Don't complain. This gives me an excuse to put my arm around you again." His right arm slipped around her waist, and she tucked her left hand in his as they moved side by side. She had to admit it felt incredibly good to be this close to him. Almost as good as it had felt being in his arms for those few moments in his kitchen.

Tanner must have been thinking the same thing, because he was unusually quiet as he directed her smoothly across the floor to the strains of a romantic ballad. They'd circled the rink a couple of times when Tanner abruptly switched position, skating backward and holding onto her as though they were dancing.

"Tanner," she said, surprise widening her eyes as he swept her into his arms. "The girls will start thinking…things if we skate like this."

"Let them."

His hands locked at the base of her spine and he pulled her close. Very close. Joanna drew a slow breath, savouring the feel of Tanner's body pressed so intimately against her own.

"Joanna, listen," he whispered. "I've been thinking."

So had she. Hard to do when she was around Tanner.

"Would it really be such a terrible thing if we were to start seeing more of each other? On a casual basis—it doesn't have to be anything serious. We're both mature adults. Neither of us is going to allow the girls to manipulate us into anything we don't want. And as far as the past is concerned, I'm not Davey and you're not Carmen."

Why, Joanna wondered, was the most important discussion she'd had in years taking place in a roller-skating rink with a top-forty hit blaring in one ear and Tanner whispering in the other? Deciding to ignore the thought, she said, "But the girls might start making assumptions, and I'm afraid we'd only end up disappointing them."

Tanner disagreed. "I feel our seeing each other might help more than it would hinder."

"How do you mean?" Joanna couldn't believe she was actually entertaining this suggestion. Entertaining was putting it mildly; her heart was doing somersaults at the prospect of seeing Tanner more often. She was thrilled, excited…and yet hesitant. The wounds Davey had inflicted went very deep.

"If we see each other more often we could include the girls, and that should lay to rest some of the fears we've had over their matchmaking efforts. And spending time with you will help satisfy Nicole's need for a strong mother figure. At the same time, I can help Kristen, by being a father figure."

"Yes, but—"

"The four of us together will give the girls a sense

of belonging to a whole family,'' Tanner added confidently.

His arguments sounded so reasonable, so logical. Still, Joanna remained uncertain. "But I'm afraid the girls will think we're serious.''

Tanner lifted his head enough to look into her eyes, and Joanna couldn't remember a time they'd ever been bluer or more intense. "I am serious.''

She pressed her forehead against his collarbone and willed her body to stop trembling. Their little kissing experiment had affected her far more than she dared let him know. Until tonight, they'd both tried to disguise or deny their attraction for each other, but the kiss had exposed everything.

"I haven't stopped thinking about you from the minute we first met,'' he whispered, and touched his lips to her temple. "If we were anyplace else right now, I'd show you how crazy I am about you.''

If they'd been anyplace else, Joanna would have let him. She wanted him to kiss her, needed him to, but she was more frightened by her reaction to this one man than she'd been by anything else in a very long while. "Tanner, I'm afraid.''

"Joanna, so am I, but I can't allow fear to rule my life.'' Gently he brushed the loose wisps of curls from the side of her face. His eyes studied her intently. "I didn't expect to feel this way again. I've guarded against letting this happen, but here we are, and Joanna, I don't mind telling you, I wouldn't change a thing.''

Joanna closed her eyes and listened to the battle raging inside her head. She wanted so badly to give this feeling between them a chance to grow. But logic told her that if she agreed to his suggestion, she'd be making herself vulnerable again. Even worse, Tanner Lund wasn't just any man—he was wealthy and successful, the half owner of an important company. And she was just a loan officer at a small local bank.

"Joanna, at least tell me what you're feeling."

"I...I don't know," she hedged, still uncertain.

He gripped her hand and pressed it over his heart, holding it there. "Just feel what you do to me."

Her own heart seemed about to hammer its way out of her chest. "You do the same thing to me."

He smiled ever so gently. "I know."

The music came to an end and the lights brightened. Reluctantly Tanner and Joanna broke apart, but he still kept her close to his side, tucking his arm around her waist.

"You haven't answered me, Joanna. I'm not going to hurt you, you know. We'll take it nice and easy at first and see how things develop."

Joanna's throat felt constricted, and she couldn't answer him one way or the other, although it was clear that he was waiting for her to make a decision.

"We've got something good between us," he continued, "and I don't want to just throw it away. I think we should find out whether this can last."

He wouldn't hurt her intentionally, Joanna realised, but the probability of her walking away unscathed from a relationship with this man was remote.

"What do you think?" he pressed.

She couldn't refuse him. "Maybe we should give it a try," she said after a long pause.

Tanner gazed down on her, bathing her in the warmth of his smile. "Neither of us is going to be sorry."

Joanna wasn't nearly as confident. She glanced away

and happened to notice Kristen and Nicole. "Uh-oh," she murmured.

"What's wrong?"

"I just saw Kristen zoom over to Nicole and whisper into her ear. Then they hugged each other like long-lost sisters."

"I can deal with it if you can," he said, squeezing her hand.

Tanner's certainty lent her courage. "Then so can I."

Ten

Joanna didn't sleep well that night, or the following two. Tanner had suggested they meet for dinner the next weekend. It seemed an eternity, but there were several problems at work that demanded his attention. She felt as disappointed as he sounded that their first real date wouldn't take place for a week.

Joanna wished he hadn't given her so much time to think about it. If they'd been able to casually go to a movie the afternoon following the slumber party, she wouldn't have been so nervous about it.

When she arrived at work Monday morning, her brain was so muddled she felt as though she were walking in a fog. Twice during the weekend she'd almost called Tanner to suggest they call the whole thing off.

"Morning," her boss murmured absently, hardly looking up from the newspaper. "How was your weekend?"

"Exciting," Joanna told Robin, tucking her purse into the bottom drawer of her desk. "I went roller-skating with fifteen eleven-year-old girls."

"Sounds adventurous," Robin said, his gaze never leaving the paper.

Joanna poured herself a cup of coffee and carried it to her desk to drink black. The way she was feeling, she knew she'd need something strong to clear her head.

"I don't suppose you've been following what's happening at Spokane Aluminum?" Robin asked, refilling his own coffee cup.

It was a good thing Joanna had set her mug down when she did, otherwise it would have tumbled from her fingers. "Spokane Aluminum?" she echoed.

"Yes." Robin sat on the edge of her desk, allowing one leg to dangle. "There's another news item in the paper this morning on Tanner Lund. Six months ago, he bought out half the company from John Becky. I'm sure you've heard of John Becky?"

"Of…course."

"Apparently Lund came into this company and breathed new life into its sagging foreign sales. He took over management himself and has completely changed the company's direction…all for the better. I've heard nothing but good about this guy. Every time I turn around, I'm either reading how great he is, or hearing people talk about him. Take my word, Tanner Lund is a man who's going places."

Joanna couldn't agree more. And she knew for a fact where he was going Saturday night. He was taking her to dinner.

"MR. LUND'S HERE," Kristen announced the following Saturday, opening Joanna's bedroom door. "And does he ever look handsome!"

A dinner date. A simple dinner date, and Joanna was more nervous than a college graduate applying for her first job. She smoothed her hand down her red-and-white flowered dress and held in her breath so long her lungs ached.

Kristen rolled her eyes. "You look fine, Mom."

"I do?"

"As nice as Mr. Lund."

For good measure, Joanna paused long enough to dab more cologne behind her ears, then she squared her shoulders and turned to face the long hallway that led to the living room. "Okay, I'm ready."

Kristen threw open the bedroom door as though she expected royalty to emerge. By the time Joanna had walked down the hallway to the living room where Tanner was waiting, her heart was pounding and her hands were shaking. Kristen was right. Tanner looked marvellous in a three-piece suit and silk tie. He smiled when she came into the room, and stood up, gazing at her with an expression of undisguised delight.

"Hi."

"Hi." Their eyes met, and everything else faded away. Just seeing him again made Joanna's pulse leap into overdrive. No week had ever dragged more.

"Sally's got the phone number of the restaurant, and her mother said it was fine if she stayed here late," Kristen said, standing between them and glancing from one adult to the other. "I don't have any plans myself, so you two feel free to stay out as long as you want."

"Sally?" Joanna forced herself to glance at the baby-sitter.

"Yes, Mrs. Parsons?"

"There's salad and leftover spaghetti in the refrigerator for dinner, and some microwave popcorn in the cupboard for later."

"Okay."

"I won't be too late."

"But, Mom," Kristen cut in, a slight whine in her

voice, "I just got done telling you that it'd be fine if you stayed out till the wee hours of the morning."

"We'll be back before midnight," Joanna informed the baby-sitter, ignoring Kristen.

"Okay," the girl said, as Kristen sighed expressively. "Have a good time."

Tanner escorted Joanna out to the car, which was parked in front of the house, and opened the passenger door. He paused, his hand still resting on her shoulder. "I'd like to kiss you now, but we have an audience," he said, nodding toward the house.

Joanna chanced a look and discovered Kristen standing in the living-room window, holding aside the curtain and watching them intently. No doubt she was memorising everything they said and did to report back to Nicole.

"I couldn't believe it when she agreed to let Sally come over. She's of the opinion lately that she's old enough to stay by herself."

"Nicole claims the same thing, but she didn't raise any objections about having a baby-sitter, either."

"I guess we should count our blessings."

Tanner drove to an expensive downtown restaurant overlooking the Spokane River, in the heart of the city.

Joanna's mouth was dry and her palms sweaty when the valet opened her door and helped her out. She'd never eaten at such a luxurious place in her life. She'd heard that their prices were outrageous. The amount Tanner intended to spend on one meal would probably outfit Kristen for an entire school year. Joanna felt faint at the very idea.

"Chez Michel is an exceptionally nice restaurant, Tanner, if you get my drift," she muttered under her breath after he handed the car keys to the valet. As a newcomer to town, he might not have been aware of just how expensive this place actually was.

"Yes, that's why I chose it," he said nonchalantly. "I was quite pleased with the food and the service when I was here a few weeks ago." He glanced at Joanna and her discomfort must have shown. "Consider it a small token of my appreciation for your help with Nicole's birthday party," he added, offering her one of his bone-melting smiles.

Joanna would have been more than content to eat at Denny's, and that thought reminded her again of how different they were.

She wished now that she'd worn something a little more elegant. The waiters seemed to be better dressed than she was. For that matter, so were the menus.

They were escorted to a table with an unobstructed view of the river. The maître d' held out Joanna's chair and seated her with flair. The first thing she noticed was the setting of silverware, with its bewildering array of forks, knives and spoons. After the maître d' left, she leaned forward and whispered to Tanner, "I've never eaten at a place that uses three teaspoons."

"Oh, quit complaining."

"I'm not, but if I embarrass you and use the wrong fork, don't blame me."

Unconcerned, Tanner chuckled and reached for the shiny gold menu.

Apparently Chez Michel believed in leisurely dining, because nearly two hours had passed by the time they were served their after-dinner coffee. The entire meal was everything Joanna could have hoped for, and more. The food was exceptional, but Joanna considered Tanner's company the best part of the evening. She'd never felt this much at ease with a man before. He made her smile, but he challenged her ideas, too. They talked about the girls and about the demands of being a parent. They discussed Joanna's career goals and Tanner's plans for his company. They covered a lot of different subjects, but didn't focus their conversation on any one.

Now that the meal was over, Joanna was reluctant to see the evening end. She lifted the delicate china cup, admiring its pattern, and took a sip of fragrant coffee. She paused, her cup raised halfway to her mouth, when she noticed Tanner staring at her. "What's wrong?" she asked, fearing part of her dessert was on her nose or something equally disastrous.

"Nothing."

"Then why are you looking at me like that?"

Tanner relaxed, leaned back in his chair, and grinned. "I'm sorry. I was just thinking how lovely you are, and how pleased I am that we met. It seems nothing's been the same since. I never thought a woman could make me feel the way you do, Joanna."

She looked quickly down, feeling a sudden shyness—and a wonderful warmth. Her life had changed, too, and she wasn't sure she could ever go back to the way things had been before. She was dreaming again, feeling again, trusting again, and it felt so good. And so frightening.

"I'm pleased, too," was her only comment.

"You know what the girls are thinking, don't you?'

Joanna could well imagine. No doubt those two would have them engaged after one dinner date. "They're probably expecting us to announce our marriage plans tomorrow morning," Joanna said, trying to make a joke of it.

"To be honest, I find some aspects of married life appealing."

Joanna smiled and narrowed her eyes suspiciously. "Come on, Tanner, just how much wine have you had?"

"Obviously too much, now that I think about it," he said, grinning. Then his face sobered. "All kidding aside, I want you to know how much I enjoy your company. Every time I'm with you, I come away feeling good about life—you make me laugh again."

"I'd make anyone laugh," she said, "especially if I'm wearing a pair of roller skates." She didn't know where their conversation was leading, but the fact that Tanner spoke so openly and honestly about the promise of their relationship completely unnerved her. She felt exactly the same things, but didn't have the courage to voice them.

"I'm glad you agreed we should start seeing each other," Tanner continued.

"Me, too." But she fervently hoped her mother wouldn't hear about it, although Kristen had probably phoned her grandmother the minute Joanna was out the door. Lowering her gaze, Joanna discovered that a bread crumb on the linen tablecloth had become utterly absorbing. She carefully brushed it onto the floor, an inch at a time. "It's worked out fine...so far. Us dating, I mean." It was more than fine. And now he was telling her how she'd brightened his life, as though *he* was the lucky one. That someone like Tanner Lund would ever want to date her still astonished Joanna.

She gazed up at him, her heart shining through her eyes, telling him without words what she was feeling.

Tanner briefly shut his eyes. "Joanna, for heaven's sake, don't look at me like that."

"Like what?"

"Like...that."

"I think you should kiss me," Joanna announced, once again staring down at the tablecloth. The instant the words slipped out she longed to take them back. She couldn't believe she'd said something like that to him.

"I beg your pardon?"

"Never mind," she said quickly, grateful he hadn't heard her.

He had. "Kiss you? Now? Here?"

Joanna shook her head, forcing a smile. "Forget I said that. It just slipped out. Sometimes my mouth disconnects itself from my brain."

Tanner didn't remove his gaze from hers as he raised his hand. Their waiter appeared almost immediately, and still looking at Joanna, he muttered, "Check, please."

"Right away, sir."

They were out of the restaurant so fast Joanna's head was spinning. Once they were seated in the car, Tanner paused, frowning, his hands clenched on the steering wheel.

"What's the matter?" Joanna asked anxiously.

"We goofed. We should have shared a baby-sitter."

The thought had fleetingly entered her mind earlier, but she'd discounted the idea because she didn't want to encourage the girls' scheming.

"I can't take you back to my place because Nicole will be all over us with questions, and it'll probably be the same story at your house with Kristen."

"You're right." Besides, her daughter would be sorely disappointed if they showed up this early. It wasn't even close to midnight.

"Just where am I supposed to kiss you, Joanna Parsons?"

Oh Lord, he'd taken her seriously. "Tanner...it was a joke."

He ignored her comment. "I don't know of a single lookout point in the city."

"Tanner, please." Her voice rose in embarrassment, and she could feel herself blushing.

Tanner leaned over and brushed his lips against her cheek. "I've got an idea for something we can do, but don't laugh."

"An idea? What?"

"You'll see soon enough." He eased his car onto the street and drove quickly through the city to the freeway on-ramp and didn't exit until they were well into the suburbs.

"Tanner?" Joanna said, looking around her at the unfamiliar streets. "What's out here?" Almost as soon as she'd spoken a huge white screen appeared in the distance. "A drive-in?" she whispered in disbelief.

"Have you got any better ideas?"

"Not a one." Joanna chuckled; she couldn't help it. He was taking her to a drive-in movie just so he could kiss her.

"I can't guarantee this movie. This is its opening weekend, and if I remember the ad correctly, they're showing something with lots of blood and gore."

"As long as it isn't *Teen Massacre*. Kristen would never forgive me if I saw it when she hadn't."

"If the truth be known, I don't plan to watch a whole lot of the movie." He darted an exaggerated leer in her direction and wiggled his eyebrows suggestively.

Joanna returned his look by demurely fluttering her lashes. "I don't know if my mother would approve of my going to a drive-in on a first date."

"With good reason," Tanner retorted. "Especially if she knew what I had in mind."

Although the weather had been mild and the sky was cloudless and clear, only a few cars were scattered across the wide lot.

Tanner parked as far away from the others as possible. He connected the speaker, but turned the volume so low it was almost inaudible. When he'd finished, he placed his arm around Joanna's shoulders, pulling her closer.

"Come here, woman."

Joanna leaned her head against his shoulder and pretended to be interested in the cartoon characters leaping across the large screen. Her stomach was playing jumping jacks with the dinner she'd just eaten.

"Joanna?" His voice was low and seductive.

She tilted her head to meet his gaze, and his eyes moved slowly over her upturned face, searing her with their intensity. The openness of his desire stole her breath away. Her heart was pounding, although he hadn't even kissed her yet. One hungry look from Tanner and she was melting at his feet.

Her first thought was to crack a joke. That had saved her in the past, but whatever she might have said or done was lost as Tanner lowered his mouth and tantalised the edges of her trembling lips, teasing her with soft, tempting nibbles, making her ache all the way to her toes for his kiss. Instinctively her fingers slid up his chest and around the back of his neck. Tanner created such an overwhelming need in her that she felt both humble and elated at the same time. When her hands tightened around his neck, his mouth hardened into firm possession.

Joanna thought she'd drown in the sensations that

flooded her. She hadn't felt this kind of longing in years, and she trembled with the wonder of it. Tanner had awakened the deep womanly part of her that had lain dormant for so long. And suddenly she felt all that time without love come rushing up at her, overtaking her. Years of regret, years of doubt, years of rejection all pressed so heavily on her heart that she could barely breathe.

A sob was ripped from her throat, and the sound of it broke them apart. Tears she couldn't explain flooded her eyes and ran unheeded down her face.

"Joanna, what's wrong? Did I hurt you?"

She tried to break away, but Tanner wouldn't let her go. He brushed the hair from her face and tilted her head to lift her eyes to his, but she resisted.

He must have felt the wetness on her face, because he paused and murmured, "You're crying," in a tone that sounded as shocked as she felt. "Dear Lord, what did I do?"

Wildly she shook her head, unable to speak even if she'd been able to find the words to explain.

"Joanna, tell me, please."

"J-just hold me." Even saying that much required all her reserves of strength.

He did as she asked, wrapping his arms completely around her, kissing the crown of her head as she buried herself in his strong, solid warmth.

Still, the tears refused to stop, no matter how hard she tried to make them. They flooded her face and seemed to come from the deepest part of her.

"I can't believe I'm doing this," she said between sobs. "Oh, Tanner, I feel like such a fool."

"Go ahead and cry, Joanna. I understand."

"You do? Good. You can explain it to me."

She could feel his smile as he kissed the corner of her eye. She moaned a little and he lowered his lips to her cheek, then her chin, and when she couldn't bear it any longer, she turned her face, her mouth seeking his. Tanner didn't disappoint her, kissing her gently again and again until she was certain her heart would stop beating if he ever stopped holding her and kissing her.

"Good Lord, Joanna," he whispered after a while, gently extricating himself from her arms and leaning against the car seat, his eyes closed. His face was a picture of desire struggling for restraint. He drew in several deep breaths.

Joanna's tears had long since dried on her face and now her cheeks flamed with confusion and remorse.

A heavy silence fell between them. Joanna searched frantically for something witty to say to break the terrible tension.

"Joanna, listen—"

"No, let me speak first," she broke in, then hesitated. Now that she had his attention, she didn't know what to say. "I'm sorry, Tanner, really sorry. I don't know what came over me, but you weren't the one responsible for my tears. Well, no, you were, but not the way you think."

"Joanna, please," he said and his hands bracketed her face. "Don't be embarrassed by the tears. Believe me when I say I'm feeling the same things you are, only they come out in different ways."

Joanna stared up at him, not sure he could possibly understand.

"It's been so long for you—it has for me, too," Tanner went on. "I feel like a teenager again. And the drive-in has nothing to do with it."

Her lips trembled with the effort to smile. Tanner leaned his forehead against hers. "We need to take this slow. Very, very slow."

That was a fine thing for him to say, considering they'd been as hot as torches for each other a few minutes ago. If they continued at this rate, they'd end up in bed together by the first of the week.

"I've got a company party in a couple of weeks; I want you there with me. Will you do that?"

Joanna nodded.

Tanner drew her closer to his side and she tucked her head against his chest. His hand stroked her shoulder, as he kissed the top of her head.

"You're awfully quiet," he said after several minutes. "What are you thinking?"

Joanna sighed and snuggled closer, looping one arm around his middle. Her free hand was laced with his. "It just occurred to me that for the first time in my life I've met a real prince. Up until now, all I've done is make a few frogs happy."

Eleven

Kneeling on the polished linoleum floor of the kitchen, Joanna held her breath and tentatively poked her head inside the foam-covered oven. Sharp, lemon-scented fumes made her grimace as she dragged the wet sponge along the sides, peeling away a layer of blackened crust. She'd felt unusually ambitious for a Saturday and had worked in the yard earlier, planning her garden. When she'd finished that, she'd decided to tackle the oven, not questioning where this burst of energy had come from. Spring was in the air, but instead of turning her fancy to thoughts of love, it filled her mind with zucchini seeds and rows of tomato seedlings.

"I'm leaving now, Mom," Kristen called from behind her.

Joanna jerked her head free, gulped some fresh air and twisted toward her daughter. "What time will you be through at the library?" Kristen and Nicole were working together on a school project, and although they complained about having to do research, they'd come to enjoy it. Their biggest surprise was discovering all the cute junior-high boys who sometimes visited the library. In Kristen's words, it was an untapped gold mine.

"I don't know when we'll be through, but I'll call. And remember, Nicole is coming over afterwards."

"I remember."

Kristen hesitated, then asked, "When are you going out with Mr. Lund again?"

Joanna glanced over at the calendar. "Next weekend. We're attending a dinner party his company's sponsoring."

"Oh."

Joanna rubbed her forearm across her cheek, and glanced suspiciously at her daughter. "What does that mean?"

"What?"

"That little 'oh.'"

Kristen shrugged. "Nothing.... It's just that you're not seeing him as often as Nicole and I think you should. You like Mr. Lund, don't you?"

That was putting it mildly. "He's very nice," Joanna said cautiously. If she admitted to anything beyond a casual attraction, Kristen would assume much more. Joanna wanted her relationship with Tanner to progress slowly, one careful step at a time, not in giant leaps—though slow and careful didn't exactly describe what had happened so far!

"Nice?" Kristen exclaimed.

Her daughter's outburst caught Joanna by surprise.

"Is that all you can say about Mr. Lund?" Kristen asked, hands on her hips. "I've given the matter serious consideration and I think he's a whole lot more than just nice. Really, Mother."

Taking a deep breath, Joanna plunged her head back inside the oven, swiping her sponge furiously against the sides.

"Are you going to ignore me?" Kristen demanded.

Joanna emerged again, gasped and looked straight at her daughter. "Yes. Unless you want to volunteer to clean the oven yourself."

"I would, but I have to go to the library with Nicole."

Joanna noted the soft regret that filled her daughter's voice and gave her a derisive snort. The kid actually sounded sorry that she wouldn't be there to do her part. Kristen was a genius at getting out of work, and she always managed to give the impression of really wishing she could help her mother—if only she could fit it into her busy schedule.

A car horn beeped out front. "That's Mr. Lund," Kristen said, glancing toward the living room. "I'll give you a call when we're done."

"Okay, honey. Have a good time."

"I will."

With form an Olympic sprinter would envy, Kristen tore out of the kitchen. Two seconds later, the front door slammed. Joanna was only mildly disappointed that Tanner hadn't stopped in to chat. He'd phoned earlier and explained that after he dropped the girls off at the library, he was driving to the office for a couple of hours. An unexpected problem had arisen, and he needed to deal with it right away.

Actually Joanna had to admit she was more grateful than disappointed that Tanner hadn't stopped in. It didn't look as though she'd get a chance to see him before the company party. She needed this short separation to pull together her reserves. Following their dinner date and the drive-in movie afterward, Joanna felt dangerously close to falling in love with Tanner. Every time he came to mind, and that was practically every minute of every day, a rush of warmth and happiness followed. Without too much trouble, she could envision them finding a lifetime of happiness together. For the first time since her divorce she allowed herself the luxury of dreaming again, and although the prospect of remarriage excited and thrilled her, it also terrified her.

Fifteen minutes later, with perspiration beaded on her forehead and upper lip, Joanna heaved a sigh and sat back on her heels. The hair she'd so neatly tucked inside a scarf and tied at the back of her head, had fallen loose. She swiped a grimy hand at the auburn curls that hung limply over her eyes and ears. It was all worth it, though, since the gray-speckled sides of the oven, which had been encrusted with black grime, were now clearly visible and shining.

Joanna emptied the bucket of dirty water and hauled a fresh one back to wipe the oven one last time. She'd just knelt down when the doorbell chimed.

"Great," she muttered under her breath, casting a glance at herself. She looked like something that had crawled out of the bog in some horror movie. Pasting a smile on her face, she peeled off her rubber gloves and hurried to the door.

"Davey!" Finding her ex-husband standing on the porch was enough of a shock to knock the breath from Joanna's lungs.

"May I come in?"

"Of course." Flustered, she ran her hand through her hair and stepped aside to allow him to pass. He looked good—really good—but then Davey had never lacked in the looks department. From the expensive cut of his three-piece suit, she could tell that his real-estate business must be doing well, and of course that was precisely the impression he wanted her to have. She was pleased for him; she'd never wished him ill. They'd gone their separate ways, and although both the marriage and the divorce had devastated Joanna, she shared a beautiful child with this man. If he had come by to tell her how successful he was, well, she'd just smile and let him.

"It's good to see you, Joanna."

"You, too. What brings you to town?" She struggled to keep her voice even and controlled, hoping to hide her discomfort at being caught unawares.

"I'm attending a conference downtown. I apologise for dropping in unexpectedly like this, but since I was going to be in Spokane, I thought I'd stop in and see how you and Kristen are doing."

"I wish you'd phoned first. Kristen's at the library." Joanna wasn't fooled—Davey hadn't come to see their daughter, although he meant Joanna to think so. It was all part of the game he played with her, wanting her to believe that their divorce had hurt him badly. Not calling to let her know he planned to visit was an attempt to catch her off guard and completely unprepared— which, of course, she was. Joanna knew Davey, knew him well. He'd often tried to manipulate her this way.

"I should have called, but I didn't know if I'd have the time, and I didn't want to disappoint you if I found I couldn't slip away."

Joanna didn't believe that for a minute. It wouldn't have taken him much time or trouble to phone before he left the hotel. But she didn't mention the fact, couldn't see that it would have done any good.

"Come in and have some coffee." She led him into the kitchen and poured him a mug, automatically adding the sugar and cream she knew he used. She handed it to him and was rewarded with a dazzling smile. When he wanted, Davey Parsons could be charming, attentive and generous. The confusing thing about her ex-husband was that he wasn't all bad. He'd gravely wounded her with his unfaithfulness, but in his own way he'd loved her and Kristen—as much as he could possibly love anybody beyond himself. It had taken Joanna a good many years to distance herself enough to appreciate his good points and to forgive him for the pain he'd caused her.

"You've got a nice place here," he commented, casually glancing around the kitchen. "How long have you lived here now?"

"Seven months."

"How's Kristen?"

Joanna was relieved that the conversation had moved to the only subject they still had in common—their daughter. She talked for fifteen minutes nonstop, telling him about the talent show and the other activities Kristen had been involved in since the last time she'd seen her father.

Davey listened and laughed, and then his gaze softened as he studied Joanna. "You're looking wonderful."

She grinned ruefully. "Sure I am," she scoffed. "I've just finished working in the yard and cleaning the oven."

"I wondered about the lemon perfume you were wearing."

They both laughed. Davey started to tease her about their early years together and some of the experimental meals she'd cooked and expected him to eat and praise. Joanna let him and even enjoyed his comments, for Davey could be warm and funny when he chose. Kristen had inherited her friendly, easygoing confidence from her father.

The doorbell chimed and still chuckling, Joanna stood up. "It's probably one of the neighbourhood kids. I'll just be a minute." She never ceased to be astonished at how easy it was to be with Davey. He'd ripped her heart in two, lied to her repeatedly, cheated on her, and still she couldn't be around him and not laugh. It always took him a few minutes to conquer her reserve, but he never failed. She was mature enough to recognise her ex-husband's faults, yet appreciate his redeeming qualities.

For the second time that day, Joanna was surprised by the man who stood on her front porch. "Tanner."

"Hi," he said with a sheepish grin. "The girls got off okay and I thought I'd stop in for a cup of coffee before heading to the office." His eyes smiled softly into hers. "I heard you laughing from out here. Do you have company? Should I come back later?"

"N-no, come in," she said, her pulse beating as hard and loud as jungle drums. Lowering her eyes, she automatically moved aside. He walked into the living room and paused, then raised his hand and gently touched her cheek in a gesture so loving that Joanna longed to fall into his arms. Now that he was here, she found herself craving some time alone with him.

Tanner's gaze reached out to her, but Joanna had trouble meeting it. A frown started to form, and his eyes clouded. "This is a bad time, isn't it?"

"No...not really." When she turned around, Davey was standing in the kitchen doorway watching them. The smile she'd been wearing felt shaky as she stood between the two men and made the introductions. "Davey, this is Tanner Lund. Tanner, this is Davey— Kristen's father."

For a moment, the two men glared at each other like

angry bears who had claimed territory and were prepared to do battle to protect what was theirs. When they stepped towards each other, Joanna held her breath for fear neither one would make the effort to be civil.

Stunned, she watched as they exchanged handshakes and enthusiastic greetings.

"Davey's in town for a real-estate conference and thought he'd stop in to see Kristen," Joanna explained, her words coming out in such a rush that they nearly stumbled over themselves.

"I came to see you, too, Joanna," Davey added in a low sultry voice that suggested he had more on his mind than a chat over a cup of coffee.

She flashed him a heated look before marching into the kitchen, closely followed by both men. She walked straight to the cupboard, bringing down another cup, then poured Tanner's coffee and delivered it to the table.

"Kristen and my daughter are at the library," Tanner announced in a perfectly friendly voice, but Joanna heard the undercurrents even if Davey didn't.

"Joanna told me," Davey returned.

The two men remained standing, smiling at each other. Tanner took a seat first, and Davey promptly did the same.

"What do you do?" her ex-husband asked.

"I own half of Spokane Aluminum."

It was apparent to Joanna that Davey hadn't even bothered to listen to Tanner's reply because he immediately fired back in an aggressive tone, "I recently opened my own real-estate brokerage and have plans to expand within the next couple of years." He announced his success with a cocky slant to his mouth.

Watching the change in Davey's features as Tanner's

identity began to sink in was so comical that Joanna nearly laughed out loud. Davey's mouth sagged open, and his eyes flew from Joanna to Tanner and then back to Joanna.

"Spokane Aluminum," Davey repeated slowly, his face unusually pale. "I seem to remember reading something about John Becky taking on a partner."

Joanna almost felt sorry for Davey. "Kristen and Tanner's daughter, Nicole, are best friends. They were in the Valentine's Day show together—the one I was telling you about...."

To his credit, Davey regrouped quickly. "She gets all that performing talent from you."

"Oh, hardly," Joanna countered, denying it with a vigorous shake of her head. Of the two of them, Davey was the entertainer—crowds had never intimidated him. He could walk into a room full of strangers, and anyone who didn't know better would end up thinking Davey Parsons was his best friend.

"With the girls being so close, it seemed only natural for Joanna and me to start dating," Tanner said, turning to smile warmly at Joanna.

"I see," Davey answered. He didn't appear to have recovered from Tanner's first announcement.

"I sincerely hope you do understand," Tanner returned, all pretence of friendliness dropped.

Joanna resisted rolling her eyes toward the ceiling. Both of them were behaving like immature children, battling with looks and words as if she were a prize to be awarded the victor.

"I suppose I'd better think about heading out," Davey said after several awkward moments had passed. He stood up, noticeably eager to make his escape.

As a polite hostess, Joanna stood when Davey did. "I'll walk you to the door."

He sent Tanner a wary smile. "That's not necessary."

"Of course it is," Joanna countered.

To her dismay, Tanner followed them and stood conspicuously in the background while Davey made arrangements to phone Kristen later that evening. The whole time Davey was speaking, Joanna could feel Tanner's eyes burning into her back. She didn't know why he'd insisted on following her to the door. It was like saying he couldn't trust her not to fall into Davey's arms the minute he was out of sight, and that irritated her no end.

Once her ex-husband had left, she closed the door and whirled around to face Tanner. The questions were jammed in her mind. They'd only gone out on one date, for heaven's sake, and here he was, acting as though...as though they were engaged.

"I thought he broke your heart," Tanner said, in a cutting voice.

Joanna debated whether or not to answer him, then decided it would be best to clear the air. "He did."

"I heard you laughing when I rang the doorbell. Do you often have such a good time with men you're supposed to hate?"

"I don't hate Davey."

"Believe me, I can tell."

"Tanner, what's wrong with you?" That was a silly question, and she regretted asking it immediately. She already knew what was troubling Tanner. He was jealous. And angry. And hurt.

"Wrong with me?" He tossed the words back at her. "Nothing's wrong with me. I happen to stumble upon the woman I'm involved with cosying up to her ex-husband, and I don't mind telling you I'm upset. But nothing's wrong with me. Not one damn thing. If there's something wrong with anyone, it's you, lady.''

Joanna held tightly onto her patience. ''Before we start arguing, let's sit down and talk this out.'' She led him back into the kitchen, then took Davey's empty coffee mug and placed it in the sink, removing all evidence of his brief visit. She searched for a way to reassure Tanner that Davey meant nothing to her anymore. But she had to explain that she and her ex-husband weren't enemies, either; they couldn't be for Kristen's sake.

''First of all,'' she said, as evenly as her pounding heart would allow, ''I could never hate Davey the way you seem to think I should. As far as I'm concerned, that would only be counterproductive. The people who would end up suffering are Kristen and me. Davey is incapable of being faithful to one woman, but he'll always be Kristen's father, and if for no other reason than that, I prefer to remain on friendly terms with him.''

''But he cheated on you...used you.''

''Yes.'' She couldn't deny it. ''But, Tanner, I lived a lot of years with Davey. He's not all bad—no one is—and scattered between all the bad times were a few good ones. We're divorced now. What good would it do to harbour ill will toward him? None that I can see.''

''He let it be known from the moment I walked into this house that he could have you back any time he wanted.''

Joanna wasn't blind; she'd recognised the looks Davey had given Tanner, and the insinuations. ''He'd like to believe that. It helps him deal with his ego.''

''And you let him?''

"Not the way you're implying."

Tanner mulled that over for a few moments. "How often does he casually drop in unannounced like this?"

She hesitated, wondering whether she should answer his question. His tone had softened, but he was obviously still angry. She could sympathise, but she didn't like having to defend herself or her attitude toward Davey. "I haven't seen him in over a year. This is the first time he's been to the house."

Tanner's hands gripped the coffee mug so tightly that Joanna was amazed it remained intact. "You still love him, don't you?"

The question hit her square between the eyes. Her mouth opened and closed several times as she struggled for the words to deny it. Then she realised she couldn't. Lying to Tanner about this would be simple enough and it would keep the peace, but it would wrong them both. "I suppose in a way I do," she began slowly. "He's the father of my child. He was my first love, Tanner. And the only lover I've ever had. Although I'd like to tell you I don't feel a thing for him, I can't do that and be completely honest. But please, try to understand—"

"You don't need to say anything more." He stood abruptly, his back stiff. "I appreciate the fact that you told me the truth. I won't waste any more of your time. I wish you and Kristen a good life." With that he stalked out of the room, headed for the door.

Joanna was shocked. "Tanner...you make it sound like I'll never see you again."

"I think that would be best for everyone concerned," he replied, without looking at her.

"But...that's silly. Nothing's changed." She snapped her mouth closed. If Tanner wanted to act so childishly and ruin everything, she wasn't about to argue with him. He was the one who insisted they had something special, something so good they shouldn't throw it away because of their fears. And now he was acting like this! Fine. If that was the way he wanted it. It was better to find out how unreasonable he could be before anything serious developed between them. Better to discover now how quick-tempered he could be, how hurtful.

"I have no intention of becoming involved with a woman who's still in love with her loser of an ex-husband," he announced, his hands clenched at his sides. His voice was calm, but she recognised the tension in it. And the resolve.

Unable to restrain her anger any longer, Joanna marched across the room and threw open the front door. "Smart move, Tanner," she said, her words coated with sarcasm. "You made a terrible mistake getting involved with a woman who refuses to hate." Now that she had a better look at him, she decided he wasn't a prince after all, only another frog.

Tanner didn't say a word as he walked past her, his strides filled with purpose. She closed the door and leaned against it, needing the support. Tears burned in her eyes and clogged her throat, but she held her head high and hurried back into the kitchen, determined not to give in to the powerful emotions that racked her, body and soul.

She finished cleaning up the kitchen, and took a long hot shower afterward. Then she sat quietly at the table, waiting for Kristen to phone so she could pick up the two girls. The call came a half hour later, but by that time she'd already reached for the cookies, bent on self-destruction.

On the way home from the library, Joanna stopped off at McDonald's and bought the girls cheeseburgers and chocolate milk shakes to take home for dinner. Her mind was filled with doubts. In retrospect, she wished she'd done a better job of explaining things to Tanner. The thought of never seeing him again was almost too painful to endure.

"Aren't you going to order anything, Mom?" Kristen asked, surprised.

"Not tonight." Somewhere deep inside, Joanna found the energy to smile.

She managed to maintain a light-hearted facade while Kristen and Nicole ate their dinner and chattered about the boys they'd seen at the library and how they were going to shock Mrs. Andrews with their well-researched report.

"Are you feeling okay?" Kristen asked, pausing in mid-sentence.

"Sure," Joanna lied, looking for something to occupy her hands. She settled for briskly wiping down the kitchen counters. Actually, she felt sick to her stomach, but she couldn't blame Tanner; she'd done that to herself with all those stupid cookies.

It was when she was putting the girls' empty McDonald's containers in the garbage that the silly tears threatened to spill over. She did her best to hide them and quickly carried out the trash. Nicole went to get a cassette from Kristen's bedroom, but Kristen followed her mother outside.

"Mom, what's wrong?"

"Nothing, sweetheart."

"You have tears in your eyes."

"It's nothing."

"You never cry," Kristen insisted.

"Something must have got into my eye to make it tear like this," she said, shaking her head. The effort to smile was too much for her. She straightened and placed her hands on Kristen's shoulders, then took a deep breath. "I don't want you to be disappointed if I don't see Mr. Lund again."

"He did this?" Kristen demanded, in a high shocked voice.

"No," Joanna countered immediately. "I already told you, I got something in my eye."

Kristen studied her with a frown, and Joanna tried to meet her daughter's gaze. If she was fool enough to make herself vulnerable to a man again, then she deserved this pain. She'd known better than to get involved with Tanner, but her heart had refused to listen.

A couple of hours later, Tanner arrived to pick up Nicole. Joanna let Kristen answer the door and stayed in the kitchen, pretending to be occupied there.

When the door swung open, Joanna assumed it was her daughter and asked, "Did Nicole get off all right?"

"Not yet."

Joanna jerked away from the sink at the husky sound of Tanner's voice. "Where are the girls?"

"In Kristen's room. I want to talk to you."

"I can't see how that would do much good."

"I've reconsidered."

"Bravo for you. Unfortunately so have I. You're absolutely right about it being better all around if we don't see each other again."

Tanner dragged his fingers through his hair and stalked to the other side of the room. "Okay, I'll admit it. I was jealous as hell when I walked in and found you having coffee with Davey. I felt you were treating him like some conquering hero returned from the war."

"Oh, honestly, it wasn't anything like that."

"You were laughing and smiling."

"Grievous sins, I'm sure."

Tanner clamped down his jaw so hard that the sides of his face went white. "All I can do is apologise, Joanna. I've already made a fool of myself over one woman who loved someone else, and frankly that caused me enough grief. I'm not looking to repeat the mistake with you."

A strained silence fell between them.

"I thought I could walk away from you and not feel any regrets, but I was wrong," he continued a moment later. "I haven't stopped thinking about you all afternoon. Maybe I overreacted. Maybe I behaved like a jealous fool."

"Maybe?" Joanna challenged. "Maybe? You were unreasonable and hurtful and…and I ate a whole row of Oreo cookies over you."

"What?"

"You heard me. I stuffed down a dozen cookies and now I think I'm going to be sick and it was all because of you. I've come too far to be reduced to that. One argument with you and I was right back into the Oreos! If you think you're frightened—because of what happened with Carmen—it's nothing compared to the fears I've been facing since the day we met. I can't deal with your insecurities, Tanner. I've got too damn many of my own."

"Joanna, I've already apologised. If you can honestly tell me there isn't any chance that you'll ever get back together with Davey, I swear to you I'll drop the subject and never bring it up again. But I need to know that much. I'm sorry, but I've got to hear you say it."

"I had a nice quiet life before you paraded into it," she went on, as though she hadn't heard him.

"Joanna, I asked you a question." His intense gaze cut straight through her.

"You must be nuts! I'd be certifiably insane to ever take Davey back. Our marriage—our entire relationship—was over the day I filed for divorce, and probably a lot earlier than that."

Tanner relaxed visibly. "I wouldn't blame you if you decided you never wanted to see me again, but I'm hoping you'll be able to forget what happened this afternoon so we can go back to being...friends again."

Joanna struggled against the strong pull of his magnetism for as long as she could, then nodded, agreeing to place this quarrel behind them.

Tanner walked toward her and she met him halfway, slipping easily into his embrace. She felt as if she belonged here, as if he were the man she would always be content with. He'd once told her he wouldn't ever hurt her the way her ex-husband had, but caring about him, risking a relationship with him, left her vulnerable all over again. She'd realised that this afternoon, learned again what it was to give a man the power to hurt her.

"I reduced you to gorging yourself with Oreos?" Tanner whispered the question into her hair.

She nodded wildly. "You fiend. I didn't mean to eat that many, but I sat at the table with the Oreos package and a glass of milk and the more I thought about what happened, the angrier I became, and the faster I shoved those cookies into my mouth."

"Could this mean you care?" His voice was still a whisper.

She nodded a second time. "I hate fighting with you. My stomach was in knots all afternoon."

"Good Lord, Joanna," he said, dropping several swift kisses on her face. "I can't believe what fools we are."

"We?" She tilted back her head and glared up at him, but her mild indignation drained away the moment their eyes met. Tanner was looking down at her with such tenderness, such concern, that every negative emotion she'd experienced earlier that afternoon vanished like rain falling into a clear blue lake.

He kissed her then, with a thoroughness that left her in no doubt about the strength of his feelings. Joanna rested against this warmth, holding onto him with everything that was in her. When he raised his head, she looked up at him through tear-filled eyes and blinked furiously in a futile effort to keep them at bay.

"I'm glad you came back," she said, when she could find her voice.

"I am, too." He kissed her once more, lightly this time, sampling her lips, kissing the tears from her face. "I wasn't worth a damn all afternoon." Once more he lowered his mouth to hers, creating a delicious sensation that electrified Joanna and sent chills racing down her spine.

Tanner's arms tightened as loud voices suddenly erupted from the direction of the living room.

"I never want to see you again," Joanna heard Kristen declare vehemently.

"You couldn't possibly want to see me any less than I want to see you," Nicole returned with equal volume and fury.

"What's that all about?" Tanner asked, his eyes searching Joanna's.

"I don't know, but I think we'd better find out."

Tanner led the way into the living room. They discovered Kristen and Nicole standing face to face, glaring at each other in undisguised antagonism.

"Kristen, stop that right now," Joanna demanded. "Nicole is a guest in our home and I won't have you talking to her in that tone of voice."

Tanner moved to his daughter's side. "And you're Kristen's guest. I expect you to be on your best behaviour whenever you're here."

Nicole crossed her arms over her chest and darted a venomous look in Kristen's direction. "I refuse to be friends with her ever again. And I don't think you should have anything more to do with Mrs. Parsons."

Joanna's eyes found Tanner's.

"I don't want my mother to have anything to do with Mr. Lund, either." Kristen spun around and glared at Tanner and Nicole.

"I think we'd best separate these two and find out what happened," Joanna suggested. She pointed toward Kristen's bedroom. "Come on, honey, let's talk."

Kristen averted her face. "I have nothing to say!" she declared melodramatically and stalked out of the room without a backward glance.

Joanna raised questioning eyes to Tanner, threw up her hands and followed her daughter.

Twelve

"Kristen, what's wrong?" Joanna sat on the end of her daughter's bed and patiently waited for the eleven-year-old to repeat the list of atrocities committed by Nicole Lund.

"Nothing."

Joanna had seen her daughter wear this affronted look often enough to recognize it readily, and she felt a weary sigh work its way through her. Hell hath no fury like a sixth-grader done wrong by her closest friend.

"I don't ever want to see Nicole again."

"But, sweetheart, she's your best friend."

"*Was* my best friend," Kristen announced theatrically. She crossed her arms over her chest with all the pomp of a queen who'd made her statement and expected unquestioning acquiescence.

With mounting frustration, Joanna folded her hands in her lap and waited, knowing better than to try to reason with Kristen when she was in this mood. Five minutes passed, but Kristen didn't utter another word. Joanna wasn't surprised.

"Does your argument have to do with something that happened at school?" she asked as nonchalantly as possible, examining the fingernails on her right hand.

Kristen shook her head. She pinched her lips as if to

suggest that nothing Joanna could say would force the information out of her.

"Does it involve a boy?" Joanna persisted.

Kristen's gaze widened. "Of course not."

"What about another friend?"

"Nope."

At the rate they were going, Joanna would soon run out of questions. "Can't you just tell me what happened?"

Kristen cast her a look that seemed to question her mother's intelligence. "No!"

"Does that mean we're going to sit here all night while I try to guess?"

Kristen twisted her head and tilted it at a lofty angle, then pantomimed locking her lips.

"All right," Joanna said with an exaggerated sigh, "I'll simply have to ask Nicole, who will, no doubt, be more than ready to tell all. Her version should be highly interesting."

"Mr. Lund made you cry!" Kristen mumbled, her eyes lowered.

Joanna blinked back her astonishment. "You mean to say this whole thing has to do with Tanner and me?"

Kristen nodded once.

"But—"

"Nicole claims that whatever happened was obviously your fault, and as far as I'm concerned that did it. From here on out, Nicole is no longer my friend and I don't think you should have anything to do with…with that man, either."

"That man?"

Kristen sent her a sour look. "You know very well who I mean."

Joanna shifted farther onto the bed, brought up her

knees and rested her chin on them. She paused to carefully measure her words. "What if I told you I was beginning to grow fond of 'that man'?"

"Mom, no!" Her daughter's eyes widened with horror, and she cast her mother a look of sheer panic. "That would be the worst possible thing to happen. You might marry him and then Nicole and I would end up being sisters!"

Joanna made no attempt to conceal her surprise. "But, Kristen, from the not-so-subtle hints you and Nicole have been giving me and Mr. Lund, I thought that was exactly what you both wanted. What you'd planned."

"That was before."

"Before what?"

"Before...tonight, when Nicole said those things she said. I can't forgive her, Mom, I just can't."

Joanna stayed in the room a few more silent minutes, then left. Tanner and Nicole were talking in the living room, and from the frustrated look he gave her, she knew he hadn't been any more successful with his daughter than Joanna had been with hers.

When he saw Joanna, Tanner got to his feet and nodded toward the kitchen, mutely suggesting they talk privately and compare stories.

"What did you find out?" she asked the minute they were alone.

Tanner shrugged, then gestured defeat with his hands. "I don't understand it. She keeps saying she never wants to see Kristen again."

"Kristen says the same thing. Adamantly. She seems to think she's defending my honour. It seems this all has to do with our misunderstanding earlier this afternoon."

"Nicole seems to think it started when you didn't order anything at McDonalds," Tanner said, his expression confused.

"What?" Joanna's question escaped on a short laugh.

"From what I can get out of Nicole, Kristen claims you didn't order a Big Mac, which is supposed to mean something. Then later, before I arrived, there was some mention of your emptying the garbage when it was only half-full?" He paused to wait for her to speak. When she simply nodded, he continued, "I understand that's unusual for you, as well?"

Once more Joanna nodded. She'd wanted to hide her tears from the girls, so taking out the garbage had been an excuse to escape for a couple of minutes while she composed herself.

Tanner wiped his hand across his brow in mock relief. "Whew! At least neither of them learned about the Oreos!"

Joanna ignored his joke and slumped against the kitchen counter with a long slow sigh of frustration. "Having the girls argue is a problem neither of us anticipated."

"Maybe I should talk to Kristen and you talk to Nicole?" Tanner suggested, all seriousness again.

Joanna shook her head. "Then we'd be guilty of interfering. We'd be doing the same thing they've done to us—and I don't think we'd be doing them any favours."

"What do you suggest then?" Tanner asked, looking more disgruntled by the minute.

Joanna shrugged. "I don't know."

"Come on, Joanna, we're intelligent adults. Surely

we can come up with a way to handle a couple of preadolescent egos.''

"Be my guest," Joanna said, and laughed aloud at the comical look that crossed Tanner's handsome face.

"Forget it."

Joanna brushed the hair away from her face. "I think our best bet is to let them work this matter out between themselves."

Tanner's forehead creased in concern, then he nodded, his look reluctant. "I hope this doesn't mean you and I can't be friends." His tender gaze held hers.

Joanna was forced to lower her eyes so he couldn't see just how important his friendship had become to her. "Of course we can."

"Good." He walked across the room and gently pulled her into his arms. He kissed her until she was weak and breathless. When he raised his head, he said in a husky murmur, "I'll take Nicole home now and do as you suggest. We'll give these two a week to settle their differences. After that, you and I are taking over."

"A week?" Joanna wasn't sure that would be long enough, considering Kristen's attitude.

"A week!" Tanner repeated emphatically, kissing her again.

By the time he'd finished, Joanna would have agreed to almost anything. "All right," she managed. "A week."

"HOW WAS SCHOOL TODAY?" Joanna asked Kristen on Monday evening while they sat at the dinner table. She'd waited as long as she could before asking. If either girl was inclined to make a move toward reconciliation, it would be now, she reasoned. They'd both had ample time to think about what had happened and to determine the value of their friendship.

Kristen shrugged. "School was fine, I guess."

Joanna took her time eating her salad, focusing her attention on it instead of her daughter. "How'd you do on the math paper I helped you with?"

Kristen rolled her eyes. "You showed me wrong."

"Wrong!"

"The answers were all right, but Mrs. Andrews told me they don't figure out equations that way anymore."

"Oh. Sorry about that."

"You weren't the only parent who messed up."

That was good to hear.

"A bunch of other kids did it wrong. Including Nicole."

Joanna slipped her hand around her water glass. Kristen sounded far too pleased that her ex-friend had messed up the assignment. That wasn't encouraging. "So you saw Nicole today?"

"I couldn't very well not see her. Her desk is across the aisle from mine. But if you're thinking what I think you're thinking, you can forget it. I don't need a friend like Nicole Lund."

Joanna didn't comment on that, although she practically had to bite her tongue. She wondered how Tanner was doing. Staying out of this argument between the two girls was far more difficult than she'd imagined. It was obvious to Joanna that Kristen was miserable without her best friend, but saying as much would hurt her case more than help it. Kristen needed to recognise the fact herself.

The phone rang while Joanna was finishing up the last of the dinner dishes. Kristen was in the bath, so Joanna grabbed the receiver, holding it between her

hunched shoulder and her ear while she squirted deter-
gent into the hot running water.

"Hello?"

"Joanna? Good Lord, you sounded just like Kristen
there. I was prepared to have the phone slammed in my
ear," Tanner said. "How's it going?"

Her heart swelled with emotion. She hadn't talked to
him since Saturday, and it felt as though months had
passed since she'd heard his voice. It wrapped itself
around her now, warm and comforting. "Things aren't
going too well. How are they at your end?"

"Not much better. Did you know Kristen had the
nerve to eat lunch with Nora this afternoon? In case
you weren't aware of this, Nora is Nicole's sworn enemy."

"Nora?" Joanna could hardly believe her ears.
"Kristen doesn't even like the girl." If anything, this
war between Kristen and Nicole was heating up.

"I hear you bungled the math assignment," Tanner
said softly, amused.

"Apparently you did, too."

He chuckled. "Yeah, this new math is beyond me."
He paused, and when he spoke, Joanna could hear the
frustration in his voice. "I wish the girls would hurry
and patch things up. Frankly, Joanna, I miss you like
crazy."

"It's only been two days." She should talk—the last
forty-eight hours had seemed like an eternity.

"It feels like two years."

"I know," she agreed softly, closing her eyes and
savouring Tanner's words. "But we don't usually see
each other during the week anyway." At least not during the past couple of weeks.

"I've been thinking things over and I may have

come up with an idea that will put us all out of our misery."

"What?" By now, Joanna was game for anything.

"How about a movie?" he asked unexpectedly, his voice eager.

"But Tanner—"

"Tomorrow night. You can bring Kristen and I'll bring Nicole, and we could accidentally-on-purpose meet at the theatre. Naturally there'll be a bit of acting on our part and some huffing and puffing on theirs, but if things work out the way I think they will, we won't have to do a thing. Nature will take its course."

Joanna wasn't convinced this scheme of his would work. The whole thing could blow up in their faces, but the thought of being with Tanner was too enticing to refuse. "All right," she agreed. "As long as you buy the popcorn and promise to hold my hand."

"You've got yourself a deal."

ON TUESDAY EVENING, Kristen was unusually quiet over dinner. Joanna had fixed one of her daughter's favourite meals—macaroni-and-cheese casserole—but Kristen barely touched it.

"Do you feel like going to a movie?" Joanna asked, her heart in her throat. Normally Kristen would leap at the idea, but this evening Joanna couldn't predict anything.

"It's a school night, and I don't think I'm in the mood to see a movie."

"But you said you didn't have any homework, and it sounds like a fun thing to do…and weren't you saying something about wanting to see Tom Cruise's latest film?" Kristen's eyes momentarily brightened, then faded. "And don't worry," Joanna added cheerfully, "you won't have to sit with me."

Kristen gave a huge sigh. "I don't have anyone else to sit with," she said, as though Joanna had suggested a trip to the dentist.

It wasn't until they were in the parking lot at the theater that Kristen spoke. "Nicole likes Tom Cruise, too."

Joanna made a noncommittal reply, wondering how easily the girls would see through her and Tanner's scheme.

"Mom," Kristen cried. "I see Nicole. She's with her dad. Oh, no, it looks like they're going to the same movie."

"Oh, no," Joanna echoed, her heart acting like a Ping-Pong ball in her chest. "Does this mean you want to skip the whole thing and go home?"

"Of course not," Kristen answered smugly. She practically bounded out of the car once Joanna turned off the engine, glancing anxiously at Joanna when she didn't walk across the parking lot fast enough to suit her.

They joined the line, about eight people behind Tanner and Nicole. Joanna was undecided about what to do next. She wasn't completely sure that Tanner had even seen her. If he had, he was playing his part perfectly, acting as though this whole thing had happened by coincidence.

Kristen couldn't seem to stand still. She peeked around the couple ahead of them several times, loudly humming the song of Heart's that she and Nicole had performed in the talent show.

Nicole whirled around, standing on her tiptoes and staring into the crowd behind her. She jerked on

Tanner's sleeve and, when he bent down, whispered something in his ear. Then Tanner turned around, too, and pretended to be shocked when he saw Joanna and Kristen.

By the time they were inside the theatre, Tanner and Nicole had disappeared. Kristen was craning her neck in every direction while Joanna stood at the refreshment counter.

"Do you want any popcorn?"

"No. Just some of those raisin things. Mom, you said I didn't have to sit with you. Did you really mean that?"

"Yes, honey, don't worry about it, I'll find a place by myself."

"You're sure?" Kristen looked only mildly concerned.

"No problem. You go sit by yourself."

"Okay." Kristen collected her candy and was gone before Joanna could say any more.

Since it was still several minutes before the movie was scheduled to start, the theatre auditorium was well lit. Joanna found a seat towards the back and noted that Kristen was two rows from the front. Nicole sat in the row behind her.

"Is this seat taken?"

Joanna smiled up at Tanner as he claimed the seat next to her, and had they been anyplace else she was sure he would have kissed her. He handed her a bag of popcorn and a cold drink.

"I sure hope this works," he muttered under his breath, "because if Nicole sees me sitting with you, I could be hung as a traitor." Mischief brightened his eyes. "But the risk is worth it. Did anyone ever tell you how kissable your mouth looks?"

"Tanner," she whispered frantically and pointed toward the girls. "Look."

Kristen sat twisted around and Nicole leaned forward. Kristen shook a handful of her chocolate-covered raisins into Nicole's outstretched hand. Nicole offered Kristen some popcorn. After several of these exchanges, both girls stood up, moved from their seats to a different row entirely, sitting next to each other.

"That looks promising," Joanna whispered.

"It certainly does," Tanner agreed, slipping his arm around her shoulder.

They both watched as Kristen and Nicole tilted their heads toward each other and smiled at the sound of their combined giggles drifting to the back of the theatre.

Thirteen

After their night at the movies, Joanna didn't give Tanner's invitation to the dinner party more than a passing thought until she read about the event on the society page of Wednesday's newspaper. The *Review* described the dinner, which was being sponsored by Spokane Aluminum, as the gala event of the year. Anyone who was anyone in the eastern half of Washington state would be attending. Until Joanna noticed the news article, she'd thought it was a small intimate party; that was the impression Tanner had given her.

From that moment on, Joanna started worrying, though she wasn't altogether sure why. As a loan officer, she'd attended her share of business-related social functions...but never anything of this scope. The problem, she decided, was one she'd been denying since the night of Nicole's slumber party. Tanner's social position and wealth far outdistanced her own. He was an important member of their community, and she was just a spoke in the wheel of everyday life.

Now, as she dressed for the event, her uneasiness grew, because she knew how important this evening was to Tanner—although he hadn't told her in so many words. The reception and dinner were all part of his becoming half owner of a major corporation and, according to the newspaper article, had been in the planning stages for several months after his arrival. All John Becky's way of introducing Tanner to the community leaders.

Within the first half hour of their arrival, Joanna recognised the mayor and a couple of members from the city council, plus several other people she didn't know, who nonetheless looked terribly important.

"Here," Tanner whispered, stepping to her side and handing her a glass of champagne.

Smiling up at him, she took the glass and held the dainty stem in a death grip, angry with herself for being so unnerved. It wasn't as though she'd never seen the mayor before—okay, only in pictures, but still... "I don't know if I dare have anything too potent," she admitted.

"Why not?"

"If you want the truth, I feel out of it at this affair. I'd prefer to fade into the background, mingle among the draperies, get acquainted with the wallpaper. That sort of thing."

Tanner's smile was encouraging. "No one would know it to look at you."

Joanna had trouble believing that. The smile she wore felt frozen on her lips, and her stomach protested the fact that she'd barely managed to eat all day. Tonight was important, and for Tanner's sake she'd do what she had to.

The man who owned the controlling interest in Columbia Basin Savings and Loan strolled past them and paused when he recognised her. Joanna nodded her recognition, and when he continued on she swallowed the entire glass of champagne in three giant gulps.

"I feel better," she announced.

"Good."

Tanner apparently hadn't noticed how quickly she'd downed the champagne, for which Joanna was grateful.

"Come over here. There are some people I want you to meet."

More people! Tanner had already introduced her to so many that the names were swimming around in her head like fish crowded in a small pond. She'd tried to keep them all straight, and it had been simple in the beginning when he'd started with his partner, John Becky, and John's wife, Jean, but from that point on her memory had deteriorated steadily.

Tanner pressed his hand to the middle of her spine and steered her across the room to where a small group had gathered.

Along the way, Joanna picked up another glass of champagne, just so she'd have something to do with her hands. The way she was feeling, she had no intention of drinking it.

The men and women paused in the middle of their conversation when Tanner approached. After a few words of greeting, introductions were made.

"Pleased to meet all of you," Joanna said, forcing some life into her fatigued smile. Everyone seemed to be looking at her, expecting something more. She nodded toward Tanner. "Our daughters are best friends."

The others smiled.

"I didn't know you had a daughter," a voluptuous blonde said, smiling sweetly up at Tanner.

"Nicole just turned twelve."

The blonde seemed fascinated with this information. "How very sweet. My niece is ten and I know she'd just love to meet Nicole. Perhaps we could get the two of them together. Soon."

"I'm sure Nicole would like that."

"It's a date then." She sidled as close to Tanner as she possibly could, practically draping her breast over his forearm.

Joanna narrowed her gaze and took a small sip of the champagne. The blonde, whose name was—she searched her mind—Blaise, couldn't have been any more obvious had she issued an invitation to her bed.

"Tanner, there's someone you must meet—that is, if I can drag you away from Joanna for just a little minute." The blonde cast a challenging look in Joanna's direction.

"Oh, sure." Joanna gestured with her hand as though to let Blaise know Tanner was free to do as he wished. She certainly didn't have any claims on him.

Tanner frowned. "Come with us," he suggested.

Joanna threw him what she hoped was a dazzling smile. "Go on. You'll only be gone a little minute," she said sweetly, purposely echoing Blaise's words.

The two left, Blaise clinging to Tanner's arm, and Joanna chatted with the others in the group for a few more minutes before fading into the background. Her stomach was twisted in knots. She didn't know why she'd sent Tanner off like that, when it so deeply upset her. Something in her refused to let him know that; it was difficult enough to admit even to herself.

Hoping she wasn't being obvious, her gaze followed Tanner and Blaise until she couldn't endure it any longer, and then she turned and made her way into the ladies' room. Joanna was grateful that the outer room was empty, and she slouched onto the sofa. Her heart was slamming painfully against her rib cage, and when she pressed her hands to her cheeks her face felt hot and feverish. Joanna would gladly have paid the entire three hundred and fifteen dollars in her savings account for a way to gracefully disappear.

It was then that she knew.

She was in love with Tanner Lund. Despite all the warnings she'd given herself. Despite the fact that they were worlds apart, financially and socially.

With the realisation that she loved Tanner came another. The night had only begun—they hadn't even eaten yet. The ordeal of a formal dinner still lay before her.

"Hello again," Jean Becky said, strolling into the ladies' room. She stopped for a moment, watching Joanna, then sat down beside her.

"Oh, hi." Joanna managed the semblance of a smile to greet the likeable older woman.

"I just saw Blaise Ferguson walk past clinging to Tanner. I hope you're not upset."

"Oh heavens, no," Joanna lied.

"Good. Blaise, er, has something of a reputation, and I didn't want you to worry. I'm sure Tanner's smart enough not to be taken in by someone that obvious."

"I'm sure he is, too."

"You're a sensible young woman," Jean said, looking pleased.

At the moment, Joanna didn't feel the least bit sensible. The one emotion she was experiencing was fear. She'd fallen in love again, and the first time had been so painful she had promised never to let it happen again. But it had. With Tanner Lund, yet. Why couldn't she have fallen for the mechanic who'd worked so hard repairing her car last winter, or someone at the office? Oh, no, she had to fall—and fall hard—for the most eligible man in town. The man every single woman in the party had her eye on this evening.

"It really has been a pleasure meeting you," Jean continued. "Tanner and Nicole talk about you and your daughter so often. We've been friends of Tanner's for several years now, and it gladdens our hearts to see him finally meet a good woman."

"Thank you." Joanna wasn't sure what to think about being classified as a "good woman." It made her wonder who Tanner had dated before he'd met her. She'd never asked him about his social life before he'd moved to Spokane—or even after. She wasn't sure she wanted to know. No doubt he'd made quite a splash when he came to town. Rich, handsome, available men were a rare commodity these days. It was a wonder he hadn't been snatched up long before now.

Five minutes later, Joanna had composed herself enough to rejoin the party. Tanner was at her side within a few seconds, noticeably irritable and short-tempered.

"I've been searching all over for you," he said, frowning heavily.

Joanna let that remark slide. "I thought you were otherwise occupied."

"Why'd you let that she-cat walk off with me like that?" His eyes were hot with fury. "Couldn't you tell I wanted out? Good Lord, woman, what do I have to do, flash flags?"

"No." A waiter walked past with a loaded tray, and Joanna deftly reached out and helped herself to another glass of champagne.

Just as smoothly, Tanner removed it from her fingers. "I think you've had enough."

Joanna took the glass back from him. She might not completely understand what was happening to her this evening, but she certainly didn't like his attitude. "Excuse me, Tanner, but I am perfectly capable of determining my own limit.''

His frown darkened into a scowl. ''It's taken me the last twenty minutes to extract myself from her claws. The least you could have done was stick around instead of doing a disappearing act.''

''No way.'' Being married to Davey all those years had taught her more than one valuable lesson. If her ex-husband, Tanner, or any other man, for that matter, expected her to make a scene over another woman, it wouldn't work. Joanna was through with those kinds of destructive games.

''What do you mean by that?''

''I'm just not the jealous type. If you were to go home with Blaise, that'd be fine with me. In fact, you could leave with her right now. I'll grab a cab. I'm really not up to playing the role of a jealous girlfriend because another woman happens to show some interest in you. Nor am I willing to find a flimsy excuse to extract you from her clutches. You look more than capable of doing that yourself.''

''You honestly want me to leave with Blaise?'' His words were low and hard.

Joanna made a show of shrugging. ''It's entirely up to you—you're free to do as you please. Actually you might be doing me a favour.''

Joanna couldn't remember ever seeing a man more angry. His eyes seemed to spit fire at her. His jaws clamped together tightly, and he held himself with such an unnatural stiffness, it was surprising that something in his body didn't crack. She observed all this in some distant part of her mind, her concentration focused on preserving her facade of unconcern.

''I'm beginning to understand Davey,'' he said, his

tone as cold as an arctic wind. "Has it ever occurred to you that your ex-husband turned to other women out of a desperate need to know you cared?"

Tanner's words hurt more than any physical blow could have. Joanna's breath caught in her throat, though she did her best to disguise the pain his remark had inflicted. When she was finally able to breathe, the words tumbled from her lips. "No. Funny, I never thought of that." She paused and searched the room. "Pick a woman then, any woman will do, and I'll slug it out with her."

"Joanna, stop it," Tanner hissed.

"You mean you don't want me to fight?"

He closed his eyes as if seeking patience. "No."

Dramatically, Joanna placed her hand over her heart. "Thank goodness. I don't know how I'd ever explain a black eye to Kristen."

Dinner was about to be served, and, tucking his hand under her elbow, Tanner led Joanna into the banquet room, which was quickly filling up.

"I'm sorry, I didn't mean that about Davey," Tanner whispered as they strolled toward the dining room. "I realise you're nervous, but no one would ever know it—except me. We'll discuss this Blaise thing later."

Joanna nodded, feeling subdued now, accepting his apology. She realized that she'd panicked earlier, and not because this was an important social event, either. She'd attended enough business dinners in her career to know she hadn't made a fool of herself. What disturbed her so much was the knowledge that she'd fallen in love with Tanner.

To add to Joanna's dismay, she discovered that she was expected to sit at the head table between Tanner and John Becky. She trembled at the thought, but she wasn't about to let anyone see her nervousness.

"Don't worry," Tanner said, stroking her hand after they were seated. "Everyone who's met you has been impressed."

His statement was meant to lend her courage; unfortunately it had the opposite effect. What had she said or done to impress anyone?

When the evening was finally over, Tanner appeared to be as eager to escape as she was. With a minimum of fuss, they made their farewells and were gone.

Once in the car, Tanner didn't speak. But when he parked in front of the house, he turned off the car engine and said quietly, "Invite me in for coffee."

It was on the tip of Joanna's tongue to tell him she had a headache, which was fast becoming the truth, but delaying the inevitable wouldn't help either of them.

"Okay," she mumbled.

The house was quiet, and Sally was asleep on the sofa. Joanna paid her and waited on the front porch while the teenager ran across the street to her own house. Gathering her courage, she walked into the kitchen. Tanner had put the water and ground coffee into the machine and taken two cups down from the cupboard.

"Okay," he said, turning around to face her, "I want to know what's wrong."

The bewilderment in his eyes made Joanna raise her chin an extra notch. Then she remembered Kristen doing the same thing when she'd questioned her about her argument with Nicole, and the recollection wasn't comforting.

Joanna was actually surprised Tanner had guessed anything was wrong. She thought she'd done a brilliant job of disguising her distress. She'd done her best to say and do all the right things. When Tanner had stood up, after the meal, to give his talk, she'd whispered encouragement and smiled at him. Throughout the rest of the evening, she'd chatted easily with both Tanner and John Becky.

Now she had to try to explain something she barely understood herself.

"I don't think I ever realised what an important man you are," she said, struggling to find her voice. "I've always seen you as Nicole's father, the man who was crazy enough to agree to a slumber party for his daughter's birthday. The man who called and disguised his voice so Kristen wouldn't recognise it. That's the man I know, not the one tonight who stood before a filled banquet room and promised growth and prosperity for our city. Not the man who charts the destiny of an entire community."

Tanner glared at her. "What has that got to do with anything?"

"You play in the big league. I'm in the minors."

Tanner's gaze clouded with confusion. "I'm talking about our relationship and you're discussing baseball!"

Pulling out a kitchen chair, Joanna sat in it and took a deep breath. The best place to start, she decided, was the beginning. "You have to understand that I didn't come away from my marriage without a few quirks."

Tanner started pacing, clearly not in the mood to sit still. "Quirks? You call what happened with Blaise a quirk? I call it loony. Some woman I don't know from Adam comes up to me—"

"Eve," Joanna inserted, and when he stared at her, uncomprehending, she elaborated. "Since Blaise Ferguson's a woman, you don't know her from Eve."

"Whatever!"

"Well, it does make a difference." The coffee had finished filtering into the pot, so Joanna got up and poured them each a cup. Holding hers in both hands, she leaned against the counter and took a tentative sip.

"Some woman I don't know from Eve," Tanner tried again, "comes up to me, and you act as if you can't wait to get me out of your hair."

"*You* acted as if you expected me to come to your rescue. Honestly, Tanner, you're a big boy. I assumed you could take care of yourself."

"You looked more than happy to see me go with her."

"That's not true. I was content where I was." Joanna knew they were sidestepping the real issue, but this other business seemed to concern Tanner more.

"You were content to go into hiding."

"If you're looking for someone to fly into a jealous rage every time another woman winks at you, you'll need to look elsewhere."

Tanner did some more pacing, his steps growing longer and heavier with each circuit of the kitchen. "Explain what you meant when you said you didn't come away from your marriage without a few quirks."

"It's simply really," she said, making light of it. "Davey used to get a kick out of introducing me to his women friends. Everyone in the room knew what he was doing, except me. I was so stupid, so blind, that I just didn't know any better. Once the scales fell from my eyes, I was astonished at what a complete fool I'd been. But when I became wise to his ways, it was much worse. Every time he introduced me to a woman, I'd be filled with suspicion. Was Davey involved with her, or wasn't he? The only thing left for me to do was hold my head high and smile." Her voice was growing tighter with every word, cracking just as she finished.

Tanner walked toward her and reached out his hands as though to comfort her. "Joanna, listen—"

"No." She set her coffee aside and wrapped her arms around her middle. "I feel honoured, Tanner, that you would ask me to attend this important dinner with you tonight. I think we both learned something valuable from the experience. At least, I know I did."

"Joanna—"

"No," she cut in again, "let me finish, please. Although it's difficult to say this, it needs to be said. We're not right for each other. We've been so caught up in everything we had in common and what good friends the girls are and how wonderful it felt to…be together, we didn't stop to notice that we live in different worlds." She paused and gathered her resolve before continuing. "Knowing you and becoming your friend has been wonderful, but anything beyond that just isn't going to work."

"The only thing I got carried away with was you, Joanna. The girls have nothing to do with it."

"I feel good that you would say that, I really do, but we both lost sight of the fact that neither one of us wants to become involved. That had never been our intention. Something happened, and I'm not sure when or why, but suddenly everything is so intense between us. It's got to stop before we end up really hurting each other."

Tanner seemed to mull over her words. "You're so frightened of giving another man the power to hurt you that you can't see anything else, can you?" His brooding, confused look was back. "I told you this once, but it didn't seem to sink into that head of yours—I'm never going to do the things Davey did. We're two entirely different men, and it's time you realised that.''

''What you say may very well be true, Tanner, but I don't see what difference it's going to make. Because I have no intention of involving myself in another relationship.''

''In case you hadn't noticed, Joanna, we're already involved.''

''Roller-skating in the couples round doesn't qualify as being involved to me,'' she said, in a futile attempt at humor. It fell flat.

Tanner was the first to break the heavy silence that followed. ''You've obviously got some thinking to do,'' he said wearily. ''For that matter, so do I. Call me, Joanna, when you're in the mood to be reasonable.''

Fourteen

"Hi, Mom," Kristen said, slumping down on the sofa beside Joanna. "I hope you know I'm bored out of my mind," she said, and sighed deeply.

Joanna was busy counting the stitches on her knitting needle and didn't pause to answer until she'd finished. "What about your homework?"

"Cute, Mom, real cute. It's spring break—I don't have any homework."

"Right. Phone Nicole then. I bet she'll commiserate with you." And she might even give Kristen some information about Tanner. He'd walked out of her house, and although she'd thought her heart would break she'd let him go. Since then, she'd reconsidered. She was dying to hear something from Tanner. Anything. But she hadn't—not since the party more than a week earlier, and each passing day seemed like a lifetime.

"Calling Nicole is a nothing idea."

"I could suggest you clean your room."

"Funny, Mom, real funny."

"Gee, I'm funny and cute all in one evening. How'd I get so lucky?"

Not bothering to answer, Kristen reached for a magazine and idly thumbed through the pages, not finding a single picture or article worth more than a fleeting glance. She set it aside and reached for another. By the time she'd gone through the four magazines resting on top of the coffee table, Joanna was losing her patience.

"Call Nicole."

"I can't."

"Why not?"

"Because I can't."

That didn't make much sense to Joanna. And suggesting that Kristen phone Nicole was another sign of her willingness to settle this rift between her and Tanner. It had been so long since she'd last seen or heard from him. Ten interminable days, and with each one that passed she missed him more. She'd debated long and hard about calling him, wavering with indecision, battling with her pride. What she'd told him that night had been the truth—they did live in different worlds. But she'd overreacted at the dinner party, and now she felt guilty about how the evening had gone. When he'd left the house, Tanner had suggested she call him when she was ready to be reasonable. Well, she'd been ready the following morning, ready to acknowledge her fault. And her need. But pride held her back. And with each passing day, it became more difficult to swallow that pride.

"You know I can't call Nicole," Kristen whined.

"Why not? Did you have another argument?" Joanna asked without looking at her daughter. Her mind was preoccupied with counting stitches. She always knitted when she was frustrated with herself; it was a form of self-punishment, she suspected wryly.

"We never fight. Not anymore. Nicole's in West Virginia."

Joanna paused and carefully set the knitting needles down on her lap. "Oh? What's she doing there?"

"I think she went to visit her mother."

"Her mother?" It took some effort to keep her heart from exploding in her throat. According to Tanner, Nicole hadn't seen or heard from Carmen in three years. His biggest worry, he'd told her, was that someday his ex-wife would develop an interest in their daughter and steal her away from him. "Nicole is with her mother?" Joanna repeated, to be certain she'd heard Kristen correctly.

"You knew that."

"No, I didn't."

"Yes, you did. I told you she was leaving last Sunday. Remember?"

Vaguely, Joanna recalled the conversation—she'd been peeling potatoes at the sink—but for the last week, every time Kristen mentioned either Tanner or Nicole, Joanna had made an effort to tune her daughter out. Now she was hungry for information, starving for every tidbit Kristen was willing to feed her.

The eleven-year-old straightened and stared at her mother. "Didn't Mr. Lund mention Nicole was leaving?"

"Er, no."

Kristen sighed and threw herself against the back of the sofa. "You haven't been seeing much of him lately, have you?"

"Er, no."

Kristen picked up Joanna's hand and patted it gently. "You two had a fight?"

"Not exactly."

Her daughter's hand continued its soothing action. "Okay, tell me all about it. Don't hold back a single thing—you need to talk this out. Bare your soul."

"Kristen!"

"Mom, you need this. Releasing your anger and

frustration will help. You've got to work out all that inner agitation and responsive turbulence. It's disrupting your emotional poise. Seriously, Mom, have you ever considered Rolfing?''

"Emotional poise? Responsive turbulence? Where'd you hear about that? Where'd you hear about Rolfing?''

Kristen blinked and cocked her head to one side, doing her best to look concerned and sympathetic. "Oprah Winfrey.''

"I see," Joanna muttered, and rolled her eyes.

"Are you or are you not going to tell me all about it?''

"No, I am not!''

Kristen released a deep sigh that expressed her keen disappointment. "I thought not. When it comes to Nicole's dad, you never want to talk about it. It's like a deep dark secret the two of you keep from Nicole and me. Well, that's all right—we're doing our best to understand. You don't want us to get our hopes up that you two might be interested in each other. I can accept that, although I consider it grossly unfair.'' She stood up and gazed at her mother with undisguised longing, then loudly slapped her hands against her sides. "I'm perfectly content to live the way we do...but it sure would be nice to have a baby sister to dress up. And you know how I've *always* wanted a brother.''

"Kristen!''

"No, Mom.'' She held up her hand as though she were stopping a freight train. "Really, I do understand. You and I get along fine the way we are. I guess we don't need to complicate our lives with Nicole and her dad. That could even cause real problems.''

For the first time, her daughter was making sense.

"Although heaven knows, I can't remember what it's like to be part of a *real* family."

"Kristen, that's enough," Joanna cried, shaking her head. Her daughter was invoking so much guilt that Joanna was beginning to hear violins in the background. "You and I *are* a real family."

"But, Mom, it could be so much better." Kristen sank down beside Joanna again and crossed her legs. Obviously her argument had long since been prepared, and without pausing to breathe between sentences, she proceeded to list the advantages of joining the two families.

"Kristen—"

Once more her daughter stopped her with an outstretched hand, as she started on her much shorter list of possible disadvantages. There was little Joanna could do to stem the rehearsed speech. Impatiently she waited for Kristen to finish.

"I don't want to talk about Tanner again," Joanna said in a no-nonsense tone of voice reserved for instances such as this. "Not a single word. Is that clearly understood?"

Kristen turned round sad eyes on her mother. The fun and laughter seemed to drain from her face as she glared back at Joanna. "Okay—if that's what you really want."

"It is, Kristen. Not a single word."

Banning his name from her daughter's lips and banning his name from her own mind were two entirely different things, Joanna decided an hour later. The fact that Nicole was visiting Carmen concerned her—not that she shared Tanner's worries. But knowing Tanner, he was probably beside himself worrying that Carmen would want their daughter to come and live with her.

It took another half hour for Joanna to build up enough courage to phone Tanner. He answered on the second ring.

"Hello, Tanner…it's Joanna." Even that was almost more than she could manage.

"Joanna." Just the way he said her name revealed his delight in hearing from her.

Joanna was grateful that he didn't immediately bring up the dinner party and the argument that had followed. "How have you been?"

"Good. How about you?"

"Just fine," she returned awkwardly. She leaned against the wall, crossing and uncrossing her ankles. "Listen, the reason I phoned is that Kristen told me Nicole was with her mother, and I thought you might be in need of a divorced-parent prep talk."

"What I really need is to see you. Lord, woman, it took you long enough. I thought you were going to make me wait forever. Ten days can be a very long time, Joanna. Ten whole days!"

"Tanner—"

"Can we meet someplace?"

"I'm not sure." Her mind struggled with a list of excuses, but she couldn't deny how lonely and miserable she'd been, how badly she wanted to feel his arms around her. "I'd have to find someone to sit with Kristen, and that could be difficult at the last minute like this."

"I'll come to you then."

It was part question, part statement, and again, she hesitated. "All right," she finally whispered.

The line went oddly silent. When Tanner spoke again there was a wealth of emotion in his words, although his voice was quiet. "I'm glad you phoned, Joanna."

She closed her eyes, feeling weak and shaky. "I am, too," she said softly.

"I'll be there within half an hour."

"I'll have coffee ready."

When she replaced the receiver, her hand was trembling, and it was as though she were twenty-one again. Her heart was pounding out of control just from the sound of his voice, her head swimming with the knowledge that she'd be seeing him in a few minutes. How wrong she'd been to assume that if she put him out of her sight and mind she could keep him out of her heart, too. How foolish she'd been to deny her feelings. She loved this man, and it wouldn't matter if he owned the company or swept the floors.

Joanna barely had time to refresh her makeup and drag a brush through her hair. Kristen had been in her room for the past hour without a sound; Joanna sincerely hoped she was asleep.

She'd just poured water into the coffee maker when the doorbell chimed.

The bedroom door flew open, and Kristen appeared in her pajamas, wide awake. "I'll get it," she yelled.

Joanna started to call after her, but it was too late. With a resigned sigh, she stood in the background and waited for her daughter to admit Tanner.

Kristen turned to face her mother, wearing a grin as wide as the Mississippi River. "It's that man whose name I'm not supposed to mention ever again."

"Yes, I know."

"You know?"

Joanna nodded.

"Good. Talk it out with him, Mom. Relieve yourself of all that inner stuff. Get rid of that turmoil before it eats you alive."

Joanna cast a weak smile in Tanner's direction, then turned her attention to Kristen. "Isn't it your bedtime, young lady?"

"No."

Joanna's eyes narrowed. "Yes, it is."

"But, Mom, it's spring break, so I can sleep in tomorrow—Oh, I get it, you want me out of here."

"In your room reading or listening to a cassette should do nicely."

Kristen beamed her mother a broad smile. "'Night, Mom. 'Night…Nicole's dad."

"'Night."

With her arms swinging at her sides, Kristen strolled out of the living room. Tanner waited until they heard her bedroom door shut, then he started across the carpet toward Joanna. He stopped suddenly, frowning. "She wasn't supposed to say my name?"

Joanna gave a weak half shrug, her gaze holding his. No man had ever looked better. His eyes seemed to caress her with a tenderness and aching hunger that did crazy things to her equilibrium.

"It's so good to see you," she said, her voice unsteady. She took two steps towards him.

When Tanner reached for her, a heavy sigh broke from his lips and the tension left his muscles. "Dear Lord, woman, ten days you left me dangling." He said more, but his words were muffled in the curve of her neck as he crushed her against his chest.

Joanna soaked up his warmth, and when his lips found hers she surrendered with a soft sigh of joy. Being in Tanner's arms was like coming home after a long journey and discovering the comfort in all that's familiar. It was like walking in sunshine after a bad storm, like holding the first rose of summer in her hand.

Again and again his mouth sought hers in a series of passionate kisses, as though he couldn't get enough of the taste of her.

The creaky sound of a bedroom door opening caused Joanna to break away from him. "It's Kristen," she murmured, her voice little more than a whisper.

"I know, but I don't care." Tanner kept her close for a moment longer. "Okay," he breathed, and slowly stroked the top of her head with his chin. "We need to settle a few things. Let's talk."

Joanna led him into the kitchen, since they were afforded the most privacy there. She automatically took down two cups and poured them each some coffee. They sat at the small table, directly across from each other, but even that seemed much too far.

"First, tell me about Nicole," she said, her eyes meeting his. "Are you worried now that she's with Carmen?"

A sad smile touched the edges of Tanner's mouth. "Not particularly. Carmen, who prefers to be called Rama Sheba now, contacted my parents at the end of last week. According to my mother, the reason we haven't heard from her in the past three years is that Carmen's been on a long journey in India and Nepal. Apparently Carmen went halfway around the world searching for herself. I guess she found what she was looking for, because she's back in the United States and enquiring about Nicole."

"Oh, dear. Do you think she wants Nicole to come live with her?"

"Not a chance. Carmen, er, Rama Sheba, doesn't want a child complicating her life. She never did. Nicole wanted to see her mother and that's understandable, so I sent her back to West Virginia for a visit with my parents. While she's there, Carmen will spend an afternoon with her.''

"What happened to…Rama Sheba and the baseball player?''

"Who knows? He may have joined her in her wanderings, for all I know. Or care. Carmen plays such a minor role in my life now that I haven't the energy to second-guess her. She's free to do as she likes, and I prefer it that way. If she wants to visit Nicole, fine. She can see her daughter—she has the right.''

"Do you love her?'' The question sounded abrupt and tactless, but Joanna needed to know.

"No,'' he said quickly, then grinned. "I suppose I feel much the same way about her as you do about Davey.''

"Then you don't hate her?'' she asked next, not looking at him.

"No.''

Joanna ran a fingertip along the rim of her cup and smiled. "Good.''

"Why's that good?''

She lifted her eyes to meet his and smiled a little shyly. "Because if you did have strong feelings for her it would suggest some unresolved emotion.''

Tanner nodded. "As illogical as it sounds, I don't feel anything for Carmen. Not love, not hate—nothing. If something bad were to happen to her, I suppose I'd feel sad, but I don't harbour any resentments toward her.''

"That's what I was trying to explain to you the afternoon you dropped by when Davey was here. Other people have a hard time believing this, especially my parents, but I honestly wish him success in life. I want him to be happy, although I doubt he ever will be.''

Davey wasn't a man who would ever be content. He was always looking for something more, something better.

Tanner nodded.

Once more, Joanna dropped her gaze to the steaming coffee. "Calling you and asking about Nicole was only an excuse, you know."

"Yes. I just wish you'd come up with it a few days earlier. As far as I'm concerned, waiting for you to come to your senses took nine days too long."

"I—"

"I know, I know," Tanner said before she could list her excuses. "Okay, let's talk."

Joanna managed a smile. "Where do we start?"

"How about with what happened the night of the party?"

Instantly Joanna's stomach knotted. "Yes, well, I guess I should be honest and let you know I was intimidated by how important you are. It shook me, Tanner, really shook me. I'm not used to seeing you as chairman of the board. And then later, when you strolled off with Blaise, those old wounds from my marriage with Davey started to bleed."

"I suppose I did all the wrong things. Maybe I should have insisted you come with me when Blaise dragged me away, but—"

"No, that wouldn't have worked, either."

"I should have guessed how you'd feel after being married to Davey."

"You had no way of knowing." Now came the hard part. "Tanner," she began, and was shocked at how thin and weak her voice sounded, "I was so consumed with jealousy that I just about went crazy when Blaise wrapped her arms around you. It frightened me to have to deal with those negative emotions again. I know I acted like an idiot, hiding like that, and I'd like to apologise.''

"Joanna, it isn't necessary."

She shook her head. "I don't mean this as an excuse, but you need to understand why I was driven to behave the way I did. I'd thought I was beyond that—years beyond acting like a jealous fool. I promised myself I'd never allow a man to do it to me again." In her own way, Joanna was trying to tell him how much she loved him, but the words weren't coming out right.

He frowned at that. "Jealous? You were jealous? Good Lord, woman, you could have fooled me. You handed me over to Blaise without so much as a hint of regret. From the way you were behaving, I thought you *wanted* to be rid of me."

The tightness in Joanna's throat made talking difficult. "I already explained why I did that."

"I know. The way I acted when I saw your ex here was the other kind of jealous reaction—the raging-bull kind. I think I see now where *your* kind of reaction came from. I'm not sure which one is worse, but I think mine is." He smiled ruefully, and a silence fell between them.

"Could this mean you have some strong feelings for me, Joanna Parsons?"

A smile quirked at the corners of her mouth. "You're the only man I've ever eaten Oreos over."

The laughter in Tanner's eyes slowly faded. "We could have the start of something very important here, Joanna. What do you think?"

"I...I think you may be right."

"Good." Tanner looked exceedingly pleased with

this turn of events. "That's exactly what I wanted to hear."

Joanna thought—no, hoped—that he intended to lean over and kiss her. Instead his brows drew together darkly over brooding blue eyes. "Okay, where do we go from here?"

"Go?" Joanna repeated, feeling uncomfortable all of a sudden. "Why do we have to go anywhere?"

Tanner looked surprised. "Joanna, for heaven's sake, when a man and a woman feel about each other the way we do, they generally make plans."

"What do you mean 'feel about each other the way we do'?"

Tanner's frown darkened even more. "You love me."

Only a few moments before, Joanna would have willingly admitted it, but silly as it sounded, she wanted to hear Tanner say the words first. "I...I..."

"If you have to think about it, then I'd say you obviously don't know."

"But I do know," she said, lifting her chin a notch higher. "I'm just not sure this is the time to do anything about it. You may think my success is insignificant compared to yours, but I've worked damn hard to get where I am. I've got the house I saved for years to buy, and my career is starting to swing along nicely, and Robin—he's my boss—let me know that I was up for promotion. My goal of becoming the first female senior loan officer at the branch is within sight."

"And you don't want to complicate your life right now with a husband and second family?"

"I didn't say that."

"It sure sounded like it to me."

Joanna swallowed. The last thing in the world she

wanted to do was argue with Tanner. Craziest of all, she wasn't even sure what they were arguing about. They were in love with each other and both just too damn proud. "I don't think we're getting anywhere with this conversation."

Tanner braced his elbows on the table and folded his hands. "I'm beginning to agree with you. All week, I've been waiting for you to call me, convinced that once you did, everything between us would be settled. I wanted us to start building a life together, and all of a sudden you're Ms Career Woman, and about as independent as they come."

"I haven't changed. You just didn't know me."

His lips tightened. "I guess you're right. I don't know you at all, do I?"

"MOM, MOM, come quick!"

Joanna's warm cozy dream was interrupted by Kristen's shrieks. She rolled over and glared at the digital readout on her clock radio. Five. In the morning. "Kristen?" She sat straight up in bed.

"Mom!"

The one word conveyed such panic that Joanna's heart rushed to her throat and she threw back her covers, running barefoot into the hallway. Almost immediately, her feet encountered ice-cold water.

"Something's wrong," Kristen cried, hopping up and down. "The water won't stop."

That was the understatement of the year. From the way the water was gushing out of the bathroom door and into the hallway, it looked as though a dam had burst.

"Grab some towels," Joanna cried, pointing toward the hallway linen closet. The hems of her long pajamas were already damp. She scooted around her daughter, who was standing in the doorway, still hopping up and down like a crazed kangaroo.

Further investigation showed that the water was escaping from the cabinet under the sink.

"Mom, Mom, here!" Dancing around, Kristen threw her a stack of towels that separated in midair and landed in every direction.

"Kristen!" Joanna snapped, squatting down in front of the sink. She opened the cabinet and was immediately hit by a wall of foaming bubbles. The force of the flowing water had knocked over her container of expensive bubble bath and spilled its contents. "You were in my bubble bath!" Joanna cried.

"I... How'd you know?"

"The cap's off, and now it's everywhere!"

"I just used a little bit."

Three bars of Ivory soap, still in their wrappers, floated past Joanna's feet. Heaven only knew what else had been stored under the sink or where it was headed now.

"I'm sorry about the bubble bath," Kristen said defensively. "I figured you'd get mad if you found out, but a kid needs to know what luxury feels like, too, you know."

"It's all right, we can't worry about that now." Joanna waved her hands back and forth trying to disperse the bubbles enough to assess the damage. It didn't take long to determine that a pipe had burst. With her forehead pressing against the edge of the sink, Joanna groped inside the cabinet for the knob to turn off the water supply. Once she found it, she twisted it furiously until the flowing water dwindled to a mere trickle.

"Kristen!" Joanna shouted, looking over her shoulder. Naturally, when she needed her, her daughter disappeared. "Get me some more towels. Hurry, honey!"

A couple of minutes later, Kristen reappeared, her arms loaded with every towel and washcloth in the house. "Yuck," she muttered, screwing her face into a mask of sheer disgust. "What a mess!"

"Did any water get into the living room?"

Kristen nodded furiously. "But only as far as the front door."

"Great." Joanna mumbled under her breath. Now she'd need to phone someone about coming in to dry out the carpet.

On her hands and knees, sopping up as much water as she could, Joanna was already soaked to the skin herself.

"You need help," her daughter announced.

The child was a master of observation. "Change out of those wet things first, Kristen, before you catch your death of cold."

"What about you?"

"I'll dry off as soon as I get some of this water cleaned up."

"Mom—"

"Honey, just do as I ask. I'm not in any mood to argue with you."

Joanna couldn't remember ever seeing a bigger mess in her life. Her pajamas were soaked; bubbles were popping around her head—how on earth had they got into her hair? She sneezed violently, and reached for a tissue that quickly dissolved in her wet hands.

"Here, use this."

The male voice coming from behind her surprised Joanna so much that when she twisted around, she lost

Fifteen

Dumbfounded, Joanna stared at Tanner, her mouth hanging open and her eyes wide.

"I got this frantic phone call from Kristen."

"Kristen?"

"The one and only. She suggested I hurry over here before something drastic happened." Tanner took one step toward her and lovingly brushed a wet tendril away from her face. "How's it going, Tugboat Annie?"

"A pipe under the sink broke. I've got it under control now—I think." Her pajamas hung limply at her ankles, dripping water onto her bare feet. Her hair fell in wet spongy curls around her face, and Joanna had never felt more like bursting into tears in her life.

"Kristen shouldn't have phoned you," she said, once she found her voice.

"I'm glad she did. It's nice to know I can be useful every now and again." Heedless of her wet state, he wrapped his arms around Joanna and brought her close, gently pressing her damp head to his chest.

A chill went through her and she shuddered. Tanner felt so warm and vital, so concerned and loving. She'd let him think she was this strong independent woman, and normally she was, but when it came to broken pipes and floods and things like that, she crumbled into bite-sized pieces. When it came to Tanner Lund, well...

"You're soaked to the skin," he whispered, close to her ear.

"I know."

"Go change. I'll take over here."

The tears started then, silly ones that sprang from somewhere deep inside her and refused to be stopped. "I can't get dry," she sobbed, wiping furiously at the moisture that rained down her face. "There aren't any dry towels left in this entire house."

Tanner jerked his water-blotched tan leather jacket off and placed it around her shoulders. "Honey, don't cry. Please. Everything's going to be all right. It's just a broken pipe, and I can have it fixed for you before noon—possibly sooner."

"I can't help it," she bellowed, and to her horror, hiccuped. She threw a hand over her mouth and leaned her forehead against his strong chest. "It's five o'clock in the morning, my expensive Giorgio bubblebath is ruined, and I'm so much in love I can't think straight."

Tanner's hands gripped her shoulders and eased her away so he could look her in the eye. "What did you just say?"

Joanna hung her head as low as it would go, bracing her weight against Tanner's arms. "My Giorgio bubblebath is ruined." The words wobbled out of her mouth like a rubber ball tumbling down stairs.

"Not that. I want to hear the other part, about being so much in love."

Joanna sniffled. "What about it?"

"What about it? Good Lord, woman, I was here not more than eight hours ago wearing my heart on my sleeve like a schoolboy. You were so casual about everything, I thought you were going to open a discussion on stock options.''

"*You* were the one who was so calm and collected about everything, as if what happened between us didn't really matter to you." She rubbed her hand under her nose and sniffled loudly. "Then you made everything sound like a foregone conclusion and—"

"I was nervous. Now, shall we give it another try? I want to marry you, Joanna Parsons. I want you to share my life, maybe have my babies. I want to love you until we're both old and gray. I've even had fantasies about us traveling around the country in a mobile home to visit our grandchildren!"

"You want grandkids?" Timidly, she raised her eyes to his, almost afraid to believe what he was telling her.

"I'd prefer to take this one step at a time. The first thing I want to do is marry you. I couldn't have made that plainer than I did a few hours ago."

"But—"

"Stop right now, before we get sidetracked. First things first. Are you and Kristen going to marry me and Nicole?"

"I think we should," the eleven-year-old said excitedly from the hallway, looking smugly pleased with the way things were going. "I mean, it's been obvious to Nicole and me for ages that you two were meant to be together." Kristen sighed and slouched against the wall, crossing her arms over her chest with the sophistication that befitted someone of superior intelligence. "There's only one flaw in this plan."

"Flaw?" Joanna echoed.

"Yup," Kristen said, nodding with unquestionable confidence. "Nicole is going to be mad as hops when she finds out she missed this."

Tanner frowned, and then he chuckled. "Oh, boy. I think Kristen could be right. We're going to have to stage a second proposal."

Feeling slightly piqued, Joanna straightened. "Listen, you two, I never said I was going to marry anybody—yet."

"Of course you're going to marry Mr. Lund," Kristen inserted smoothly. "Honestly, Mom, now isn't the time to play hard to get."

"W-what?" Stunned, Joanna stood there staring at her daughter. Her gaze flew from Kristen to Tanner and then back to Kristen.

"She's right, you know," said Tanner.

"I can't believe I'm hearing this." Joanna was standing in a sea of wet towels, while her daughter and the man she loved discussed her fate as though she was to play only a minor role in it.

"We've got to think of a way to include Nicole," Tanner said thoughtfully.

"I am going to change my clothes," Joanna murmured, eager to escape.

"Good idea," Tanner answered, without looking at her.

Joana stomped off to her bedroom and slammed the door. She discarded her pajamas and, shivering, reached for a thick wool sweater and blue jeans.

Tanner and Kristen were still in the bathroom doorway, discussing details, when Joanna reappeared. She moved silently around them and into the kitchen, where she made a pot of coffee. Then she gathered up the wet towels, hauled them onto the back porch, threw them into the washer and started the machine. By the time she returned to the kitchen, Tanner had joined her there.

"Uh-oh. Trouble," he said, watching her abrupt angry movements. "Okay, tell me what's wrong now."

"I don't like the way you and my daughter are planning my life," she told him point-blank. "Honestly, Tanner, I haven't even agreed to marry you, and already you and Kristen have got the next ten years all figured out."

He stuck his hands in his pants pockets. "It's not that bad."

"Maybe not, but it's bad enough. I'm letting you know right now that I'm not about to let you stage a second proposal just so Nicole can hear it. To be honest, I'm not exactly thrilled about Kristen being part of this one. A marriage proposal is supposed to be private. And romantic, with flowers and music, not...not in front of a busted pipe with bath bubbles popping around my head and my family standing around applauding."

"Okay, what do you suggest?"

"I don't know yet."

Tanner looked disgruntled. "If you want the romance, Joanna, that's fine. I'd be more than happy to give it to you."

"Every woman wants romance."

Tanner walked toward her then and took her in his arms, and until that moment Joanna had no idea how much she did, indeed, want it.

Her eyes were drawn to his. Everything about Tanner Lund fascinated her, and she raised her hand to lightly caress the proud strong line of his jaw. She really did love this man. His eyes, blue and intense, met hers, and a tiny shiver of awareness went through her. His arms circled her waist, and then he lifted her off the ground so that her gaze was level with his own.

Joanna gasped a little at the unexpectedness of his action. Smiling, she looped her arms around his neck.

Tanner kissed her then, with a hunger that left her weak and clinging in its aftermath.

"How's that?" he asked, his voice husky.

"Better. Much better."

"I thought so." Once more his warm mouth made contact with hers. Joanna was startled and thrilled at the intensity of his touch. He kissed her again and again, until she thought that if he released her, she'd fall to the floor and melt at his feet. Every part of her body was heated to fever pitch.

"Joanna—"

She planted warm moist kisses across his face, not satisfied, wanting him until her heart felt as if it might explode. Tanner had awoken the sensual part of her nature, buried all the years since her divorce, and now that it had been stirred back to life, she felt starved for a man's love—this man's love.

"Yes," she breathed into his mouth. "Yes, yes, yes."

"Yes what?" he asked in a breathless murmur.

Joanna paused and smiled gently. "Yes, I'll marry you. Right now. Okay? This minute. We can fly somewhere...find a church... Oh, Tanner," she pleaded, "I want you so much."

"Joanna, we can't." His words came out in a groan, forced from deep inside him.

She heard him, but it didn't seem to matter. She kissed him and he kissed her. Their kiss continued as he lowered her to the floor, her body sliding intimately down his.

Suddenly Joanna realized what she'd just said, what she'd suggested. "We mustn't. Kristen—"

Tanner shushed her with another kiss, then said, "I know, love. This isn't the time or place, but I sure wish…"

Joanna straightened, and broke away. Shakily, she said, "So do I…and, uh, I think we should wait a while for the wedding. At least until Nicole gets back."

"Right."

"How long will that be?"

"The end of the week."

Joanna nodded and closed her eyes. It sounded like an eternity.

"What about your job?"

"I don't want to work forever, and when we decide to start a family I'll probably quit. But I want that promotion first." Joanna wasn't sure exactly why that was so important to her, but it was. She'd worked years for this achievement, and she had no intention of walking away until she'd become the first female senior loan officer.

Tanner kissed her again. "If it makes you happy keep your job as long as you want."

At that moment, however, all Joanna could think about were babies, family vacations and homemade cookies.

"THAT'S HER PLANE now," Tanner said to Kristen, pointing toward the Boeing jet that was approaching the long narrow landing strip at Spokane International.

"I get to tell her, okay?"

"I think Tanner should do it, sweetheart," Joanna suggested gently.

"But Nicole and I are best friends. You can't expect me to keep something like this from her, something we planned since that night we all went to the Pink Palace.

If it weren't for us, you two wouldn't even know each other.''

Kristen's eyes were round and pleading as she stared up at Tanner and Joanna.

"You two would have been cast adrift in a sea of loneliness if it hadn't been for me and Nicole," she added melodramatically.

"All right, all right," Tanner said with a sigh. "You can tell her."

Poised at the railing by the window of the terminal, Kristen eagerly studied each passenger who stepped inside. The minute Nicole appeared, Kristen flew into her friend's arms as though it had been years since they'd last seen each other instead of a week.

Joanna watched the unfolding scene with a quiet sense of happiness. Nicole let out a squeal of delight and gripped her friend around the shoulders, and the two jumped frantically up and down.

"From her reaction, I'd guess that she's happy about our decision," Tanner said to Joanna.

"Dad, Dad!" Nicole raced up to her father, and hugged him with all her might. "It's so good to be home. I missed you. I missed everyone," she said, looking at Joanna.

Tanner returned the hug. "It's good to have you home, cupcake."

"But everything exciting happened while I was away," she said, pouting a little. "Gee, if I'd known you were finally going to get rolling with Mrs. Parsons, I'd never have left."

Joanna smiled blandly at the group of people standing around them.

"Don't be mad," Kristen said. "It was a now-or-never situation, with Mom standing there in her pajamas and everything.''

Now it was Tanner's turn to notice the interested group of onlookers.

"Yes, well, you needn't feel left out. I saved the best part for you,'' Tanner said, taking a beautiful solitaire diamond ring out of his pocket. "I wanted you to be here for this.'' He reached for Joanna's hand, looking into her eyes, as he slowly, reverently, slipped it onto her finger. "I love you, Joanna, and I'll be the happiest man alive if you marry me.''

"I love you, Tanner,'' she said in a soft voice filled with joy.

"Does this mean we're going to be sisters from now on?'' Kristen shrieked, clutching her best friend's hand.

"Yup,'' Nicole answered. "It's what we always wanted.''

With their arms wrapped around one another's shoulders, the girls headed toward the baggage-claim area.

"Yours and mine,'' Joanna said, watching their two daughters.

Tanner slid his arm around her waist and smiled into her eyes.

LONE STAR LOVIN'

One

"**Y**ou're a long way from Orchard Valley," Sherry Waterman muttered to herself as she stepped out of her GEO Storm and onto the main street of Pepper, Texas. Heat shimmered up from the black asphalt.

Drawing a deep breath, she glanced around with an appraising eye at this town, which was to be her new home. Pepper resembled any number of small mid-Texas towns she'd driven through in the past twenty-four hours.

The sun was pounding down with a vengeance, and Sherry wiped her brow with her forearm, looking for someplace to buy a cold drink. She was a couple of weeks early; she'd actually planned it this way, hoping to get a feel for Pepper and the surrounding ranch community before she took over her assignment. In an hour or so she would drive on to Houston, where she'd visit her friend Norah Cassidy for a couple of weeks, then double back to Pepper. Although it was considerably out of her way, she was curious about this town—and the job she'd accepted as a physician's assistant, sight unseen, through a medical-employment agency.

Her small car didn't have air-conditioning, and she'd rolled down both windows in an effort to create a cooling cross-draft. It had worked well enough, but along with the breeze had come a fine layer of dust, and a throat as dry as the sun-baked Texas street.

Clutching her purse and a folded state map, she headed for the Yellow Rose café directly opposite. A red neon sign in the window promised home cooking.

After glancing both ways, she jogged across the street and hurried into the, thankfully, air-conditioned café. The counter was crowded with an array of cowboy types, so she seated herself by the window and reached for the menu tucked behind the napkin canister.

A waitress wearing a pink gingham uniform with a matching ruffle fixed in her hair strolled casually toward Sherry's table. "You're new around these parts, aren't you?" she asked by way of greeting.

"Yes," Sherry answered noncommittally, looking up from the menu. "I'll have an iced tea with extra lemon and a cheeseburger, without the fries." No need to clog her heart arteries with extra fat. The meat and cheese were bad enough.

"Iced tea and a cheeseburger," the waitress repeated. "You wanna try our lemon meringue pie? It's the best this side of Abilene."

"Oh, sure, why not?" Sherry said, giving up the cholesterol battle without a fight. The waitress left and returned almost immediately with the iced tea. Sherry drank long and gratefully, then spread the map across the table and charted her progress. With luck, she should be able to reach Houston by midafternoon the following day. Right on schedule. Her friend, Norah Cassidy, wasn't expecting her before Wednesday, so Sherry could make a leisurely drive of it—though she'd enjoy the drive a whole lot more if it wasn't so hellishly hot.

The waitress brought Sherry's cheeseburger on a

thick, old-fashioned ceramic plate. A mound of onion and tomato slices, plus lettuce and pickles, were neatly arranged next to the open burger.

"Don't see too many strangers coming this way," the waitress commented, plopping down containers of mustard and ketchup. "Most folks stick to the freeway."

"I prefer driving the back roads," Sherry said, popping a pickle slice into her mouth.

"You headed for San Antonio?"

"Houston. I'm a physician's assistant and—"

"I don't suppose you're looking for a job?"

Sherry smiled to herself. "Not exactly. I already have one." She didn't add that the job was right here in Pepper.

"Oh." The eager grin faded. "The town council's been advertising with one of those employment agencies for over a year."

Apparently the waitress hadn't heard that they'd hired someone. "I'm also a nurse and a midwife," Sherry added, although she wasn't sure why she felt obliged to list her credentials for the woman. The physician's assistant part was a recent qualification.

The waitress nodded. "I hear lots of women prefer to have their babies at home these days. Most everyone around Pepper comes to the hospital, though."

"You have a hospital here?" This was welcome news. The town didn't look large enough to support more than a café, a couple of taverns and a jail.

"Actually it's a clinic. But Doc's made sure we've got the best emergency-room facilities within two hundred miles. Last year one of the high-school boys lost an arm, and Doc was able to save the arm *and* the kid.

Wouldn't have been able to do it without all that fancy equipment. We're right proud of that clinic.''

"You should be." Sherry gazed longingly at her lunch. If the waitress didn't stop chattering, it was going to get cold.

"You have family in Houston?"

Sherry added the rest of her condiments, folded the cheeseburger closed and raised it toward her mouth as a less-than-subtle hint. "No, just a good friend."

The woman's eyes brightened. "I see." She left and returned less than a moment later, a tall, potbellied older man in tow.

"Howdy," he said with a lazy drawl. "Welcome to Texas."

Sherry finished chewing her first bite. "Thank you. It's a wonderful state."

"What part of the country you from?"

Sherry's gaze lingered on her burger. "Oregon. A little town called Orchard Valley."

"I hear it's real pretty up there in Or-ee-gon."

"It's beautiful," Sherry agreed, dropping her gaze to her plate. If she was lucky, this cowpoke would get the message and leave her to her lunch.

"'Course living in Texas has a lot of advantages."

"That's what I understand."

"Suppose I should introduce myself," he said, holding out his hand. "Name's Dan Bowie. I'm Pepper's duly elected mayor."

"Pleased to meet you." Sherry wiped the mustard from her fingertips and extended her hand. He shook it, his eyes gleaming, then without waiting for an invitation, pulled out the chair opposite her and made himself comfortable.

"Little Donna Jo here was telling me you're a physician's assistant."

"That's true."

"She also said you already have a job."

"That's true too, but—"

"It just so happens that Pepper badly needs a qualified physician's assistant. Now, we've finally hired one, but she's not due to get here for a coupla weeks yet. So-o-o..."

Sherry abruptly decided to discontinue her charade. "Well, she's here. It's me." She smiled brightly. "I'm early, I know, but—"

"Well, I'll be! This is great, just great. I wish you'd said something sooner. We'd've thrown a welcome party if we'd known, isn't that right, Donna Jo?"

"Actually I was on my way to Houston to visit a friend, but curiosity got the better of me," Sherry explained. "I thought I'd drive through town and get a look at Pepper."

"Well, what do you think?" He pushed back his Stetson and favored her with a wide smile. "You can stay for a little while, can't you?" he asked. "Now you finish your lunch," he said as Donna Jo set a towering piece of lemon meringue pie in front of Sherry and replenished her iced tea. "Your meal's on us," he announced grandly. "Send the tab to my office, Donna Jo."

"Thank you, but—"

"Soon as you're done, Miz..."

"Waterman. Sherry Waterman."

"Soon as you're done eating, I aim to show you around town. We'll mosey by the clinic, too. I want Doc Lindsey to meet you."

"Well...I suppose." Sherry hoped she didn't sound

ungracious. She finished her meal quickly and in silence, acutely conscious of Mayor Bowie's rapt and unwavering gaze.

The second she put her fork down, he took hold of her elbow and lifted her from the chair. He'd obviously regained his voice, because he was talking enthusiastically as he guided her out the café door.

"Pepper's a sweet little town. Got its name from Jim Pepper. Don't suppose you ever heard of him up there in Or-ee-gon. He died at the Alamo, and our forefathers didn't want the world to forget what a fine man he was, so they up and named the town after him. What most folks don't know is that he was darn near blind. He couldn't have shot one of Santa Ana's men if his life depended on it, which unfortunately it did."

"I'm sure his family was proud."

They strolled down the road and turned left onto a friendly-looking, tree-lined street. Sherry noticed a huge old white house with a wide porch and dark green shutters and guessed it must be the clinic.

"Doc Lindsey's going to be mighty glad to meet you," the mayor was saying as he held open the gate of the white picket fence. "He's been waiting a good long while for this. Yes, indeed. A good long while."

"I'm looking forward to meeting him, too," Sherry said politely. And it was true. She'd spent the better part of two years going to school part-time in order to train for this job. She was looking forward to beginning her new responsibilities. But not quite yet. She did want to visit Norah first.

She preceded the mayor up the porch steps to the screen door. He opened it for her, and led her inside, walking past a middle-aged receptionist, who called out a cordial greeting.

"Doc's in, isn't he?" Dan asked over his shoulder, without stopping to hear the reply.

Apparently, whether or not Doc was with a patient was no concern to Pepper's duly elected mayor. Guiding her by the elbow, he knocked loudly on a polished oak door and let himself in.

An older white-haired man was sitting in a comfortable-looking office chair, his feet propped on the corner of a scarred desk. His mouth was wide open, his head had fallen back. A strangled sound came from his throat, and it took Sherry a moment to realize he was snoring.

"Doc," Dan said loudly. "I brought someone for you to meet." When the old man didn't respond, Dan said it again, only louder.

"I think we should let him sleep," Sherry whispered.

"Nonsense. He'll be madder'n blazes if he misses meeting you."

Whereas the shouting hadn't disrupted Don Lindsey's nap, Sherry's soft voice did. He dropped his feet and straightened, blinking at Sherry as if she were an apparition.

"Who in tarnation are you?"

"Sherry Waterman," she said. "Mayor Bowie wanted us to meet."

"What ails you?"

"I'm in perfect health."

"She's that gal we hired from Or-ee-gon."

"Why in heaven's name didn't you say so sooner?" Doc Lindsey boomed, vaulting to his feet with the energy of a man twenty years younger. "About time you got here."

"I'm afraid there's been some misunderstanding...." Sherry began, but neither man was listening. Doc slapped the mayor across the back, reached behind the door for his fishing pole and announced he'd be back at the end of the week.

He hesitated on his way out of the office. "Ellie Johnson's baby is due anytime now, but you won't have a problem with that. More'n likely I'll be back long before she goes into labor. She was two weeks late with her first one."

"Don't you worry," the mayor said, following Doc out the door. "I heard Sherry tell Donna Jo she's a midwife too."

Doc shook hands with the mayor, and chortled happily. "You outdid yourself this time, Danny-boy. See you in a week."

"Dr. Lindsey!" Sherry cried, chasing after him. He was already outside and on the sidewalk. "I'm not staying! I'm on my way to Houston to meet a friend." She scrambled down the steps so fast she nearly stumbled.

Apparently Doc didn't hear her. The mayor seemed to have developed a hearing problem, too.

Doc tossed his fishing pole into the bed of his truck and climbed into the front seat.

"I can't stay!" she shouted. "I'm not scheduled to start work for another two weeks. I've made other plans!"

"Seems to me you're here now," Doc said. "Might as well start. Good to have you on the team. I'll see you..." The roar of the engine drowned out his last words.

Sherry stood on the lawn, her heart pounding as she watched him drive away. Frowning in frustration, she knotted her fists at her sides. Neither man had taken the trouble to listen to her; they just assumed she would willingly forgo her plans. But darn it, she wasn't going to be railroaded by some hick mayor and a doctor who obviously spent more time sleeping and fishing than practicing medicine.

"I can't stay," she announced, annoyed as much with herself as she was with the mayor for the mess she was in. This was what she got for being so curious.

"But you can't leave now," Mayor Bowie insisted. "Doc won't be back for a week. Besides, he's never been real good with time—a week could turn out to be ten days or more."

She pushed a stray lock of shiny brown hair off her forehead, and her blue eyes blazed. "That's unfortunate, because I'm meeting my friend in Houston and I can't be late." That wasn't entirely true but she didn't intend to start work until the agreed date. On top of that, she couldn't shake the feeling that there was something not quite right about the situation here in Pepper. Something was going on.

"If you could only stay the week, we'd all be mighty grateful," the mayor was saying.

"I'm sorry but no," Sherry stated emphatically, heading back down the street toward her car.

The mayor dogged her heels. "I'm sure your friend wouldn't mind. Why don't you phone and ask her? The city will pay for the call."

Great, Sherry thought, there were even perks. "No thanks," she said firmly.

The mayor continued to plead. "I feel right bad about this," he said. "But a week, why, only seven days, and Doc hasn't had time off like this in months."

Sherry kept walking, refusing to allow him to work on her sympathies. He seemed to have forgotten about the possibility of Doc's absence lasting as long as ten days, too.

"You have to understand," he went on, "that with Doc away there isn't anyone within miles for medical emergencies."

Sherry stopped and turned to glare at him. "It's unfortunate that the pair of you didn't think of that sooner. I told you when you introduced yourself that I was on my way to Houston. My contract doesn't start for two weeks."

"I know." He removed his hat and looked at her imploringly. "Surely a week isn't too much to ask."

"Excuse me, miss." A stocky police officer dressed in a tan uniform had come out of the café and moseyed over to her. The town sheriff, she decided. He was chewing on a toothpick and his thumbs were tucked in his belt buckle, which hung low under his protruding belly. "I don't suppose you happen to own that cute little GEO Storm, just there, do you?" He pointed at her car, about twenty feet away.

"As a matter of fact, I do."

His nod was slow and deliberate. The toothpick was smoothly transferred to the other side of his mouth. "I was afraid of that. As best I can tell, it's parked illegally."

"It most certainly is not," Sherry protested as the three of them reached the GEO. The slot was clearly marked and she had pulled in between two other vehicles.

"See how your left rear tire is over the yellow line?" the sheriff asked, pointing.

"I suppose that carries a heavy fine?" Good grief, she thought. Before long some cowpoke was going to suggest they get a rope and hang her from the nearest tree. In which case she was okay, since she hadn't seen anything but brush for the last hundred miles.

"There isn't a fine for illegally parking your car," he said, grinning lazily. "But jaywalking carries a hefty one, and I saw you cross that street with my very own eyes."

"There wasn't a crosswalk," she protested.

"Sure there is," he said, still grinning. "It's down the street a bit, but it's there. I painted it myself no more'n ten years ago."

"You're going to fine me, then," she said reaching into her bag for her wallet. "Great. I'll pay you and be done with it." She was going to head straight for the freeway, and when she reached Houston, she would reconsider this job offer.

"There isn't any fine."

"But you just said there was!" Actually, Sherry was greatly relieved. Her cash was running low and she doubted that the sheriff would accept a check.

"No fine, but the jail term—"

"Jail term!" she exploded.

"Now, Billy Bob," the mayor said, placing himself between the two of them, "you don't really intend to put our doc's helper in jail, do you?"

Billy Bob rubbed his hand across the underside of his jaw as if needing to contemplate such a monumental decision.

"You'd give Pepper a bad name," the mayor continued, "and we wouldn't want that, would we?"

"You staying in Pepper, miss?" the officer asked.

Sherry's gaze connected with Mayor Bowie's. "It appears I don't have much choice, do I?"

The minute she had access to a phone, Sherry vowed, she was going to call her friend's husband, Rowdy Cassidy. Rowdy, the owner of one of the largest computer software companies in the world, had a large legal staff at his fingertips. He'd be able to pull a few strings for her. By the end of the day, these folks in Pepper would be facing so many lawsuits, they'd throw a parade when she left town.

"I'll walk you back on over to the clinic," the mayor said, smiling as though he hadn't a care in the world. "I'm sure Mrs. Colson'll be happy to give you a tour of the place."

Sherry ground her teeth and bit back a tart reply. Until she had the legal clout she needed, there was no use in voicing any more protests.

Instead, Billy Bob himself escorted her down the street and around the corner to the clinic. The middle-aged receptionist introduced herself as Mrs. Colson and greeted Sherry with a warm smile. "I'm so pleased you decided to stay."

"You make her welcome now," the sheriff instructed.

"You know I will," Mrs. Colson told him, standing and coming around the short counter. "There's no need for you to stay," she told Billy Bob and, taking him by the elbow, escorted him out the door. She turned to Sherry. "Billy Bob can outstare a polecat, but beneath that tough hide of his, he's as gentle as a baby."

Sherry bit back a retort as the receptionist went on to extol the sheriff's virtues.

"One of those multitalented folks you read so much about. Not only does he uphold the law around these parts, but he makes the best barbecue sauce in the state. Just wait till you taste it. Everyone thinks he should bottle and sell it, but I doubt he will."

"How unfortunate," was the best Sherry could manage.

Her mood didn't improve as Mrs. Colson gave her

the grand tour. Despite her frame of mind, Sherry was impressed with the clinic's modern equipment and pleased with the small apartment at one end of the building that would serve as her living quarters.

"Doc's sure glad to get away for a few days," Mrs. Colson said amicably, ignoring Sherry's sour mood. "I can't even remember the last time he had more than a day to himself. He talks about fishing all the time—gets a pile of those magazines and catalogs. In the twenty years I've known him, I don't believe I've seen him livelier than he was today after you arrived. Guess he was thinking he'd best skedaddle before you changed your mind. I'm sure glad you didn't."

Sherry's answering smile was weak. Between Dan Bowie, Doc Lindsey and Billy Bob, she'd been completely hog-tied.

"So Dr. Lindsey has been practicing in Pepper for twenty years?" She wondered if, like her, he'd innocently driven into town and been snared. This could be something straight out of "The Twilight Zone."

"Thirty years, in fact, maybe more. Most folks think of him as a saint."

Some saint. Sherry thought. With little more than a nod of his head, he'd abandoned Pepper and her.

Mrs. Colson led her to Doc's office. "Now make yourself at home. Do you want a cup of coffee?"

"No, thanks," Sherry answered, walking over to the desk. The telephone caught her eye. As soon as she had a minute alone, she would call Houston.

But the moment Mrs. Colson left there was a knock at the office door. Sherry groaned. She hadn't even had time to sit down.

"Come in," she called, thinking it must be the receptionist.

In walked a tall, rawboned cowboy with skin tanned the color of a new penny. He wore jeans, a checkered shirt and a pair of scarred boots. A Stetson hat hooded his dark eyes, and somehow, with the red bandana around his neck, he looked both rough and dangerous.

"You're not Doc Lindsey," he said accusingly.

"No," she agreed tartly, "I'm not."

"Oh, good," Mrs. Colson said, following him into the room. "I see your one-o'clock appointment is here."

"*My* one o'clock appointment?"

"Where's Doc?" the cowboy demanded.

"He's gone fishing. Now you sit down," Mrs. Colson directed in steel tones. "You're Miz Waterman's first patient, and I don't want her getting a bad impression about the folks in Pepper."

"I ain't talkin' to no woman about Heather."

"Why not? A woman would be far more understanding than Doc."

Personally, Sherry agreed with the cowboy.

"Don't you argue with me, Cody Bailman," Mrs. Colson said, arms akimbo. "I'll have your hide if you make trouble for Miz Waterman. She's a real sweetheart."

Cody shifted his hat farther back on his head and scratched his brow. "It ain't gonna work."

"That's right enough. It ain't gonna work unless you try." The receptionist took Cody by the elbow and marched him to the chair on the other side of the desk. "Now sit. You, too, Sherry." Neither of them bothered to comply, but that didn't disturb the receptionist. "Cody's here to talk about his daughter. She's twelve and giving him plenty of grief, and he comes for advice because...well, because his wife died about ten years back and he's having a few problems understanding what's happening to Heather now that she's becoming a young woman.''

''Which means I'm not talkin' to some stranger about my personal affairs,'' Cody said.

''It'll do you good to get everything out,'' Mrs. Colson assured him. ''Now sit down. Sherry, you sit, too. If you stand, it'll make Cody nervous.''

Sherry sat. ''What am I supposed to do?'' she whispered.

''Listen,'' the older women instructed. ''That's all Doc ever does. It seems to help.''

Doc Lindsey apparently served as Pepper's psychologist, too. Sherry had received some training along those lines, but certainly not enough to qualify as a counselor.

''I'm not talkin' to a woman,'' Cody said.

''Did you ever consider that's the reason you're having so many problems with Heather?'' Mrs. Colson pointed out, then stalked over to the door. As she reached for the knob, her narrowed gaze moved from Cody to Sherry, and her tight features relaxed into a reassuring smile. ''You let me know if Cody gives you any problems, but I doubt he will. He's a dear once you get to know him.'' She dropped her voice. ''What Heather really needs is a mother, and to my way of thinking, Cody should remarry.''

''You volunteering for the job, Martha?'' Cody said.

Mrs. Colson's cheeks pinkened. ''I'm old enough to be your mother, and you darn well know it.'' With that she left the room, closing the door behind her.

Cody laughed and to Sherry's surprise sat down in the chair across from her, took off his hat and relaxed.

As he rested one ankle on top of his knee and stared at Sherry, the humor drained out of his face.

She wasn't sure what she should do. If she hadn't felt so intimidated by this dark-haired cowboy, she'd have sent him on his way.

"You married?" He asked suddenly.

Her mouth dropped open. When she finally managed to speak, her words stumbled over one another. "No, I'm not, I...that is..." She knew she sounded breathless and inane.

"Don't look so worried. I wasn't expecting you to volunteer as my wife."

"I realize that," she said with as much dignity as she could muster. Unfortunately it wasn't much.

"Then how are you supposed to know about kids?"

"I have two younger brothers and a sister," she said, wondering why she thought she had to defend herself. By all that was right, she *should* be sending him on his way. She sighed. The more this day progressed, the more convinced she was that she'd somehow stepped out of time. The man sitting across from her might have come from another century.

"So you know about girls?"

"I was one not so long ago myself," she said wryly. Resigning herself to the situation, she asked, "Why don't you tell me something about Heather and I'll see if I can help?"

Cody seemed to need time to think over her suggestion. "Well, first off, Heather's doing things behind my back."

"What sort of things?"

"Wearing makeup and the like. The other night I went in to check up on her and I swear she had on so much silver eye shadow her lids glowed in the dark."

Sherry swallowed her impulse to laugh.

"No more'n about six months ago," he continued, clearly confused by what was happening with his daughter, "Heather was showing signs of being one of the best cowhands I'd ever seen, but now she doesn't want to have anything to do with ranching. Besides that, she's getting bigger on top."

"Have you bought her a bra?"

He flushed slightly beneath his tan. "I didn't have to—she bought her own. Ordered it right out of the catalog before I even knew what she'd done. From what I can see, she didn't have a clue about what she was doing, because the one they sent was five sizes too big. Rather than admit she didn't know about such things, she's wearing it and as best I can tell stuffing it with something. Heaven only knows what."

"My guess is tissue." That had worked for Sherry when she was a teenager!

Cody's dark eyes narrowed in concentration. "Could be. I asked her about it, and she nearly bit my head off."

Mrs. Colson was right, the poor girl did need a mother.

"Has Heather got a boyfriend?" Maybe Cody was jealous of some boy. It sounded like a good theory anyway.

Cody frowned. "Ever since she's been wearing this bra, she'd got a whole passel of boys hanging around. The thing is, she doesn't like all this attention. You have to understand that until recently Heather was a tomboy."

"Heather's growing up, Cody," Sherry told him softly. She leaned back and crossed her arms. "She doesn't understand what's happening to her body. My guess is she's frightened by the changes. Trust me, she isn't any happier about the things that are taking place than you are. Give her a little time and a little space, and you'll be surprised by how well she adjusts.''

Cody eyed her as if he wasn't sure he should believe her.

''Does she have any close friends?'' she asked.

''Wally and Clem, but she doesn't seem to be getting along with them as well as she used to.''

''What about girlfriends?''

''She has a couple, but they live here in town and we're twenty miles away. What she really needs is to talk to someone—you know, a woman, someone older than thirteen, who knows a bit more about things like bras and other girl stuff. And then there was this business with the 4-H—all of a sudden my daughter wants to run my life.''

''The 4-H? Your life?''

''Never mind,'' he said, groaning heavily.

''Would you like me to try talking to her?'' Sherry offered. ''I…I don't know if I'd be able to accomplish anything, but I'd be willing.''

''I'd like it a whole lot,'' he said, his eyes softening with gratitude. He frowned again. ''She's been acting like a porcupine lately, so don't be offended if she seems a bit unfriendly.'' Cody hesitated, looked away and sighed. ''Then again, she might be overly friendly. Just don't be shocked by anything she says or does, all right?''

''I won't be,'' Sherry promised. ''I'm sure we'll get along just fine.'' She wasn't as confident as she sounded, but she found she liked Cody Bailman. It hadn't been easy for him to discuss such private matters with a stranger, a woman, no less, yet he'd put his concern for his daughter first. She was impressed.

"I found something the other day. I'm sure Heather didn't mean for me to see it. Frankly, it's got me worried."

"What was it?"

"A book. She had it tucked between the cushions in the sofa. It was one of those romance novels you women like so much. I tell you right now, it's got me concerned."

"Why?"

"Well, because I don't think it's a good idea for her to be clouding her head up with that sort of nonsense." He muttered something else, but Sherry didn't catch it. Apparently he didn't think highly of romance.

"I'll bring it up with her if you want," Sherry offered. "Of course, I won't let her know you found the book."

Cody stood. "I appreciate this, Miz…"

"Waterman. But please, call me Sherry."

"Sherry," he repeated. He held out his hand and she took it. Was it her imagination, or did he maintain contact a moment longer than necessary? Her gaze fell to their clasped hands, and he released her fingers as if he suddenly realized what he was doing. "It's been a pleasure."

"Thank you. Do you want to bring Heather in to see me tomorrow afternoon, or would you rather I paid a visit to your ranch?"

"Could you? It'd be best if this visit appeared casual-like. If Heather ever found out I was talking to anyone about her, she'd be madder than a mule with a mouthful of bees."

"I'll get directions from Mrs. Colson and be there shortly after lunch—say one o'clock?"

"Perfect."

Cody lingered at the door and seemed to assess her. "Are you thinking of sticking around Pepper?"

"I was hired last month but wasn't scheduled to start work for another two weeks. But it seems I'm starting early."

Sherry couldn't believe she'd said that. Until the minute Cody Bailman had walked in the door she'd been intent on demanding her two weeks. Now, she wasn't so sure.

"I'll see you tomorrow, then," Cody said, grinning broadly.

"Tomorrow," she agreed.

Still he stayed. "Might as well come by around lunchtime. The least I can do is feed you."

With a slight nod of her head, she accepted his off-hand invitation.

The phone on the desk pealed, breaking the silence and the spell that seemed to have taken hold of them both. Then the ring was cut off. Apparently Mrs. Colson had picked it up.

As Cody was just about to leave, the receptionist burst through the door, a look of panic in her eyes. "That was Luke Johnson. Ellie's having labor pains, and he's scared to death he's gonna have to deliver that baby on his own. You'd better get over there quick as you can."

"Where?" Sherry demanded.

"Rattlesnake Ridge," Cody supplied. "Come on," he said gripping her elbow. "I'll drive you. You'd never find it on your own."

Two

"Rattlesnake Ridge?" Sherry muttered under her breath as she hurried with Cody toward his pickup truck. He opened the passenger door and helped her inside. Although slender, Sherry wasn't the sort of female who generally required assistance, but her comparatively meager height—five foot five, as opposed to Cody's six-two—meant she needed help this time. The tires on his truck looked as if they belonged on a tanker trailer.

It was impossible to determine the color of the vehicle, and Sherry was convinced it hadn't been washed since it'd been driven off the showroom floor. Maybe, she thought, the dirt helped the rust hold the thing together.

Once she situated herself inside the cab, Cody raced around the front and leapt inside. His door made a cranking sound when he opened and closed it. He shoved the key into the ignition and the engine roared to life. She couldn't help but notice all the papers clipped to the dash; it looked as if he stored the majority of his paperwork there. She couldn't suppress a smile at his fingertip filing system.

"I'll need some things from my car," she told him. "It's parked over by the café." Cody stopped on Main

Street, directly in front of her GEO and answered her unasked question.

"It's the only car I didn't recognize," he said as he opened the door and jumped down, then came around to give her a hand.

By the time Sherry was back in the pickup and fumbling with her seat belt, they were racing out of town.

Over the years Norah had written her long letters about life in Texas saying that the men here were as unique as the trucks they drove. Sherry had been amused and intrigued enough to move here herself. She was beginning to understand what Norah had meant about the men.

"I wish I'd talked to Luke myself," Cody muttered. He glanced at Sherry as if she were somehow to blame for his friend's discomfort. "That man's so besotted with Ellie he'd lose his head completely if anything ever happened to her."

Sherry grinned. "Isn't that the way a man *should* feel about his wife?"

Cody didn't answer right away. "Some men with some women, I suppose," he said several moments later as though it pained him to admit it.

"Are there really rattlesnakes out there on Rattlesnake Ridge?" Sherry asked conversationally.

Cody grinned. "In Texas we tend to call a spade a spade. We don't pretty up the truth, and the truth is there's rattlers on that ridge. Notice it ain't named Buttercup Hill."

"I see." She swallowed tightly. "Are snakes a real problem around here?"

"You afraid of snakes?" His gaze momentarily left the road.

"Not particularly," she said, trying to make her tone

light. Norah hadn't said anything about snakes. "Tell me what you know about Ellie. Doc said she'd gone two weeks beyond her due date with the first pregnancy. Do you remember the baby's birth weight?"

Cody glanced at her again, as if puzzled by her prying.

"If I'm going to be delivering this baby, every bit of information is helpful," she said. "Is Ellie small and delicate?"

"Aren't all women?"

Sherry could see that Cody wasn't going to be much help. "What else can you tell me about her?"

"Well, she's real cute."

"Young?"

"Mid-twenties, maybe younger. Luke wasn't much interested in marriage until Ellie came to visit her grandparents a few years back. He took one look at her and he hasn't been the same since. I swear he walked around like a sick calf from the moment he met her." Cody frowned before he continued, "Unfortunately, his condition hasn't improved much since. It's been a long while since I've seen a man as smitten as Luke." He said this last part as if he had little patience with the emotion. "My bet is that Ellie's the calm one now."

"Her first pregnancy was normal?"

"I wouldn't know."

"Boy or girl?"

"Girl. Christina Lynn. Cute as a bug's ear, too."

"Was she a big baby?"

"Not that I recall, but then I wouldn't know much about that sort of thing."

"How old is Christina Lynn?"

"She must be a year or so." He paused. "Is that bad?"

"Why?" His question surprised her.

"Because you frowned."

Sherry hadn't realized she had. "No, it's just that they didn't wait long before Ellie became pregnant again."

"No, but if you want the truth, I don't think this one was planned any more than Christina Lynn was. As I said earlier, Luke's besotted. Got his head in the clouds where Ellie's concerned."

Sherry found that all rather endearing. She liked his terminology, too. Smitten, besotted. Here she was in her late twenties and no man had ever felt that way about her—nor she about any man. This was one of the reasons she'd decided to move away from Orchard Valley. If she stayed, she had the sinking feeling the rest of her life would have gone on just as it had been. She'd been content, but never excited. Busy, but bored. Liked, but not loved.

Her entire life had been spent in Orchard Valley, a small town where neighbors were friends and the sense of community was strong. It was one of the reasons Sherry had accepted the position in Pepper.

Norah had made the transition from Orchard Valley to Houston without a lot of difficulty, but Sherry wasn't sure she'd have done nearly as well. She didn't have a big-city mentality. But, Norah's letters about the Lone Star state had intrigued her, and if she was going to make a change, she couldn't see doing it by half measure. So she'd answered the agency's advertisement with a long letter and a detailed résumé. They phoned almost immediately, and she was hired so fast, without a personal interview, her head spun. She did learn from Dr. Colby Winston, Norah's brother-in-law, that her references had been checked and this eased her mind.

They'd been driving about twenty minutes when Cody braked suddenly to turn off the main road and onto a rugged dirt-and-gravel one. Sherry pitched forward, and without the restraint of the seat belt, would have slammed against the dash.

"You all right?"

"Sure," she said, a bit breathless. "How much farther?"

"Ten miles or so."

Sherry groaned inwardly and forced a smile. Even if they'd been driving at normal speed, the road would have been a challenge. Sherry felt like a yo-yo doing a round-the-world spin. Her body pitched one way and another, and she was forced to grip the seat with both hands.

When at last Cody pulled into the ranch yard, the road smoothed out. He eased to a stop in front of a two-story white house, which to Sherry looked like a desert oasis, standing out in a sort of warm welcome from the heat and barrenness. The windows were decorated with wide bright blue shutters, and brilliant red geraniums bloomed in the boxes out front. The wrap-around porch was freshly painted. Sherry watched as the front door swung open and a tall, rangy cowman barreled out and down the steps.

"What took you so damn long?" he hollered. "Ellie's in pain."

Sherry was still fiddling with her seat belt when Cody opened the door for her. His hands fit snugly around her waist as he helped her down from the cab.

"Sherry, meet Luke," Cody said.

"Where's Doc?" Luke demanded.

"Fishing," Sherry explained, holding out her hand. "I'm Sherry Waterman and I—"

Luke's hand barely touched hers as his gaze moved accusingly to Cody, interrupting her introduction. "You brought some stranger out here for Ellie? Cody, this is my wife! You can't bring just anyone to—"

"I'm a midwife, as well as a physician's assistant," Sherry supplied. "I can do just about everything Dr. Lindsey does, including prescribe medication and deliver babies. Now, where's your wife?"

"Cody?" Luke looked at his friend uncertainly.

"Do you want to deliver Ellie's baby yourself?" Cody asked him.

Luke went visibly pale and shook his head mutely.

"That's what I thought." Cody's hand cupped Sherry's elbow as he escorted her into the house. "You'll have to forgive Luke," he whispered. "As I said earlier, he's been screwy ever since he met Ellie."

The door led into the kitchen. A toddler was sitting in a high chair grinning happily and slamming a wooden spoon against the tray.

"Christina Lynn, I assume," Sherry said.

The toddler's face broke into a wide smile. At least Luke's daughter seemed pleased to see her.

"Where's Ellie?" Sherry asked Luke.

"Upstairs. Hurry, please!" Luke strode swiftly toward the staircase.

Sherry followed, taking the stairs two at a time, Cody right behind her.

When Sherry reached the hallway, Luke led the way into the master bedroom. Ellie was braced against the headboard, her eyes closed, her teeth gnawing on her lower lip. Her hand massaged her swollen abdomen as she breathed deeply in and out.

Luke fell to his knees and reached for her free hand,

kissing her knuckles fervently. "They're here. There's nothing to worry about now."

Ellie acknowledged Sherry's and Cody's presence with an absent nod. Sherry waited until the contraction had ebbed before she asked, "How far apart are they?"

"Five minutes," Ellie said. "They started up hard, right after my water broke."

"How long ago was that?"

"An hour or so."

"I better check you, then." Sherry set her bag down at the foot of the bed and reached for a pair of rubber gloves.

"Cody?" Once again Luke pleaded for his friend's advice.

"Cody," said Ellie, "kindly keep my big oaf of a husband entertained for a while." She motioned toward the door. "Make him tend to Christina Lynn—she shouldn't be left alone, anyway. Whatever you do, keep him out of this room."

"But, Ellie, you need me!" Luke protested.

"Not right now I don't, honey. Cody, do as I say and keep Luke out of here."

Cody virtually pushed Luke out of the room. After the pair had left, Ellie looked to Sherry. "Whoever you are, welcome. I couldn't be more pleased to see another woman."

Sherry smiled. "Sherry Waterman. I'm new to Pepper. Doc was so excited by my arrival that he took off fishing. He said you weren't due for another couple of weeks."

"I'm not, but then we miscalculated with Christina Lynn, too."

"I'll wash my hands and be right back." By the time Sherry returned, Ellie was in the middle of another contraction. She waited until Ellie had relaxed, then adjusted her pillows to make her as comfortable as possible.

"How am I doing?" Ellie asked after the pain receded. Her brow was covered with a thin sheen of perspiration. She licked her dry lips.

"You're doing just great," Sherry told her, wiping the woman's face with a wet rag.

"How much longer will it take?"

"A while," Sherry told her gently. "Maybe several hours yet."

Ellie's shoulders sagged. "I was afraid of that."

Twenty minutes later, Cody appeared after knocking lightly on the bedroom door. "How's everything going up here?"

"Great," Sherry assured him. "Ellie's an excellent patient."

"I wish I could say the same for Luke. Is there anything I can get you?"

"Pillows and a cassette player." At his frown, she elaborated, "Soothing music will help relax Ellie during the contractions. I have tapes with me."

Cody nodded and looked at Ellie. "Don't worry about Christina Lynn. She's in her crib now and sound asleep. I phoned the ranch, and our housekeeper's staying with Heather, so everything's been taken care of at my end."

"Whatever you do, keep Luke out of here," Ellie said. "You'd think I was the only woman ever to suffer labor pains. He was a wreck by the time Christina Lynn was born. Doc Lindsey had to spend more time with him than me."

"I'll keep him in line," replied Cody, ducking back out of the room.

Sherry remembered more than one birth where the father required full-time attention. It always warmed her that men could be so greatly affected by the birth of their children.

"Talk to me," Ellie requested before the next powerful contraction gripped her body.

Sherry told the woman about her introduction to the good people in Pepper. About meeting Mayor Bowie and Doc Lindsey and Billy Bob. Ellie laughed softly, then as the pain came again, she rolled onto her side and Sherry massaged the tightness from the small of her back, all the while murmuring encouragingly.

"I'm a transplant myself," Ellie spoke when she could. "I was a college sophomore when I came here to visit my grandparents. They've lived in Pepper for as long as I can remember. I only intended on staying a few days, but then I met Luke. I swear he was the most pigheaded, most ill-behaved man I'd ever known. I told myself I never wanted to have anything to do with the likes of him. To be truthful, I was a bit sweet on Cody Bailman, but only at first."

"Obviously your opinion of Luke changed."

"My sweet Luke. You've never seen anyone more crusty on the outside and more gentle on the inside. I'll never forget the afternoon he proposed. I'd decided to drive back home to Dallas—good grief, I'd spent two weeks longer than I'd originally intended. Luke didn't want me to leave, but I really didn't have any choice. I had a job waiting for me and was signed up for classes in the fall. Grandma sent me off with enough food to last me into the following month."

Sherry chuckled and waited for Ellie to work her way through the next contraction.

"I was five miles out of town when I saw this man

on a horse galloping after me as if catching me was a matter of life or death. It was Luke.'' She shook her head remembering. ''When I pulled over to the side of the road, he jumped off his horse, removed his glove and fell to one knee and proposed. I knew then and there I wasn't ever going to find a man who would love me as much as Luke Johnson. Suddenly nothing mattered without him, not anymore. I know my parents were disappointed I didn't finish college, but I'm happy and that's what counts.''

''You don't mind living so far away from town?''

''At first, just a little. Now I'm happy about it.''

''That's wonderfully romantic story.''

Ellie smiled. ''Is there a special man in your life?''

Sherry exhaled slowly. ''I've never fallen in love. Oh, I had a few crushes, the way we all do when we're young. I dated a doctor for a while, but both of us knew it wasn't going anywhere.'' Sherry smiled to herself remembering how difficult it was for Colby Winston to admit he was in love with Valerie Bloomfield.

In the hours that followed, Cody came up to check on their progress twice more and give a report of his own. Luke, he said, had worn a path in the living-room carpet pacing back and forth, but thus far, Cody had been able to restrain him from racing up the stairs. He doubted that Luke would have much hair left though before the ordeal was over; he'd jerked his hands through the thick mop so many times there were grooves in his hairline.

''He loves me,'' Ellie said softly.

When Sherry walked Cody to the bedroom door, he asked quietly, ''Will it be much longer? Luke's a mess.''

''Another couple of hours.''

Cody nodded and his eyes briefly held hers. "I'm glad you're here." He turned and headed down the stairs. A surge of emotion gripped her, but she wasn't sure how to read it. All she knew was that she felt *alive*, acutely sensitive to sounds and colors, and she had the impression Cody experienced the same thing.

"I'm glad you're here, too," Ellie said from behind her.

Sherry moved back to the bed. "Doc would have done just as well."

"Perhaps, but it helps that you're a woman."

The second stage of labor arrived shortly after midnight, and Ellie arched against the bed at the strength of her contractions, panting in between. Sherry coached her as she had so many others. And then, at last, with a shout of triumph, Ellie delivered a strong, squalling son.

The baby was barely in his mother's arms when the door burst open and Luke barged into the room.

"A son, Luke," Ellie whispered. "We have a son."

Luke knelt beside the bed and stared down at the angry infant in his wife's arms. The baby was a bright shade of pink, his legs and arms kicking in protest. His eyes were closed and he was yelling for all his worth. "He looks just like you when you get mad," Ellie told her husband.

Luke nodded and Sherry noticed his eyes were bright with tears as he bent forward and kissed his son's wrinkled brow. Then he gently placed his hand over Ellie's cheek and kissed her. "Never again," he vowed. "Our family's complete now."

Ellie's eyes drifted shut. "That's what you said after Christina Lynn was born."

"True," Luke admitted, "but that was because I

couldn't bear to see you suffer again. This time it's for me. I don't think I could go through this another time. And, I nearly lost my best friend.''

"You were a long way from that, partner," Cody said from the doorway.

"I don't care. Two children are plenty, understand, Ellie? I know you said you'd like four, but I won't hear of it. You agree with me now, don't you?"

Sherry moved behind the big, rangy cattleman and looked down at Ellie. "You're exhausted. You need some sleep." Gently lifting the baby from her arms, Sherry placed him in a soft blanket, marveling at the perfectly formed tiny person in her hands.

"Come on," Cody urged Luke. "It's time to celebrate. Let's break open that bottle of expensive scotch you've been saving."

"She's going to do it, you know," Luke said to no one in particular. "That woman knows I can't refuse her a damn thing. Before I even figure out how it happened, we're going to have four young ones running around this house."

Sherry finished her duties and found Luke and Cody in the living room each holding a shot of whiskey. "Ellie and Philip are sound asleep," she assured them.

"Philip," Luke repeated slowly, and a brightness came into his eyes. "She decided to name him Philip, after all."

"A family name?" Cody asked him.

Luke shrugged. "Actually, it's mine. I never much cared for it as a kid and dropped it when I entered school, insisting everyone call me by my middle name."

"Ellie says your son looks like a Philip," Sherry put in.

A wide grin split Luke's face. "I think she's right—he does." He looked down into the amber liquid in his glass. "A son. I've got myself a son."

Sherry smiled, then found herself yawning. It had been a long day. She'd been up since dawn, not wanting to travel in the worst heat of the day, and now it was well past two in the morning.

"Come on," Cody said, setting his glass down, "I'd better drive you back into town."

Sherry nodded and covered her mouth when yet another wide yawn escaped. She was weary through and through.

"Thank you," Luke said, his eyes bright. He took her limp hand and pumped it several times to show his gratitude. He seemed to have forgiven her for being a stranger.

"I'll be in touch with you both tomorrow," Sherry promised. "Ellie did a beautiful job with this baby."

"I know." Luke dropped his gaze as if embarrassed by his behavior earlier. "I knew the minute I saw that woman I was going to love her. What I didn't know was how damn lucky I was that I convinced her to marry me."

"From what Ellie told me, she considers herself the lucky one." Luke grinned hugely at Sherry's words.

"Come on, Sherry, you're beat," Cody said, cupping her elbow. "Good night, Luke."

"Night." Luke walked with them to the front door. "Ellie's mother is on her way and should be here by morning. She'll be a big help. But thanks again."

By the time Sherry was inside Cody's truck, she was dead on her feet. She dreaded the long, rough drive back into town, but there was no help for it.

"SHERRY." Her name seemed to come from a long distance away. The bottom of a well, perhaps. It was then that she realized she'd been asleep.

She'd meant to stay awake, but apparently she was more tired than she realized, for she'd slept through that dreadful ten miles before they hit the main road. Cody must have driven the stretch with infinite care.

To compound her sense of disorientation, she found her head neatly tucked against his shoulder. It felt warm and comfortable there, she wasn't inclined to move.

"We're in town already?" she asked, slowly opening her eyes.

"No. I couldn't see taking you all the way into Pepper when you're so tired."

Sherry straightened and looked around. They were parked outside a barn beside an enormous brick house with arched windows on the main floor and four gables jetting out from the second. The place, which was illuminated by several outdoor lights, resembled something from a prime-time soap opera.

"Where are we?" she asked.

"My place, the Lucky Horseshoe. I figured you could spend what's left of the night here. I'll drive you back into town first thing in the morning."

Sherry was too tired to argue, not that she wanted to. She liked and trusted this cattleman, and when he came around to help her from the cab, she found herself almost eager to feel his hands on her waist again.

Cody helped her down, and if he was feeling any of what Sherry was, he didn't show it.

"I hope I didn't make a pest of myself falling asleep on you that way," she said.

He mumbled something she couldn't quite make out. But apparently she hadn't troubled him. He led the way into the big country kitchen, turning on lights as he went.

Without asking, he took down two large glasses from the cupboard and filled them with milk from the refrigerator. "You didn't have any dinner."

Sherry had to stop a moment and think about it. He was right. She hadn't had anything since the cheeseburger and pie at lunchtime. It surprised her to realize she wasn't the least bit hungry.

"Here," he said, handing her the glass of milk. "This'll tide you over till breakfast."

"Thanks."

He pulled out a chair for her, then twisted the one across from it around and straddled it. They didn't seem to have a lot to say to each other, yet the room was charged with electricity.

"So," he ventured, "you're planning to stay in Pepper?"

Sherry nodded. She liked the gruff quality of his voice. She liked his face, too, not that he was turn-her-bones-to-water handsome. His features were tough and masculine, browned by the sun and creased with experience, some of it hard, she guessed.

"You'll like it here. Pepper's a good town."

Everything about Cody Bailman fascinated her. A few strands of thick dark hair fell over his high forehead, giving him a little-boy look. It was so appealing that Sherry had to resist leaning forward and brushing the hair away.

"The guest bedroom's upstairs," Cody said abruptly, and stood. He drained the last of his milk in three gulps and set the empty glass in the sink.

Sherry drank the last of her own and stood, too. She'd forgotten how tired she was.

"This way," Cody whispered, leading her up the gently curving stairway off the entryway.

Sherry paused and glanced around at the expensive furnishings, the antiques and works of art. "Your home is lovely."

"Thanks."

Sherry followed him to the top of the stairs and then to the room at the far end of the hallway. He opened the door and cursed under his breath.

"Is something wrong?" Sherry asked.

"The bed isn't made up. Heather had a friend stay here last night and she'd promised to change the sheets and make up the bed herself. Apparently she forgot. Listen, I'll make do in here and you can sleep in my room. Janey, our housekeeper, changed the sheets just today."

"That isn't necessary," she protested. It would only take a matter of minutes to assemble the bed.

"You're dead on your feet," Cody returned. "Here." He reached for her hand and led her down to the other end of the hallway.

Had she possessed the energy, Sherry would have continued to protest, but Cody's evaluation of her state was pretty accurate.

"Call me if you need anything, and don't argue, understand?"

Sherry nodded.

Whether it was by impulse or design, she didn't know, but before he turned away, Cody leaned down and casually brushed her lips with his.

They both seemed taken back by the quick exchange. Neither spoke for what seemed the longest moment of Sherry's life. Her pulse was pounding wildly in her throat, and Cody reached out and pressed his fingertip to the frantic throbbing. Then, before she could encourage or dissuade him, he bent his head and brushed her mouth with his a second time.

Her moist lips quivered beneath the gentle contact. He moved toward her and she toward him, and soon they were wrapped in each other's arms. The kiss took on an exploring, demanding quality as if this moment was all they'd be granted and they'd best make the most they could of it.

Sherry nearly staggered when he released her. "Good night, Sherry," he said, then she watched as his giant strides ate up the length of the hallway. He paused when he reached the opposite end and turned back to look at her. Even from this distance, Sherry could read the dilemma in his eyes. He didn't want to be attracted to her, hadn't wanted to kiss her, and now that he had, he wasn't at all sure what to do about it.

Sherry was experiencing many of those same feelings herself. She opened the door and stepped inside his room, angry with herself for not insisting on the guest room. For everything about these quarters shouted of Cody. From the basalt fireplace to the large four-poster bed.

She pulled back the sheets and undressed. She'd thought she'd be asleep before her head hit the pillow, but she was wrong. She tossed and turned till dawn, the image of Cody standing at the end of the hallway staring at her as if he regretted ever having met her burned in her brain. At last she fell into a troubled sleep.

"HOT DAMN."

Sherry opened one eye and saw a pretty girl of about twelve, dressed in jeans and a red plaid shirt, standing just inside the doorway. Dark braids dangled across her shoulders.

"Hot damn," the girl repeated, smiling as if it was Christmas morning and she'd found Santa sitting under the tree waiting for her.

Sherry levered herself up on one elbow and squinted against the light. "Hello."

"Howdy," the girl greeted eagerly with a wide grin.

"What time is it?" Sherry rubbed her eyes. It seemed she'd only been asleep a matter of minutes. If it hadn't been rude to do so, she would have fallen back against the thick down pillow and covered her face with the sheet.

"Eight-thirty. Where's Dad?"

"Uh…you're Heather?"

"So he mentioned me, did he?" she asked gleefully. The girl walked into the room and leapt onto the mattress, making it bounce.

"I think you have the wrong impression of what's going on here," Sherry felt obliged to tell the girl.

"You're in my dad's bed, aren't you? That tells me everything I need to know. Besides, you're the first woman I've seen him bring home. I think I got the picture. How'd you two meet?" She tucked her knees up under her chin and looped her arms around them, preparing herself for a lengthy explanation.

"Heather!" Cody's voice boomed from the end of the hallway.

"In here!" she shouted back with enough force to cause Sherry to grimace.

Cody appeared as if by magic two seconds later, his large frame filling the doorway.

"Dad," Heather said with a disappointed sigh, "you've been holding out on me."

Three

"Gee, Dad, when's the wedding?"

"Heather!" Cody ground out furiously. He looked as if he'd dressed in a hurry. He was in jeans and barefoot, and his Western-style shirt was left open, exposing his hard chest and abdomen, and an attractive spattering of dark, curly hair.

"But, Dad, you've comprom—" she faltered "—ruined your friend's reputation! Surely you intend on making an honest woman of her."

Sherry laughed. She couldn't help it, although it was clear Cody wasn't amused by his daughter badgering. Heather's clear blue eyes sparkled with mischief.

"So," the girl continued, "how long has this been going on?"

"You will apologize to Miz Waterman," Cody insisted, his voice hard as cable.

"Sorry, Miz Waterman," Heather said. She didn't sound at all contrite. "I take it you're new in town?"

Sherry nodded and thrust out her hand. "Call me Sherry. I'll be working with Doc Lindsey."

"Wow. That's great. Real great!"

"I was with Ellie Johnson last night," Sherry said.

"Ellie had her baby?" Heather's excited gaze shot to her father.

"A boy. They named him Philip," Cody answered.

Heather slapped her hand against the mattress. "Hot damn! Luke never said anything, but I know he was hoping for a boy. But then, Luke's so crazy about Ellie he'd have been happy with a litter of kittens."

Cody rubbed his forehead. "We didn't get back to the house till after two. The guest bed wasn't made up." He looked accusingly at his daughter.

"Oops." Heather slapped her fingers against her lips. "I said I'd do that, didn't I? Sorry about that."

Sherry cleared her throat. "Uh, I'd better see about getting back to town." With Doc gone she was responsible for any medical emergency that might arise. Not that she intended to be manipulated into staying. She still intended on taking the time entitled to her, with or without the Sheriff's approval.

"You want me to see if Slim can drive her for you?" Heather asked her father.

"I'll do it," Cody said casually, turning away from them. "But first we'll have breakfast."

"Breakfast," Heather repeated meaningly. She wiggled her eyebrows up and down several times before climbing off the bed. "He's going to drive you back into town himself," she added, grinning at Sherry. Her smile grew wider and the sparkle in her eyes was bright enough to light a fire. "Yup," she said. "My dad's sweet on you. Real sweet. This could be downright interesting. It's about time he started listening to me."

"I... We only met yesterday," Sherry explained.

"So?"

"I mean, well, isn't it a little soon to be making those kind of judgments."

"Nope." Heather plopped herself down on the edge of the bed once more. "How do you feel about him? He's kinda handsome, don't you think?"

"Ah..."

"You'll have to be patient with him, though. Dad tends to be a little dumb when it comes to dealing with women. He's got a lot to learn, but between the two of us, we should be able to train him, don't you think?"

Sherry had gotten the impression from talking to Cody that Heather was a timid child struggling with her identity. Ha! This girl didn't have a timid bone in her body.

"I love romance," Heather said on a long drawn-out sigh. She looked behind her to be sure no one was listening, then lowered her voice. "I've been waiting a long time for Dad to come to his senses about marrying again. My mom died when I was only two, so I hardly even remember her, and—"

"Heather, your father and I've only just met," Sherry reminded her. "I'm afraid you're leaping to conclusions that could be embarrassing to both your father and me."

The girl's face fell. "You think so? It's just that I'm so anxious for Dad to find a wife. If he doesn't hurry, I'll be grown up before there're any more babies. In case you haven't guessed, I really like babies. Besides, it's not much fun being an only child." She hesitated and seemed to change her mind. "Sometimes it is, but sometimes it isn't. You know what I mean?"

Sherry would have answered, given the chance, but Heather immediately began speaking again.

"You like him, don't you?"

Sherry pushed the hair away from her face with both hands. She didn't need to look in a mirror to know her cheeks were aflame. "You're father's a very nice man, but as I said before—"

"Heather!" Cody boomed again.

"He wants me to leave you alone," Heather translated with a grimace. "But we'll have a chance to talk later, right?"

"Uh...sure." Sherry was beginning to feel dizzy, as if she'd been caught up in a whirlwind and wasn't exactly sure when she would land—or where.

It was impossible not to like Cody's daughter. She was vibrant and refreshing and fun. And not the least bit timid.

"Great. I'll talk to you soon, then."

"Right."

Fifteen minutes later, Sherry walked down the stairs and into the kitchen. Cody and Heather were sitting at the table and a middle-aged woman with thick gray braids looped on top of her head smiled a warm welcome.

"Hello," Sherry said to the small gathering.

"Sherry, this is Janey," Cody said. "She does the cooking and the housekeeping around here."

Sherry nodded when introduced and noticed the eager look exchanged between Heather and the cook. Heather, it appeared, hadn't stopped smiling from the moment she'd discovered Sherry sleeping in her father's bed. The housekeeper looked equally pleased.

"Janey's been around forever," Heather explained as she stretched across the table to spear a hot pancake with her fork.

Janey chuckled. "I'm a bit younger than Heather believes, but not by much. Now sit down and I'll bring you some cakes hot off the griddle."

Cody didn't have much to say during their breakfast, although Sherry was certain he was convinced bringing her to the ranch was a big mistake.

Breakfast was delicious. Cody didn't contribute

much to the conversation, not that Sherry blamed him. Anything he said was sure to be open to speculation. A comment on the weather would no doubt send Heather into a soliloquy about summer being the perfect time of year to have a wedding. The girl seemed determined to do whatever she could to arrange a marriage for her father. Sherry's presence only worsened the situation.

After they'd finished eating, Cody said he needed a few minutes to check with his men. Sherry took the opportunity to phone the Johnson ranch and see how Ellie and the baby were doing. She spoke to Luke who said that everything was well in hand, especially since Ellie's mother had arrived that morning. Once again, he thanked Sherry for her help.

"You ready?" Cody asked when she hung up the phone.

"All set. Just let me say goodbye to Janey."

When Sherry walked into the yard a few minutes later, Cody was waiting for her. Heather had gone with her, and the girl paused when she saw her father standing outside the pickup. "You aren't driving her back in that old thing, are you? Dad, that truck's disgusting."

"Yes, I am," Cody said in a voice that defied arguing. It didn't stop Heather, however.

"But Sherry's special. I'd think you'd want to take her in the Caddie."

"It's fine, Heather," Sherry insisted, opening the door of the truck herself. Unfortunately she was at least six inches too short to boost herself into the cab. Cody's aid seemed to come grudgingly. Maybe he regretted not accepting Heather's advice about which car to drive, she thought.

Sherry waved to the girl as they pulled out of the yard. Heather, with a good deal of drama, crossed her hands over her heart and collapsed, as if struck by how very sweet romance could be. With some effort, Sherry controlled her amusement.

Cody's ranch was huge. They'd been driving silently for what seemed like miles and were still on his spread. She asked him a couple of questions, to which he responded with little more than a grunt. Apparently he was something of a grouch when he didn't get a good night's sleep.

About ten minutes outside of town he cleared his throat as if he had something important to announce. "I hope you didn't take anything Heather said seriously."

"You mean about your making an honest woman of me?"

He snorted. "Yes."

"No, of course I didn't."

"Good."

He was so serious it was all she could do not to laugh.

"The kiss, too," he added, his brow folded into a thick frown.

"Kisses," she reminded him, making sure he understood there had been more than one.

Despite her restless sleep, Sherry honestly hadn't given the matter much thought. She did so now, concluding that they'd both been exhausted and rummy, high on the emotional aftermath of the birth of Philip and the roles they'd each played in the small drama. Being attracted to each other was completely understandable, given those circumstances. The kisses had been a sort of celebration for the new life they'd helped usher into the world. There hadn't been anything sexual about them, had there?

"Let's call them a breech of good judgment," Cody suggested.

"All right." That wasn't how Sherry would define them, but Cody seemed comfortable with the explanation—and pleased with her understanding.

They remained silent for the rest of the trip, and Sherry grew thoughtful. She found she agreed with him in principle. Their evening together had been a step out of time. Nevertheless, disappointment spread through her. It was as though she'd been standing on the brink of a great discovery and had suddenly learned it was all a hoax.

Her entire romantic career had followed a similar sorry pattern. Just when she thought perhaps she'd found her life's partner in Colby Winston, she discovered she experienced no great emotion toward him. Certainly nothing like what Ellie had described to her.

Sherry knew precious little of love. Four years earlier, she'd watched the three Bloomfield sisters back home in Orchard Valley find love, all within the space of one short summer. Love had seemed explosive and chaotic with each sister. Valerie and Colby had both been caught unaware, each fighting their attraction and each other. Sherry had stood by and watched the man she'd once seriously dated herself fall head over heels in love. She knew then that this was what she wanted for herself.

Then Valerie's sister Steffie had returned from Italy. She and Charles were brought back together after a three-year separation and they, too, had seemed unprepared for the strength of their feelings. They were married only a matter of weeks after Valerie and Colby.

But the Bloomfield sister who had surprised Sherry the most was Norah. They'd been schoolmates, sharing the same interests and often the same friends. A smile never failed to appear on Sherry's face whenever she thought of Norah and Rowdy. The lanky millionaire Texan hadn't known what hit him when he fell for Norah, and the amusing thing was Norah hadn't, either. All of Orchard Valley had seemed to hold its collective breath awaiting the outcome of their romance. But Norah and Rowdy made the ideal couple, Sherry had thought. Nothing, outside of love, would have convinced Norah to leave Orchard Valley.

In the years since Norah had left Oregon, Sherry had been busy studying and working toward her degree, too absorbed in her goal to find time for relationships. But now she was ready. She wanted the love her friends had found, the excitement, the thrill of finding that special someone, of being courted and treasured. She was looking for a man who felt about her the way Luke felt about Ellie. She wanted a man to look at her the way Colby Winston looked at Valerie Bloomfield.

Cody eased the truck to a stop behind Sherry's GEO. Sherry unbuckled the seat belt and reached for her purse and medical bag.

"I really appreciate the ride," she said, holding out her hand for him to shake.

"You're welcome." He briefly took her hand, then leapt from the cab and came around to help her down. When his hands came to encircle her waist, his eyes captured hers. For the longest moment she didn't move, couldn't move, as if his touch had caused a strange paralysis. But when he shifted his gaze away, she placed her hands on his shoulders and allowed him to lift her to the ground. As she met his gaze again, she read surprise and a twinge of regret there.

Cody eased away from her, and Sherry watched as an invisible barrier was erected between them. Irritation seemed to flicker through him. "I'm not going to apologize for kissing you last night," he said softly.

"But you regret it?"

"Yes, more so now than before."

The harsh edge to his voice took her by surprise. "Why?" The word was little more than a throaty whisper.

"Because it's going to be damn difficult to keep from doing it again." With that, he stalked back to the driver's side of the pickup, climbed in and roared off.

Sherry got into her car and drove the short distance to the clinic, parking in the small lot behind the building. When she walked around and went in the front door, Mrs. Colson broke into a wide smile. "Welcome back."

"Thanks. Ellie had a beautiful baby boy."

"So I heard. Word spreads fast around these parts. Ellie claims she'll never have another baby without you there. She thinks you're the best thing to happen to Pepper since we voted in sewers last November."

Sherry laughed. "I don't suppose you've heard from Doc Lindsey?"

"Yes. He called this morning to see if everything was working out."

Sherry was relieved. At least the physician had some sense of responsibility. "I want to talk to him when he phones in again."

"No problem. He wants to talk to you, too. Apparently there's a misunderstanding—you weren't scheduled to begin work for another two weeks."

"That's what I've been trying to tell everyone," Sherry said emphatically. "I made the mistake of driving through town, and everyone assumed that because I was here I was starting right away."

Mrs. Colson fiddled with a folder from the file drawer, pulling out a sheet of paper and glancing through its contents. "Doc's right. It's here as plain as day. So, why *are* you here so early?"

Briefly Sherry wondered if a megahorn would help the good people of Pepper hear her. "I was just passing through on my way to Houston," she explained patiently. "Mayor Bowie assumed I was here to stay and so did Doc. Before I could stop him, he was out the door with his fishing pole in hand."

"You should've said something."

Sherry resisted the urge to scream. "I tried, but no one would listen."

"Well, Doc told me to tell you he'll be back in town sometime this afternoon. He claims the fish don't bite this early in the season, anyway."

"I'll need to call my friends and tell them I'm going to be late," Sherry said.

"Sure, go right ahead. The town'll pay for the call."

Sherry decided to wait until she'd showered and changed clothes before she contacted Norah. It was midmorning before she felt human again.

"I'm in Pepper," Sherry explained once she had Norah on the line. "It's a long story, but I won't be able to leave until later this afternoon, which will put me in Houston sometime late tomorrow."

"That's no problem," Norah was quick to assure her. "I'm so pleased you're coming! I've missed you, Sherry."

"I've missed you, too."

"So how do you like Texas so far?" Norah wanted to know.

Given Sherry's circumstances, it was an unfair question. "I haven't been here long enough to form an opinion. The natives seem friendly enough, and with a little practice I think I'll be able to pick up the language."

Norah chuckled. "Oh, Sherry, I am so looking forward to seeing you! Don't worry, I've decided to give you a crash course on the state and the people once you arrive. You're going to love it—just the way I do."

Sherry didn't comment on that. "How's Rowdy?" she said, instead.

"Busy as ever. I swear that man runs circles around me, but that's all right. It's me he comes home to every night and me he sits across the dinner table from, and me he loves. He's such a good father and an even better husband."

"Val and Steffie send their love. Your dad, too."

"Talking to you makes me miss them even more. Rowdy promised me we'd fly to Orchard Valley sometime this fall, but I doubt Dad's going to wait that long. I half expect him to drop by for a visit before the end of the summer."

Sherry chuckled. "Well, at least I'll be there before he is."

"It wouldn't matter," Norah said. "You're welcome anytime."

Sherry felt a lot better after talking to her friend. But Norah sounded so happy she couldn't quite squelch a feeling of envy. Norah and Rowdy had two small children and were looking into adopting two more. Norah had always been a natural with children. Sherry never did understand why her friend with her flair with youngsters, hadn't chosen pediatrics.

In an effort to help the time pass till Doc's arrival, Sherry read through several medical journals in his office. When she looked up, it was well past noon.

Mrs. Colson stuck her head in the door, "Do you want me to order you some lunch?" she asked.

"No thanks." Her impatience for Doc to arrive had completely destroyed her appetite.

"I'm going to order a salad for myself. The Yellow Rose is real good about running it over here to me. You sure I can't talk you into anything?"

"I'm sure."

Donna Jo stopped off fifteen minutes later with a chef salad and plopped herself down on a chair in the reception area. Mrs. Colson was behind the counter, and Sherry was sitting on another chair with her purse and suitcase all ready to go. "The Cattlemen's Association's in town for lunch," Donna Jo explained to the receptionist, removing her shoe and massaging her sore foot. She eyed Sherry with the same curiosity she had a day earlier. "I hear you delivered Ellie's baby last night."

Word had indeed gotten around. Sherry nodded.

"You must have spent the night out there with her and Luke, because Mayor Bowie came into the café this morning looking for you. You weren't at the clinic."

"Actually, Cody Bailman drove me over to his house."

"You stayed the night at Cody's?" Donna Jo asked. Both the waitress's and Mrs. Colson's interest was piqued.

"It was after two by the time I finished. I was exhausted, and so was Cody." She certainly didn't want to give the two the wrong impression. "Nothing happened. I mean, nothing that was, uh…'' She gave up trying to find the words. ''Cody was the perfect gentleman.''

''Isn't he always?'' Donna Jo winked at Mrs. Colson.

''Is there something wrong about my spending the night at Cody's?''

''Not in the least,'' Mrs. Colson was quick to assure her. ''Cody's a gentleman.''

''As much of a gentleman as any Texan gets,'' Donna Jo amended. ''Martha, are you going to tell her, or am I?''

''Tell me what?'' Sherry said.

Donna Jo and Mrs. Colson shared a significant look.

''What?'' Sherry demanded again.

''I don't think so,'' Mrs. Colson said thoughtfully after a long moment. ''She'll find out soon enough on her own.''

Donna Jo nodded. ''You're right.''

''What will I find out on my own?'' Sherry tried a third time, but again her question was ignored.

''Martha here tells me you're bent on leaving town,'' the waitress said conversationally. ''Stop in at the café on your way out and I'll pack you a lunch to take along. You might not be hungry now, but you will be later.''

''Thanks, I'll do that.''

Doc arrived around two that afternoon, looking tired and disgruntled. ''I've been up since before dawn,'' he muttered. ''It didn't make sense that I wasn't reeling in fifteen-inchers until I realized it was too early in the month.''

''I'll be back in less than two weeks,'' Sherry promised, ''and next time the fish are sure to be biting.''

"I hope so," Doc grumbled. "You might've said something about arriving early, you know."

Sherry nearly had to swallow her tongue to keep from reminding him she'd done everything but throw herself in front of his truck to keep him from leaving.

Sherry had almost passed the café when she remembered her promise to Donna Jo and pulled to a stop. The waitress was right; she should take something to eat with her, including several cold sodas. Already it was unmercifully hot. She chuckled, remembering Donna Jo's remark that the ones who escaped to Colorado for the summer weren't real Texans. Apparently folks were supposed to stay in Texas and suffer.

The café was nearly empty. Sherry took a seat at the counter and reached for the menu.

"What'll you have?" Donna Jo asked.

"Let's see… A turkey sandwich with tomato and lettuce, a bag of chips and five diet sodas, all to go."

Donna Jo went into the kitchen to tell the chef. When she came back out her eyes brightened. "Howdy, Cody."

"Howdy." Cody slipped onto the stool next to Sherry and ordered coffee.

"Hi," he said, edging up his Stetson with his index finger as if to get a better look at her.

"Hi." It was silly to feel shy with him, but Sherry did. A little like she had in junior high when Wayne Pierce, on whom she'd had a crush, sat next to her in the school lunchroom. Her mouth went dry and she felt incapable of making conversation.

"I was wondering if I'd run into you this afternoon."

"Cody's in town for the local cattlemen's meeting," Donna Jo explained as she placed a beige ceramic mug full of steaming coffee in front of Cody.

"Doc's back," Sherry said, although she wasn't certain he understood the significance. "He said the fishing was terrible, but then, it generally is about now."

He shrugged, not agreeing or disagreeing with her. "You're having a rather late lunch, aren't you?"

Donna Jo set a brown paper bag on the counter along with the tab. "I was planning to eat on the road," Sherry said, thanking Donna Jo with a smile. She slipped her purse strap over her shoulder and opened the zipper to take out her wallet.

A frown crowded Cody's features. "You're leaving?"

"For Houston."

His frown deepened. "So soon?"

"I'll be back in a couple of weeks." She slid off the stool and was surprised when Cody slapped some coins on the counter and followed her to the register.

"Actually I was hoping to talk to you," he said, holding open the café door for her.

"Oh?" She headed for her car.

Cody followed. "Yeah, it's about what I said this morning." His eyes refused to meet hers. "I was thinking about it on my way back to the ranch, and I realized I must have sounded pretty arrogant about the whole thing."

"I didn't notice," Sherry lied, but it was only a small one. She found it rather charming that he wanted to correct the impression he'd made.

"It's just that Heather's on this kick, but you were so terrific with Ellie and everything else."

"We both agreed it was a lapse in judgment," she reminded him. "So let's just forget it ever happened."

He jammed his fingers into his pockets as Sherry

opened her car door. "I wish I could," he said so low Sherry wasn't sure she heard him correctly.

"Pardon?" she said, looking up to him and making a feeble attempt at a smile.

"Nothing," he said gruffly. "I didn't say anything."

"You wish you could what?" she pressed, refusing to allow him off lightly.

He looked away from her and his wide shoulders moved up and down with a labored sigh. "I wish I could forget!" he said forcefully. "There. Are you happy now?"

"No," she returned softly. "I'm confused."

"So am I. I like you, Sherry. I don't know why, but I do, and I don't mind telling you it scares the living daylights out of me. The last time I was this attracted to a woman I was—" he stopped and rubbed the side of his jaw—"a hell of a lot younger than I am now. And you're leaving."

"But I'll be back." The rush to reach Houston at the earliest possible moment left her. Nothing appealed to her more than exploring what was happening between her and Cody Bailman at this moment.

"But you won't be back for two weeks." He made it sound like an eternity. His face tightened. "By the time you're back it won't be the same."

"We don't know that."

"I do," he said with certainty.

Sherry was torn. "Are you asking me to stay?"

His nostrils flared at the question. "No," he said forcefully, and then more softly, "No." He moved a step closer to her. "Aw, what the hell," he muttered crossly. He reached for her, wrapped his arm around her waist, dragged her toward him and kissed her soundly.

Tentatively, shyly, her lips opened to his until the kiss blossomed into something wanting and wonderful. At last he pulled away slightly and sighed. "There," he said, his breath warm against her face. "Now go, before I make an even bigger fool of myself."

But Sherry wasn't sure that she was capable of moving, let alone driving several hundred miles. She blinked and tried to catch her breath.

"Why'd you do that?" she demanded, pressing her fingertips to her lips.

"Damned if I know," Cody admitted, sounding none too pleased with himself.

Sherry understood the reason for his consternation when she looked around her. It seemed the entire town of Pepper, Texas, had stopped midmotion to stare at them. A couple of men loitering outside the hardware store were staring. Several curious faces filled the window at the Yellow Rose, including Donna Jo's. The waitress, in fact, looked downright excited and gave Sherry a thumbs-up.

"We've done it now," Cody muttered, staring down at her as if she was to blame. "Everyone's going to be talking."

"I'd like to remind you I wasn't the one who started the kissing."

"Yeah, but you sure enjoyed it."

"Well, this is just fine, isn't it," she said, glad for an excuse to be on her way. "I'm outta here. Tossing her lunch bag onto the passenger seat, she slipped inside the car.

"Sherry, dammit, don't leave yet."

"Why? What else have you planned?"

"Okay, okay, I shouldn't have kissed you, I'll be the first to agree." He rubbed his hand along the back of his neck as if considering his words. "As I said before, I like you."

"You have a funny way of showing it."

He closed his eyes and nodded. "Already I've made a mess of this, and I haven't even known you for a whole day. Listen, in two weeks Pepper's going to hold its annual picnic and dance. Will you be there?" He gave her the date and the time.

She hesitated, then nodded.

"If we still feel the same way, then we'll know," he said, then spun on his heel and walked away.

Four

"What can I tell you about Texas?" Norah asked Sherry as they sat by the swimming pool in the yard behind her sprawling luxury home. Both three-year-old Jeff and baby Grace were napping, and Norah and Sherry were spending a leisurely afternoon soaking up the sun. "Texas is oil wells, cattle and cotton. It's grassy plains and mountains."

"And desert," Sherry added.

"That, too. Texas is chicken-fried steak, black-eyed peas and hot biscuits and gravy. Actually, I've discovered," Norah added with a grin, "that most Texans will eat just about anything. They've downed so many chili peppers over the years that they've burned out their taste buds."

"I've really come to love this state," Sherry admitted, sipping from her glass of iced tea. "Everyone's so friendly."

"It's not only known as the Lone Star state, but a lot of folks call it the Friendship state."

That didn't surprise Sherry.

"The men are hilarious," Norah continued, her eyes sparkling with silent laughter. "Oh, they don't mean to be, but I swear they've got some of the craziest ideas about…well, just about everything. To give you an example, they have this unwritten code, something that has to do with *real* Texans versus everyone else in the world. A real Texan would or wouldn't do any number of things.''

''Such as?''

''Well, a real Texan believes strongly in law and order, except when the law insists upon a fifty-five-mile-an-hour speed limit. They consider that downright unreasonable. Clothes are something else. A real Texan wouldn't dream of decorating his Stetson with feathers or anything, with the possible exception of a snake band, but only if he'd killed the snake and tanned the skin himself. And the jeans! I swear they refuse to wash them until they can stand up on their own.''

Sherry laughed. She'd run into a few of those types herself on her journey across the vast state. But no one could compete with the characters she'd met in Pepper. Mayor Bowie, Donna Jo and Billy Bob. The way that man had manipulated her into remaining in town!

And Cody Bailman kept drifting into her mind, although she'd made numerous attempts to keep him away. Especially the thought of their last meeting, when he'd kissed her in broad daylight in front of half the town. But nothing helped. No matter how hard she tried, Cody Bailman was in her head day and night. It didn't seem possible for a man she'd known for so short a while.

''Sherry.''

Sherry looked up and realized Norah was waving a hand in front of her face. ''You're in another world.''

''Sorry, I was just thinking about, uh, the folks back in Pepper.''

''More than likely it's that cattleman you were telling me about.''

Sherry lowered her gaze again, not surprised Norah

had read her so easily. "I can't stop thinking about him. I thought that once I was with you I'd be able to get some perspective on what happened between us. Not that anything really did—happen, I mean. Good heavens, I was only in town a little more than twenty-four hours."

"You like him, don't you?"

"That's just it," Sherry said, reaching for her drink and gripping it tightly. "I don't know how I feel about him. It's all messed up in my mind. I don't know Cody well enough to form an opinion, and yet..."

"And yet, you find yourself thinking about him, wishing you could be with him and missing him. All this seems impossible because until a few days ago he wasn't even in your life."

"Yes," Sherry returned emphatically, amazed at the way Norah could clarify her thoughts. "That's exactly what I'm feeling."

"I thought so." Norah relaxed against the cushion on the patio chair and sighed softly, lifting her face to the sun. "It was that way with me after Rowdy was released from the hospital and went home to Texas. My life felt so empty without him. It was like a giant hole had opened up inside me.... He'd only been in the hospital a couple of weeks, but it already seemed as if my whole world revolved around him."

"Rowdy, fortunately, felt the same way about you," Sherry said, knowing Cody was as perplexed as she was by the attraction *they* shared.

"Not at first," Norah countered. "I amused him, and being stuck in traction the way he was, the poor guy was desperate for some comic relief. I happened to be handy. Being Valerie's sister lent to my appeal, too. You know, he actually came to Orchard Valley to break up her engagement to Colby! I don't think it was until much later that he fell in love with me—later than he's willing to admit now, at any rate.''

''Don't be so sure.'' Sherry still remembered the chaos Rowdy Cassidy had brought into the tidy world of Orchard Valley General. His plane had crashed in a nearby field and he'd been taken, seriously injured, to Emergency. He'd been a terrible patient—demanding and cantankerous. Only one nurse could handle him.... Sherry had known he was in love with Norah long before he ever left the hospital, even if he wasn't aware of it himself. Norah's feelings had been equally clear to her. It seemed she could judge another's emotions better than her own.

''I'm rather sorry you took this position in Pepper,'' Norah said softly. ''I know it's pure selfishness on my part, but I was hoping if you moved to Texas you'd settle closer to Houston.''

''I don't think I realized how large this state is. Central Texas didn't look that far from Houston on the map. I found out differently when I had to drive it.''

''I wish you'd taken the time to stop in San Antonio. Rowdy took me there for our first anniversary, and we fell in love all over again. Of course, it might have had something to do with the flagstone walks, the marvelous boutiques and the outdoor cafés.'' Norah sighed longingly with the memory. ''The air was scented by jasmine. If I close my eyes I can almost smell it now.''

Norah's face grew wistful.

''We rode in a river taxi down the San Antonio River and...oh, I swear it was the most romantic weekend we've ever spent together.''

''I'll make a point of visiting San Antonio soon,'' Sherry said.

"Don't go alone," Norah insisted. "It's a place meant for lovers."

"Okay. I'll make sure I'm crazy in love before I make any traveling plans."

"Good." Norah was satisfied.

Rowdy returned home from the office earlier than usual with wonderful news. He and Norah were hoping to adopt two small children who'd been orphaned the year before. Because of some legal difficulties, the adoption had been held up in the courts.

"It looks like we're going to be adding to our family shortly," Rowdy explained, kissing Norah's cheek before claiming the chair next to her and reaching for her hand.

It was almost painful for Sherry to see these two people so deeply in love. It reminded her how very alone she was, how very isolated her life had become as more and more of her friends found their life's partner. Sherry felt like someone on the outside looking in.

"Grace's new tooth broke through this afternoon," Norah told Rowdy after she poured him a glass of iced tea and added a slice of lemon.

"This I've got to see," he said, heading toward the house.

"Rowdy," Norah called after him. "Let her sleep. She was fussy most of the afternoon."

"I thought I'd take her and Jeff swimming."

"You can, but wait till they wake up from their naps." Norah looked to Sherry and sighed softly. "I swear Rowdy's nothing more than a big kid himself. He's looking for someone to play with."

"He's wonderful. I could almost be jealous."

"There's no need," Norah said, reaching over and

squeezing Sherry's arm. "Your turn's coming, and I think it's going to be sooner than you expect."

"I hope so," Sherry said, but she didn't have any faith in her friend's assessment.

"Sherry," Rowdy said, turning back from the house. "I did a bit of checking on that cattleman you mentioned the other night." He removed a slip of paper from his inside pocket. "Cody James Bailman," he read, "born thirty-five years ago, married at twenty-one, widowed, one daughter named Heather. Owns a ten-thousand-acre spread outside of Pepper. He was elected president of the local Cattlemen's Association three years running."

"That's it?" Norah pressed.

"He raises quarter horses, as well as cattle."

That didn't tell Sherry much more than she already knew.

"He seems decent enough. I spoke to a man who's known Bailman for several years and he thinks real highly of him. If you want my advice, I say marry the fellow, present him with a couple of kids in the next few years and see what happens."

"Rowdy!" Norah chastised.

"That's what you did to me, and everything worked out, didn't it?"

"Circumstances are just a tad different, dear," Norah said, glancing apologetically toward Sherry.

"Marriage would do them both good," Rowdy continued. He looked at Sherry and nodded as if the decision had already been made. "Marry the man."

"Marry the man." As Sherry drove toward Pepper several days later, Rowdy's words clung to her mind. Cody's parting words returned to haunt her, as well.

Then we'll know. But what could they possibly have learned from their two weeks apart? Sherry hadn't a clue.

Because of a flat tire fifty miles on the other side of nowhere, followed by a long delay at the service station, Sherry was much later than she'd hoped. In fact, she was going to miss a portion of the scheduled festivities, including the parade. But with any luck she'd be in town before the dance started.

She'd tried phoning Cody's ranch from the service station, but there hadn't been any answer. No doubt everyone was enjoying the community celebration. With nothing left to do, she drove on, not stopping for lunch, until she arrived in Pepper.

The town had put on its best dress for this community event. A banner stretched across Main Street, declaring Pepper Days. The lampposts were decorated with a profusion of blue bonnets, and red, white and blue crepe paper was strung from post to post.

Several brightly painted cardboard signs directed her toward the city park and the barbecue. As soon as she turned off Main and onto Spruce, Sherry was assailed by the scent of mesquite and roasting beef. Several signs directed participants and onlookers to the far side of the park where a chili cook-off was in progress. Sherry was fortunate to find a parking space on a side street. Country-and-western music blared from loudspeakers, and colorful Chinese lanterns dotted the cottonwood trees.

People were milling around the park, and Sherry didn't recognize anyone. She would have liked to freshen up before meeting Cody, but she was already late and didn't want to take the time. Besides, her calf-length denim skirt, cowboy boots and Western shirt with a white leather fringe were perfect for the festivities. The skirt and shirt had been a welcome-to-Texas gift from Norah.

"Sherry!"

She twirled around to see Cody's daughter waving and racing toward her. Not quite prepared for the impact as Heather flung herself at her, throwing her arms around her waist and squeezing tightly, Sherry nearly toppled backwards but caught herself just in time.

"I knew you'd come! I never doubted, not even for a second. Have you seen my dad yet?"

"No, I just arrived."

"He didn't think you were going to come. Men are like that, you know. It's all a way to keep from being disappointed, don't you think?"

But Cody's attitude disappointed Sherry. "I said I'd be here."

"I know, but Dad didn't have a lot of faith that you'd show. I did, though. What do you think of my hair?" Heather looked extremely pretty with her thick dark hair loose and curling down her back. She whipped back the curls and tossed her head as if she were doing a shampoo commercial. She looked up at Sherry, her eyes wide and guileless, as though she'd practiced the look countless times in front of the bathroom mirror. "Come on, let's go find my father before he pines away."

It didn't take long for Sherry to spot Cody. He was talking to a group of men who were gathered in a circle. Their discussion appeared to be a heated one, and Sherry guessed the topic was politics. It wasn't until she was closer that she realized they were contesting the pros and cons of adding jalapeño peppers to Billy Bob's barbecue sauce.

"They're just neighbors," Heather whispered as they approached. "Dad can talk to them anytime."

Unwilling to interrupt him, Sherry stopped the girl's progress.

"But this could go on for hours!" Heather protested, apparently loud enough for her father to hear, because at that moment he turned and saw them.

His eyes moved from his daughter to Sherry, and he looked as if he couldn't believe she was really there. He excused himself to his friends and began walking toward her.

"Hello, Cody." The words seemed to stick like tar in Sherry's throat.

"I didn't think you were going to come," he said.

"I had a flat tire on the way, and it took ages to repair. I phoned, but I guess everyone at the Lucky Horseshoe had already left for the picnic."

"Are you hungry?"

"Starved," she admitted.

Cody pulled a wad of bills from his pocket, peeled off several ones and handed them to Heather. "Bring Sherry a plate of the barbecue beef."

"But, Dad, I wanted to talk to her and—"

Cody silenced the protest with a single look.

"All right, I get the picture. You want to be alone with her. How long do you want me to stay away?" The question was posed with an elaborate sigh. "An hour? Two?"

"We'll be under the willow tree," Cody said, ignoring her questions and pointing to an enormous weeping willow about fifty feet away.

"The willow tree," Heather repeated, her voice dipping suggestively. "Good choice, Dad. Real good. I couldn't have thought of a better place myself."

Cody gave a sigh of relief as Heather trotted off. "You'll have to forgive my daughter," he said shaking his head. Then he smiled. "She was as eager for you to return as I was."

His words and smile went a long way toward reassuring Sherry. Their separation had felt like a lifetime to her. Two weeks away from a man she'd known only briefly; it didn't make sense, but then, little did any longer.

All at once Sherry felt scared. Scared of all the feelings that were crowding up inside her. Scared of being with Cody again, of kissing him again, of making more of this attraction than he intended or wanted. Her feelings were powerful, alien. At first she attributed them to being with Norah and Rowdy and seeing how happy they were.

Now here she was with Cody, sitting under the shadowy arms of a weeping willow, and her confusion returned a hundredfold. This man touched her in a thousand indescribable ways, but she was troubled; she wasn't sure her feelings were because of Cody himself. Maybe it was the warm promise he represented. The happiness waiting for her just around the corner, out of reach. She desperately wanted the joy her friends had found. She was tired of being alone. Tired of walking into an empty apartment. Tired of being a bridesmaid, instead of bride. She wanted a husband, a home and a family. Was that so much to ask?

Cody spread out a blanket for them to sit on. "How were your friends?"

"Very much in love." It wasn't what Sherry had meant to say, but the first thing that sprang to her lips. She looked away embarrassed.

"Newlyweds?"

She shook her head. "They've been married four years and have two children. Within a few weeks they'll be adding two adopted ones to the family."

"They sound like a compassionate, generous couple."

His words warmed her heart like a July sun. Rowdy and Norah *were* two of the most generous people Sherry had ever known. It was as if they were so secure in their love for each other that it spilled over and flowed out to those around them.

"What's wrong?"

This man seemed to read her so accurately that nothing less than the truth would do. "I'm scared to death of seeing you again, of feeling the things I do for you. I don't even know you, and I feel… That's just it, I don't know what I feel."

He laughed. "You're not alone. I keep telling myself this whole thing is nuttier than a pecan grove. I don't really know you, either. Why you, out of all the women I've met over the years?"

"I'm not interrupting anything, am I?" Heather burst through the hanging branches and stepped onto the blanket. She crossed her legs and slowly lowered herself on the ground before handing Sherry a plate heaped high with potato salad, barbecued chicken and one of the biggest dill pickles Sherry had ever seen.

Heather licked her fingertips clean. "They've run out of beef. I told Mayor Bowie this was for Sherry, and he wanted me to ask you to save a dance for him. He's been cooking all afternoon, and he says he's looking forward to seeing a pretty face, instead of a pot of Billy Bob's barbecue sauce."

"This smells heavenly," Sherry said, taking the plate and digging in.

Cody looked pointedly at his daughter, expecting her to make herself scarce, but she looked just as pointedly back. "So, have you come to any conclusions?" Heather asked.

"No. But then we haven't had much time *alone,* have we?"

"You've had enough."

Cody closed his eyes. "Heather, please."

"Are you going to ask Sherry to dance, or are you going to wait for Mayor Bowie to steal her away from you? Dad, you can't be so nonchalant about this courting business. Aren't you the one who insists the early bird catches the worm? You know Mayor Bowie's fond of Sherry."

"The mayor's a married man."

"So?" Heather said, seeming to enjoy their exchange. "That didn't stop Russell Forester from running off with Milly You-know-who."

If the color in his neck was any indication, Cody's frustration level was quickly reaching its peak. But Sherry welcomed the intrusion. She needed space and time to sort through her feelings. Everything had become so intense so quickly. If Heather hadn't interrupted them when she had, Sherry was certain she'd have been in Cody's arms. It was too soon to cloud their feelings with sexual awareness.

"The chicken was delicious," Sherry said, licking her fingers clean of the spicy sauce. "I can't remember ever tasting any better."

"Cody Bailman, are you hiding Sherry under that tree with you?" The toes of a pair of snakeskin boots stepped on the outer edges of the blanket just under the tree's protective foliage.

Heather cast her father a righteous look and whispered heatedly, "I *told* you Mayor Bowie was going to ask her to dance first."

Cody stood and parted the willow's hanging branches. "She's eating."

"Howdy, Mayor," Sherry said, looking up at him, a chicken leg poised in front of her mouth. "I understand you're the chef responsible for this feed. You can cook for me anytime."

"I'm not a bad dancer, either. I thought I'd see if you wouldn't mind taking a spin with an old coot like me."

She laughed. "You're not so old."

"What'll your wife think?" Cody asked, his tone jocular, but with an underlying...what? Annoyance? Jealousy? Sherry wasn't sure.

Pepper's mayor waved his hand dismissively. "Hazel won't care. Good grief, I've been married to the woman for thirty-seven years. Besides, she's talking to her friends, and you know how that bunch loves to idle away an afternoon gossiping. I thought I'd give them something to talk about."

"Sherry?" Cody glanced at her as if he expected her to decline.

Frankly, Sherry was flattered to have two men vying for her attention, even if one of them was old enough to be her father and looked as if he'd sampled a bit too much of his own cooking over the years.

"Why, Mayor, I'd be delighted."

Cody didn't look at all pleased.

"I told you something like this was going to happen," Heather reminded him indignantly. "Your problem, Dad, is that you never listen to me. I read romance novels, I know about these things."

A laugh hovered on Sherry's lips. She hoisted herself

up and accepted Mayor Bowie's hand as he led her to the dancing platform.

Cody and Heather followed close behind. Because Mayor Bowie was chatting, she couldn't quite make out the conversation going on between father and daughter, but it seemed to her Heather was still chastising her father for his tardiness.

Although it was still early evening, the dance floor was already crowded. Willie Nelson was crooning a melodic ballad as the mayor deftly escorted Sherry onto the large black-and-white-checkered platform. He tucked his hand at her waist and stretched her arm out to one side, then smoothly led her across the floor.

"How're you doin', Sherry?" Said a woman's voice.

She turned to see Donna Jo dancing with the sheriff. Sherry waved with her free hand. Doc Lindsey danced by with Mrs. Colson, first in one direction and then another in what looked like a crazy version of a tango.

Mayor Bowie was surprisingly light on his feet, and he whirled Sherry around so many times she started to get dizzy. When the dance ended, she looked up to find Cody standing next to the mayor.

"I believe this dance is mine," he said.

"Of course." The mayor gracefully stepped aside and turned to Heather. Tucking his arm around his middle, he bowed and asked the giggling twelve-year-old for the pleasure of the next dance.

Heather cast Sherry a proud look and responded with a dignified curtsy.

"So, we meet again," Sherry said, slipping her left arm onto Cody's shoulder.

"You should have danced with me first," he muttered.

"Why?" She wasn't sure she approved of his tone

or his attitude. Mayor Bowie certainly couldn't be seen as competition!

"If you had, you'd have saved me a lecture from my daughter. She seems to have been doing research on romance, and apparently I've committed several blunders. According to Heather, my tactics aren't the way to ensnare today's sophisticated woman." He made a wry grimace.

Sherry couldn't help but notice they were doing little more than shuffling their feet, while other couples whirled around them. Cody seemed to notice the same thing and he exhaled sharply.

"That's another thing." he said. "My own daughter suggested I take dancing lessons." He snorted. "Me, as if I have the time for that kind of nonsense. Listen, if you want to date a man who's light on his feet, you better know right now I'm no Fred Astaire and never will be."

Actually Sherry had figured that out for herself, not that it mattered. Cody sighed again.

"Is something else troubling you?" Sherry asked.

"Yes," he admitted grudgingly. "You feel damn good in my arms. I'm probably breaking some romance code by telling you that. Damned if I know what a man's supposed to say and what he isn't."

Sherry pressed the side of her head to his chin and closed her eyes. "That was very sweet."

Cody was silent for the next few moments. "What about you?" he asked gruffly.

Sherry pulled back enough for him to read the question in her eyes. His own were dark and troubled.

"It'd help matters if you told me the same thing," he said. "That you...like being with me, too." He shook his head. "I've got to tell you, I'm feeling real silly."

"I do enjoy being with you."

He didn't seem to hear. "I feel like a pinned and mounted Monarch butterfly on display for everyone to inspect."

"Why's that?"

He looked away, but not before she read his frown. "Let me just say that kissing you in public didn't help matters any. It was the most ridiculous thing I've done in my thirty-four years. I made a damn fool of myself in front of the entire town."

"I wouldn't say that," she whispered, close to his ear. "I liked it."

"That's the problem." He grunted. "So did I. You know what I think? This is all Heather's doing. It started with that crazy project of hers. I swear that kid is going to ruin me yet."

"Heather's project?"

"Forget I said that."

"Why are you so angry? Is it because I danced with the mayor?"

"Good heavens, no. This has nothing to do with that."

"Then what *does* it have to do with?"

"You," he grumbled.

Dolly Parton's tremulous tones were coming out of the speakers now. It was a fast-paced number, not that Cody noticed. He didn't alter his footwork, but continued his laborious two-step.

"Cody, maybe we'd better sit down."

"We can't."

"Why not?" she asked.

"Because the minute we do, someone else is sure to ask you to dance, and I can't allow that."

She stared up at him, growing more confused by the moment. "Why not? Cody, you're being ridiculous."

"I don't need you to tell me that. I've been ridiculous ever since I saw you holding Ellie's baby in your arms. I've been behaving like a lovesick calf from the first moment I kissed you. I can understand what caused a normally sane, sensible man like Luke Johnson to chase after a sports car with his horse because he couldn't stand to let the woman he loved leave town. And dammit, I don't like it. Not one bit."

What had first sounded rather romantic was fast losing its appeal. "I don't like what I feel for you, either, Cody Bailman. I had a perfectly good life until you barged in."

"So did I!"

"I think we should end this whole thing," she said, pulling away from him. "Before we say something we'll regret." She dropped her arms to her sides and stared up at him.

"Great," he muttered. "Let's just do that."

With so many couples whirling about, Sherry found it difficult to make her way off the dance floor, but she managed, sidestepping her way. To her consternation, Cody followed close behind her.

Spotting Ellie sitting beneath the shade of an oak tree, Sherry headed in that direction, determined to ignore Cody. She was halfway across the park when she heard him call out after her.

"Sherry! Dammit, woman, wait up for me!"

She didn't bother to turn around to see what had

Five

"Cody infuriates me," Sherry announced, plopping herself next to Ellie Johnson on the blanket under the tree. She wrapped her arms around her knees and exhaled sharply in frustration.

"Men have infuriated women since the dawn of time. They're totally irrational beings," Ellie said calmly while gently patting her infant son's back. Philip was sleeping contentedly against her shoulder.

"Irrational isn't the word for it. They're insane."

"That, too," Ellie agreed readily.

"No one else but Cody could use a compliment to insult someone!"

"Luke did when we first started dating," Ellie told her. "He'd say things like 'You're not bad-looking for a skinny girl.'"

Despite her annoyance with Cody, Sherry laughed.

Cody had been waylaid by Luke, Sherry noticed. Luke carried Christina Lynn on his shoulders, and the toddler's arms were reaching toward the sky in an effort to touch the fluffy clouds. Sherry hoped Ellie's husband was giving Cody a few pointers about relationships.

Forcing her thoughts away from the cattleman, Sherry sighed and watched Ellie with her baby son. Philip had awoken and she turned him in her arms, situated a receiving blanket over her shoulder, then bared her breast.

"He's thriving," Ellie said happily. "I can't thank you enough for being with me the night he was born. Having you there made all the difference in the world."

"It wasn't me doing all the work," Sherry reminded her.

"Then let's just say we make an excellent team." Ellie stroked her son's face with her index finger as he sucked greedily at her breast. "I'm really pleased you're going to live in Pepper. I feel like you're a friend already."

Sherry glanced up to discover Heather marching her way, hands on hips. Her eyes were indignant as she stopped and briefly talked to her father and Luke before tossing her hands in the air and striding over to Ellie and Sherry.

"What did he do now?" Cody's daughter demanded. "He said something stupid, right?" In a display of complete disgust, she slapped her hands against her sides and lowered herself to the blanket next to Sherry. "I tried to coach him, but a lot of good that did." She eyed her father angrily. "No wonder he's never re-married. The man obviously needs more help than me and romance novels can offer him."

Ellie and Sherry shared a smile. "Don't try so hard, Heather."

"But I want Dad to remarry so I can have a baby brother or sister. Or one of each."

"Heather," Sherry said, "your father said something about a project you were involved in, and then he immediately seemed to regret mentioning it."

"He's never going to let me forget it, either," the girl muttered. "Neither is anyone else in this town."

"You have to admit, it was rather amusing," Ellie added.

"Oh, sure, everyone got a big laugh out of it—at my expense, too."

"Out of what?" Sherry wanted to know.

"My 4-H project. I've been a member for several years and each spring we work on a single project for the following twelve months. One year I raised rabbits, and another I worked with my horse, Misty. This spring I gave the whole town a big laugh when I decided I wanted my project to be helping my dad find himself a wife."

"You weren't serious!" Sherry was mortified.

"I was at the time, but now I can see it was all pretty silly," Heather continued. "Anyway, everyone talked about it for days. That's one of the worst things about living in a small town. Dad was furious with me, which didn't help."

Sherry wasn't sure what to think. "That's why you were so excited when you met me."

"You're darn right, especially when I found you sleeping in Dad's bed."

Sherry shot a glance at Ellie and felt her face grow warm. "Cody slept in the guest room."

"My friend, Carrie Whistler, spent the night before with me, and I was supposed to have changed the sheets, but I forgot," Heather explained further to Ellie, then turned her attention back to Sherry. "You're just perfect for Dad, and I was hoping you might grow to, you know, love him. I think you'd make a terrific mother."

Sherry felt tears burn the back of her eyes. "I don't know when anyone's paid me a higher compliment, Heather, but love doesn't work that way. I'm sorry. I can't marry your father just because you want a baby brother and sister.''

"But you like him, don't you?"

"Yes, but—"

"Until he said something stupid and ruined everything." Heather's face tightened.

"Why don't you let those two work matters out for themselves?" Ellie suggested to the girl. "Your interference will only cause problems."

"But Dad won't get anything right without me!"

"He married your mother, didn't he?" Ellie reminded her. "It seems to me he'll do perfectly fine all on his own."

"I *like* Sherry, though. Better than anyone, and Dad does, too. His problem is he thinks love's a big waste of time. He told me he wanted to cut to the chase and be done with it."

"He said that?" Sherry glared over at him. Cody must have sensed it, because he glanced her way and grimaced at the intensity of her look. He said something to Luke, who turned their way, also. Luke's shoulders lifted in a shrug. Then he patted Cody's back and the two of them headed in the direction of the cook-off area.

"He said he's too busy with the ranch to date anyone."

"I'm sure that's true," Sherry said. She felt like a complete fool for having constructed this wild romantic fantasy in her mind. Cody had never been interested in her. From the very first, he'd been looking to mollify his daughter. She just happened upon the scene at a convenient moment. Sherry felt sick to her stomach. This was what happened when she allowed herself to believe in romance, to believe in love. It seemed all so easy for her friends, but it wasn't for her.

"I've had a long day," Sherry said, suddenly feeling weary. "I think I'll go unpack my bags, soak in the tub and make an early night of it."

"You can't!" Heather protested. "I signed you and Dad up for the three-legged race, the egg toss and the water-balloon toss. They have the races in the evening because it's too hot in the afternoon."

"I don't think your father's interested in having me as a partner."

"But he is," Heather insisted. "He's won the egg toss for years and years, and it's really important to him. It's one of those ego things."

"Unfortunately, he's already got egg on his face," Sherry muttered to Ellie who laughed outright.

"Please stay," Heather pleaded. "Please, please, please. If you don't, I can't see myself ever forgiving Dad for ruining this golden opportunity."

Sherry was beginning to understand Cody's frustration with his daughter. "Heather, don't play matchmaker. It'll do more harm than good. If your father is genuinely interested in dating me, he'll do so without you goading him into it. Promise me you'll stay out of this."

Heather looked at the ground and her pretty blue eyes grew sad. "It's just that I like you so much and we could have so much fun together."

"We certainly don't need your father for that."

"We don't?"

"Trust me," Ellie inserted, "a man would only get in the way."

"Would you go school-clothes shopping with me? I

mean, to a real town with a mall with more than three stores, and spend the day with me?''

"I'd love it."

Heather lowered her gaze again, then murmured. "I need help with bras and...and other stuff."

Sherry smiled. "We'll drive into Abilene and make it a day."

Heather's eyes lit up like sparklers on the Fourth of July. "That'd be great!"

"So, I'll leave you to partner your dad on the egg toss."

The glimmer in her eyes didn't fade. "I was thinking the same thing." She looked mischievous. "This could well be the year Dad loses his title as the egg champion."

"Heather," Sherry chastised, "be nice to your father."

"Oh, I will," she promised, "especially since you and I have reached an understanding."

"Good. Then I'm heading over to the clinic now."

"You're sure you won't stay? There's a fireworks display scheduled for tonight. It's even better than the one we had on the Fourth."

"I think Sherry's seen all the fireworks she wants for one night," Ellie put in.

"You're right, I have. We'll talk later, Heather. Goodbye, Ellie." She leaned over and kissed the top of Philip's head. "Let's make a point of getting together soon."

"I'd like that," Ellie said.

Sherry was halfway back to her car when Cody caught up with her. He fell into step with her. "I didn't mean to offend you." He said after a moment.

Sherry sighed and briefly closed her eyes. "I know."

"But you're still mad?"

"No, discouraged perhaps, but not mad." She reached her car and unlocked it. "I talked to Heather and she told me about her 4-H project. It explained a lot."

"Like what?"

"Like why you're interested in me. Why you chose to drive me to the ranch, instead of town after Ellie's baby was born."

"That had nothing to do with it. We were both dog-tired, and my place was a lot closer than town."

"You don't need to worry," Sherry said, not the least bit interested in getting into another debate with him. She was truly weary and not in the best of moods, fighting the heat, disappointment and the effects of an undernourished romantic heart. "I had a nice chat with Heather. You've done a wonderful job raising her, Cody. She's a delightful girl. Unless you object, I'd like to be her friend. She and I already made plans to go clothes shopping in Abilene."

"Of course I don't object."

"Thank you." She slipped inside her car and started the engine. She would have driven away, but Cody prevented her from closing the door.

He scratched his temple and frowned darkly. "I don't mean to be obtuse, but what does all this mean?"

"Nothing, really. I'm just cutting to the chase," she said, "and explaining that it isn't necessary for you to play out this charade any longer."

"What charade?"

"Of being attracted to me."

"I *am* attracted to you."

"But you wish you weren't."

He opened and closed his mouth twice before he

answered. "I should have known you'd throw that back in my face. You're right. I don't have time for courtin' and the like. I've got a ranch to run, and this is one of the busiest times of the year."

Sherry blinked, not sure what to make of Cody. He seemed sincere about not meaning to offend her, and yet he constantly said and did things that infuriated her.

"The problem is," Cody continued, still frowning, "if I don't stake my claim on you now, there'll be ten other ranchers all vying for your attention."

"Stake your claim?" He made her sound like an acre of water-rich land.

"You know," he said. "Let everyone in town see you're my woman."

"I'm not *any* man's woman."

"Not yet, but I'd like you to think about being mine." He removed his hat; Sherry guessed that meant he intended her to take him seriously. "If you'd be willing to run off and get married, then—"

"Then *what?*"

"Then we'd be done with it. See, I don't have the time or energy to waste on courtin' a woman."

Sherry nodded slowly, all the while chewing on the inside of her cheek to keep from saying something she'd regret. So much for romance! So much for sipping champagne and feeding each other chocolate-covered strawberries in the moonlight, a fantasy Sherry had carried with her for years. Or a romantic weekend in San Antonio, the way Norah had described. No wonder Heather was frustrated with her father. The girl must feel as if she was butting her head against a brick wall.

"Well?" Cody demanded.

Sherry stared at him for several moments. "You aren't serious, are you?"

"I'm dead serious. I like you. You like me. What else is there? Sure we can spend the next several months going through the ridiculous rituals society places on couples, or we can use the common sense God gave us and be done with this romance nonsense."

"And do what?" Sherry asked innocently.

"Marry, of course. I haven't stopped thinking about you in two weeks. You didn't stop thinking about me, either. I saw it in your eyes no more'n an hour ago. You know what it's like when we kiss. Instead of playing games with each other, why not admit you want me as much as I want you? I never did understand why women need to complicate a basic human need with a bunch of flowery words. If you want kids, all the better. I certainly won't object."

Sherry carefully composed her response. Apparently she took longer than he thought necessary.

"Well?" he pressed.

She looked up at him, her gaze deliberately calm. "I'd rather eat fried rattlesnake than marry a man who proposed to me the way you just did."

Cody stared at her as if not sure what to make of her response, then slammed his hat back on his head. "This is the problem with you women. You want everything served to you on a silver platter. For your information, fried rattlesnake happens to be pretty good. Doesn't taste all that much different from chicken."

"Well, I wouldn't eat it even if it *was* served on a silver platter." Sherry snapped. This conversation was over. He'd only frustrated her before, but now she was really angry.

"That's your decision, then?"

"That's my decision," she said tightly.

"You're rejecting my proposal?"

"Yup."

"I should have figured as much," Cody said. "I knew even before I opened my mouth that you were going to be pigheaded about this."

"Don't feel bad," she said with feigned amiability. "I'm sure there're plenty of women who'd leap at your offer. I just don't happen to be one of them." She reached for the handle of the still-open door, and he was obliged to move out of the way.

"Good night, Cody."

"Goodbye," he muttered, and stalked away. He turned back once as if he wanted to argue with her some more, but apparently changed his mind. Sherry threw the GEO into gear and drove off.

"WHAT HAPPENED between my dad and you after we talked?" Heather asked in a whisper over the telephone. She'd called Sherry first thing the following morning.

"Heather, I'm on duty. I can't talk now."

"Who's sick?"

"No one at the moment, but—"

"If there's no one there, then it won't hurt to talk to me for just a couple of minutes, will it? Please?"

"Nothing happened between your dad and me." Which of course wasn't true. She'd been proposed to, if you could call it that, for the first time in her life.

"Then why is Dad acting like a wounded bear? Janey threatened to quit this morning, and she's been working for Dad since before I was born."

"Why don't you ask your father?"

"You're kidding, right? No one wants to talk to him. Even Slim's staying out of his way."

"Give him time. He'll cool down."

"If I was willing to wait, I wouldn't be calling you."

"Heather," Sherry said, growing impatient, "this is between your father and me. Let's just leave it at that, all right?"

"You don't want my help?"

"No," Sherry returned emphatically, "I don't. Please, leave this to us to settle."

"All right," the girl agreed reluctantly. "I'll drop whatever it is that *didn't* happen that you don't want to talk about."

"Thank you."

"I hope you realize what a sacrifice this is."

"Oh, I do."

"You might think that just because I'm a kid I don't know certain things. But I know more than either you or Dad realize. I—"

Sherry rolled her eyes. "I need to get off the phone."

Heather released a great gusty sigh. "All right. We're still going shopping for school clothes, aren't we? Soon, too, because school starts in less than two weeks."

"You bet." Sherry suggested a day and a time and reminded Heather to check with her father. "I'll make reservations at a nice hotel, and we'll spend the night."

"That'll be great! Oh, Sherry, I really wish you and Dad could get along, because I think you're fabulous."

"I think you're pretty fabulous yourself, honey. Now listen, I must go. I can't tie up the line."

"I understand. Next time I call, I'll have Mrs. Colson take a message. You can call me back later when you're not on duty.''

"That sounds perfect."

SHERRY HAD JUST FINISHED with her first patient of the afternoon, a four-year-old with a bad ear infection, when Mrs. Colson handed her a telephone message. Sherry should have suspected something wasn't right when the receptionist smiled so broadly.

Sherry took the slip and stuck it into the pocket of her white uniform jacket, waiting until she was alone to read it. When she did, she sank into a chair and closed her eyes. The call was from Heather. She'd talked to her father, and he apparently had business in Abilene that same weekend and was making arrangements for the three of them to travel together.

This was going to be difficult. Knowing Cody, he'd turn a simple shopping trip into a test of her patience and endurance. She'd have to set some ground rules.

CODY WAS SCHEDULED to pick her up at the clinic early Saturday morning, and she was standing on the porch waiting for him. It'd been a week since she'd last seen him, four days since their stilted conversation on the phone—and a lifetime since she'd dreaded any trip more.

Her heart sank to the deepest pit of her stomach when the white Cadillac pulled to a stop in front of the clinic's porch, where she was waiting.

Cody got out of the car and climbed the steps. Sherry saw Heather scramble over the front seat and into the back.

"Hello," Sherry said, her grip on her overnight case punishing.

"Hello." His voice was devoid of emotion as he reached for her bag.

"I thought we should talk before we leave," she said when he was halfway back down the steps.

"All right." He didn't sound eager.

"Let's call a truce. It shouldn't be difficult to be civil to one another, should it? There isn't any reason for us to discuss our differences now or ever again, for that matter."

"No," he agreed, "it shouldn't be the least bit difficult to be civil."

And surprisingly, it wasn't. The radio filled in silence during the long drive, and when the stations faded, Heather bubbled over with eager chatter. Cody seemed to go out of his way to be amiable, and Sherry found her reserve melting as the miles slipped past.

The hotel Cody chose in Abilene was situated close to a large shopping mall. Heather was ready to head for the shops the minute they checked into their spacious two-bedroom suite.

"Hold your horses," Cody insisted. He had his briefcase with him. "I probably won't be back until later this evening."

"What about dinner?" Heather wanted to know. "I've got an appointment."

"Don't worry about us," Sherry told him. "Either we'll order something from room service or eat downstairs. If we're feeling adventurous, we'll go out, but I don't imagine we'll go far."

"What time will you be back, Dad?"

Cody paused. "I can't say. I could be late, so don't wait up for me."

"Can I watch a movie?" She stood in front of the color television and read over the listings offered on the printed card.

"If Sherry doesn't object, I can't see any reason why not."

Heather hugged her father and he kissed the crown of her head. "Have fun, you two."

"We will," Sherry said.

"Spend your money wisely," he advised on his way out the door, but the look he cast Sherry assured her he trusted her to guide Heather in making the proper selections.

The girl waited until her father was out of the room before she hurled herself onto the beige sofa and carelessly tossed out both arms. "Isn't this great? You brought your swimsuit, didn't you? I did."

Sherry had, but she wasn't sure there'd be enough time for them to use the large hotel pool.

"It's almost as if we were a real family."

"Heather..."

"I know, I know," she said dejectedly, "Dad already lectured me about this. I'm not supposed to say anything that would in any way insin...insinuate that the two of you share any romantic interest in each other." She said this last bit in a voice that sounded as if it were coming from a robot.

"At least your father and I understand one another."

"That's just it. You don't. He really likes you, Sherry. A lot. He'd never admit it, though." She sighed and cocked her head. "Men have a problem with pride, don't they?"

"Women do, too," Sherry said, reaching for her purse. "Are you ready to shop till we drop, or do you want to discuss the troublesome quirks of the male psyche?"

It didn't take Heather more than a second to decide. She bolted from the sofa. "Let's shop!"

Sherry couldn't remember an afternoon she enjoyed more. The mall near the hotel consisted of nearly fifty stores, of which twenty sold clothing, and they made it a matter of pride to visit each and every one. When they were back in the hotel, their arms laden with packages, Sherry discovered they'd bought something in more than half the stores they'd ventured into.

Heather was thrilled with her purchases. She removed the merchandise from the bags and spread the outfits over the twin beds in their room, quickly running out of space. The overflow spilled out onto the sofa and love seat in the living room. Two pairs of crisp jeans and several brightly colored blouses. A couple of jersey pullovers and a lovely soft cardigan. Two bras—the right size for Heather's still-developing figure—and matching panties. Sherry had talked Heather into buying a couple of dresses, too, although the girl insisted the only place she'd ever wear them was to church. Their biggest extravagance had been footwear—five pairs altogether. Boots, sneakers, dress shoes—to go with her Sunday dresses—a sturdy pair for school and a fun pair of bedroom slippers.

Sherry wasn't immune to spending money on herself, and she'd purchased a lovely black crepe evening dress. The top was studded with rhinestone chips that flashed and glittered in the light. Heaven only knew where she was going to wear it, but she'd been unable to resist.

"I have an idea!" Heather announced. "Let's dress up really nice for dinner. I'll wear my dress and new shoes and you can wear *your* new dress, and then we'll go down and order lobster for dinner and charge it to the room so Dad'll pay for it."

An elegant dinner to celebrate their success held a certain appeal—and gave Sherry an unexpected chance to wear her new finery—but charging it to the room didn't seem fair to Cody. "I don't know, Heather..."

"Dad won't mind," Heather assured her. "He's grateful you're willing to shop with me, and he'll be even more pleased now that I have bras that fit me. So, come on—what do you think?"

"I think dinner's a marvelous idea." They could work out the finances later.

"Great." Heather rummaged through the bags stacked on Sherry's bed until she found what she was looking for. "We should do our nails first, though, shouldn't we?"

They'd discovered the hottest shade of pink fingernail polish Sherry had ever seen. Heather had fallen in love with it and convinced Sherry her life wouldn't be complete without it.

"Our hair, too."

"Why not?" If they were going to do themselves up fancy there was no point in half measures. Heather was filled with such boundless enthusiasm Sherry couldn't help being infected with it, too.

Using jasmine-scented bubble bath, Sherry soaked in the tub, washed her hair and piled it high on her head in a white towel. Wrapping herself in a thick terry-cloth robe supplied by the hotel, she rendezvoused with Heather, who'd made use of the second bathroom, back in the living room.

Heather, also wrapped in a thick terry-cloth robe, eagerly set the bottle of hot-pink polish on the table.

"Only for our toes, not our fingers," Sherry instructed.

Heather was clearly disappointed, but she nodded. She balanced one foot then the other against the edge of the coffee table, and Sherry painted her toenails, then had Heather paint hers. They were halfway through this ritual when the key turned in the lock. They both looked up to see Cody stroll casually into the room.

"Dad!" Heather bounded to her feet and raced over to her father. "We had a fabulous day. Wait'll you see what we bought."

Cody set down his briefcase and hugged his daughter. "I take it you had a fun afternoon."

"It was wild. I spent oodles of money. Sherry did, too. She bought this snazzy black dress with diamonds on top, not real ones of course, but they look real. It wasn't on sale, either, but she said she had to have it. When you see her in it, you'll know why."

Cody didn't comment on that. His gaze narrowed when he noticed his daughter's feet. "What have you done to your toes?"

"Isn't it great?" Heather said rhapsodically, wiggling her toes for his inspection.

"Will they make your feet glow in the dark?"

"No, silly!"

Sherry finished painting the last of her own toenails and screwed the top back on the bottle of polish. "We were going to dress up in our new outfits and go downstairs and have dinner in the dining room," she said. "That's all right, isn't it?"

"Anything you want. Dinner's on me."

"Even lobster?" Heather asked, as though she wasn't entirely sure how far his generosity would stretch.

"Even lobster. I just sold off the main part of my herd for the best price I've gotten in years."

"Congratulations." Sherry stood and tightened the cinch of her robe.

"Then you're all through with your business stuff?" Heather asked.

"I'm finished."

"That's even better! You'll join us for dinner, right? You don't mind if Dad comes, do you, Sherry?"

Cody's eyes connected with Sherry's and his smile was slightly cocky, as if to suggest the ball was in her court.

"Of course I don't mind." There wasn't anything else she could say.

"You'll wear your slinky new dress," Heather insisted. "Dad," she turned her attention to her father "—your eyeballs are going to pop out of your head when you see Sherry in it."

Cody's gaze was on his daughter when he spoke. "It's too late for that. They popped out of my head the first minute I saw her."

Six

Sherry wasn't sure why she felt so nervous. Maybe it had something to do with her new outfit. She had a feeling it was a mistake to wear that particular dress with this particular man.

She arranged her glossy brown hair carefully, piling it on top of her head with dangling wisps at her temples and neck. She wished she could tame her heart just as easily. She tried not to place any credence on this evening out, tried to convince herself it was just a meal between friends. That's all they were. Friends. The promise of more had been wiped away from everyplace but her heart. Yet none of her strategies were succeeding. They hadn't even come close to succeeding. She was falling in love with this no-nonsense cattleman, despite the fact there wasn't a romantic bone in his body.

When they'd finished dressing, the three of them met back in the living room. Sherry endured—or was it thrilled to?—Cody's scrutiny. The dress was modest, sleeveless with a dropped waist. The skirt flared out at her hips in a triple layer of sleek ruffles. The high-heeled black sandals were the perfect complement.

"Doesn't Sherry look like a million bucks?" Heather asked.

Without taking his eyes from Sherry, Cody nodded. "Very nice."

"Heather, too," Sherry said.

Cody seemed chagrined that he needed to be reminded to compliment his daughter. His eyes widened with appreciation as he gazed at his daughter.

"Heather," he murmured. "Why…you seem all grown-up."

"I'm nearly thirteen, you know, and that means I'm almost a woman."

"You certainly look like one in that pretty dress." The glance he flashed at Sherry was filled with surprised gratitude. He seemed to be asking how she'd managed to convince his daughter to buy something other than jeans and cowboy boots.

Seeing Cody in a smart sport jacket with a crisp blue shirt and a string tie had a curious effect on Sherry. She couldn't look at him and not be stirred. As much as she hated to admit it, he was a handsome devil. When they'd first met, she'd been struck by the sense of strength and authority she sensed in him. Those same traits were more prominent than ever now.

"Are we going to dinner, or are we going to stand around and stare at each other all evening?" Heather said bluntly, looking from her father to Sherry and then back again.

"By all means, let's eat," Cody put in.

"Yes, let's." Sherry was surprised by how thin and wavery her voice sounded. Apparently she wasn't the only one who noticed, because Heather cast her a curious look, then grinned broadly.

Dinner was an elegant affair. The small dining room was beautifully decorated with antique fixtures and furnishings. The tables were covered with crisp, white linen tablecloths, and the lights were muted. Both Heather and Sherry ordered the lobster-tail dinner while Cody opted for a thick T-bone steak. When a three-piece musical ensemble started to play, Heather glanced at both her father and Sherry.

"You're going to dance, aren't you?" she said.

"The music is more for mood than dancing," Sherry explained, although she wouldn't have objected if Cody had offered. But she knew he didn't much care for dancing, so an offer wasn't likely.

Their salads arrived, all Caesars with big crusty croutons. Heather fairly gobbled hers, and when Sherry looked her way, silently suggesting she eat more slowly, the girl wiped the dressing from the corner of her mouth and shrugged. "I'm too hungry to linger over my food the way you and Dad seem to want to."

Sherry's appetite was almost nil, a stark contrast to an hour earlier—before Cody had returned to the suite. She was almost sorry he was with them, because she couldn't seem to enjoy her food. But although she was uncomfortably aware of his presence, she was still glad to be sharing this time with him and Heather.

Their entrées arrived, and Sherry was grateful to Heather, who singlehandedly carried the dinner conversation. She chattered almost nonstop between bites of lobster, relating the details of the afternoon. Cody concentrated almost entirely on his food, occasionally murmuring a brief response to his daughter's recitations.

But whatever was happening between Cody and her, if indeed anything was, felt strange to Sherry. Cody seemed withdrawn from her both physically and emotionally. A sort of sultry tension filled the air about them, as if they were both waging battles against themselves, against the strong pull of the attraction they shared. Thank goodness, she thought, for Heather's easy banter.

Sherry barely touched her meal, but nothing went to waste, because after Heather downed her own dinner, she polished off what remained of Sherry's.

When their dinner plates had been taken away and Heather was waiting for the blueberry-swirl cheesecake she'd ordered, Sherry excused herself and retreated to the ladies' room. She applied fresh lipstick and lingered. She was uncertain of so many things. Cody had told her how much he *didn't* want to be attracted to her, and she'd found his words faintly insulting. Now she understood. She was attracted to him, and she didn't like it, either, didn't know how to deal with it. What troubled her most was that she seemed to be weakening toward him. She'd always thought of herself as strong-willed, but now her defenses were crumbling. She feared that, as the evening progressed, it would become increasingly difficult to hide her feelings—and that could prove disastrous.

Sherry had rejected his less-than-flattering proposal. Cody made it sound as if he was too busy rounding up cattle to date her properly. But it was much more than that. He wasn't willing to make an emotional commitment to her and their relationship, and Sherry would accept nothing less.

She was on her way back into the dining room when a tall, vaguely familiar-looking man approached her. His eye caught hers, and he hesitated a moment before speaking.

"Excuse me," he said, smiling apologetically, "but don't I know you?"

Sherry studied him, sharing the same feelings, but

unable to decide where or when she'd met him. "I'm not from this area," she said. "This is my first time in Abilene."

He frowned and introduced himself, but that didn't help. "It'll come to me. Do I look familiar to you?"

Sherry studied him. "A little, but I can't place you."

"Or me you. I'm sorry to have disturbed you."

"No problem."

When she reached the table, Cody's eyes were filled with questions. "Do you know that man?"

"I'm not sure. He said his name was Jack Burnside." She paused. "He thought we'd met before. We might have, but neither of us can remember when or where. I'm generally good about remembering people. It's a little embarrassing."

Cody snickered. "Don't you know a come-on when you hear one? That guy's never met you—he was just looking for an excuse to introduce himself. His ploy's as old as the hills. I thought you were smarter than that."

"Apparently not," Sherry admitted, refusing to allow Cody the pleasure of irritating her.

"I think you should dance with Sherry," Heather suggested once more, glancing at the minuscule dance floor where several other couples were swaying to the music.

"I'm sure your father would rather we—"

"As it happens, I'd be more than happy to give it a try." Cody's gaze seemed to hold a challenge.

Sherry blinked. Cody had managed to surprise her once again. She stood when he pulled out her chair. His hand felt warm at the small of her back as he guided her to the polished wooden floor.

He turned her into his arms with a bit of flair, causing

her skirt to fan out from her knees. Then he brought her close to him, so close she was sure she could feel his heart beating.

Sherry wasn't fooled; she knew exactly what he was doing, although she doubted he'd ever admit it. He hadn't asked her to dance because of any great desire to twirl her around the floor, but to make sure Jack Burnside understood she was with him. He was placing his brand on her.

His attitude angered her, yet in some odd way pleased her, too. She was gratified to realize the attraction was mutual.

While Cody may have escorted her onto the dance floor to indicate clearly she was with *him*, Sherry was convinced he was as unprepared as she was for the impact of the physical closeness. His hold on her gradually grew more possessive. His hand slid upward from the dip of her waist until his fingers were splayed across her back. Of its own volition, her head moved closer to his until her temple rested against the lean strength of his jaw. Her eyes drifted closed, and she breathed in the scent of spicy after-shave. The music was pleasant, easy and undemanding. Romantic.

As soon as she realized what she was doing, allowing herself to be drawn into the magic of the moment, she pulled her head away from his and concentrated on the music. Cody didn't attempt anything beyond a mere shuffling of his feet, which suited Sherry just fine.

She quickly saw her mistake. With her head back, their eyes inevitably met, and neither seemed inclined to look away. They continued to gaze at each other, attempting to gauge all that remained unspoken between them. The longer they continued to stare at each other the more awkward it became. Warm seconds ripened into warmer minutes....

It was Sherry who could bear it no longer, who was the first to look away. Cody's hand eased her head back toward his, and she sighed as her temple again unerringly came to rest against his jaw. Her eyes had just drifted shut when, out of the blue, she remembered where she'd met Jack Burnside.

"College," she said abruptly, freeing herself from Cody's embrace. She glanced about the restaurant until she spotted Jack. "I do know him," she said. "We met in Seattle several years ago." Taking Cody by the hand, she led him off the dance floor to a table at the far side of the restaurant, where Jack was eating alone. He stood at their approach.

"Jack," she said, slightly breathless, "you're right, we do know each other. I'm Sherry Waterman. Your sister and I were roommates in our junior year at college. You were in Seattle on business and took us both to dinner. That must have been eight or more years ago now."

Jack's face broke into a wide grin. "Of course. You're Angela's friend. I was certain we'd met."

"Me, too, but I couldn't remember where."

"So, how are you?"

"Fine," Sherry replied, "I'm living in Texas now."

"As a matter of fact, so am I. Small world, isn't it?" His gaze moved fleetingly to Cody.

"Very small," Sherry agreed.

Jack seemed especially pleased to have made the connection. "I never forget a face, especially one as pretty as yours."

Sherry blushed at the compliment. "This is Cody Bailman."

The two men exchanged brisk handshakes. "Please join me," Jack invited, gesturing toward the empty chairs at his table.

"Thanks, but no," said Cody. "My daughter is with us and she's rather shy. She'd be uncomfortable around a stranger, I'm afraid." Cody refused to meet Sherry's baffled glance. Heather—shy?

The three of them spoke briefly for a few minutes longer, and then Sherry and Cody returned to their table and an impatient Heather.

Sherry knew that the reason she'd dragged Cody off the dance floor was more than the opportunity to prove she was right about Jack. It was a means of breaking the romantic spell they'd found themselves under. Cody had made her feel vulnerable, and she'd seized the opportunity to show him she was not.

"Who were you talking to?" Heather asked, craning her neck. "I didn't think you two were ever going to come back."

"The man who approached me earlier," said Sherry. "I remembered who he was, so we went over to speak to him. He's a friend of mine. Actually, his sister and I are friends. Jack and I only met once."

"Apparently your time with him was memorable," said Cody. Sherry caught the hint of sarcasm in his voice and was amused.

He paid the tab, and the three of them began to head out of the dining room. Cody glanced in Jack's direction, then back to Sherry, and said stiffly, "You're welcome to stay and visit with your friend, if you like."

"I've visited enough, thanks," she said, following him and Heather to the elevators.

They weren't back in the suite more than thirty seconds before Heather changed out of her dress and into her pajamas and new fuzzy slippers. The girl plopped herself down in front of the television set, studying the movie guide. She checked out her selection with Cody, who gave his approval.

Sherry changed out of the evening gown and into a comfortable pair of jeans and a cotton T-shirt, then wandered back into the living room to sit on the sofa with Heather. Her mind wasn't on the first-run movie the girl had opted for; it was on Cody and what had transpired between them while they were dancing.

When they'd left Pepper, the emotional distance between them had felt as wide and deep as the Grand Canyon. Now she wasn't sure what to think. She glanced at him. He was sitting at the table, with his briefcase open in front of him. He reached for the phone and ordered a pot of coffee from room service.

What made matters so difficult was how strongly she was attracted to him. It saddened her to realize there was little chance for a truly loving relationship between them. His life was ranching. He needed a woman in his life to appease Heather—though certainly there were beneficial side effects. It wouldn't be a one-sided relationship. Cody would be generous with her in every way except the one that mattered. With himself.

Sherry wanted a man who cherished her, a man who was willing to do whatever was necessary to win her heart, even if it meant courting her during the busiest time of the year. She wanted a husband who would withhold none of himself from her. And Cody couldn't offer that.

"Something troubling you?" he asked, looking up from his paperwork.

The question snapped her out of her reverie. "No," she said abruptly. "What makes you ask?"

"You look like you're about to cry."

Strangely that was exactly how she felt. She managed a chuckle. "Don't be silly."

Heather fell asleep halfway through the movie. When Cody noticed his daughter had curled up on the sofa and nestled her head in Sherry's lap, he stood, and turned off the TV after a nod from Sherry, and gently lifted the twelve-year-old into his arms. Heather stirred and opened her eyes as if she wanted to scold him for treating her like a little girl, but she must have thought better of it for she let him carry her to bed.

Sherry pulled back the covers, and Cody gently placed his daughter, who seemed to have fallen right back to sleep, on the mattress. Silently they moved from the room and then paused as if each was suddenly aware they were now alone.

Luckily Sherry had remembered to bring a book along with her, and she opted to sit on the couch and bury herself in it. Although Cody sat at the table to the side, busy with his own affairs, Sherry had never been more aware of him. Agreeing to the suite had been a mistake. She should have insisted upon two rooms on different floors.

"Would you like some coffee?" Cody's question cut into the silence.

"No, thanks." If it wasn't so early, she'd make her excuses and go to bed too, but it would look ridiculous for her to turn in at nine-thirty.

Unexpectedly Cody released a beleaguered sigh. "All right," he said, "let's air this once and for all and be done with it."

"Air what?" she asked, innocently.

"What's happening between us."

"I wasn't aware anything was now."

He closed his briefcase with a deliberate lack of haste, then stood and walked over to the sofa. He sat down on the end opposite her, as far removed from her as he could get and still be on the same piece of furniture. "I've had more than a week to give your rejection of my proposal ample consideration."

Sherry spoke softly. "I shouldn't have said what I did."

He brightened and cocked his head as if he thought it was about time she'd shown some sense. "You mean you've changed your mind and decided to marry me?"

"No." She didn't like to be so blunt, but it seemed the only way to reach Cody. "I regret saying I'd rather eat fried rattlesnake."

"Oh." His shoulders slumped. "I should have known it wouldn't be that easy," he muttered. He reached for a pen and pad. "All right, I'd like to know exactly what it is you find so objectionable about me."

"Nothing, really. You're honest, hardworking, trustworthy. My grandmother, if she were alive, would call you a salt-of-the-earth kind of guy, and I'd agree with her. It would be very easy to fall in love with you, Cody. Sometimes I think I already have, and that terrifies me."

"Why?" His expression was sincere.

"Because you don't love me."

His face fell. "I *like* you. I'm attracted to you. That's a hell of a lot more than many other couples start out with."

"Love frightens you, doesn't it? You lost Heather's mother, and you've guarded your heart ever since."

"Don't be ridiculous." He stood and walked to the window, stuffing his hands in his pants pockets and staring out at the night. His back was to her, but that didn't prevent Sherry from hearing the pain in his voice. "Karen died ten years ago. I hardly even remember what she looked like anymore." He turned to gaze at her. "That's the problem with you women. You read a few magazine articles and romance novels and then think you're experts on relationships."

"You loved her, didn't you?"

"Of course, and I grieved when she died."

"You opted not to remarry," she told him softly, afraid of agitating him further.

"I didn't have the time, and to be truthful, my life was plenty full without letting a woman dominate my time. That's why I want to set the record straight right now. I'm not about to let a wife put a collar around my neck and lead me around like a puppy."

"Karen did that?"

"No." He scowled fiercely. "But I've seen it happen to plenty of other men, including Luke."

"Ellie doesn't seem the type to do such a thing."

Cody frowned. "I know—Luke put the collar around his own neck." He walked over to the table, made a notation on the pad and glanced her way. "I was thinking you and I might reach some sort of compromise."

"Is that possible?"

"I don't know," he answered. "But it might be if we try."

"Before we go any further, I want it understood I have no intention of changing who you are, Cody. That's not what marriage is about."

His look told her he didn't believe her. Sherry, however, had no intention of arguing with him. He'd believe whatever he wanted.

"Already this isn't working," Cody said, brushing the hair from his face in an agitated movement. "I was hoping to make a list, so I'd know exactly what it is you want from me.''

''For what?''

He slapped the pen he still held on top of the table. ''So we can be done with this foolishness and get married!''

She hadn't meant to be obtuse, but their conversation had taken so many twists she wasn't clear on exactly what it was they were discussing.

''You still want to marry me?''

''Obviously, otherwise I wouldn't be willing to make a fool of myself a second time.''

''Why?'' she asked, genuinely curious.

''Damned if I know,'' he snapped. He took a moment to compose himself and come to grips with his temper. ''Because I like the way you feel in my arms. I like the way you taste. Your mouth is sweet, and kissing you reminds me of eating an orange when it's ripe and juicy. It's the kind of kiss a man could get addicted to.''

''That's all?'' she asked.

''No. I also want to marry you because my daughter clearly adores you. On top of that, you're not hard on the eyes, you're intelligent and well-read.''

''Ah,'' Sherry said.

Her response seemed to succeed in making him angrier. ''Dammit, there's electricity between us—you can't deny it.''

This man had the most uncanny way of insulting her with compliments. He made it impossible for her to be angry, and luckily she was more amused than offended.

''We've only kissed on two occasions,'' she reminded him.

"Only two?" He sounded as if that were impossible. "Well, honey, I guess you pack quite a wallop."

Sherry decided to accept that as a compliment, and she smiled softly. He was in front of her suddenly, his hands reaching for hers, drawing her up so that she stood before him. "I can't stop thinking about how good you taste," he whispered. His mouth was mere inches from her own.

A kiss, Sherry realized, would muddle her reasoning processes, but then again, they were already so tangled it shouldn't matter.

He pulled her closer. For one crazy moment all they did was stare at each other. Then Cody spoke. "It's been a hell of a long time since I've kissed a woman the way I want to kiss you." His words were low and heavy with need.

"I'm not afraid," Sherry said simply.

"Maybe not, but I sure as hell am." His arms went around her, folding her into his chest. How right this felt, Sherry thought. How perfectly their bodies fit together, as if they'd been crafted for one another.

His voice was ragged and oddly breathless when he instructed. "You kiss me."

Sherry didn't hesitate, not for an instant. She placed her hands on either side of his head and drew it down toward hers. Their lips met in an uncomplicated kiss. Sweet, gentle, undemanding. Then it changed in intensity. What had seemed so sweet and simple a moment earlier took on a magnitude and power that left her head swimming and her lungs depleted of air.

Cody groaned and his mouth slanted hard over hers. Sherry felt herself opening up to him in ways she never had before. Her mouth opened to him, her arms and, most frightening of all, her heart.

This wasn't the type of kiss that burned itself out, that made the gradual transformation from passionate to a series of sweet pecks. This kiss was a long way from being complete before it grew too hot, too heady for either of them to handle.

Sherry wasn't sure who moved first, but they broke apart and stepped back. Space, she needed space, and from the look of him, so did Cody. Sherry's chest was heaving, her heart pounding, and her emotions threatened to fly out of control.

Cody spoke first. "I think," he said raggedly, "that it's a fair assumption to say we're sexually compatible."

Sherry nodded mutely. This brief experiment with the physical realm of their relationship proved to be more potent than she'd thought possible. She raised her trembling fingers to her lips and investigated them for herself.

Suddenly, standing seemed to require a great amount of energy, so Sherry moved back to the sofa and sat, hoping she looked composed and confident. She felt neither.

Cody waited a moment, then joined her as he had earlier—on the far end of the sofa where there wasn't any possibility of them accidentally touching.

He reached for the same pad and pencil. "Thus far your main objection to our marrying is..." He hesitated, then reviewed his notes and set aside the pad as if all this was beyond him.

"I want to be sure of something," Sherry said when she was reasonably sure her voice would sound even and steady. "Heather's 4-H project."

Cody's gaze shot to hers, and she read the remorse in their dark depths.

"This sudden desire for a wife—does it have anything to do with that?"

His shoulders squared defensively. "Yes and no. To be fair, I hadn't given much thought to marrying again until this past year, and Heather had a lot to do with that decision. She's at the age now when she needs someone's influence other than Janey's. Someone younger. She realized it herself, I think, before I did. Otherwise she wouldn't have come up with that crazy project idea."

"I see." Sherry found the truth painful, but was pleased he hadn't lied.

"But that doesn't mean anything. I didn't meet you and immediately decide you'd be a perfect mother for Heather. I looked at you and decided you were perfect wife for *me,* with one exception."

"What's that?"

"You want everything sugar-coated."

"Cody, it's much more than that."

He shook his head. "I'm not the type to decorate something with a bunch of fancy words. Nor do I have the time to persuade you I'm decent enough to be your husband. If you haven't figured that out by now, then flowers and candy ain't going to do it."

"Don't be so sure," she teased.

"That's what you want, is it?" He was frowning so mightily, his lips were white.

"I want a man who's willing to make an emotional commitment to me, and that includes time to come to know one another properly. I'm not willing to settle for anything less. If you're serious about marrying me, Cody Bailman, then you're going to have to prove to me you're sincere. I'm not willing to accept some…some offhand proposal."

Cody muttered something under his breath that Sherry couldn't catch, but from the look of him it was just as well she didn't.

"You're looking for romance, aren't you?" he asked.

"That and much more," she told him, her tone intense. "I need to know I'm important to you, that this attraction isn't just a passing thing."

"I asked you to marry me, didn't I?" He sounded thoroughly disgusted. "Trust me, a man doesn't get any more serious than that."

"Perhaps not," Sherry agreed. "But a woman needs a little more than a proposal that talks about cutting to the chase and being done with it."

"You want me down on one knee with my heart on my sleeve, telling you I couldn't survive without you?"

She considered that for a moment. "That would be a good start."

"I thought so." Cody stood and marched over to his briefcase. He cast his pen and pad inside, then slammed down the lid. "Well, you can forget it. I'm willing to compromise, but that's as far as it goes. Take it or leave it, the choice is up to you."

Sherry closed her eyes to her mounting frustration. "I believe we've both made our choices."

Seven

Sherry sat in a booth at the Yellow Rose, sipping coffee and mulling over the events of the weekend in Abilene. Doubts assailed her from all sides. Twice now, her heart in her throat, she'd rejected Cody's marriage proposal.

The irony of the situation didn't escape her. For years she'd longed for a husband and family. She'd been looking for a change in her life. This was the very reason she'd uprooted herself and moved halfway across the country.

She'd been in Texas less than a month, and in that time she'd been held captive by a community, helped deliver a beautiful baby boy and received a marriage proposal. This was some kind of state.

Cody. She wished she could think clearly about him. That she'd meet a man who attracted her so powerfully came as a shock. That he should feel equally captivated by her was an unexpected bonus.

Donna Jo strolled over to the booth and refilled her coffee. "You're looking a little under the weather," the friendly waitress commented. "How'd your weekend with Cody and Heather go?"

It was no surprise that Donna Jo knew she'd spent the weekend with the Bailmans. "We had a lot of fun."

Donna Jo set the glass pot on the table and pressed

her hands into her hips. She shifted her weight from one foot to the other as if what she had to say was of momentous importance. "Take my word, honey, that man's sweet on you."

Sherry's only response was a weak smile. "I heard about Heather's 4-H project. That's what you and Mrs. Colson wanted me to find out on my own, wasn't it?"

Donna Jo did a poor job of hiding her amusement. "I wondered how long it'd take for you to learn about that. Cody's kid's got a good head on her shoulders. Heather figured that suggesting she find him a wife herself guaranteed her father's attention, and by golly she was right." Donna Jo laughed at the memory. "Cody was shocked. He's lived so long without a woman that I don't think remarrying so much as entered his mind. You're sweet on him, too, aren't you?'

"He's a good man." Sherry tried to sound noncommittal.

"Cody's one of the best. He can be cantankerous, but then he wouldn't be a man if he wasn't. Now, I don't have any dog in this fight, but—"

Sherry stopped her. "You don't have a dog? They fight dogs in Texas?"

"Of course not. It's an old Texan saying, meaning I don't have a stake in what happens between you and Cody. I've been married a whole lot of years myself, and personally I'd like to see Cody find himself a decent wife." Her smile widened. "Folks in the Yellow Rose been talking about you two, and everyone agrees Cody should marry you. Are we going to have a fall wedding?"

"Uh…"

"Leave Doc's helper alone," the sheriff called out

from his perch at the counter, ''and bring that coffee over here.''

''Hold your horses, Billy Bob. This is the kind of information folks come into the Yellow Rose for. Trust me, it isn't the liver-and-onion special they're after, it's gossip, and everyone wants to know what's happening between Cody and Sherry.''

It seemed everyone in the café was staring at Sherry, expecting a response.

''I hear you and Heather traveled with him to Abilene.'' The sheriff said, twisting around to face her. ''That sounds promising. Right promising.''

''Sure does,'' someone else agreed.

''The way I see it,'' said a second man—Sherry hadn't formally met him, but she knew he was the local minister ''—a man wasn't meant to be alone, a woman neither. Now I know there're plenty of folks who'd argue with me, but it seems if you're both wanting the same thing, then you should get on with it.''

With everyone looking at her so expectantly, Sherry felt obligated to say something, anything. ''I… Thanks for the advice. I'll take it into consideration.'' She couldn't get out of the café fast enough. It seemed everyone had a curious question or some tidbit of wisdom.

By the time Sherry reached the clinic, she regretted opening her mouth. She had no idea so many people would be interested in what was happening between her and Cody.

Mrs. Colson looked up from her desk when Sherry came through the front door. ''Good morning,'' the receptionist greeted cheerfully, her gaze full of questions.

''Morning,'' Sherry said, hurrying past. Her eagerness to escape didn't go unnoticed.

"How was your weekend with Cody and Heather?" Mrs. Colson craned her neck and called after her.

"Great." Sherry reached behind the examination room door for her jacket and was buttoning up the front when the receptionist let herself in. "I heard first thing this morning that Cody popped the question. I don't even think Donna Jo's heard this yet. Is it true?"

Sherry's hands fumbled with the last button and her heart zoomed straight to her knees. "Who told you that?"

"Oh, you know—the grapevine."

"You should know by now how unreliable that can be," Sherry said as unemotionally as she could, unwilling to swallow the bait.

Mrs. Colson wiggled her brows. "Not this time. My source is pure as the driven snow. I have my ways of learning certain things."

"This town's worse than Orchard Valley," Sherry muttered. "I barely know Cody Bailman. What makes you think he'd ask a casual acquaintance to marry him, and furthermore, what makes you assume I'd accept?"

"Casual acquaintance, is it?" Mrs. Colson asked, tapping her index finger against her lips. "It seems to me you know him well enough to dance cheek to cheek in some fancy hotel restaurant, don't you?"

"You know about that, too?" Sherry's lower jaw dropped. "Is nothing sacred in this town?"

"Morning." Doc Lindsey strolled into the room, and spying Sherry, he paused and grinned broadly. "I hear you're marrying Cody Bailman. He's a damn good man. He'll make you a good husband." He patted Sherry's back and sauntered out of the room.

Sherry balled her hands into fists and looked toward the ceiling while she counted to ten. Apparently the folks in Pepper had nothing better to do than speculate on Cody's love life.

"Cody's waited a long time to find the right woman," Mrs. Colson stated matter-of-factly on her way out the door. "I only hope his stubbornness doesn't ruin everything."

"Mrs. Colson," Sherry said, placing the stethoscope around her neck. "I don't mean to be rude or unfriendly, but I'd rather not discuss my personal affairs with you or Donna Jo, or Billy Bob or anyone else."

"The mayor's got a good ear if you change your mind."

Sherry grit her teeth in her effort not to lose her temper. Something was going to have to be said, and soon; the situation was getting totally out of hand.

Sherry saw several patients that morning, the majority for physicals before the start of the school year, which was only a week away. Rather than risk another confrontation with Donna Jo and the lunch crowd at the Yellow Rose, she ordered a chef salad and had it delivered.

At one, Mrs. Colson ushered her into Doc's office, where a tall, regal-looking older woman in a lovely blue suit was waiting for her. The woman's hair was white with a smattering of gray, and she wore it in an elegant French roll.

"Hello," Sherry said. The woman sat, her legs crossed at the ankle, her designer purse clenched in her lap.

"You must be Sherry. I'm Judith Bailman, Cody's mother. I've made the trip from Dallas to meet you."

Sherry felt an overwhelming urge to sit down. "I'm pleased to make your acquaintance, Mrs. Bailman."

"The pleasure is mine. I understand there are several items we need to discuss."

For the life of her, Sherry couldn't make her mouth work. She twisted around and pointed toward the door in a futile effort to explain that she was on duty. Unfortunately, no patients were waiting at the moment.

"Mrs. Colson's arranged for us to have several minutes of privacy, so you needn't worry we'll be interrupted."

"I see." Sherry claimed Doc's chair, on the other side of the desk, nearly falling into it. "What can I do for you, Mrs. Bailman?"

"I understand my son's proposed to you?" She eyed Sherry speculatively.

Sherry didn't mean to sound curt, but after everything else that had happened that day, she was in no mood to review her private life with anyone. "I believe that's between Cody and me."

"I quite agree. I don't mean to be nosy. I hope you'll forgive me. It's just that Cody's been single all these years, so I couldn't help getting excited when Heather mentioned—"

"Heather?" Sherry interrupted. That explained everything.

"Why, yes. My granddaughter phoned me first thing this morning." A smile tempted the edges of her mouth. "She's concerned her father's going to ruin her best chance at being a big sister, and knowing my son, I strongly suspect she's right."

"Mrs. Bailman—"

"Please, call me Judith."

"Judith," Sherry said, "don't get me wrong, I think the world of Cody and Heather. Your son did ask me to marry him in a sort of offhand cavalier way."

The woman's mouth tightened. "That sounds like Cody."

"If you must know, I turned him down. Cody makes marriage sound about as appealing as a flu shot."

Judith laughed softly. "I can see I'm going to like you, Sherry Waterman."

"Thank you." She wasn't accustomed to having an entire town and now the man's mother involved in her affairs. At least when she lived in Orchard Valley, her life was mostly her own. It seemed that the minute she'd been hired to work in Pepper, her personal business was up for grabs.

"I hope you'll forgive me for being so blunt, but are you in love with Cody?"

Sherry meant to explain that she was strongly attracted to Judith's son, then add how much she respected and liked him, but instead, she found herself nodding.

The full impact of the truth took her by storm. She closed her eyes and waited several moments for the strong waves of emotion to pass.

Judith smiled and sighed with apparent relief. "I guessed as much. I tried speaking to him about you, but he refused. If the truth be known, I would have been surprised had he listened," she muttered. "That boy's more stubborn than a mule and always has been."

The description was apt, and Sherry found herself smiling.

"If he knew I was here, I don't know he'd ever forgive me, so I'm going to have to ask for your discretion."

"Of course." Sherry glanced worriedly at the door. "You needn't worry that Martha Colson will say anything. We've been friends for years.'' She sighed and looked past Sherry and out the window. ''Be patient with him, Sherry. He's closed himself off from love, and knowing him the way I do, he's fighting his feelings for you with the full strength of his will. Which, I might add, is formidable.''

How well Sherry knew. She'd bumped heads with it more than once, and each time she'd come away shaken.

''Cody deserves your love,'' Judith said softly. ''Sure he has his faults, but believe me, the woman my son loves will be happy. When he falls in love again, it'll be with his whole heart and soul. It may take some time, but I promise you the wait will be well worth the effort.''

Sherry wasn't sure how to respond. ''I'll remember that.''

''Now—'' Judith gave a deep sigh and stood ''—I must be on my way. Remember, not a word of my visit to either my son or granddaughter.''

''I promise.''

Judith hugged her and said softly. ''Be patient with Cody. He'll make you a wonderful husband.''

''I'll try,'' Sherry promised.

Cody's mother left by the back door. When Mrs. Colson returned, her sparkling eyes met Sherry's and she said, ''This visit will be our little secret.''

''What visit?'' she answered.

FRIDAY EVENING, Sherry sat out on the porch in front of the clinic enjoying the coolness. The wooden bench swung gently in the breeze, creaking now and again. Crickets telegraphed greetings to one another, the sound almost musical in the still of the night.

Evenings were her favorite time. Sherry loved to sit outside and think about her day. Her life was falling into a pattern now as she adjusted to the good people of Pepper. Often she read, or wrote letters home, mentioning as Norah had done the peculiarities she saw in day-to-day life in the Lone Star state. No doubt she was the peculiar one with her Northern ways, but folks here had accepted her readily. Norah's birthday was coming up soon, and Sherry had spent the earlier part of the evening writing her a long, chatty letter.

Her heart seemed to skip a beat when Cody's pickup eased to a stop in front of the clinic. She stood and walked over to the steps, leaning against the support beam while he climbed out of the cab and came toward her.

"Hi, Sherry," he said, looking a bit sheepish. He stopped in front of the gate.

"Hi, Cody."

He stared at her for several seconds as if trying to remember the purpose of his visit. Sherry decided to make it easier for him. "Would you care to sit a spell?" She motioned toward the swing.

"Don't mind if I do." He'd recently shaved and the familiar scent of his after-shave floated past her as he moved to the swing.

They sat side by side, swaying gently back and forth. Neither seemed eager to talk.

"I was on my way to playing poker with a few friends," he said at last, "when I saw you sitting here."

"I do most evenings. Nights are so beautiful. I love stargazing. It's one of the reasons I'd never be happy in a big city. Sometimes the sky's so full it's impossible to look away."

"Have you had a good week?" he asked.

"A busy one. What about you?"

"The same." His gaze found hers. "Any problems?"

"Such as?"

He shrugged and looked past her to the street. "I thought there might have been some talk about, you know, us."

"There was definitely some heavy speculation after our trip last weekend."

"Anyone pestering you?"

"Not really. What about you?"

He laughed lightly. "You mean other than Heather and Janey?"

The bench squeaked in the quiet that followed.

"I've been thinking about what you said about romance," he admitted after a moment.

"Oh?"

"To my way of thinking, it's pure foolishness."

Sherry frowned. "So you've said." Countless times, but reminding him of that would have sounded petty and argumentative. The moment was peaceful, and she didn't want to ruin it.

"Tell me what you want and I'll do it." He said decisively, as if he was filling an order for ranching supplies.

"You want a list?"

"It'd help. I'm not much good at this sort of thing, and I'm going to need a few instructions."

Sherry turned to look at him. She pressed her hand to his cheek and held it there. "That's really very sweet, Cody. I'm touched."

"If that's the only way I can convince you to marry me, then what the hell, I'll do it. Just tell me what it is you want, so I don't waste a lot of time."

Sherry wasn't sure what to say. "I...I hate to disappoint you, but having me give you instructions would ruin it. It has to come from your heart, Cody." She moved her hand to his chest and pressed it there. "Otherwise it wouldn't be sincere."

A frown quickly snapped into place. "You want me to do a few mushy things to prove my feelings are sincere, but you aren't willing to tell me what they are?"

"You make it sound silly."

"As far as I'm concerned, it is. Damnation, woman, you seem to think I'm a mind reader. Well, I've had about all the—"

Their peace was about to be destroyed, and Sherry was unwilling to let it happen. So she acted impulsively and stopped him the only way she knew would work.

She kissed him.

The instant her mouth covered his, she felt his anger melt away. His arms gripped her shoulders and his kiss was both tender and fierce. His breath was warm and his lips hot and eager, and the kiss left her trembling.

Then he began kissing her neck, from the underside of her chin to the top of her slender shoulder. As always happened when he touched her, Sherry felt like Dorothy caught up in the tornado, her world spinning out of control, before landing in a magical land. When he raised his head from hers, she was left feeling utterly bereft.

Cody started to say something, then changed his mind. He raised his finger to her face and brushed it down her cheek. "I have to go."

She wanted him to stay, but wouldn't ask it of him.

"The fellows are waiting for me. They're counting on me."

"It's all right, Cody. I understand."

He stood and stuffed his hands in his jeans pockets, as if to stop himself from reaching for her a second time. The thought that this was probably the case helped lighten the melancholy she experienced at his leaving.

"It was good to see you again," he said stiffly.

"Good to see you, too," she returned just as stiffly.

He hesitated at the top step and turned back to face her. "Uh, you're sure you don't want to give me a few tips on, you know, romance?"

"I'm confident you aren't going to need them. Follow your heart, Cody, and I promise you it'll lead directly to mine."

He smiled, and Sherry swore she'd never seen anything sexier.

SHE DIDN'T HEAR from Cody all day Saturday, which was disappointing. She'd hoped he'd taken her words to heart and understood what she'd been trying to say.

Yes, she wanted to be wooed, courted the way women had been courted for centuries. But she also wanted to be loved. Cody was more afraid of love than he was marriage.

Late that night when she was in bed reading, she heard something or someone outside her bedroom window. At first she didn't know what to make of it. The noise was awful, loud and discordant as if someone was rocking a chair over a cat's tail. Several moments passed before she realized it was someone playing a guitar, or rather, attempting to play a guitar.

She reached over and pulled open the blinds. She stared out to see Cody standing on the lawn in front of her window, crooning for all he was worth.

"Cody," she shouted, jerking up the window and sticking out her head, "what in heaven's name are you doing?"

He started to sing even louder than before. Sherry winced. She couldn't help it. His singing was even worse than his guitar playing. Holding up the window with one hand, she covered her ear with the other.

"Cody," she shouted once more in an attempt to get him to stop.

"You wanted romance," he called back and then repeatedly strummed the guitar in a burst of energy. "Sweetheart, this comes straight from the heart, just the way you wanted."

"Have you been drinking?"

He laughed and tossed back his head, running his fingers over the guitar strings with hurried, unpracticed fingers. "You don't honestly believe I'd attempt this sober, do you?"

"Cody!"

The sound of a police siren in the background startled Sherry. It was the first time she could remember hearing it in Pepper. Apparently there was some kind of trouble, but Sherry didn't have the time to think about that now, not with Cody serenading her, sounding like a sick bull.

"Cody!" she shouted once more.

"What's the matter?" he called back. "You said you wanted romance. Well this is as good as it gets."

"Give me a minute to get dressed and I'll be right out." She started to lower the window, then thought better of it. Sticking her head out again, she brushed the hair away from her face and slowly shook her head. "Don't go away, and for the love of heaven, stop playing that guitar."

"Anything you want," he said strumming for all his worth.

Even lowering the window didn't help. Cody knew as much about guitar playing as she did about mustering cattle. Donning jeans and a light sweater, she stuffed her feet into tennis shoes and hurried out the door without bothering to brush her hair.

As she came out onto the front porch, she was gratified to realize he'd stopped playing. It wasn't until she'd reached the bottom step that she noticed the police car was parked in front of the clinic.

Hurrying around to the side of the building, she met up with Cody and a sheriff's deputy. His flashlight was zeroed in on her romantic idiot.

"Is there a problem here?" Sherry asked. She hadn't met this particular deputy, but the small gold name tag above his shirt pocket read Steven Bean.

"No problem, isn't that right, Mr. Bailman?"

"None whatsoever," Cody said, looking as sober as a judge. If it wasn't for the cocky smile he wore, it would have been impossible to know he'd been drinking. "I only had a couple of shots of whiskey," he explained. "It was necessary, or else I'd never have had the guts to pull this off."

"Are you arresting Mr. Bailman?" Sherry asked.

"We had three calls within the last five minutes," Deputy Bean explained. "The first call claimed there was a wounded animal in town. The second one came from Mayor Bowie. He said we had the authority to do whatever was necessary to put an end to that infernal racket. Those were his precise words."

"I may not be another Willie Nelson, but my singing isn't that bad," Cody protested.

"Trust me, Bailman, it's bad. Real bad."

Cody looked to Sherry for vindication. Even though he was serenading her in the name of romance, even though he was suffering this supreme embarrassment on her behalf, she couldn't bring herself to lie.

"I think it'd be better if you didn't sing again for a while," she suggested tactfully.

He gave her an injured look. "Are you going to take me to the jail?" Cody demanded.

"I could, you know," Deputy Bean told him.

"On what grounds?" Sherry challenged.

"Disturbing the peace, for starters."

"I didn't know it was unlawful to play the guitar."

"It is the way you do it," Deputy Bean muttered.

"He won't be doing it again," Sherry promised, looking to Cody for confirmation. "Right?"

"Right." Cody held up his right hand.

The Deputy sighed and lowered his flashlight. "In that case, why don't we drop the whole matter and let it go with a warning."

"Thank you," Sherry said.

The deputy started to turn away, but Cody stopped him. "Will there be a report of this in the paper on Wednesday?"

The officer shrugged. "I suppose. The *Weekly* reports all police calls."

"I'd appreciate it if you could see that this one doesn't make it to the paper."

"I can't do that, Mr. Bailman."

"Why not?"

"I'm not the one who turns the calls over to Mr. Douglas. He comes in every morning and collects them himself."

"Then make sure he doesn't have anything to collect," Cody said.

The deputy shrugged. "I'll do my best, but I'm not making any promises. After all, we got three calls, you know."

Cody waited until the patrol car had disappeared into the night before he removed his Stetson and slammed it against his leg. He stared at his mangled hat and attempted to bend it back into shape.

"I've damn near ruined the best hat I've ever had because of you," he grumbled.

"Me?"

"You heard me."

"Are you blaming me for this…this fiasco?"

"No!" he shouted back. "I'm blaming Luke. He was the one who suggested I serenade you. He claimed it didn't matter that I couldn't play the guitar or sing. He said women go crazy for this kind of thing. I should've known." He indignantly brushed off the Stetson before setting it back on his head, adjusting the angle.

"It was very sweet, Cody, and I do appreciate it."

"Sure you do. Women get a real kick out of seeing a grown man make a jackass out of himself in front of the whole town."

"That's not fair!" Sherry protested.

"I'll have you know," Cody barked, waving his arms, "I was well respected and liked in this town before you came along making unreasonable demands on me. All I want is a wife."

"*You're* being unreasonable."

Cody ignored her. "The way I see it, you're waiting for some prince to come along and sweep you away on his big white charger. Well, sweetheart, it isn't going to be me."

For a moment, Sherry was too stunned to respond. "I didn't ask you to serenade me."

"Oh, no," he said, walking away from her. He stopped in front of the gate. "That would have been too easy. On top of everything else, I'm supposed to be psychic. You won't tell me what it is you want. It's up to me to read your mind."

"That's not fair."

"You said it, not me."

"Cody—" She stopped herself, not wanting to argue with him. "Maybe it'd be best if we dropped the whole thing. You're right. I'm way out of line expecting a man who asks me to marry him to love me, too."

Cody apparently didn't hear her, or if he had, he chose to ignore her and the sarcasm. "Luke. That's where I made my mistake," he muttered. "I assumed my best friend would know all the answers, because for all his bumbling ways, he managed to woo Ellie."

"You're absolutely right," Sherry said, marching up the front steps. "You could learn a lesson or two from your friend. At least he was in love with the woman he wanted to marry and wasn't just looking for someone to warm his bed and keep his daughter content."

Cody whirled around and shook his finger at her. "You know what I think?"

"I don't know and I don't really care."

"I'm going to tell you, anyway, so listen."

She crossed her arms and heaved an exasperated sigh.

"Cancel the whole thing!" Cody shouted. "Forget I was fool enough to even ask you to marry me!"

"Cody," someone hollered in the distance. Sherry looked up in time to see a head protruding from the upstairs window of the house across the street. "Either you shut up or I'm calling the sheriff again."

"Don't worry," Cody hollered back, "I'm leaving."

Eight

"Is it true?" Heather asked the following morning as Sherry walked out of church. "Did you nearly get my dad arrested?"

Sherry closed her eyes wearily. "Did Cody tell you that?"

"No." Heather's eyes were huge and round. "I heard Mrs. Ellis telling Mrs. James about it. They said Dad was standing under your bedroom window singing and playing the guitar. I didn't even know Dad could play the guitar."

"He can't. I think you should ask your father about what happened last night," Sherry suggested, unwilling to comment further. She couldn't. Cody would find some way of blaming her.

"He didn't come to church this morning. He had Slim drive me into town because he said his head hurt."

Served him right, thought Sherry.

"School starts tomorrow," Heather announced. "Do you want to know what I'm going to wear for the first day? My acid-washed jeans, that lavender T-shirt and my new shoes."

"Sounds perfect," Sherry told her.

"I've got to go." Heather glanced across the parking lot. "Slim's in the pickup waiting. When are you going to come out to the house again? I was kind of hoping you would last week. I was thinking of having my hair cut and found this rad style in my friend Carrie's magazine. I wanted to show it to you.''

"Ask your father if you can stay after school one afternoon this week, and I'll drive you home,'' Sherry suggested. "But tell him—'' she hesitated, ''—I won't be able to stay. Be sure he knows that. I'll drop you off and be gone.''

"Okay,'' Heather said, walking backward for several steps. "That'd be really great. Do you mind if my friend Carrie comes along? She wants to meet you, too, and her ranch isn't all that far from mine.''

"Sure.''

"Thanks.'' Heather's smile rivaled the afternoon sun. "I'll call and let you know which day.''

Sherry waved and the girl raced toward the pickup. Sighing, Sherry started toward her own car. She hadn't gone more than a few steps when she heard Ellie Johnson call her.

"Sherry,'' Ellie said, walking toward her. "It's good to see you.''

"You too.''

"I've been meaning to call on you all week, but with the baby and everything else, it slipped my mind. I know it's short notice, but I'd love for you to come over to the house for dinner tonight—I've got a roast in the slow cooker. Luke's so busy these days I'm starved for companionship.''

"I'd love to.''

"That's great.'' Ellie seemed genuinely pleased. "You won't have any problems finding your way, will you?''

Sherry was sure she wouldn't. As it happened she

was eager for a bit of female companionship. With El-lie, Sherry could be herself. She didn't worry that she'd have to suffer an inquisition or make explanations for herself and Cody.

When Sherry arrived at the ranch an hour or so later, Ellie came out onto the porch to greet her. Year-old Christina Lynn was thrilled to have company, and she raced excitedly.

After giving Ellie's daughter the proper attention, Sherry asked about Philip. "He's sleeping," she was assured. "I fed him and put him down. Christina Lynn's due for her nap, too, but I promised her she could visit with you first." The friendly toddler climbed into Sherry's lap and investigated, with small probing fingers, the jeweled pin she wore.

It had been several weeks now since Sherry had spent time with Norah and her little ones, and she'd forgotten how much she enjoyed children. Christina Lynn seemed equally infatuated with her.

While Sherry devoted herself to the world of a small child, Ellie poured them tall glasses of iced tea and delivered them to the kitchen table.

"I suppose you heard what happened?" Sherry asked, needing to discuss the events of the night before. After all, there was sure to be some sort of backlash, since Cody seemed to blame Luke as much as he did her.

"There were rumors at church this morning. Is it true Cody was nearly arrested?"

"Yes. For disturbing the peace."

A smile wobbled at the edges of Ellie's mouth. "Serves him right. I'm afraid Cody Bailman has several lessons yet to learn when it comes to wooing a woman."

"I would have thought his first wife, Karen, had taught him all this."

"I never knew her, of course," Ellie said, reaching for her sweating glass, "but apparently Luke did. I asked him about her once."

"What did he tell you?" Sherry was more than curious. The key to understanding Cody was rooted in his first marriage, however brief.

"From what I remember, Cody met Karen while in college. He was away from home for the first time and lonely. Luke was surprised when he married her—at least that's what he told me. She was something of a tomboy, even at twenty. In many ways I suspect she was the perfect rancher's wife. She loved riding the range and working with the cattle. The way I hear it there wasn't anything she couldn't do." Ellie hesitated and looked away as if carefully judging her words. "Luke also said Karen wasn't much of a wife or mother. She resented having to stay home with the baby.

"From what Luke told me they had some drag-out fights about it. Karen died in a car accident after one of them. She threatened to leave Cody and Heather, but Luke doubts she was sincere. She mentioned divorce on a regular basis, dramatically packing her bags and lugging them out to the car. No one will ever know if she meant it that time or not because she took a curve too fast and ran off the road. She died instantly."

"How sad."

"I know Cody loved Karen," Ellie continued. "I admire him for picking up the pieces of his life and moving forward."

"I do, too. I didn't realize his first marriage had been so traumatic."

"It wasn't always unhappy. Don't misunderstand me. Cody cared deeply for his wife, but I don't think he was ever truly comfortable with her, if you know what I mean."

Sherry wasn't sure that she did, but she let it pass.

"He's at a loss when it comes to showing a woman how he feels now. The only woman he ever loved was so involved in herself that there was little love left over for anyone else, including him or Heather."

"He's afraid," Sherry whispered, and for none of the reasons she'd assumed. After learning he was a widower, Sherry believed he'd buried himself in his grief. Now she understood differently. Cody feared if he loved again, that love would come back to him empty and shallow.

"Be patient with him," Ellie advised.

Sherry smiled. "It's funny you should say that. A few days ago someone else said the same thing."

"Cody's so much like Luke. I'd like to shake the pair of them. Luke was the same way when we first met. He assumed that if he loved me he'd lose a part of himself. He put on this rough-and-tough exterior and was so unbelievably unreasonable that…suffice to say we had our ups and downs, as well."

"What was the turning point for you and Luke?"

Ellie leaned back in her chair, her expression thoughtful. "My first inclination is to say everything changed when I decided to leave Pepper. That's when Luke raced after my car on his horse and proposed, but it happened about a week before then." She sighed and sipped her tea. "To hear Luke tell it, we fell in love the moment we set eyes on each other. Trust me, it didn't happen like that. For most of the summer we did little more than argue. He seemed to think I was his exclusive property, which infuriated me.''

''What happened?''

''Oh, there wasn't any big climactic scene when we both realized we were destined for each other. In fact, it was something small that convinced me of his love—and eventually mine for him.

''Luke had taken me horseback riding, and I'd dared him to do something stupid. I can't even remember what it was now, but he refused, rightly so, I should add, but it made me mad, so I took off in a gallop. I'm not much of a horsewoman and hadn't gone more than a few feet before I was thrown. Luckily I wasn't hurt, but my pride had taken a beating and Luke made the tragic mistake of laughing at me.

''I was so furious I took off, deciding I'd rather walk back to the ranch than ride. Naturally, it started to rain—heavily—and I was drenched in seconds, Luke, too. I was so angry with him and myself I refused to speak to him. Finally Luke got down off his horse and walked behind me, leading the two mares. He wouldn't leave me, although heaven knew I deserved it. I thought about that incident for a long time afterward, and I realized this was the kind of man I wanted to spend the rest of my life with.''

''But you decided to leave Pepper shortly after that.''

''Yes,'' Ellie admitted cheerfully. ''It was the only way. He seemed to think marriage was something we could discuss in three or four years.''

''It's something Cody wants to discuss every three or four minutes.''

Ellie laughed. ''Do you love him?''

''Yes,'' Sherry agreed softly. ''But that's not the problem.''

"Cody's the problem. I know what you mean."

"He wants me to marry him, but he doesn't want to get emotionally involved with me. He makes the whole thing sound like a business proposition, and I'm looking for much more than a…an arrangement."

"You frighten him."

"Good, because he frightens me, too. We met that first day I arrived in town, and my life hasn't been the same since."

Ellie patted Sherry's hand. "Tell me, what's all this business about your insisting upon romance? I overheard Cody talking to Luke yesterday afternoon. I wish I could've recorded the conversation, because it was really very funny. Luke was advising Cody on a variety of ways to win your heart."

"That's the problem. Cody already has my heart. He just doesn't know what to do with it."

"Give him time," Ellie suggested. "Cody's smarter than he looks."

A little later, Sherry helped her friend with the dinner preparations. Christina Lynn awoke from her nap and gleefully "helped" Sherry arrange the silverware around the table. A few minutes before four, Luke returned home, looking hot and dusty. He kissed his wife and daughter, showered and joined them for dinner.

They sat around the big kitchen table and after the blessing, Luke, handing Sherry the bowl of mashed potatoes, said, "I understand Cody came to see you last night." He cast a triumphant smile at his wife. His cocky grin suggested that if Sherry and Cody wed anytime soon, he'd readily accept the credit for getting them together.

"Honey," Ellie said brightly, "Luke was nearly arrested for disturbing the peace. From what Sherry told me, Cody blames you.''

''Me? I wasn't the one out there making a first-class fool of myself.''

''True, but you were the one who suggested he do it.''

''That shouldn't make any difference.'' Luke ladled gravy over his meat and potatoes before reaching for the green beans. ''As long as Sherry was impressed with his romantic soul, it shouldn't matter.'' He glanced at Sherry and nodded as if to accept her gratitude.

''Well, yes, it was, uh…''

''Romantic,'' Luke supplied, looking hopeful.

''It was romantic, yes.''

''It was ridiculous,'' Ellie inserted.

''A man's willing to do ridiculous things for a woman if that's what she wants.''

''I don't, and I never said I did,'' Sherry was quick to inform the rancher. ''It bothers me that Cody would think I wanted him to do anything so…''

''Asinine,'' Ellie supplied.

''Exactly.''

Luke was grinning from ear to ear. ''Isn't love grand?''

''No, it isn't,'' a male voice boomed from the doorway. It was Cody, standing on the other side of the screen. He swung it open and stepped inside, eyeing Luke as if he was a traitor who ought to be dragged before a firing squad.

''Cody!'' Ellie greeted him warmly. ''Please join us for dinner?''

''No, thanks, I just ate. I came over to have a little

heart-to-heart with Luke. I didn't realize you had company."

"If it makes you uncomfortable, I'll leave," Sherry offered.

"Don't be silly," Ellie whispered.

Cody's gaze swung to Sherry and it seemed to bore into her very soul. He was angry; she could feel it.

"Come in and have a coffee at least," Ellie said, reaching for the pot and pouring him a cup. Cody moved farther into the kitchen and sat down at the table grudgingly.

"I suppose you heard what happened?" Cody's question was directed at Luke and filled with censure. "The next time I need advice about romance, you're the last person I'm gonna see."

Sherry did her best to concentrate on her meal and ignore both men.

"I assumed because you and Ellie were so blissfully in love," Cody went on, "you'd know the secret of keeping a woman happy."

"He does!"

Three pairs of eyes moved to Ellie. "He loves me."

"Love." Cody spat the word as if he found the very sound of it distasteful.

"That could be the reason a smart woman like Sherry hesitates to marry you," Ellie offered.

"I don't suppose she mentioned the fact I've withdrawn my offer. I've decided the whole idea of marriage is a mistake. I don't need a woman to make a fool out of me."

"Not when you do such a good job of it yourself," Ellie said dryly.

Sherry's grip on her fork tightened at the flash of

pain that went through her. It hurt her to think she'd come this close to love only to lose it.

"Anyway," Ellie went on, "I'm sorry to hear you've changed your mind, Cody." Then she grinned. "I've got apple pan dowdy for dessert. Would you care for some?"

"Apple pan dowdy?" Cody's eyes lit up. "I imagine I might find room for a small serving."

Sherry wasn't sure how Ellie arranged it, but within a matter of minutes she was alone in the kitchen with Cody. Philip began to cry and Ellie excused herself. Then Luke made some excuse to leave, taking Christina Lynn with him.

"Would you like some more coffee?" Sherry asked.

"Please."

She refilled his cup, then carried the pot back to the warmer. Never had she been more conscious of Cody than at that moment.

"Heather said something about her stopping off and visiting you one day after school." He was holding his mug with both hands and refusing to look at her.

"If you don't object."

"Hell, no. You've been the best thing to happen to that girl in a long time. I never thought it was possible to convince her to wear a dress."

"She just needed a little guidance is all." Sherry moved about the kitchen, clearing off the table and stacking dirty dishes in the sink. At last she said, "I hope that whatever happens between you and me won't affect my relationship with Heather."

"Don't see why it should. I hope you'll always be friends."

"I hope so, too."

They didn't seem to have much to say after that.

Sherry was the first one to venture into conversation again. "I'm sorry about what happened last night."

He shrugged. "I'll get over it some day." The beginnings of a smile touched his mouth. He stood then and carried his mug to the sink. "I need to get back to the ranch. Give Ellie and Luke my regards, will you?"

Sherry nodded, not wanting him to leave but unable to ask him to stay. She walked him to the door. Cody hesitated on the top step and frowned.

"It'd help matters a whole lot if you weren't so damn pretty," he muttered before turning toward his truck. His strides quickly ate up the distance.

"Cody," Sherry called after him, moving out the door and onto the top step. When he turned back to her, she wrapped her arms around her middle and said, "Now *that* was romantic."

"It was? That's the kind of thing you want me to say?"

"Yes," she said.

"But that was simple."

She smiled. "It came from the heart."

He seemed to stiffen. "The heart," he repeated, placing his hand on his chest. He opened the door of his truck, then looked back at her. "Do you want me to say things like 'God robbed heaven of one of its prettiest angels the day you were born' and mushy stuff like that?"

"That's very sweet, Cody, but it sounds like a line that's been used before."

"It has been," he admitted, his eyes warming with silent laughter. "But I figured it couldn't hurt, especially since it's true."

"Now that was nice."

With an easy grace he climbed into the pickup and

closed the door. Propping his elbow against the open window, he looked back to her once more, grinning. "Plan on staying for dinner the night you bring Heather home with you."

"All right, I will. Thanks for the invitation."

Sherry watched him drive away. The dust had settled long before she realized she wasn't alone.

"He's coming around," Ellie commented. "I don't think he realizes it himself yet, but he's falling in love with you hook, line and sinker."

It was exactly what Sherry wanted to hear. Hope blossomed within her and she sighed in contentment.

MONDAY EVENING, Sherry was again sitting in the porch swing, at the clinic, contemplating the events of the weekend. She'd written a long letter to her parents, telling them all about Cody and their rocky relationship.

When she saw his Cadillac turn the corner and pull to a stop in front of the clinic, she wasn't sure what to think. Heather leapt out of the passenger's side and raced up the walkway.

"Dad needs you!"

The girl's voice was high and excited, but her smile discounted any real emergency.

"It's nothing, dammit," Cody said, walking toward her. A box of chocolates was clenched under his arm and he held a bouquet of wildflowers, a mixture of bluebonnets and white-and-yellow daisies.

"The flowers are for you," Heather explained. "Dad picked them himself."

"If you don't mind, I prefer to do my own talking," Cody growled. He jerked up the sleeve of his shirt and started scratching at his forearm.

"Both his arms are a real mess," Heather whispered.

"Heather!" Cody barked.

"He's in one of his moods, too."

"Here," Cody said, thrusting the flowers and candy at Sherry.

Sherry was too flabbergasted to respond right away. "Thank you."

"That's real romantic, isn't it?" his daughter prompted. "Dad asked me what I thought was romantic, and I said flowers and chocolate-covered cherries. They're my favorite, and I bet you like them, too."

"I do." She returned her gaze to Cody.

"What did you get into? Why are you so itchy?"

"This is why he needs you," Heather said in a loud whisper. A cutting look from Cody silenced her.

"I picked the flowers myself. The bluebonnets are the state flower, and I thought you might like the daises. They're plentiful enough around here."

"It looks like you might have tangled with something else," she said, reaching for his arm and moving him toward the light so she could get a better view. "Oh, Cody," she whispered when she saw the redness and the swelling.

"Poison ivy," he told her.

"Let me give you something for that."

"He was hoping you would." Heather said. "He's real miserable. But we can't stay long, because I need to get over to Angela Butterfield's house and pick up my algebra book by eight o'clock."

Sherry led Cody into the clinic and brought out a bottle of calamine lotion, swabbing the worst of the swelling with that. She gave him something for the itch, as well.

Heather sat in the corner of the room, the chocolates

in her lap. "Janey says you should give Dad an *A* for effort. I think so, too." This last bit was added between bites of candy. "Did you know you can hold the chocolate in your mouth like this—" she demonstrated "—then suck the cherry out and leave the chocolate intact?"

"Heather, I didn't buy those damn chocolate-covered cherries for you," Cody said irritably.

"I know, but Sherry doesn't mind sharing them, do you?"

"Help yourself."

"She already has," Cody muttered.

Sherry put the lotion away while Cody rolled down his sleeves and snapped them closed at the wrists. "Heather, don't you have something to occupy yourself with outside?"

"No."

"Yes, you do," he said pointedly.

"I do? Oh, I get it, you want some time alone with Sherry. Gee, Dad, why didn't you just say so?"

"I want some time alone with Sherry."

"Great." Heather read her watch. "Is fifteen minutes enough, or do you need longer? Just remember I need to be at Angela's by eight."

Cody sighed expressively, and Sherry could tell his patience was tattered. "Fifteen minutes will be fine. I'll meet you on the porch."

"I can take the chocolates?"

"Heather!"

"All right, all right, I get the message." She tossed him an injured look on her way outside. "I know when I'm not wanted."

"Not soon enough, you don't," her father tossed out after her.

Now that they were alone, Cody didn't seem to know what it was he wanted to say. He paced the room restlessly, without speaking.

"Cody?"

"I'm thinking."

"This sounds serious," Sherry said softly, amused.

"It *is* serious. Sit down." He pulled out a chair, escorted her to it and sat her down, then stood facing her.

"I'm sorry about the poison ivy," Sherry ventured.

He shrugged. "It's my own fault. I should have noticed it, but my head was in the clouds thinking about you."

"I know it's painful."

"It won't be as bad as the razzing I'm going to take when folks learn about this—on top of my behavior last Saturday night."

"Oh, Cody," she whispered, feeling genuinely contrite, knowing her demands that he be romantic had prompted his actions. He was trying hard to give her what she wanted, yet he didn't seem to understand what she was really asking for. Yes, she wanted the sweet endearing things a man did for a woman he was courting, but she wanted him to trust her and open up to her.

"Listen, I know I said I was withdrawing my proposal of marriage, but we both know I wasn't serious."

Sherry hadn't known that at all, but was pleased he was willing to say so.

"I don't know what to do anymore, and every time I try to give you what you say you need, it turns into another disaster."

He squatted down in front of her and claimed her hands in both of his. She noted how callused they were, the knuckles chafed, yet to her they were the most beautiful male hands she'd ever seen.

"You wanted romance, and I swear to you, Sherry, I've given it my best shot. If it's romantic to be nearly arrested for a woman, then I should get some kind of award, don't you think?"

She nodded.

"I don't blame you for my stumbling into a patch of poison ivy—that was my own fault. I wanted to impress you with the bluebonnets. I could have brought you a bouquet of carnations and that fancy grass that goes with them from the market. Les Gilles sells them for half price after seven, but I figured you'd think those wildflowers were a lot more romantic."

"I do. They're beautiful. Thank you."

"I've done every romantic thing I can think of for you. I don't know what else it is you want. I've sung to you, I've brought you candy—I know Heather's the one eating it, but I'll buy you another box."

"Don't worry about it."

"I am worried, not about the chocolates, but about everything else." He shook his head as if to clear the cobwebs. "I know you're concerned that Heather was the one who prompted the proposal, her wanting a baby brother and sister and all. In a way I suppose she did—in the beginning. I'm asking you to marry me again, only this time it's for me."

"Five minutes." Heather's voice thrilled from the other side of the door.

Cody briefly closed his eyes, stood and marched over to the door. "Heather, I asked for some time alone with Sherry, remember?"

"I'm just telling you you've used up ten of those minutes, and you only have five more. I can't be late,

Dad, or Angela will be gone and my algebra book with her.''

''I remember.''

''Dad, you've wasted another whole minute of that time lecturing me.''

Cody shook his head helplessly and returned to Sherry's side. ''Now, where was I?''

''We were discussing your proposal.''

''Right.'' He wiped his face as if that would help him say what he wanted to say. ''I don't know what more it is you want from me. I've made a first-class fool of myself over you. I've done my damnedest to be the kind of man you want, but I can't be something when I don't have a clue what you're asking me to be. I don't know how to be romantic. All I know is how to be me. I'm wondering if that'll ever be good enough for you.''

''Stop.'' She raised both hands. ''Go back to what you were saying before Heather interrupted you.''

He looked confused.

''You said you were asking me to marry you, not for Heather's sake, but for yourself.''

''So?''

''So,'' she said, scooting forward in her chair, ''are you trying to tell me you love me?''

He stopped his pacing and rubbed his hand along the back of his neck. ''I'm not going to lie to you, Sherry— that would be too easy. I don't know if I love you, but I know there hasn't been a woman in the last decade who makes me feel the things you do. I've swallowed my pride for you, nearly been arrested for you. I'm suffering a bout of poison ivy because all I think about is you.''

His words sounded like the lyrics of a love song. Sherry was thrilled.

"Dad!"

"All right, all right," Cody said impatiently. "I'm coming."

Sherry got to her feet, not wanting him to leave. "I'll be over at the ranch one afternoon this week," she volunteered hastily. "That'll give us both time to think about what we want."

Cody smiled and briefly touched her face. "I'll do what I can to keep Heather out of our hair."

"I heard that!"

Cody chuckled and, leaning forward, kissed Sherry gently on the lips. "Your kisses are sweeter than any chocolate-covered cherries."

"Hey, Dad, that was good," Heather announced on her way through the door. "I didn't prompt him, either," she said to Sherry.

Nine

"I hate to impose on you," Ellie said for the third time.

"You're not imposing," Sherry insisted also for the third time. "Christina Lynn and I will get along royally, and Philip won't even know you're gone." As if to confirm her words, Christina Lynn crawled into Sherry's lap and planted a wet kiss on her cheek. "Now go," Sherry said, tucking the toddler against her hip and escorting Ellie to the door. "Your husband wants to celebrate your anniversary."

"I can't believe he arranged all this without my knowing!"

Luke appeared then, dressed in a dark suit, his hair still damp beneath his hat. His arm went around Ellie's waist. "We haven't been out to dinner in months."

"I know, but..."

"Go and enjoy yourself," Sherry insisted. The more she got to know Luke and Ellie, the more she grew to enjoy them as a couple. Luke wasn't as easy to know as his wife, but Sherry was touched by the strength of his love for Ellie and his family. Luke had contacted her early Tuesday morning to ask if she'd mind sitting with the children Wednesday night while he surprised Ellie with dinner to celebrate their third wedding anniversary. Sherry had been honored that he'd want her.

He then told her there wasn't anyone he'd trust more with his children.

Later, when she arrived at the ranch and Ellie was putting the finishing touches on her makeup, Luke had proudly shown Sherry the gold necklace he'd purchased for his wife. Sherry knew her friend would be moved to tears when she saw it and told him so. Luke had beamed with pleasure.

"If Philip should wake," Ellie said, "there's a bottle of formula in the refrigerator."

"Ellie," Luke said pointedly, edging her toward the door. "We have a dinner reservation for six."

"But—"

"Go on, Ellie," Sherry urged. "Everything will be fine."

"I know. It's just that I've never left Philip before, and it seems a bit soon to be cutting the apron strings."

Sherry laughed and bounced Christina Lynn on her hip. "We're going to have a nice quiet evening all by ourselves."

"You're sure…"

"*Go*," Sherry said again. She stood on the porch with Christina Lynn as Luke and Ellie drove off. The little girl waved madly.

For the first half hour, Christina Lynn was content to show Sherry her toys. She dragged them into the living room and proudly demonstrated how each one worked. Sherry oohed and ahhed at all the appropriate moments. When the toddler finished, Sherry helped her return the toys to the treasure chest that Luke had made for his daughter.

Having grown tired of her game, Christina Lynn lay down on the floor and started to fuss. "Mama!" she demanded as if realizing for the first time that her mother wasn't there.

"Mommy and Daddy have gone out to eat," Sherry explained patiently. Thinking Christina Lynn might be hungry, she heated her dinner and set the little girl in her high chair. But apparently Christina Lynn wasn't hungry, because the meal landed on the floor in record time.

"Mama!" Christina yelled, banging her little fists on the high-chair tray.

"Mommy's out with Daddy, sweetheart."

Christina Lynn's lower lip started to wobble.

"Don't cry, honey," Sherry pleaded but to no avail. Within seconds Christina Lynn was in full voice.

Sherry lifted her from the high chair and carried her into the living room. She sat in the rocker trying to soothe the child, but Christina Lynn only wept louder.

Inevitably her crying awoke Philip. With Christina Lynn gripping her leg for all she was worth, Sherry lifted the whimpering infant from his bassinet and changed his diaper. Lifting him over her shoulder, she gently patted his back, hoping to urge him back to sleep.

That, however, proved difficult, especially with Christina Lynn still at full throttle. The little girl was wrapped around Sherry's leg like a plaster and, both she and Philip were wailing loud enough to bring down the house. And this was how Sherry was when Cody found her.

She didn't hear Cody come in so was surprised to turn and find him standing in the hallway outside the children's bedroom, grinning hugely.

"Hi," he said. "Luke told me you were sitting with

the kids tonight. It looks like you could use a little bit of help.''

"Christina Lynn," Sherry said gratefully, "look— Uncle Cody's here."

Cody moved into the room and dislodged the toddler from Sherry's leg, lifting her into his arms. Christina Lynn buried her face in his shoulder and continued her tearful performance.

"What's wrong with Philip?" Cody asked over the din.

"I think he might be hungry. If you keep Christina Lynn occupied, I'll go heat his bottle."

They met in the living room, Sherry carrying the baby and the bottle. Cody was down on the floor, attempting to interest the toddler in a five-piece wood puzzle, but the little girl wanted none of it.

Philip apparently felt the same way about the bottle. "He's used to his mother breast-feeding him," Sherry said. "The nipple on the bottle is nothing like Ellie. Besides, I don't think he's all that hungry. If he was, he'd figure out this nipple business quick enough."

She returned the bottle to the kitchen and sat down in the chair with Philip, rocking him until his cries abated. Christina Lynn's wails turned to soft sobs as she buried her face in the sofa cushions.

"It looks like you've got your hands full."

Sherry gave a weary sigh. "Imagine Ellie handling them both, day in and day out. The woman's a marvel."

"So are you."

"Hardly." Sherry didn't mean to discount his compliment, but she was exhausted, and Luke and Ellie hadn't been gone more than a couple of hours. "I don't know how Ellie does it."

"Or Luke," Cody added. He slumped onto the end of the sofa and lifted an unresisting Christina Lynn into his arms. She cuddled against him, burying her face in his shirt.

At last silence reigned. "Come sit by me," Cody urged Sherry, stretching his arm along the back of the couch.

Sherry was almost afraid to move for fear Philip would awake, but her concern proved groundless. The infant didn't so much as sigh as she moved over to Cody's side. As soon as she was comfortable, Cody dropped his arm to her shoulder and pulled her closer. It was wonderful to be sitting this way with him, so warm and intimate.

"Peace at last," he whispered. "I'm wondering if I dare kiss you."

Sherry smiled softly. "You like to live dangerously, don't you?" She lifted her head and Cody's mouth brushed hers. Softly at first, moving back and forth several times, creating an exciting friction between them. Then he deepened the kiss, his lips urging hers apart until she was so involved in what was happening between them she nearly forgot Philip was in her arms.

She broke off the kiss and exhaled on a ragged sigh. "You're one powerful kisser."

"It isn't me, Sherry. It's us."

"Whomever or whatever, it's dangerous." She nestled her head against his shoulder. "I don't think we'd better do that again."

"Oh, I plan to do it again soon, and often."

"Cody," she said, lifting her head so their eyes could meet, "I'm not here to, uh, make out with you."

"Shh." He pressed his finger to her lips.

She pressed her head back against his shoulder. His

arm was about her, anchoring her to him. She enjoyed the feeling of being linked to him, of being close, both physically and emotionally. It was what she'd sought from the beginning, this bonding, this intimacy.

She closed her eyes, savoring the warm, vital feel of him. Cody rubbed the underside of his jaw over the top of her head and she felt his breathing quicken. She straightened and read the hunger in his eyes, knowing it was a reflection of her own need. He lowered his mouth to hers, claiming her with a kiss that left her weak and clinging.

She was trembling inside and out. Neither of them spoke as they kissed again and again, each one more potent than the last. After many minutes, Sherry pulled back, almost gasping with pleasure and excitement.

"I can't believe we're doing this," she whispered. Each held a sleeping child in their arms. They were in their friends' home and could be interrupted at anytime.

"I can't believe it, either," Cody agreed. "Damn, but you're beautiful."

They didn't speak for a few minutes, just sat and savored the silence and each other.

"Sherry, listen—" Cody began.

He was interrupted by the shrill ringing of the telephone. Philip's piercing cry joined that of the phone. Christina Lynn awoke, too, and after taking one look at Cody and Sherry, burst into tears and cried out for her mom.

Cody got up to answer the phone. He was back on the couch in no time. He cast Sherry a frustrated look. "That was my daughter. She heard I was over here helping you baby-sit Christina Lynn and Philip, and she's madder than hops that I left her at home."

"It seems to me," Sherry said, patting Philip's back, "she got her revenge."

Cody grinned. "It was selfish of me not to bring her, but I wanted to be alone with you."

"We aren't exactly alone," she said. Her gaze moved to Luke and Ellie's children, who had miraculously calmed down again and seemed to be drifting off.

"True, but I was counting on them both being in bed asleep. Luke thought they would be and—"

"Luke," Sherry interrupted, pretending to be offended. "Do you mean to tell me this was all prearranged between you and Luke?"

"Well…"

"Did you?" Sherry could have sworn Cody was blushing.

"This all came about because of you and the fuss you made over wanting romance. Luke got a bit whimsical and thought he'd like to do something special for his and Ellie's anniversary. Then he worried that Ellie wouldn't want to leave the kids. It's hard to be romantic with a pair of kids around."

Sherry looked at Christina Lynn and Philip and smiled. "They didn't seem to deter us."

"True, but we're the exception." After a pause he said, "Put your head back on my shoulder." He looped his arm around her. "It feels good to have you close."

"It feels good to me, too."

He kissed the crown of her head. Sherry closed her eyes, never dreaming she'd fall asleep, but she must have, because the next thing she heard was Luke and Ellie whispering.

She opened her eyes and her gaze met Ellie's smiling features. "They were a handful, weren't they?"

"Not really," Sherry whispered.

"All four of you are worn to a frazzle. Even Cody's asleep."

"I'm not now," he said, yawning loudly.

Ellie removed Philip from Sherry's arms, and Luke lifted his daughter from Cody's. The two disappeared down the hallway to the children's room, returning momentarily.

"How was your dinner?" Sherry asked.

"Wonderful." Ellie's eyes were dreamy. She sat in the rocking chair while Luke moved into the kitchen. He reappeared a few moments later carrying a tray with four mugs of coffee.

"I can't remember an evening I've enjoyed more." Ellie's hand went to her throat and the single strand of gold that Luke had given her for their anniversary. "Thank you, Sherry."

"I'll be happy to watch the kids anytime."

"I don't mean for watching the kids—I mean, I certainly appreciate it, but there's more. Luke told me I should thank you because it was Cody talking to him about love and romance that made him realize he wanted our anniversary to be extra special this year."

Luke moved behind the rocking chair and leaned forward to kiss his wife's cheek.

"I think it's time we left," Cody suggested, "before this turns into something serious, or worse yet, something private."

"You could be right," Sherry agreed.

With eyes only for each other, Ellie and Luke didn't appear to notice they were leaving until Sherry was out the front door.

"Stick around, you two," Luke protested. "You haven't drunk your coffee."

"Another time," Cody answered, leading Sherry down the steps.

"Night," Sherry said to her friends.

"Night, and thanks again," Ellie said, standing in the doorway, her arm around her husband's waist, her head against his shoulder.

Cody escorted Sherry to her car, then hesitated before turning away. "I'll see you soon," he said frowning.

She was puzzled by the frown. She watched him as his gaze swung back to Luke in the doorway and then again to her. At last he sighed, rubbed his eyes and stepped away.

Sherry would gladly have given her first month's wages to know what Cody was thinking.

"DAD WAS FURIOUS with me," Heather announced when she stopped in at the clinic early the following afternoon. "He told me I had the worst sense of timing of anyone he's ever known. First the night he brought you the candy and flowers, and then when you were watching Christina Lynn and Philip.

"Slim got kicked by a horse once," the girl continued. "He was walking along behind this gelding, minding his own business, and the horse reared back and got him good. He was in a cast for six weeks. I reminded Dad of that, and he said my timing was even worse than Slim's."

"It's all right," Sherry assured her. "Your father and I'll get everything straightened out sooner or later." But Cody hadn't mentioned anything about them marrying lately, and Sherry was beginning to wonder.

"I'm not supposed to butt into your and Dad's business, and I don't mean to, but I really do hope you decide to marry us. I don't even care about the babies so much anymore. I really like you, Sherry, and it'd be so much fun if you were always around.''

"I'd enjoy that, too."

"You would?" Sherry instantly brightened. "Can I tell Dad you said that, because I know he'd like to know and—"

"That might not be a good idea." Sherry removed her jacket and tossed it into the laundry container. She was finished for the day and eager to see Cody.

"I thought your friend Carrie was going to stop by with you," Sherry said.

"She couldn't. That's why I can't show you the way I want my hair cut."

"Oh, well. I'll see the magazine another time."

"Especially if you're going to be around awhile." Heather pressed her books against her chest and her eyes grew wistful. "I can hardly wait for you to move in with us."

"I didn't say I was moving in with you, Heather. Remember what Ellie told you at the picnic?"

Heather rolled her eyes exasperatedly as if reciting it for the hundredth time. "If I interfere with you and Dad, I could hurt more than help."

"You got it."

Before leaving the clinic, Sherry ran a brush through her hair and touched up her makeup. "You're sure Janey and your father are expecting me tonight?"

"Of course. Dad specifically suggested I stop by this evening and invite you out, but if you can't come, that's fine, too, because Slim's in town and he can take me home."

The phone rang just then, and Sherry let Mrs. Colson answer. The receptionist came back for Sherry.

"It's a nice-sounding young man asking for you."

This surprised Sherry. The only "nice sounding young man" who interested her was Cody Bailman, but Mrs. Colson would have recognized his voice.

She walked into her office and reached for the telephone. "This is Sherry Waterman."

"Sherry, it's Rowdy Cassidy. I know it's short notice, but I was wondering if you could fly to Houston for dinner tonight?"

"Fly to Houston? Tonight?"

"It's Norah's birthday, and I'd love to surprise her."

"But there isn't a plane for me to catch, and it'd take you hours for you to fly to Pepper to get me."

"I'm here now, at the airstrip outside of town."

"Here?" Norah's husband was full of surprises.

"Yeah, I flew into Abilene this morning and I got to thinking on my way home about bringing you back with me. I know it's a lot to ask on such short notice, but it'd give Norah such a boost. She loves Texas, but after your visit, she got real homesick. It'd mean a lot to her if you'd come and help her celebrate her birthday."

Sherry hesitated and looked at Heather, not wanting to disappoint Cody's daughter, either. "I need to be back by nine tomorrow morning."

"No problem. I can have one of my men fly you back tonight. What do you say?"

"Uh…" Sherry wished she had more time to think this over. "Sure," she said finally. "Why not?" Norah was her best friend, and she missed her, too.

They made the arrangements to meet, and Sherry hung up. "You heard?" she asked Heather.

Heather lowered her gaze dejectedly and nodded.

"It's for a surprise. Norah's the reason I moved to

Texas, and she'd do it for me. Besides, you said Slim can take you back to the ranch.''

"Yeah, I know.''

"How about if you stop by after school tomorrow?'' Sherry asked, hating to disappoint Heather. "It'd be even better, wouldn't it, because Carrie might be able to come.''

Once more Heather nodded, but not with a lot of enthusiasm. "You're right. It's just that I was really looking forward to having you out at the ranch again. I think Dad was, too.''

"There'll be lots of other times, I promise. You'll explain to your father, won't you?''

Heather nodded. Sherry dropped her off at the feed store where Slim's pickup was parked. She stayed long enough to be sure the older man was available to drive Heather back to the ranch.

From there she drove to the landing strip where Rowdy was waiting. How like a man to think of this at the last minute!

After greetings and hugs, Sherry boarded Rowdy's company jet and settled back in the cushioned seat.

"So how's Pepper been treating you?'' Rowdy asked.

"Very well. I love Texas.''

"Any progress with that cattleman?''

She smiled. "Some.''

"Norah's going to be glad to hear that.'' He slapped his knee. "She's going to be very surprised to see you, but she's going to be even more surprised to see her father. He arrived earlier this afternoon. My driver picked him up at the airport and is going to give him a quick tour of Houston and Galveston Island. If everything goes according to schedule, we should arrive at the house at about the same time.''

''You thought all this up on your own?''

''Yep.'' He looked extremely proud of himself. ''I talked to Norah's father a couple of months back about flying out, but as I explained, having you join us was a spur-of-the-moment idea. Norah's going to be thrilled. I love surprising her.''

To say that Norah was surprised was putting it mildly. As Rowdy predicted, David Bloomfield arrived within minutes of her and Rowdy. They'd waited in the driveway for him, and the three of them walked into the house together.

Rowdy stood in the entryway and, his eyes twinkling, called, ''Norah, I'm home!''

Norah appeared and Rowdy threw open his arms. ''Happy birthday!'' he shouted, and stepped aside to reveal David Bloomfield and Sherry, standing directly behind him.

''Daddy!'' Norah cried, enthusiastically hugging her father first. ''Sherry!'' Norah wrapped her arms around her and squeezed tight, her eyes bright with tears.

''You thought I forgot your birthday, didn't you?'' Rowdy crowed.

Norah wiped the moisture from her face and nodded. ''I really did. I had the most miserable day. The kids were both fussy, and I felt like I'd moved to the ends of the earth and everyone had forgotten me.''

''This is a long way from Orchard Valley,'' her father said, putting his arm around his youngest daughter's shoulder, ''but it isn't the end of the world—although I think I might be able to see it from here.''

Norah chuckled. ''Oh, Dad, that's an old joke.''

''You laughed, didn't you?''

"Come on in and make yourselves comfortable," Rowdy invited, ushering them into the living room. "I certainly hope you didn't go to any trouble for dinner," he said to his wife.

"No. I was feeling sorry for myself and thought we'd order pizza. It's been that kind of day."

"Good—" Rowdy paused and looked at his watch. "—because the caterer should arrive in about ten minutes."

Norah was floored. "Is there anything else I should know about?"

"This?" He removed a little velvet box from his pocket, then put it back. "Think I'll save that for later when we're alone."

David laughed and looked around. "Now, where are those precious grandchildren of mine?"

"Sleeping. They're both exhausted. But if you promise to be quiet, I'll take you upstairs for a peek. How long are you staying? A week, I hope."

David and Sherry followed Norah upstairs and tiptoed into the children's rooms. Sherry was fond of David Bloomfield and loved watching his reaction as he looked at his grandchildren. Sherry remembered several years back when David had suffered a heart attack and almost died. His recovery had been nothing short of miraculous.

By the time they came back downstairs, the caterer had arrived and the table was set for an elegant dinner. The candles were lit and the appetizers served.

"Rowdy did this once before," Norah said, reaching for her husband's hand. Rowdy brought her fingers to his mouth and brushed his lips over them. "He wanted something then. Dinner was all part of a bribe to get me to leave Orchard Valley and be his private nurse."

Rowdy laughed. "It didn't work, either. Norah didn't believe I loved her, and I can't say I blame her, since I didn't know it myself. All I knew was that I couldn't imagine my life without her. You led me on quite a merry chase—but I wouldn't have had it any differently."

"Are you looking to bribe my daughter this time?" David asked.

Rowdy shook his head. "Nope. I have everything I need."

The shrimp appetizer was followed by a heart-of-palm salad. Norah turned to Sherry. "How's everything going between you and Cody?"

Sherry shrugged, unsure how much she should say. "Better."

"I have to tell you, I got a kick out of your last letter. He actually proposed to you by saying he wanted to cut to the chase?"

"Sounds like a man who knows what he wants," Rowdy commented.

"Cody's come a long way since then. He's trying hard to understand what I want, but I don't think he's quite figured it yet." She lowered her gaze and sighed. "Currently he's suffering from the effects of poison ivy. He ran into a patch of it while picking wildflowers for me."

"Well, he's certainly trying hard."

"I wish now I'd been more specific," Sherry said, smoothing her napkin. "I love Cody and I want romance, yes, but more than that, I want him to share himself with me, his thoughts and ideas, his dreams for the future. What troubles him most is the fear that if he loves me he'll lose his identity. He says he isn't willing to let any woman put a collar around his neck."

"Sounds reasonable." David said.

"He's really very dear." Sherry wanted to be sure everyone understood her feelings.

"You love him?"

Sherry nodded. "I did almost from the first."

"Let me talk to him," Rowdy offered, "man to man."

"It wouldn't do any good," Sherry said, trying to sound upbeat. "His best friend, who's happily married, tried, and Cody just thinks Luke's lost his marbles."

"He'll feel differently once he's married himself."

"Didn't you tell me Cody has a twelve-year-old daughter?" Norah asked.

Sherry nodded. "I don't know a lot about his marriage, just enough to know they were both pretty immature. His wife was killed in an automobile accident years ago."

"And he's never thought about marrying again until now?" David inquired.

"Heather had a lot to do with his proposing to me, but—" She stopped, remembering how Cody had told her that the first time he'd asked her to marry him it'd been for Heather's sake, but now it was for his own. "With time, I believe he'll understand it isn't wildflowers that interest me, or serenading me in the dead of night—it's trusting and sharing. It's a sense of belonging to each other."

"It's sitting up together with a sick baby," Norah added.

"And loving your partner enough to allow them to be themselves," Rowdy continued.

"And looking back over the years you were together and knowing they were the best ones of your life," David added thoughtfully.

Sherry hoped that in time Cody would understand all this. His mother had asked her to be patient, and Ellie had given her the same advice. It was difficult at times, but she held on to the promise of everything eventually working together.

Sherry left early the following morning. Norah walked out to the car with her, dressed in her robe, her eyes sleepy. "I wish you could stay longer."

"I do, too."

"If you ever want to get away for a weekend, let me know, and I'll have Rowdy send a plane for you."

"I will. I promise."

The flight back to Pepper seemed to take only half the time the ride into Houston had. Her car was waiting for her when she arrived at the airfield. She glanced at her watch, pleased to see she had plenty of time before she was on duty at the clinic.

Driving down Main Street, Sherry was struck once more by the welcome she felt in Pepper. It was as if she belonged here and always would. The sight of Cody's pickup parked in front of the clinic came as a surprise. She pulled around to the back of the building to her appointed slot and came in the back door.

Cody wasn't anywhere in sight. "Mrs. Colson," she asked, walking out front. "Have you seen Cody?"

"No, I was wondering that myself. His truck's here, but he doesn't seem to be around."

Stepping onto the porch, Sherry glanced around. A movement, ever so slight, from Cody's truck caught her eye. She moved down the walkway to discover Cody fast asleep in the cab.

"Cody," she called softly through the open window, not wanting to startle him. "What are you doing here?"

"Sherry?" He bolted upright, banging his head on

the steering wheel. "Damn!" he muttered, rubbing the injured spot. He opened the door and nearly fell onto the street in his eagerness.

"Have you been drinking?" she demanded.

"No," he returned angrily. "Where the hell have you been all night?"

"With my friend in Houston," she told him, "although where I was or who I was with isn't any of your business."

"Some hotshot with a Learjet, from what I heard."

"Yes. As I understand it, Rowdy's something of a legend."

"I see." Cody slammed his hat onto his head. "What are you trying to do? Make me jealous?"

"Oh, for crying out loud, that's the stupidest thing you've ever said to me, Cody Bailman, and you've said some real doozies. Rowdy's married."

"So you're flying off with married men now?"

"Rowdy's married to my best friend, Norah. It was her birthday yesterday, and on his way home from Abilene, he decided to surprise Norah by bringing me home with him."

Cody frowned as if he didn't believe her. "That's not the story Heather gave me. She said I had to do something quick, because you were seeing another man." Cody paced the sidewalk in front of her like a caged bear. "This is it, Sherry. I'm not willing to play any more games with you. I've done everything I know to prove to you I'm sincere, so if you want to run off with a married man at this point—"

"I didn't run off with a married man!" she said hotly. "For you to even suggest I did is ridiculous."

"I spent the entire night sleeping in my pickup, waiting for you to get back, so if I happen to be a bit short-tempered, you can figure out why."

"Then maybe you should just go home and think this through before you start throwing accusations at me."

"Maybe I should," he growled.

Sherry was mortified to glance around and notice they had an audience. Mrs. Colson was standing on the front porch enthralled with their conversation. The woman across the street who'd been watering her roses had long since lost interest in them and was inadvertently hosing down the sidewalk. Another couple rocking on their porch seemed to be enjoying the show, as well.

"I'm serious, Sherry. This is the last time I'm going to ask." Cody jerked open the truck door and leapt inside. "Are you going to marry me or not, because I've had it."

"That proposal's about as romantic as the first."

"You know what I think of romance." He started the engine and ground the gears.

He'd pulled away from the curb when she slammed her foot down on the pavement. "Yes, you idiot!" she screamed after him. "I'll marry you!"

Ten

"I don't think he heard you, dear," the lady watering the roses called, looking concerned.

"I don't think he did, either," the older man on the porch agreed, standing up and walking to his gate to get a better look at Sherry.

"Cody would never have driven away," Mrs. Colson said. "That dear man's beside himself for want of you. Cody may be stubborn, but he isn't stupid. Mark my words, he'll come to his senses soon."

Sherry wasn't sure she wanted him to. The man was too infuriating, suggesting she was seeing a married man behind his back.

"Do you want me to phone Cody for you, dear, and explain?" Mrs. Colson suggested as Sherry marched up the stairs and in the front doorway.

Sherry turned and glared angrily at the receptionist.

"It was only a suggestion." Mrs. Colson muttered.

"I prefer to do my own talking."

"Of course," Mrs. Colson said pleasantly, clearly not offended by the reprimand. "I'm positive everything will work out between you and Cody. Don't give a moment's heed to what he said earlier. Everyone knows he can be as stubborn as a mule."

"I'm not the least bit positive about anything having to do with that man," Sherry returned. Cody had been telling her for weeks that this was her last opportunity to marry him, and he wasn't going to ask her again.

A half hour later, when Sherry came out of her office reading a file Doc Lindsey had left for her to review, she heard Mrs. Colson speaking softly into the telephone.

"I swear you've never seen anyone so angry in all your life as Cody Bailman was this morning," she said. "He left half his tire on the street peeling out of here the way he did, and all because he's so crazy about—"

"Mrs. Colson," Sherry said.

The receptionist placed her hand over the receiver and barely glanced upward. "I'll be with you in just a minute." She put the receiver to her ear once more and continued, "And dear, dear Sherry, why she's so overwrought that she can hardly—"

Mrs. Colson froze, swallowed once, tightly, and then looked at Sherry. "Is there anything I can do for you?" she managed, her face flushing crimson.

"Yes," Sherry said. "You can kindly stop gossiping about me."

"Oh, dear, I was afraid of that. You've got the wrong impression. I never gossip—ask anyone. I have been known to pass on information, but I don't consider that gossiping." Abruptly she replaced the receiver.

Sherry glanced at the phone, wondering what the person on the other end was thinking.

"I was only trying to help," Mrs. Colson insisted. "Donna Jo's known Cody all his life and—"

"You were speaking to Donna Jo?" It amazed Sherry that anyone got any work done in this town.

"Why, yes. Donna Jo's friends with Cody's mother same as I am. She has a vested interest in what happens between you two. So do Mayor Bowie and the sheriff, and we both know those two spend a lot of time over there at the Yellow Rose."

"What's my schedule like this morning?" Sherry asked wearily.

Mrs. Colson flipped through the pages of the appointment book. "Mrs. O'Leary's due at ten, but she's been coming to see Doc for the past three years for the same thing."

"What's her problem?"

Mrs. Colson sighed heavily. "Mrs. O'Leary's over seventy and, well, she wants a nose job. She's convinced she lost Earl Burrows because her nose was too big, and that was more'n fifty years ago."

"Did she ever marry?"

"Oh, yes. She married Larry O'Leary, but I don't think it was a happy union, although she bore him eight sons. Doc says it's the most ridiculous thing he's ever heard of, a woman getting her nose done when she's seventy. When she comes in, he asks her to think about it for another six months. She's been coming back faithfully every six months for three years."

"If she sees me, I'll give her a referral. If she's that set on a new nose, then she should have it."

"I told Doris you'd feel that way—that's why I set the appointment up with you," Mrs. Colson said, looked pleased with herself. "If you want, I can save Doris the trouble of coming in and give her the name of the referral."

"All right. I'll make a few calls and be back to you in a couple of minutes. Am I scheduled to see anyone else?"

"Not until this afternoon." The receptionist looked almost gleeful with the news. "You're free to go for a long drive, if you like." She looked both ways, then added, "No one would blame you for slipping out for a few hours...."

Sherry wasn't sure if she was slipping out or flipping out. She made a couple of calls, gave the names of three plastic surgeons for Mrs. Colson to pass on to her first patient of the day and then reached for her purse.

She was halfway to the door when it burst open and Donna Jo rushed in. "I'm so glad I caught you!" she said excitedly. "You poor, poor girl," she said with liquid eyes, "you must be near crazy with worry."

"Worry?"

"About losing Cody. Now, you listen here, I've got some womanly advice for you." She paused, inhaled deeply and pressed her hand over her generous bosom. "Sherry Waterman, fight for your man. You love him—folks in town have known that for weeks—and we're willing to forgive you for leaving in that fancy jet with that handsome cowboy. By the way, who *was* that?"

"Rowdy Cassidy, and before you say another word, I didn't leave with him the way you're suggesting."

"We know that, dear."

"Rowdy Cassidy?" Martha Colson whispered, and nodded when Donna Jo's eyes questioned her. "Not *the* Rowdy Cassidy?"

"That's who she said," Donna Jo muttered irritably. "Now let her talk."

"There's nothing more to say." Sherry didn't want to spend what time she had talking about her excursion of the night before, although both women were eager for details. "I'm going to do as you suggest and take a long drive this morning."

"Now you be sure and stop in at the café and let me

know what happens once you're through talking to Cody," Donna Jo instructed.

"Who said I was going to talk to Cody?"

"You *are* going to him, aren't you?" Donna Jo said. "You must. That poor dear is all thumbs when it comes to dealing with love and romance. Personally, I thought you did a smart thing, asking for a little romance first, but everyone agrees that the time's come for you to put Cody out of his misery."

"He's suffered enough," Mrs. Colson added.

"Who would have believed Cody Bailman would be like this with a woman. I will say it took a mighty special one," Donna Jo concluded, winking at Sherry.

With half the town awaiting the outcome, Sherry hopped in her car and drove out to Cody's ranch. Odds were he was working out on the range, so she wasn't sure what good her visit would do. Nevertheless, she had to try.

She saw Cody almost immediately. He was working with a gelding in the corral when she arrived, leading him by the reins around the enclosed area.

Climbing out of her car, Sherry walked over to the fence and stood for several moments, waiting for Cody to notice her. He seemed preoccupied with the task at hand, putting the gelding through his paces. Sherry was certain he knew she was there, and she was willing to be ignored for only so long.

Five of the slowest minutes of her life passed before she stepped onto the bottom rung of the fence and braced her arms on the top one.

"Cody!"

He turned to face her, his eyes blank.

This was much harder than Sherry had expected. On the drive out to his ranch, she'd envisioned Cody's eyes lighting up with pleasure at the sight of her. She'd imagined him hugging her, lifting her from the ground and swinging her around, his eyes filled with love and promises.

"Yes?" he said at last.

"When you drove away this morning, I...I didn't think you heard me," she offered weakly.

Cody led the gelding over to one of his hired hands, removed his hat long enough to wipe his brow with his forearm and then strolled toward her as if he had all the time in the world.

Sherry found it impossible to read him. He revealed no emotion. He might as well have been an android.

"I...don't think you're ready to talk yet," Sherry said.

"You were the one who suggested I go home."

"I know, but I was hoping you'd have thought things out by now and realized I would never date my best friend's husband." Or anyone else when she was so desperately in love with Cody. It seemed as if their time together with Christina Lynn and Philip had been forgotten.

"It was Rowdy Cassidy you left with, wasn't it?"

Sherry nodded.

"I must say you certainly have friends in high places."

"It's Norah I know, not Rowdy."

"Yet you left on a moment's notice with a man who is virtually a stranger."

Sherry closed her eyes and prayed for patience. "Would you stop being so damn stubborn! If you honestly believe I'm the type of woman to run around with a married man, then you don't know me at all."

"*My* stubbornness!" he exploded. "Do you realize

what I've gone through because of you? I've been the brunt of jokes for weeks. My reputation with the other ranchers is in shambles, and furthermore I'm still scratching.'' He removed his glove, rolled up a sleeve and scraped his fingernails across his forearm. "I've done everything I know to earn your love, and I'm finished. I've gone as far as I'm willing to go.''

"That's the problem. You want my love, but you aren't willing to give me yours. It wasn't romance I was looking for, Cody, it was love. I wanted you to care enough for me that you'd be willing to do whatever it took to win my heart.'' She pressed her hand over her heart and felt it beating hard and strong against her palm. "You never understood that. From the first you've been looking for the shortcut, because you didn't want to be bothered. No woman wants to be considered an annoyance.''

"So that's what you think of me.''

"What am I supposed to think with you saying the things you do?''

"That's just fine and dandy.''

He turned away from her as if this was the end of their conversation, as if everything that needed to be said had been said. Sherry knew a brush-off when she saw one. Whatever more she might say would fall on deaf ears.

She walked over to her car, climbed in and started the engine. She'd shifted into gear and started to drive away when she changed her mind. Easing the car into reverse, she pulled alongside the corral fence and stuck her head out the open window intending to shout at him, but in her frustration, no words came.

She pulled out of the yard hell-bent for leather. It had been a mistake to try to reason with Cody. Her better judgment insisted she wait several days and let matters cool before she attempted to reopen communication. She should have listened to her own heart instead of Mrs. Colson's and Donna Jo's eagerly offered advice.

Sherry wasn't sure what caused her to look in her rearview mirror, but when she did, her breath jammed in her throat. Cody was riding bareback after her, atop the gelding he'd been working with moments earlier. The horse was in full gallop, and Cody looked as if he were riding for the pony express, whipping the reins across the animal's neck. Sherry was astonished that he managed to stay astride.

She eased to a stop, and so did the gelding. Cody leapt off his back and jerked open her car door.

"Are you going to marry me or not?" he demanded. He was panting harshly.

Sherry eyed him calmly. "Do you love me?"

"After everything I've been through, how can you ask me a question like that!" he snapped. "Yes, I love you. You've been carrying my heart with you for weeks. What does it take to convince you I'm sincere? Blood?"

"No," she whispered, biting her trembling lower lip.

"I love you, Sherry Waterman," he said. "Would you do me the supreme honor of being my wife?"

She nodded through her tears.

"Hot damn!" he shouted, then hauled Sherry into his arms so fast her breath fled her lungs. His mouth was over hers as if he were starving and she were bread hot from the oven.

His kiss left her weak. "Cody..." she said, breaking away from him. "You maniac. You chased after my car on a horse just the way Luke came after Ellie, and you always said that was such a stupid thing to do.''

He opened his mouth as though to deny it, then realized it was true. He blinked several times, then smiled sheepishly. "So I did. Guess this is what love does to a man.''

"Do you really love me?''

"Love you?'' he cried. "Yes, Sherry, I love you.''

"But you—''

"Don't even say it. Damn, but you led me on a crazy chase, woman.'' He kissed her again, this one far less urgent, more…loving. After a few minutes he released her and said, "Let's go.''

"Where?'' she asked.

"Where else? A preacher. You're not going to get the opportunity to change your mind.''

She looped her arms around his neck again. "I'm not going to, not ever.'' It was Sherry who did the kissing this time, and when they finished, Cody was leaning against the side of her car. His eyes were closed and his breaths were deep, heavy. Then he reached for her again and swung her off the ground.

"Put me down,'' Sherry said, "I'm too heavy.''

"No, you're not,'' Cody declared. "I'm calling the preacher right now and we'll get the license this afternoon.''

"Cody,'' she said, "Put me down!''

He finally did so, then eyed her firmly. "I've waited ten long years for you, sweetheart, and I'm not putting this wedding off for another moment. If you want one of those big fancy weddings, then…'' he paused as if he wasn't sure what he'd do.

"A small ceremony is fine.'' She grinned.

"With a reception big enough to fill the state of Texas, if that's what you want."

"I want my family here."

"I'll have airplane tickets waiting for them by noon."

"Cody, are we crazy?"

"Yes, for one another, and that's just the way it's supposed to be. Luke told me that, and I didn't understand it until I met you. By heaven, woman, what took you so damn long?"

She stared at him and felt the laughter bubble up inside her. Wrapping her arms around his neck, she kissed him soundly. "For the life of me I don't know."

SHERRY RETURNED to the office sometime later to find both Mrs. Colson and Donna Jo standing on the porch, eagerly waiting for her.

Sherry greeted them warmly, as she strolled past.

"How'd it go with Cody?" Donna Jo asked urgently. The pair followed her into the clinic.

"Everything went fine," Sherry said, enjoying keeping them guessing.

"Fine?" Mrs. Colson repeated. She looked at Donna Jo. "What does 'fine' tell us?"

"Nothing," the waitress responded. "I learned a long time ago not to listen to the words, but to study the expression. 'Fine' to me, the way Sherry just said it, says there's going to be a wedding in Pepper real soon."

"Isn't the lunch crowd at the café by now?" Sherry asked.

"Ellen can handle it," Donna Jo said, sitting in the closest chair.

"She's not wearing a diamond," Martha Colson said.

"No diamond?" Donna Jo looked incredulous. "I was sure you'd come back sporting the biggest rock this side of Mexico."

"You mean one this size?" Sherry dug into her purse and pulled out the one Cody had given her. She slipped it in her finger feeling heady with joy and excitement. Mrs. Colson and Donna Jo screamed with delight and Sherry hugged them both.

"When's the wedding?"

"Soon, just the way you said," Sherry told them, her heart warming. They'd contacted Sherry's family and made what arrangements they could over the phone. Afterward, Cody had given her the ring, one he'd been patiently carrying with him for weeks.

Sherry wasn't able to explain more. The front door opened, and Heather let out a cry and vaulted into her arms.

"Who told you?" Sherry asked when she got her breath. Cody had planned to pick his daughter up after school and bring her over to the clinic so they could tell her together.

"Dad," Heather explained. "He came by the school. Men are so funny—they can't keep a secret at all."

Cody walked into the clinic, looking sheepish. "You don't mind, do you?"

"Of course not." Sherry hugged her soon-to-be-daughter.

"Hey, I need a hug, too," Cody said, wrapping his arms around Sherry and holding her against him. With her hands at either side of his face, she pulled.

"Now that's romantic," Mrs. Colson sighed.

"I could just cry," Sherry heard Donna Jo say.

"How soon do you think it'll be before Sherry has a baby?" Heather whispered.

"A year," Mrs. Colson suggested.

"Give them that at least that long," Donna Jo agreed.

"A year," Cody said, lifting his head and casting a weary eye toward his audience. He smiled down at Sherry and winked. "I don't think it'll take nearly that long."

HARLEQUIN *Super*ROMANCE

CREATURE COMFORT

A heartwarming new series by

Carolyn McSparren

Creature Comfort, the largest veterinary clinic in Tennessee, treats animals of all sizes—horses and cattle as well as family pets. Meet the patients—and their owners. And share the laughter and the tears with the men and women who love and care for all creatures great and small.

#996 THE MONEY MAN
(July 2001)

#1011 THE PAYBACK MAN
(September 2001)

Look for these Harlequin Superromance titles coming soon to your favorite retail outlet.

HARLEQUIN®
Makes any time special®

C'mon back home to Crystal Creek with
a BRAND-NEW anthology from

bestselling authors
Vicki Lewis Thompson
Cathy Gillen Thacker
Bethany Campbell

Return to Crystal Creek

**Nothing much
has changed in
Crystal Creek...
till now!**

The mysterious Nick Belyle has shown up in town,
and what he's up to is anyone's guess. But one
thing is certain. Something big is going down in
Crystal Creek, and folks aren't going to rest till
they find out what the future holds.

*Look for this exciting anthology,
on-sale in July 2002.*

Coming in August...

UNBREAKABLE BONDS

by

Judy Christenberry

Identical twin brothers separated at birth. One had every
opportunity imaginable. One had nothing, except the ties of
blood. Now fate brings them back together as part of the
Randall family, where they are thrown into a maelstrom of
divided loyalties, unexpected revelations and the knowledge that
some bonds are simply unbreakable.

**Dive into a new chapter of the bestselling series
Brides for Brothers with this unforgettable story.**

Available August 2002 wherever paperbacks are sold.

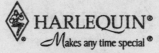

HARLEQUIN®
Makes any time special ®

Visit us at www.eHarlequin.com

PHUB-R